LOST IN TRANSLATION

MARGARET BALL

LOST IN TRANSLATION

This is a work of fiction. All the characters and events portrayed in this book are fictional, and any resemblance to real people or incidents is purely coincidental.

A Baen Books Original

Baen Publishing Enterprises
P.O. Box 1403
Riverdale, NY 10471

ISBN: 0-671-87688-0

Cover art by Courtney Skinner & Newell Convers

First printing, October 1995

Distributed by Simon & Schuster
1230 Avenue of the Americas
New York, NY 10020

Typeset by Windhaven Press, Auburn, NH
Printed in the United States of America

CHAPTER ONE

Allie had never liked Dad's office, with its whirring, blinking machines and expanses of shiny smooth metal and plastic surfaces. She tuned out his voice, let her eyes cross slightly and rested her unfocused gaze on the blinking red eye of some piece of office machinery: a slim black thing with many push-buttons, like a super remote control for the world's greatest synthesizer deck. Only knowing Dad, it wouldn't be anything that interesting. More likely a direct link to the stock market, or a device for monitoring the brain-wave activity of his employees in case any of them stopped scurrying around like lab rats, or . . .

"And *look* at me when I'm talking to you!" Dad snapped.

Allie uncrossed her eyes and looked. Like always, there wasn't much to see; he'd been chainsmoking while he lectured her, lighting one cigarette before the next one went out. By now his pinched face and thinning hair were half hidden behind a veil of blue smoke.

"Smoke makes my eyes water. Do you mind if I open a window?" She said it as politely as she could after half an hour of standing and listening—or trying not to listen—to his complaints about her character, politics, study habits, hair, and taste in music and boyfriends.

But of course it didn't matter how politely she said it, Dad had to take it as a challenge.

"The windows don't open," he said. "The computers

need a climate-controlled environment. You'd know that if you'd studied something useful like engineering instead of, what is it this year, Down With Dead White Males, or whatever they call your artsy-fartsy curriculum."

Allie considered asking him whether the computers liked to operate in smoke-filled rooms, like politicians. She considered telling him that at least she'd had enough biology to know how he was rotting his lungs with that filthy habit. She even considered pointing out that UC Vista View's new major in Non-Western Philosophies was considered such hot shit that a prof from Harvard had come to take notes on their curriculum plan.

None of these responses seemed likely to end the scene any time soon, so she shrugged and said nothing. Dad sucked on his latest-lit cancer stick until the end glowed red. "Dammit, I wish you'd say something once in a while instead of just staring at me like a zombie!"

"You did tell me to look at you," Allie said before she could stop herself.

Dad put down the shredded coffin nail and launched into Diatribe, Phase IV. Allie nodded and tried to look intelligent as he tore apart her latest boyfriend's character, strip by strip. Actually she sort of agreed with most of what he was saying. Luke *was* lazy, and the way he and his friends wanted to lounge out at the beach drinking beer all day instead of going to class was already getting old before Dad yanked her out of Vista View College in California and brought her all the way to New York to lecture her on the subject. In fact, Allie thought while Dad explained what would have happened in his day to any young man who slouched around campus sporting the Grunge Look plus triple diamond ear studs, Luke was almost as boring as her father.

Not that either of them would have been pleased by the comparison.

"What are you thinking?" Dad demanded. Allie blinked, startled. Last time she could remember her father wanting to know what she thought about something, she'd been six and he'd still been living with her and Mom and the topic had been Christmas presents. Well, score one for old Luke, then; at least he'd helped her get Dad's complete attention. Maybe she could sort of, like, break off with Luke but make the parents think she was still going with him . . .

"Alexandra, I asked you a question." Dad's voice was taut.

"I could tell you I totally agree with everything you've said," Allie said chirpily, "but I wouldn't want you to have a heart attack from shock."

He snorted. It was the most human sound she'd heard in a long time. A lot more human than the constant twittering and beeping of the machines around the office. "Don't worry. I'm not stupid enough to believe you'd pay one second's attention to any of my views. But here's something you will pay attention to." He held up a multipart form covered with typing, and Allie felt a quiver of apprehension.

"What's that?"

"Your transfer," he said. The lighted cigarettes in the ashtray beside him smoldered, unnoticed, sending up five thin blue trails of smoke that joined the ambient cloud. "You're leaving UC Vista View. No more California hippy-liberal-humanist mis-education. I had to pull a lot of strings to do this, but I've got you enrolled at the Université de Massat in Castelnau-le-Quercy, in the south of France. Starting," he finished triumphantly, "day after tomorrow."

"You have to be kidding!" Allie stared at her father and prayed for disbelief. "I *like* UC Vista View."

"I," he said, "do not. And since I'm paying the exorbitant tuition, I think I have some right to make my views known. What do you know about Moliere? Thucydides? Epictetus?"

He snapped the names out so quickly that Allie couldn't follow him. "Huh?"

"I rest my case," he said. "Twelve thousand a year in tuition, and that's all you can say about the great writers of Western civilization. You're a barbarian and an ignoramus. And I'm transferring you to a real university where you'll get a real education."

"But I don't speak French!" Allie yelped.

"Five years of French at that girls' school and you don't speak the language?" Dad shook his head. "Progressive education," he mourned. "Never mind, something must have soaked in. Anyway, the local dialect isn't like Parisian French. They talk more slowly in the south. I'm sure you'll pick it up quickly enough." His smile showed too many teeth. "You'll have to."

"Passport," Allie babbled, "shots, airline tickets . . ."

"All arranged."

"No university takes student transfers in the middle of spring semester."

"This one does." That toothy smile again. "I had to endow two lecture halls and a chamber music quartet, but they're taking you and they're going to civilize you."

"*Chamber music*," Allie repeated. She had a vision of pimply European boys in tight suits, seriously playing that tweedely deedely violin crap. "That settles it. I'm not going. I can't go," she remembered with relief, "Luke and I have tickets to hear Toad the Wet Sprocket next week, and . . ."

Dad snarled.

Allie reconsidered her words. "If, um, if I promised not to go with Luke?"

"No need," said Dad. "You won't be going anywhere with Luke. By next week you'll be studying literature at the Université de Massat. I would have enrolled you in something real, like math or sciences," he explained, "but you seem to resemble your mother in intellectual capacity."

"You think I can't hack it?"

He laughed indulgently. "Well, really, Alexandra. Look at you now! Terrified at the prospect of using a foreign language you've supposedly studied for five years, overwhelmed at being taken out of your familiar little rut. If I also expected you to study something requiring more than the minimum of intellectual effort, you'd accuse me of cruel and unusual punishment."

"There *is* a difference," Allie said between her teeth, "between being terrified and being furious at the way you're jerking me around." But just at the moment she wasn't quite sure what the difference was.

Aigar of Coindra, Dean of the College of Magical Arts and Sciences, liked to tell incoming students that he was happiest when he could shed the cares and responsibilities of the deanship and slip into his private laboratory to spend a few hours with hands-on magic. Even when his spells blew up in his face or littered the lab with magical toads, ha ha. (The bachelors and masters of Magical Arts, having learned what was expected of them, always tittered politely at this point). Aigar liked introducing these little notes of levity, *grace* notes as you might say. Ha! There was a fine conceit. He'd have to work it in at the next administrative meeting, point out that these grace notes helped to humanize him for the students, to reduce their awe at meeting someone in so lofty a position and of such renown.

Besides, it was true. Aigar hummed the opening measures of the Magestreams Chant under his breath and fiddled with the network of fine silken threads suspended over a bowl of solid crystal. The quartz crystal was cloudy white, laced with fine intersecting lines of rust-red, netted again with the shadows of the silk threads. This time, Aigar thought happily, *this* time surely his modification of the standard transportation spell would work. He stepped outside the protective circle of sprinkled salt and lifted his voice in the full sequence of the chant. His fingers danced across a line of hanging glass bubbles and called forth high vibrating notes that blended with his own weak voice to strengthen and amplify his chant across the space between the worlds.

❖❖❖❖❖

Flaubert Duval liked to work the Paris Metro during rush hour. When commuters were streaming off the trains he raised his voice in a throat-straining howl to ensure that he would be noticed, if not appreciated. When the crowd thinned he rested his throat and improvised sequences of chords.

For a moment, just before the roar of the next train filled the tunnel, he thought he heard someone or something joining in with him. Almost unconsciously he adjusted his chords to blend with the high humming tones that swirled about him.

The guitar strings vibrated, muted, floated ethereally away. So did the guitar.

Aigar scowled at the strange flat-bottomed lute that had appeared in the protected circle of salt. It looked like something from another world, all right—indisputably alien, with its bands of bright impossible color, its peculiarly metallic strings. For a moment he was distracted by wondering what kind of beast had guts of a consistency so like wire. Never mind that, he told himself irritably; the point was that the spell had only half worked. He needed something with a soul, not an alien construct. He would have to try again. Maybe this time he'd get the lutenist instead of the instrument.

The white rats in Room 04 (Basement) of the Centre Experimentale twittered and chirped with interest as the air around them shimmered with unworldly energies. 44A and 44B reared up, bandaged forepaws in the air, and stared with quivering noses and twitching whiskers. 45A, B, and C, having just come back from the experimental lab, were feeling too ill to pay much attention to the change. And 46A and B, who were scheduled for lab tomorrow and had been feeling sick with apprehension, went over the top at this last disturbance. "Stop shaking the cage!" 46A snarled at 46B.

"*You* stop!" 46B squealed back before launching herself at 46A. They rolled over and over, biting and scratching wildly, until 46A sank her teeth into 46B's left ear. The resulting high squeak of pain hung in the air for several seconds.

In the non-space between the worlds, 46B's squeak rang precisely three octaves above the top note of Aigar's chant. As the vibrations matched in perfect harmony, the cage containing 46A and B faded from view. The other lab rats began fighting and squeaking and shrilling for all they were worth. They didn't know where 46A and B had gone, but it had to be better than *this* place.

Aigar shook his head in disgust. Perhaps it had been too long since he'd attempted any laboratory magic. True, the spell *was* working. But to what end? What was he to do with a malformed lute and two ghostly white rats with demon-red eyes? Invoking the transport spell with no clear vision of the other end felt rather like reaching through a black curtain with a pair of tweezers, but—

Aigar chuckled. "That's it! Can't pick up a large two-legged mammal with tweezers, can you? I need to adjust for size." His long ink-stained fingers unwove the silk net and recreated it in a larger form, one that draped over the quartz bowl and flowed almost to the floor. Aigar knelt and carefully swept up the lines of salt that spiraled around his work area, then traced a much larger pattern that included most of the clear floor space as well as the quartz bowl, the silk net, the cauldron of earth and the double-pronged glass knife that lay ready for use. His joints were aching by the time he stood straight again. He should have had a laboratory assistant to do this work for him. It had been careless to dispose of Janifer. Of course, at the time he hadn't realized the need to bring a soul from the Elder World. No matter. Lack of foresight was inexcusable in magical arts; Aigar wouldn't have excused it in a student, and now he shook his head sadly at his own folly.

No matter, no matter! If it weren't for the foolish prejudice against experimental work of this kind, he could have got a research grant to refine his spell on the basis of the preliminary results alone. But then there'd have been Masters of Arts and Clerks of the Seal poking and prying and wanting to know exactly what he was doing every step of the way. He couldn't afford that. Not now. Later, perhaps, after the Elder World soul had been trained to do his bidding? Ah, but then he'd be renowned for an achievement far greater than restoring contact with the Elder World. Aigar of Coindra, the man who saved Escorre from the landmonsters. "Only one who is both Landsenser and Mage, a Master of both Arts and Sciences, one who has selflessly devoted his life and his great creative talents to the service of our land . . ." Aigar could write the speech in his head; only he couldn't decide who was to deliver it. To accept accolades from the Seignors would be like admitting their suzerainty over the University, something he'd fought all his adult life. The Vice-Chancellor of Coindra might do, but he'd look like a fool accepting an award from a pudgy little man six inches shorter than he; besides, after this great work succeeded, Aigar intended to be Chancellor and Regent. Perhaps he'd better give the speech himself. In that case the tone should change; modest, even humorously self-deprecating . . . *Grace notes*. Aigar gave the silken net one last adjustment with a flick of his fingers, stepped back and began chanting the spelltones. This time surely he would catch something large enough to have a soul.

Madelon Machaut left the keys in her Renault and the motor running while she dashed into the corner bakery for the day's loaf of fresh bread. She didn't dare turn it off here, the Rue Normande was totally flat and her Renault needed a long downslope to coax it into starting. Please please please let it keep running till I get back, she prayed while the store clerk rang up her purchase.

Outside, the engine shifted up half a tone into that irritating whine that meant it was about to cough and expire. The two high-pitched notes wobbled back and forth, for a moment achieving perfect harmony with the plainchant of Aigar's spell. Madelon glanced out the window just in time to see the car go transparent. Slowly and gracefully, like a cloud dissolving, the transparent image of the Renault wobbled like a Jello sculpture, then vanished completely.

"My *car*!" she screamed.

"What car?" said the store clerk.

Aigar snatched his quartz bowl out of the way just in time. As he leaped backward, he knocked over the wire box containing the demonic white mini-rats. It hit the floor with an ominous clang followed by small rattling sounds, as if various pieces had been knocked loose.

Aigar had no attention to spare for the rat-demons. The wobbling, translucent shape that covered two-thirds of his laboratory floor sighed, rattled, and seemed to settle a few inches as it became completely solid and subject to Escorre's gravity. A coughing noise came from somewhere deep inside the—chest? Throat? Finally it expelled clouds of noxious blue smoke and then sat quiet, doing nothing at all.

Coughing, Aigar approached the object. It seemed quiescent now. Was this the mouth, the round pipe that had spat blue smoke at him? He touched it gingerly and leaped back, sucking his finger. The thing was *hot*.

The white lab rats (46A and B) discovered that the side of their cage was open. Squeaking encouragement to one another, they ventured out to explore the interesting textures and smells of this new environment. (Aigar had left an apple core and the end of a cheese pastry behind his work table several days ago. He was used to having Janifer clean up such odds and ends. But, of course, Janifer was no longer in shape to do these little chores for him.)

Aigar wasted half a day refocusing a transport spell that would move the large metal monster out of his lab and to a remote spot in the mountains south of Coindra where it might go unnoticed for some time. Moving something that heavy, without the benefit of the University journey-maze to start the energies or a destination pad to focus them, was an exhausting task; by nightfall he felt as though he had personally carried every chunk of metal and wood and fabric and strange black otherworldly substance down to the river with his own hands. A man should have a lab assistant for these menial tasks . . .

He glowered at the crudely shaped lump of pottery that rolled around on a high shelf, chattering and whispering at him while he worked through the transport spells. "A lot of help you are now," he told it. "I can't even set you on guard."

Instead, Aigar activated the old keyspell. That closed the laboratory to everyone except him and Janifer; effectively, now, to everybody except him. If he ever hired a new assistant he'd have to modify the spell. Another of the nuisances caused by his loss of Janifer. Mumbling mild curses, he trudged off to his rooms and a good fire and a flask of Brefania Red. A man needed restoration after a day like this.

In the morning, with his mouth stale from the aftertaste of the Brefania, the answer appeared to him with perfect shining clarity. He couldn't risk having his lab wrecked by any more bulky soulless things like the one that had appeared last night. Very well; he would continue the work outside. The meadow just across the south bridge would do very well. A soggy piece of ground too damp to build on and too rocky even for the students to loiter in, it had been left fallow through Aigar's long tenure as Dean. The weeds and wild flowers grew waisthigh there, absorbing any surges of excess landvirtue that might coil up through the scanty mountain earth to wash against Coindra. Today the tall weeds could also serve the much more important purpose of screening Aigar's experimental setup from curious eyes. And if another useless large object showed up, instead of a soul all alive, he would simply move to another part of the field and cast another salt-circle.

If he had to keep sprinkling salt, of course, the meadow's fertility would be impaired. And if nothing could grow there, they might have landmonsters rising out of the once-fertile earth. Aigar grinned. He liked a challenge. It would be a race to see whether he could bring forth a soul to serve him before the landmonsters stirred out of the salted earth.

Allie was not quite sure, in retrospect, how she had wound up on the Paris-bound airplane. She'd been quite clear that Dad couldn't jerk her around like that. What was this, the Middle Ages or something? She just wouldn't show up at the airport. She'd *leave*. What could he do—have her locked up in a convent? She could take care of herself.

It was just that part of taking care of herself seemed to involve making it absoutely clear to him that she was *not* scared to go to a university abroad. Nope. No way. What, her, Allie, the scourge of Vista View's hockey team, scared of a bunch of short dark guys with bad skin who talked funny? It was just that—

She didn't want to spend the rest of the semester without hearing any real music.

"There are probably rock bands in Europe," Dad pointed out. "Unfortunately. And I assume you're taking that . . . device?"

"You bet I am," Allie said, wrapping both arms around her Walkman and glaring at him. "I mean, I would if I were going, but I'm not."

"You'll probably want some tapes of your favorite noisemakers to keep you from getting homesick," he suggested, and handed her his charge card. "Here. I'll finance the last day's shopping spree. And get yourself some decent clothes, too," he threw in. "If you know how."

She could have left right then, used his charge card to finance her return to UC Vista View and Luke. But it wasn't . . . Allie wriggled in her airplane seat, crossed and uncrossed her legs, picked at the artistically raveled hole in the knee of her new stonewashed jeans, and exhaled a long sigh. It wouldn't have been fair. If he *hadn't* given her the charge card, she told herself, she could have run out on him any minute. If he had only understood that she wasn't the least bit nervous or any jazz like that, it was just that she wasn't going to stand for his high-handed ways . . .

Instead, she'd wound up with $176.85 worth of Pearl Jam, Sonic Youth, and Dead Can Dance tapes. And batteries. Remembering how fast her Walkman ate up batteries, and with some vague idea that electricity in Europe worked differently from here, Allie had stuffed her backpack with batteries.

Ha! She should have been stuffing her mind with ideas on how to get out of this. There should have been *some* way short of three months in exile to prove to Dad that she was neither afraid of a new experience nor academically incompetent to keep up with a European university curriculum. Of course she could hack it if she wanted to. It was just that she didn't want to . . . but then, nobody back home in California seemed to care whether she came back or not . . . Mom was all involved with her new yoga instructor. Somehow that idea had come across clearly during a long confusing telephone conversation in which the only other clear message was that Allie at UC Vista View was her darling daughter, but Allie at home, without a college degree or any job skills, would be just a little bit in the way. And Dad, of course, wasn't springing for any more twelve-thousand-dollar years at Vista View.

Not that she was the kind of helpless sorority twit who had to have a safe little dorm room or a place at

Mommy's house, Allie assured herself. It was just that
. . . well . . . Luke wasn't answering his phone, and Mom
had other stuff going on, and she had felt somehow as
though the whole California scene had already closed
behind her without a trace. And she'd bought all those
tapes and the new funky jeans and oversized shirt and
a waterproof jacket because she'd heard it got cold in
Europe. With Dad's charge card. Which seemed to obli-
gate her to *something*.

But not to half a semester wasted in France! That was
excessive. It really was. Yet here she was. At first it was
a relief to stand up and stretch her cramped legs, but
the relief wore thin as she shuffled behind the other
passengers in one interminable line after another. For
such a small airport, Orly certainly had a lot of lines and
confusion. Customs. Passport control. Flickering lights.
Shop windows with glittering displays, jewelry and cut-
glass perfume bottles and liquor and a whole bunch of
other stuff Allie didn't even want to window-shop for.
Lines dividing into three and then weaving back together
again. Children crying. Old tourists pushing luggage carts
the size of a Mack Truck. More lines. Fast pattering
French and a bubble of panic in her stomach: it didn't
sound at all like Mrs. Trailer in French III.

Allie rubbed her eyes and turned around three times
where she stood. All the lights and windows and mirrors confused her; she couldn't tell what was real and
what was reflection. She wished she didn't have to change
planes at Orly; she was too sleepy to read signs and follow
directions and she couldn't even ask for help because
everybody talked too fast.

And her feet hurt. The new jogging shoes were just
a little bit tight, and she'd been sitting too long. Allie
glared around at the other passengers, who were shoving their luggage and children along or gazing at the
shiny window displays of the shops. They all seemed too
preoccupied to care what she did. She sat down against
a wall, took off her shoes, peeled off the smelly socks

and stuffed everything into the backpack. Tried to, anyway. The shoes wouldn't go in until she took her Walkman out. Fine. She needed some good music to get her through the rest of this hideous day. Allie clipped the Walkman to the waistband of her jeans, adjusted the headphones, and set off down the nearest tunnel with Sonic Youth ringing good and loud in both ears.

To keep her spirits up and herself awake, Allie chirped along with the tape, not quite on key with its music. But she liked the variation she was improvising. She whistled cheerfully, eyes half closed. If she didn't quite look, the lights and reflections didn't dazzle her so much. And with the music in her ears, she could almost pretend she was in some normal place where people spoke English and you could get a tofu sprout sandwich.

The regular rhythm of her own footsteps was almost hypnotic. Allie walked and drowsed and didn't quite bump into anything, wandered through a vague dream of being somehow back in California telling Luke about her studies abroad, imagined the airplane moving backward into the sunset, into the glow of light all around her . . .

She blinked and shook her head sharply. What was she doing? Falling asleep while she walked? Had she already been on the second plane, her dreams transmuting it into a backwards fall through time and space? Queer dream: she'd felt herself fading out of the hall like a ghost . . .

The brilliant electric lights and their reflections were dark; the walls of Orly were dark and somehow not quite *there*, and the crowds around her weren't there either. Perhaps she was still asleep, or jet-lagged; dreaming herself down this long dark tunnel that wasn't really there.

But there was sunshine somewhere ahead, and grass blowing in the wind. Allie gave a little sob of relief and ran barefoot through dark nothingness to the blinding display of the sun and the tall weeds waving waist-high around her. How strange, coming out of the airport right into the countryside like this. She must have been so sleepy that she forgot all about changing planes. She *had* changed planes, hadn't she? Yes, she must have. Because when she looked past this waving sea of green grass and gold and white flowers, there was a river with a little arched bridge, and a city upon a hill: towers glowing golden in the stone, red peaked roofs, a cluster of tall narrow wooden houses between the towers and the water's edge. And two boys in long black robes leaning on the parapet of the bridge, arguing and waving their hands.

Allie scuffled her bare feet over sun-warmed soil and soft green weeds. She felt as though strength and awareness were traveling through her from the soles of her feet right up to the top of her head, pouring from her eyes and joining her with the golden town on the hillside. It looked like no place she'd ever been, but it *felt* familiar. It was Berkeley and Vista View and Santa Cruz. It was a university town, full of young people arguing and reading and cutting classes and flunking tests, and how different could it be, really, from UC Vista View? Already Allie felt comfortable.

She stepped out through the tall meadow grass. The ground was damp and yielding under her feet, and with every step she felt taller and stronger. She took deep breaths of cool fresh mountain air that almost intoxicated her; it was like drinking from an icy stream, it was like golden wine in the sun, it was like being a tree drawing life from earth and water and light. She felt each breath deep within her, felt the answering vibration of her footsteps, the gentle whispering caress of the grasses bending around her, and everything felt exactly right.

"No smog in Europe," she decided. "Clean air. More oxygen in the blood. Makes you feel better."

And she was so proud of herself for this bit of scientific reasoning, so delighted to be feeling more awake than ever before in her life, that she walked all through the meadow toward the bridge without even noticing the middle-aged man behind her. The one holding the double-bladed glass knife.

The man who had been, when the time came, so slow to react that he didn't move after his new-caught soul until it was already too close to the bridge and the damned students who'd chosen that morning of all mornings for an early walk.

Aigar cursed himself and his folly and his slowness. Then he cursed the soul from Elder World who hadn't been bound by his circle of salt or any of his other wards. That was what he'd wanted, a soul that wouldn't suffer Escorrean constraints. But why, why, *why* hadn't he thought through the consequences?

He would just have to get himself another one. No. Wait. That one who'd just come through—he couldn't leave it wandering loose in Coindra. People would wonder where it had come from. He'd have to chase it down and dispose of it quickly, before it drew suspicion on itself.

And now it was *talking* to those blasted boys on the bridge! "Why does everything go wrong for me?" Aigar mourned. He slashed at the wild flowers in front of him with his glass knife.

One of the sharp tips caught in a thick, milky stem and snapped off with a ringing sound.

It was just not his day.

CHAPTER TWO

The arched bridge over the Verenha river had been a favorite gathering place for generations of young scholars to walk and argue and watch the cool rushing water. Domerc found the view of Coindra from the bridge very soothing: high golden stone houses, red-tiled roofs, arches and passageways carved out of the native stone on which the town was built, and everywhere the green vines and flowers and slender shade trees that grew wherever a scrap of soil could be found. If he thought about Coindra as a pleasant place to argue philosophy and not as a kind of exile after the debacle of last spring, he could be—briefly—almost content while he lounged on the bridge.

And listening to Fabre's attempts to argue philosophy gave him just enough diversion to keep his mind off more depressing subjects. Fabre was studying law; he didn't have the background for true philosophy, but ignorance never stopped him from getting embroiled in a good argument. Domerc was enjoying Fabre's passionate defense of Arriaga's *Cursus Philosophicus* when he stopped, mouth open, and stared wildly past Domerc's fluttering black gown. One could almost imagine that landmonsters had arisen from the fallow fields that lay on the far side of the Verenha. But the head-high flowers and weeds that grew unchecked there should absorb all the landvirtue, and—anyway, one didn't need to think about the Guild of Landsensers and their responsibilities. Not any longer.

17

❀❀❀❀❀

"Do go on," Domerc said kindly when Fabre closed his mouth without continuing what might charitably have been referred to as his line of reasoning. "Have you forgotten where you were? I *think* you were going to argue that Horneius supports Arriaga in the third proposition, and then of course the examiners will ask you to account for the existence of sublunary comets, and I assume you are planning to counter that by claiming that such phenomena are merely natural exhalations which burst into flames. And then you'll quote Arriaga against Aristotle, and argue that comets are miracles rather than natural phenomena. Not that they're likely to pay much attention to such piddling arguments. But you'll do yourself no good at all if you dry up in the preamble like that."

Fabre aimed a half-hearted kick at Domerc's shins. "You don't know anything about it," he said, still staring at the meadow full of weeds on the far side of the bridge, "everybody accepts Arriaga nowadays. He's proved conclusively that the heavens are solid and that the sun is opaque behind, so that it may better transmit light to us. Look at that, will you?"

Domerc glanced over his shoulder. The girl coming towards them was hardly taller than the yellow starflowers that brushed her face. She wasn't wearing a gown over her peculiar tight garments, which would get her in trouble if the proctors caught her, but it wasn't *his* trouble. "It seems to be a girl. You can't let little things like that distract you in the middle of a good preamble, Fabre."

"Oh, she's a little thing, all right," Fabre crooned, "and ever so distracting. And where *did* she come from, do you suppose?"

"If she was lying down in the weeds, as your tone suggests," said Domerc, "she's already earned her slashes with someone else and will feel no need to make *your* acquaintance, my lad. Now, about the *Cursus Philosophicus*—" He broke off as the cause of Fabre's distraction marched onto the bridge. Fabre stepped quickly into the middle of the way, bowed and swirled his tattered black gown about him with a gallant air that somehow managed to block the girl's progress completely.

"Aren't you forgetting something?" he inquired.

The girl stopped, opened her mouth two or three times without saying anything, and stared at Fabre.

"Your gown," Fabre elucidated.

"I don't wear a nightgown," the girl said. "And what business is it of *yours*, anyway?"

"The proctors will make it their business," Fabre pointed out, "if they catch a scholar abroad in daylight without her gown. I was only trying to help." He sounded injured.

Up close, the girl was as distracting to Domerc as she'd been at first to Fabre. It must, he thought, have been some trick of the sun reflecting off yellow flowers and rippling water that made her seem to glow like a Landsenser who'd just absorbed enough virtue to heal an entire community. From her strange black headgear to her dusty bare feet, she seemed to vibrate like a plucked lute string. There was even a tinny hint of music around her: not music exactly, but some discordant, rhythmic noise, like the songs of invisible demons dancing at her service.

And between the curly red hair and the naked feet, she was as outlandish a sight as ever Domerc had beheld: clad in tight-fitting garments of marvelously supple weave, with the nether portions slashed and worn through like the gown of an extremely experienced student.

"He's right, you know," Domerc said at last, seeing that the girl still stood bewildered and without the sense to push Fabre out of her way. "That is, *do* you come here as a scholar?" Fabre had assumed she was already enrolled among the scholars of Coindra; Domerc doubted it. She had about her the slightly bemused air of someone who had just traveled a very long way.

Slowly she nodded.

"Then," he said, "you must put on your gown before you cross the bridge. Your tutors were remiss not to have informed you of our customs." Not that it really mattered; but if a proctor saw the girl, she'd be fined, and if some of the rowdier scholars saw her she'd be teased and hustled unmercifully. A rough way to start one's studies. Domerc, who'd had a much rougher beginning altogether, found to his mild surprise that he didn't want to let this fledgling-scholar walk into the trouble she was setting up for herself.

Allie pushed the earphones of the Walkman to the back of her head and looked up at the taller of the two young men who'd blocked her way. The other one, short and snub-nosed and grinning, might have been playing some elaborate joke on her. This one seemed to mean what he was saying; and he didn't look as though he ever made jokes. With anybody. Which, Allie thought fleetingly, was rather a pity . . .

"I'm sorry," she said, "I don't understand. At least, I understand your *words*, and what a relief that is, because after the airport I thought Dad was right about my five years of French being a dead loss, but I can understand what you're saying perfectly well."

"Then quickly, demoiselle, don your gown before a proctor chances to pass this way!" the short one urged.

"Except that I don't *understand*," Allie said.

"Is she touched with the sun, do you think, Domerc?" the short one appealed to his friend.

"Too early for that, Fabre," the dark one replied. "Perhaps a landmonster has stolen away her wits. You did not eat any fruit in the meadow, did you, demoiselle?"

This was more complication than Allie was prepared to cope with. "You were saying something about a gown. Is there some kind of rule about wearing uniforms? Nobody told me anything."

"Negligent tutors. I said as much." The one called Fabre wagged his head.

"No, you didn't, I did," Domerc pointed out.

"I, er, I came away in rather a hurry," Allie said before they could get into an argument and forget about her problems. "What exactly are the rules? If you'll tell me where the student store is, I'll buy a uniform—oh, blast." She had been so dreamy and confused in the airport that she'd forgotten to change any money. "No, I can't buy anything now."

"Ha! No gown, no money. I can read this riddle," Fabre announced.

"That's not quite—" Allie tried to interrupt. She *had* money, at least fifty dollars cash and a very large check from Dad to see her through the semester's expenses. It was just that she needed to change some currency before she did anything else.

But Fabre was in full cry and quite unstoppable. "She wasn't *sent* here, she *came*. Probably a Seignor's daughter trying to disguise herself as a peasant, run away from home to get the New Learning."

"A *what*?" Allie demanded.

"No wonder she's shy about telling us her name."

"You never asked me!"

But Fabre was talking again and didn't seem to have heard her. "Never mind, Coppercurls, we'll see you right. You'll want a place to stay—"

"The dorms," Allie said in a small voice that went quite unheard.

"—a job, and a scholar's gown. Nothing to it," Fabre assured her. "Ma Blood-Puddings will let you roost in the attic room until you've found work and have a few Dracs to rub together, won't she, Domerc?"

"I don't think—"Domerc and Allie said together.

Fabre waved his hand as if to brush away their objections. "Of course she will. Nothing to it; you just don't know how to talk the old bag round, Domerc. And she can wear Liuria's spare gown."

Domerc's long, narrow mouth twitched with the first hint of amusement Allie had seen. "She could wear it *twice*," he said, "or halved, if she doesn't want to be lost in the folds."

And somehow that seemed to be settled. Fabre took Allie's arm and led her up the cobbled street that rose precipitously from the far side of the bridge, alternating chatter about the university customs with hissed warnings to Domerc to look out for proctors. "What are you studying? Arts, Law, or Magic? I'm Law myself, but Domerc here can tell you all about the Arts course."

Windows composed of many little, thick glass panes leaned out over the street, and there were flowers everywhere. They passed a well whose wooden cover was green and purple with flowering vines; Allie breathed in the strong, sweet smell of the flowers and wished the street were not so narrow. She was beginning to lose that sense of glowing wellbeing that she'd felt at first, walking barefoot through the meadow . . . and come to think of it, what had happened to the airport? Why had she found herself in a meadow instead of a parking lot?

Fabre's chatter gave her no time to collect her wits. "F'that matter, Domerc can tell you all about *anything*, whether he knows it or not. He's your all-round expert on anything from the *Decretals* of Prospero to Geniver's *Quaere*, with a little light reading of the Lydian Romances thrown in, and of course any music from broadside ballads to Duhem's latest string quartets."

They turned into an unpaved lane even narrower than the street. No shop windows here, only the forbidding backs of wooden houses, their boards gray and silky with age, and an occasional high window or an arch blocked by double wooden doors, and the ubiquitous flowering vines. "You'd best take my arm here, Rougette, the lane's slippery," Fabre suggested, slipping his arm round her waist. What did you say you were called again?"

"Can you really major in magic?"

"College of Magical Arts. Is that what you came here to study?"

"I think I'm supposed to be studying Literature." The lane *was* slippery; Allie couldn't decide whether the puddle she'd just skirted was fish guts or rotting potato peels. Her stomach heaved and she looked up. A larger pile of refuse blocked the entire lane.

"Arts, you mean," Fabre corrected. "Here, I'll lift you over." And he did, surprisingly neatly and competently for a boy no taller than she. There must be strong arms and shoulders under that enveloping black gown with all the slashes.

Domerc's mouth twitched once again. "There's a perfectly good dry street up the hill," he pointed out, "but that wouldn't give you an excuse to fondle her, would it?"

"Just being a gentleman," Fabre said with an injured look, taking his hands away from Allie's waist. "Anyway, we daren't go on the Rue Jauzion, too many folk abroad at this time of day. Do you want the poor child to be seized upon by a proctor for going out without her gown?"

"She could pass for a servitor or a merchant's apprentice."

Fabre snorted. "Not without knowing the first thing about Coindra, she couldn't. Only a fledgling scholar could be this ignorant. She doesn't even know what she's studying."

"Arts, I think we decided."

Allie was feeling very ignorant indeed after hearing Fabre rattle off so many names she'd never even heard of. But she also had the sense of new and dazzling possibilities opening up before her; not to mention an excellent way to *really* annoy Dad.

"That was the plan," she said, "but I've decided to change to—what did you say? Magical Sciences?"

"Magical Arts," Fabre corrected, "you don't want to get mixed up with those strange lost souls who practice the black sciences." He paused and tilted his head back as if to study the vine-covered wall that sloped upward from the lane here. Just above Allie's head was an open casement window; the diamond shapes of the ironwork filling the window argued with the circular lines of the green glass panes. Inside, someone was plucking out a complicated tune that made Allie's feet want to dance.

"Lost souls. What a great way to describe them," Allie said. She'd always considered engineering students boring nerds. She'd have to remember that one.

"But if she's inscribed as an Arts student, she'll have to go to the Dean's office for a conversion," Domerc objected, "and speaking of lost souls—"

"Can you reach the window if I make a step?" Fabre interrupted.

Allie looked doubtfully at the expanse of tangled green vines and peeling gray paint before her. The window seemed even higher than it had a moment ago; but the strange tinkling music called to her. What *was* that instrument? Not a guitar. Something weird. But she kind of liked it.

"She could just go in the front—" Domerc began to say.

"No, she couldn't, you don't want Ma Blood-Puddings to see her without a gown. Up you go, little featherweight." Fabre's hands closed over her waist again and Allie found herself standing on Domerc's broad shoulders, scrabbling at vines and then at the rotting sill of the window. She gripped the inner edge of the sill and chinned herself, tucked her head and rolled forward to land on something hard that shifted under her.

"*Mind* the inkwell!" said a sharp voice, just as the table swayed and deposited Allie on the floor amid a slithering stack of papers. Something trickled over her head; Allie put one hand up and it came away damp with brownish-green stains.

An irritated fold of black cloth whisked past her; somebody leaned out the window. "Domerc, when did Fabre corrupt you into smuggling girls into the house, and why can't she use the stairs? Well, get up, girl," the room's inhabitant went on with no discernable change of tone, "don't just sit there dripping ink into my essay. What *are* you doing here? Fabre's newest acquisition, I assume?"

Allie looked up at a young woman as tall and black-browed as Domerc.

"My name," she said unsteadily, "is Allie. And I think I'm supposed to borrow your second-best gown."

Subjected to the confusing barrage of Domerc's and Fabre's explanation, Liuria was surprisingly agreeable. Resigned, even. Apart from a few tart remarks about Domerc's propensity for rescuing waifs, she really didn't object to the shambles he and Fabre and Allie had made of her essay, her table, or her morning's study time. "You can clean up the room later," she told Domerc.

"You going to let your little sister bully you?" Fabre demanded of Domerc.

He shrugged. "She outranks me. She's a third-year scholar. I'm only a fledgling."

"Only because—"

"I prefer not to discuss it," Domerc said in freezing tones. "As you well know."

Fabre subsided into discontented mutterings about the state of Liuria's room before they'd invaded it, and was she going to expect them to dust the shelves and polish her fencing foils and tune her lute and arrange her books in order as well as cleaning up the spilled ink?

"You *do* want to borrow my gown?" Liuria inquired even as she was draping the black swath of fabric over Allie. "And no, you don't have to tune my lute. I wouldn't trust your ear." Liuria knelt and started pinning up her second-best gown so that Allie wouldn't trip over it on her way to the Dean's office. "Of course she can have the gown. At least she won't be so conspicuous that way."

Fabre snorted. "You mean, they'll assume she's as experienced as you."

"Better than having them all queuing up to get the first slash. Though they will anyway, once she has her own gown."

"She can do what I do," Domerc said, "ignore them."

"She's not tall enough to look down her long patrician nose the way you do!"

"What are you talking about?" Allie demanded. "Do you think I'll tear your gown, Liuria? I promise to be *very* careful with it."

Liuria grinned up from where she knelt at the partially pinned-up hem. "I know you will. Don't pay any attention to Fabre. There's only room in his tiny mind for one thing, and you can tell what *that* is."

"Anyway," Fabre grumbled, "there's hardly room for another slash. Which makes your coldness to me all the less forgivable, Liuria!"

Allie had to agree with the first part of that statement, even if she didn't quite follow the second. Liuria's gown rippled from neck to pinned-up hem with long vertical slashes, just like the one she had draped over Allie. On Liuria, the black fabric billowed open to reveal a shimmer of brilliant colors; on Allie, it hung and gapped over her washed-out T-shirt.

"What happened to your gowns?" she asked. "Were you in some sort of accident, or what?" Perhaps Fabre had been in the same accident; his gown was nearly as tattered as these two of Liuria's. Perhaps European Laundromats were excessively hard on clothes. Perhaps, Allie thought wildly, people in Massat didn't have Laundromats, perhaps they pounded their clothes on stones at the river's edge. *Sharp* stones.

Fabre seemed obscurely amused at her question. "Accident, indeed," he said, "I make it my life's work to earn another slash for my gown."

"Some of us," said Liuria very sweetly, "don't have to work at it. We have only to select."

"Which makes it all the more cruel that you don't select *me* just once. What's the matter, are you afraid I'd inspire you to fidelity?"

"Right," Liuria said. "I'd fall victim to your charms, waste away in pining while you flitted on like a butterfly. It's my greatest fear in life." She picked up a dish of thick brass-colored pins and worked industriously at pinning up the gown until the new, temporary hem came only half-way between Allie's knees and the floor.

"You're pinning it too short," Fabre complained. "All the new class wear their gowns just brushing the floor."

"Not my gown, they don't," Liuria said sweetly, "filthy fashion that it is. Besides, if the child's seeing Aigar, she'd best be ready to run."

"I shouldn't suppose that will be necessary," Domerc put in. "One of the clerks in his office should be able to seal her conversion request. It's just a formality. The more important thing is finding her a job."

Once Allie was decently covered by Coindra standards, Domerc and Fabre and Liuria showed her the shortcut to campus, through the baker's shop and across the Rue Jauzion to a cluster of golden stone halls and towers. Fountains played everywhere, and instead of sidewalks there were paths of narrow green turf bordered by flowers. Several guys looked at Allie with evident interest, and she heard some girls singing together in one of the courtyards they passed: a high complex melody that nearly fried her brain until she figured out that they were singing two different songs at once, somehow fitting words and tunes together into a confusing whole.

"Haven't you ever heard a double ballade before?" Fabre demanded. "Don't they have any real music in your village? Oh, it is going to be fun introducing you to Coindra, Coppertop."

Allie thought about the backpack full of tapes she had left in Liuria's room and thought that the introduction could go both ways. She hadn't heard anything but acoustic music since she got here. She couldn't wait to see

Fabre's face when he put on her earphones and heard Electric Nadir rip forth. What she had playing now, barely audible with the earphones pushed to the back of her head, was a quiet meditative drumming by Skreena Freena; soothing, but not what she wanted to use to show Fabre what *she* considered "real" music.

After being discussed and dressed and pinned together like a new lifesize doll, Allie was a little surprised to find that her new friends didn't intend going any closer to the Dean's office than the carved stone fountain three courtyards away.

"Trust me," Domerc said, "it'll do you no good in the College of Magical Arts to be seen with me or any of my friends."

"You worry too much," said Fabre.

Liuria gave him a freezing glance. "Wait till it happens to you, my lad, and then see what *you* think."

"Until what happens?" Allie asked.

"Personally," Domerc said, "I'd recommend guarding your back at all times."

"Pity you didn't take your own advice earlier," said Liuria.

"When?" Allie asked.

"Just go straight on through the arches," Fabre told her. "It's no good hanging about trying to get any sense out of those two; they can go on about it for hours."

"About what?"

"We'll wait for you here," Domerc said.

"Good plan," said Fabre, "We can go on to the Blue Pigeon for a drink afterwards."

Allie passed under the first arch into a courtyard where roses grew in tangled profusion about a worn column of golden stone. Beyond the riot of crimson and magenta blossoms, a second arch beckoned in fine-grained gray stone. Here the cobblestones were gray and black and white under her feet, and a rainbow arc of water splashed between two black stone basins, and the gray walls were covered with creeping lichens all gray and green and rusty gold. And through the dazzle of sun on water she could just see a third arch of glossy black marble, all grained and swirled with patterns of white and gray that seemed to dance in the sunlight.

Under that arched way she entered a shadowy, smoky remoteness of rustling papers and whispered words. She stood blinking, irresolute, until she could separate shapes from shadows, the hissing voices of the clerks within the office from the coo and rustle of doves at the fountain outside.

There were only two clerks, after all, a boy about her own age and an older woman with a pale, pinched face. Neither of them had the authority to seal her conversion request.

"Should have brought the admissions record from the Arts office," said the woman.

"Couldn't seal it if she had brought it," the boy pointed out. "Too late in the semester."

They wrangled in hushed voices like the slithering of snakes until Allie cleared her throat and leaned on the counter. "I'm ever so sorry to be a nuisance," she said sweetly, "but you see, I'm a foreign student and I don't know where the Arts office is and my father said specifically that everything was arranged and that he'd be sending on the rest of his donation to the building fund as soon as I'd registered for classes, so perhaps I could just look through the . . ."

How odd. She knew what she meant to say, the big book where all the classes and rules for everything were listed, every university must have one, but for some reason the word escaped her.

"Well, anyway," she went on quickly, "I'm sure it must be somewhere in your lists, so I'll just come and have a look, shall I? I can explain everything, you see it was a very sudden transfer and we didn't have time to get all the paperwork done. But you see, I've been through nearly two years of lectures at UC Vista View . . ."

"And what might *that* be?"

European snobs. "It's a university," Allie said stiffly. "In California. In fact, it's part of the state university system, which is *very* good. It's small, of course, so you might not know about my campus, but surely you've heard of California? UCLA? Berkeley? Vista View is part of the same system, you see, so I'm sure my academic credits will be accepted here as soon as—"

"Never mind, you'll have to see the dean," the woman said with a weary sigh.

"That way." The boy pointed to an open doorway through which flashes of light and wisps of blue smoke and the high-pitched twitter of machines drifted into the outer office.

Allie strode forward, keeping her grin to herself. At least some of the techniques she'd learned at Vista View still worked. If you talked nonsense long enough and looked like being a major interruption to the day's work, they would send you on to somebody else. And when they ran out of somebody elses to send you to, the last one would sign whatever it was needed signing just to get you to go away.

She passed through a narrow, book-lined room with a writing stand at one side and an empty desk pulled up by the window. Nobody here to sign her papers, which she hadn't got anyway. But beyond the rows of dusty books there was light, and a sense of space. This Dean must be in there. Unless he was out to lunch. Allie took a deep breath, coughed on the mixture of dust particles and sweetish smoke that filled the air, and went on through the last open doorway.

Mirrors and prisms dangled from the ceiling of the large, light room in which she found herself, catching the sun in the pointed arches of the window openings and sending it on a dazzling, dizzying dance over the jumbled furnishings of the room. Stray beams of light choked on a cloud of blue smoke that rose from a tray somewhere near the front of the room. Allie fanned one hand before her face and hoped she wouldn't have to inhale too much secondary smoke in the course of this interview.

She looked around the room for the Dean of the College of Magical Arts. She'd been, without consciously thinking of it, expecting a large desk and a sour-faced middle-aged man behind it. Instead she saw marble table tops and a litter of glass beakers, clay statuettes, sharp glittering blades, tangled threads of white and scarlet silk, plates with scraps of food going stale and soft on them, three beautiful glass beakers full of cold dark liquid that had already begun forming promising mold cultures, an acoustic guitar, and an overturned wire cage that looked as though it had come from some biology laboratory.

The floor was white marble instead of the dark grainy stone of the outer office. Where it was visible, it reflected the sunlight and added to the unsettling play of light and shadow in a room where nothing seemed to hold perfectly still. However, most of the floor was covered with strange, clunky books bound in ribbons and clasped with ornate silver devices, and the wide central space was a disgusting mess of spilled salt and some kind of grease, with a bowl of plain dirt in the middle. It looked more like a parking space where somebody's broken-down car had been sitting than like the floor of an important University administrator's office.

There was a flurry of movement in the far corner, where more stacks of books teetered precariously on a table that something was shaking. Allie heard a muffled voice cursing vermin and scholars in a way that suggested the two categories were approximately equivalent in the speaker's mind.

"You're going to knock those books over if you don't watch it," she said, the memory of her own descent on Liuria's study still fresh in her mind.

At the sound of her voice, a gray-robed figure backed out from under the table, too fast, and something banged against the top of the table. The highest stack of books teetered and swayed ominously; Allie jumped for them, hands out, and scored a perfect catch.

The man who'd been under the table stood, rubbing his shoulder, and glared at her. "You startled me."

Allie instinctively backed up a step, then held her ground. This guy was old and kind of scruffy-looking, with straggly gray hair and beard around a deeply lined, hawk-nosed face. His gown looked as if it had originally been purple rather than black, but it was so stained and shabby that she couldn't be quite sure. This must be the janitor; nobody to be afraid of, even if his eyes did seem to pierce right through her. So, a bad-tempered janitor; surely she could deal with that. "I'm sorry," Allie said, "but I was looking for the Dean. And don't you think he's going to be annoyed when he comes back and sees what a mess you've left in his rooms?"

The janitor chuckled, not at all nicely, and Allie felt cold. "Young woman, I am the Dean. It is my province to make magic, not to push a broom. And I do it very well indeed, I must say," he said, looking her up and down in a way that made her feel even more peculiar than before, "else you would not have come to my call."

Allie set the books down and backed up a step. "I didn't hear anything."

"You wouldn't. But you came anyway."

Was this guy crazy, or what? Allie took another step back. Her left ankle knocked into something hard and solid. Oh, yes, the bowl of dirt. Sparks of pain writhed up the back of her leg. "Never mind," she said. "It's hopeless. I think I'm in the wrong place."

The gray-haired man leaned forward, suddenly taut in a way that made her want to turn around and run. *Don't be a hysterical fool*, she told herself. "What do you mean?"

"It's wrong here, it's all wrong!" Allie cried. All the little things she had managed not to notice, or to brush aside as being Different in Europe, came crowding in on her now with an intolerable weight of details that added up to—what? She couldn't think, but she knew something was terribly wrong. "Everybody wears funny clothes, and I know you have blue jeans in Europe, it's in the paper about how everybody wants to buy American jeans—no, that's Russia, but if *they* want them *you* must have heard of them here in France. And there's no cars and no telephones and no computers and the air smells wrong . . ." She even missed the stink of asphalt and car exhaust; it was part of home. "*I want to go home!*" she finished, ashamed to hear the tremble in her voice.

The Dean was playing with his bits of mirrored glass; they flashed in her eyes. "Do you now," he murmured, half singing. "Do you? Do you now? Do you not? Do you know? Know you not?"

He touched a row of glass globes and soft humming sounds fluttered around his words like a flock of moths. Allie's eyelids felt heavy. Why had she been afraid of this man? He was kind and good. He hadn't told her to stop whining, the way Dad would have if . . . She frowned, trying to remember Dad's sharp impatient face; the effort sent a stab of pain through her head.

"Do you know or do you not? Do you know or do you not?"

"I . . . don't . . . know," Allie said thickly. The sweet-smelling smoke that filled the room coated her tongue and the back of her throat. It was like being in Dad's office; flashing lights and smoke and feeling like an idiot. Except not quite . . . What had made the flashing lights in Dad's office? Not hanging mirrors . . . but she couldn't remember, now.

"It doesn't matter," the Dean said.

"It doesn't matter," Allie repeated.

"You belong here now."

"I belong here now." A small warmth began to blossom somewhere deep within her. It had never been like that with Dad . . . Allie began to feel light and happy. Of course she belonged here; what had she been thinking of?

The Dean leaned against one of his cluttered marble

tables and played with another piece of glass, something long and thin that seemed to reflect more light than it could possibly have found in those shadows.

"It was so nice of Fabre and Domerc to bring me here," Allie said happily. "I just know I'm going to love studying with you—studying Magical Arts, I mean." Probably the Dean wouldn't lower himself to teach mere undergraduates. It was a pity; he was such a nice kind man. Maybe she'd stay here and go on to graduate school. Why shouldn't she? She felt as though she were floating in a lovely, lovely bubble where nothing could touch her or hurt her. "Isn't it strange how sometimes you meet somebody and just know you're going to be friends? First Fabre and Domerc, and now you. I feel as if I could tell you anything." She heard her own words with some surprise. Undergraduates didn't chatter away like this to senior faculty members. But the Dean didn't seem offended.

"Fabre and Domerc," the Dean repeated. "Domerc Cantatz ve Falheiras Assombre?"

"Oh, do you know him? He's been so helpful about explaining the rules, and he promised to wait and show me a good place to eat after I got the conversion sealed here . . ." Actually Fabre had been the one who wanted to take Allie out to eat, but it was almost the same thing. Wasn't it?

The glass thing slipped out of the Dean's hand and shattered on the marble floor. Allie gasped in horror. He would *never* seal her conversion request now; first she startled him and made him bump his shoulder on the table and now he'd broken what must be a valuable laboratory instrument and she was sure somehow it was really her fault. Babbling incoherent apologies, she knelt and started gathering up the pieces; so many needle-sharp shards of glass, and they felt disgusting too, as if they were covered with something slimy that you couldn't see or quite wipe off. If this was Magic, she wasn't sure she wanted any part of it.

"Don't you have a wastebasket?" she said when her hands were full.

The Dean pointed wordlessly at a tight-woven wicker basket under the table. His face seemed as gray as his long gown.

The basket was overflowing, of course. Allie trod the crumpled papers down firmly, then thought better of it and rescued the topmost paper to wrap the glass shards in. "There, now the janitor won't spill any of them and cut himself when he takes the trash out."

"I don't have a janitor," the Dean said. He was almost recovered from the shock of the accident, some color coming back into his face, and that strange glittering look in his eyes again. "Too many valuable experiments going on in here. Must be undisturbed. Can't have somebody ignorant destroying my arrangements."

"Well, *somebody* has to clean in here," Allie said firmly, "or ought to. That floor is a disgrace and a hazard to anybody's health. Not to mention the food scraps and the ongoing biology experiment over here." She gestured at the beakers full of parti-colored molds.

The Dean looked at the mess as though he had not quite seen it before. "I used to have a laboratory assistant," he said sadly, "but he's no longer . . . in shape to do the work."

A furious chittering and squeaking came from the corner where the Dean had been under a table, and Allie jumped.

"Rats," the Dean said, even more sadly. "Demonic white rats with glowing red eyes. They got away, you see." He waved at the broken lab cage. "I had some hopes that they'd dispose of all this," he said, looking at the beakers and the plates of stale food scraps, "but it doesn't seem to have worked out."

Allie felt the strength that had filled her when she first walked through the fields outside Coindra. She could stay close to the Dean even if she wasn't senior enough to take classes from him. She could *help* him, this

wonderful man, what a privilege! How lucky that she'd
never been the kind of wimpy girl who screeched and
ran when a boy showed her a mouse or a spider. Rats
she could deal with.

And she needed a job.

"Do you," she breathed, "do you by any chance, I
mean, are you perhaps looking for another lab assistant?"

The Dean looked startled. She rushed into enumer-
ating her qualifications before he could think of a reason for not hiring her. "Because I can scrub and clean.
And I'd be most terribly careful of all your books and
papers. And I'm not scared of rats. If you don't want
them killed I'll get a humane trap and take them down
to the river and let them go, and once all this food stuff
is cleaned out they won't be wanting to come back." Not
with all the delicious garbage heaps she'd seen in the
alley behind Ma Blood-Puddings' boarding house, and
come to think of it that alley was probably full of rats
too and maybe she should have inspected the room a
little more carefully.

And the Dean was smiling. Allie didn't quite like his
smile, it made him look different and showed too many
teeth and reminded her of something unpleasant that
she couldn't quite put her finger on. But if it meant that
he would hire her . . .

She crossed her fingers behind her back. Everything
might, just might, be working out perfectly. And it would
serve Dad right. *Show* him.

"You'd have to come here every day," the Dean said
finally. "First thing in the morning, before lectures."

"I like getting up in the morning," Allie lied. The only
thing was, how much did the job pay? She hadn't put
herself in a good position for bargaining, practically
begging for the work like that. Oh, well. The Dean didn't
look like a man you bargained with, anyway. The wreath-
ing smoke coiled in her hair and left a stale taste in the
back of her throat, and she heard herself agreeing to
all the conditions he laid out, strange though some of

them seemed, as though she had no choice but to do what he said. Maybe if she worked really well he would approve of her. For some reason that seemed terribly important.

And when he finally mentioned the salary, of course he talked in terms of Dracs and Hawks and Griffons, which Allie supposed must be the local currency, and she had no idea what it was in real money. She was even a little disappointed at the bag of small change he handed her as an advance on her pay. But then, it was good of him to trust her at all, a total stranger coming into his lab and insulting his housekeeping and begging for a job. Maybe he was flattered that she wanted to major in Magical Arts. Maybe, Allie thought, hugging the secret warmth to herself, maybe he could tell from looking at her and talking to her that she was really an okay person. That he didn't have to yell at her like a stupid, refractory child. That she would do the right thing without being bullied and insulted first.

It seemed like all she'd ever wanted.

And he wrote and sealed her Conversion Request, right there on the spot, and handed her the strange thick paper with the dangling wax seals to turn in at the Vice-chancellor's office. She walked out of the cluttered lab with the distinct sensation that her feet were at least two inches above that hard, cold marble floor.

Aigar watched her go with a twinge of regret. What if she never came back? It had seemed too risky to dispose of her now, not with that black-browed young fool Domerc knowing exactly where she'd gone. But wasn't it a greater risk to allow his new-caught soul to wander free? Nonsense, he told himself. Of course she would be back. And next time, he'd find a pretext to spill a little of her blood. It wouldn't take much; just enough to bind some part of her soul to him, so that thereafter she'd be drawn back to the lab will she, nil she, until the time came when he could accomplish his purpose with no enemies watching to raise a cry of murder against him.

If she came back . . . if Domerc didn't poison her mind against him . . . She *would* return. She had to. She needed him. Who else would see her fed and clothed? He smiled at the memory of her fumbling around, pretending she knew what was happening. She had been so unwilling to recognize that she'd been whirled into a different world; it had been easy to cloud her mind with the slightest of confusion-cantrips. How strange and barbaric she'd seemed, with that outlandishly decorated shirt beneath her borrowed student gown! And she seemed ignorant of the simplest things; look how she'd fingered the paper of her conversion request, running a fingertip over the raised pattern of the wax seal as though she'd never seen such a thing before. Perhaps she hadn't. Perhaps the people of the old world had lapsed into barbarism, had forgotten how to beat linen rags into paper. Aigar lapsed into a dream of a world in which the knowledge of writing had been lost, in which barbarian nomads clad in gaudy colored pictures wandered the plains and communicated the wisdom of their tribes through elaborate sequences of song and ritual, carrying singing ghosts in black boxes wherever they went.

Domerc and Liuria had gone on to their lectures by the time Allie came out, but Fabre was waiting for her. He weighed her bag of small change in his hand and whistled approvingly. "You must be the first person who ever went into Dean Aigar's toils and came out better off than you went in."

"I know," Allie said. "He was very kind."

"He was fool-generous." Fabre tossed a glittering coin from the bag and slapped his hand over it as it came down on his arm.

"He was?"

"Pinions," Fabre said in disgust, lifting his hand to show

the face of the coin. A scaly winged form slithered serpent-like around the inner circle. "I never toss Beaks. Well, *I* think it's pretty good pay for sweeping up a lab. You'll be able to fork over your week's rent to Ma Blood-Puddings *and* treat us all to dinner at the Blue Pigeon."

"I will?"

Fabre gave her the same mock-disgusted look he'd given the uncooperative coin. "And you'll want to, if you've any sense. Wait till you eat at her table tonight. She didn't get that nickname for serving Salmistren haute cuisine, you know."

"Oh!" Allie wondered exactly what a pudding made of blood would taste like. It sounded nasty.

"Nourishing, Ma says," Fabre remarked, "and they are good and solid with all the meal she stirs in. But with a windfall like that, we can afford the Blue Pigeon tonight." He looked her up and down, for once without innuendo. "I just wonder what Aigar expects of you, if he's paying so well."

"He said something about extra tuition so I can catch up with the other students in his College," Allie said primly. "And so that I can help him in the lab with his spells."

Fabre exploded in laughter. "Extra tuition! Ha! Extra work is more like it! That's it, he thinks he can exploit you by teaching you all Janifer's spells and making you do the magical work of the lab as well as the scrubbing. He's not paying half enough for *that* class of work."

"More than enough," Allie contradicted, still without any idea what the flashing Dracs and Hawks in her coin purse represented in Escorrean buying power. But it didn't matter. Fabre had said it was enough to live on, and—Dean Aigar must think her talented, and worth teaching. That was better than the money.

Late that night, after a riotous tipsy supper of fried fish and Brefania wine, Allie reeled back to the boardinghouse with her new friends and parted from each of them on the narrow stairs; first Liuria, who had the

first-floor study, then Fabre and Domerc who shared
the room above, and then one more flight of winding
stairs to her own narrow attic room with its sloping roof
and one tall pointed window. She leaned on the windowsill. The flowering vine that covered all that side of
the house nodded in at the open window and brushed
her cheek. One fading white flower trembled in the night
breeze and released a heady fragrance that almost covered up the smell of the midden heaps in the lane below.
There was a group of people singing in the baker's shop
across the lane, and from somewhere farther away came
the sweet melody of something that was almost, but not
quite, a flute. All right, thought Allie. *All right*.

She looked out across the dark peaked shapes of tiled
roofs, to the rippling star-reflecting darkness that was
the river, and to the low rolling hills that stretched down
and away from Coindra beyond the river. Funny, you
couldn't see the airport at all from here. She must have
mistaken the direction she'd come from. She'd been so
sleepy and confused that morning.

If anybody'd shown her a picture of Coindra yesterday she would have called it quaint and funny and backward and no place where she was going to put in a year
in exile. But already she felt comfortable here. Almost
as if she really belonged here.

And the Dean was going to tutor her himself.

Yawning hugely, Allie pushed Liuria's second-best gown
off her shoulders—she would have to ask Fabre tomorrow if the Dean's advance pay was enough to pay for
her own student gown—fumbled in the hip pocket of
her jeans, and brought out a tightly folded scrap of paper
that had traveled with her all the way from New York.

"Do not fold, spindle, or mutilate," she chanted to the
night sky, holding up the check Dad had written to see
her through the first semester's living expenses. Her
fingers worked busily for a minute and then she sighed
with satisfaction. *That* would show him!

The torn scraps of the check floated down from her

high window like a flock of tiny winged insects, swirled in the vagaries of the night breeze, then spread themselves out over the sleeping town to rest and rot and dissolve in vines, on rooftops, on the bridge and the river. One airborne scrap caught an upward current and whirled across the river to come to rest in the field of bright weeds.

CHAPTER THREE

Allie's first few days at the university passed in a whirl of confusion. Between her hours doing laboratory chores for the Dean, she had to find out what lectures she was expected to attend, get reading lists, find the campus bookstore (there wasn't one, but a printshop in the Newmarket served the purpose) and figure out how to get her laundry done (this she never did figure out in detail, but she did learn that for a few extra Hawks the landlady would take away baskets of dirty clothes and return more or less clean ones).

It was all strangely familiar to her, and also disturbingly strange. Half the time she felt as though she'd always been a scholar at the Université de Massat. Liuria and Fabre and Domerc formed the nucleus of a group of lively, chattering young people who drew her in without effort, and the pattern of her life wasn't that different from what it had been at UC Vista View.

During the day she attended lectures in Philosophy, Algebra, Fundamentals of Magical Theory, and Introductory Art of Casting (Laboratory Section). Philosophy and Magical Theory worked just like classes at UC Vista View; all she had to do was scribble down the big important-sounding words the lecturer used and rearrange them in some syntactically pleasing order. That didn't work in Algebra, any more than it had at home. When Liuria found Allie groaning over her first Algebra assignment she patiently led Allie through the maze of letters and cabalistic signs and things called "formulas" and "equations."

"This is a lot more like magic than anything in Radegond's Fundamentals of Magical Theory lectures," Allie groaned.

"That's because you scholar-fledglings start with a survey course while they try to cram you with the background you'll need for the practicum," Liuria said. "When you get to the second-year lab courses you'll need algebra, trust me." Then she went back to groaning and scratching out and rewriting phrases of an overdue term paper. The sight of the work she was putting in convinced Allie that by the third year, Magical Arts scholars had to do considerably more than repeat jumbled versions of Radegond's long meaningless definitions. But what did it matter? She wasn't going to be here long enough to take Advanced Magical Arts. She'd finish out the semester and be back in California before she knew it.

In those first few days, what with lectures, exploring the narrow cobbled streets and market stalls of the town, informal student parties and listening to the strange complex music, Allie hardly had a moment to be homesick. Once or twice she was seized with a longing for Vista View, for mountains and redwood trees and the sound of crashing surf. On these occasions she went to her room at the top of the house, put on her Walkman and immersed herself in waves of Pearl Jam or Sonic Youth for an hour or two.

Once she offered Fabre the earphones. He fumbled as if he'd never seen such devices, recoiled from the music, asked something incomprehensible about how these people could farspeak without something called voicebubbles, and suggested that a kiss and a cuddle might cheer her up more than listening to these peculiar noises.

"I don't call *your* music peculiar noises," Allie said, pushing him away, "and most of it doesn't make any more sense to me than Toad the Wet Sprocket does to you."

Fabre tried to put his arm around her and she dug a finger into his ribs. "That tickles!" he yelped. "Spoils the mood."

"That," Allie said demurely, "was the idea."

Fabre sighed. "Oh, all right. Let's go down to Liuria's room and interrupt her. She studies too much anyway. We'll make music and she'll explain it to you and you can indulge your hopeless passion for Domerc's profile while he plays the vielle."

"I don't have a hopeless passion," Allie said.

"Contradictory wench. I've seen how you look at him when you think nobody's watching you."

"I'm not hopeless. Yet."

"Oh, all right, all right, but don't say I didn't warn you. Better women than you have tried and failed to come between Domerc and the Cazraeus vielle, Allie. I think that's the only time he's really happy now; when he's playing the vielle he forgets . . ."

"Forgets what?"

"Never mind. If he wants to talk about it, he will. And when you get tired of waiting," Fabre grinned, "maybe you'll be so exhausted you'll fall into my arms."

"If they're not full of every other unattached female in this university!" Allie retorted.

So she listened while Liuria and Domerc played the two intertwining melodies of a double ballade, and without the two sets of words to distract her she could sense how the lines of music interwove, and she began to feel at home in this place full of flowers and stone arches and black-gowned students and music.

And the next morning she went to Radegond's lectures and felt once again like a stranger observing the customs of an incurably alien culture. She'd never even heard of most of the authorities Radegond mentioned in this survey course. Even talking presented occasional difficulties. She *almost* knew the language, but things she said kept coming out wrong, or she would have trouble remembering vital words.

When Liuria banged on her door to borrow a pot of ink, Allie tried to ask why she didn't use a computer to type her papers instead of writing them out by hand. But for some reason she couldn't think of the word *computer* in this language, and when she used the English word Liuria looked totally blank. "You know," Allie said, "like a *PC* or a *Mac* or even an old Apple?"

Liuria shrugged faintly. "I prefer pears," she said, with such a straight face that Allie didn't catch the pun until a moment after Liuria had gone back to work in her own room. And then she stopped in mid-laugh and shook her head. *Had* that been a joke?

She shrugged and went back to her list of basic readings by authors she'd never heard of: Arriaga and Chesnecophorus, de Heuqueville and Gassendi. One of the other students in Fundamentals of Magical Theory had obligingly told her what they were supposed to have read in the first semester. Absolutely none of the names were familiar to her. At first she'd thought he was pulling her leg, making up imaginary homework to tease a new student. But when she asked Fabre about the books, he told her not to waste her money at the printshop when he and Domerc between them could come up with nearly everything on the list. True to his word, he'd climbed the attic stairs that night with a pile of battered textbooks almost heavy enough to justify his claims of exhaustion and his attempt to "rest" on Allie's bed.

So. The books were real enough, not somebody's complex practical joke on the stupid exchange student. And she could read them, which was a relief; reading the lecturer's handwriting was entirely beyond her. She supposed that narrow, spiky script was just another of the strange things about Europe, like no cars around the university and no typewriters, let alone computers, available to students. But Aigar had explained all that . . . hadn't he? She couldn't quite remember what he had said now; trying to think about it made her head hurt.

Allie shrugged and went back to her studies. At least

the printed books, although bulky with their creamy thick paper and black with their strange ornamental letterings, were legible. Barely. Making sense of what they said, though, was another matter. Allie slammed de Heuqueville shut, tucked the ink-stained book under her arm and went clattering down the flights of stairs to Liuria's room. On this sunny morning, with air and light and birdsong and flower scent coming in through her high narrow window, it was impossible to study in her room anyway. She might as well ask Liuria to explain why de Heuqueville was talking about magic and superstition and spells as though he were listing recipes in a cookbook.

It was, Allie discovered without too much disappointment, going to be even more difficult to study in Liuria's spacious first-floor room. Books and notes and the rickety writing table had all been pushed to the sides of the room; an amazing collection of wooden goblets, metal fencing foils and short swords, inkstands and penknives and quills and sheets of coarse paper crowded atop the tall leaning bookcases that lined one wall. The bed was disheveled enough to suggest that Liuria hadn't spent the night alone, but the brown and cream quilt with its complex geometrical pattern of stars and wheels had been spread more or less neatly over the tumbled sheets.

The casement window was pushed open; the same flowering vine that invaded Allie's attic room nodded in here, sending pale green tendrils and lavender-blue flowers over the cracked and rotting sill, and filling the room with its heady scent.

In the middle of the floor stood three wooden music stands. Fabre and Liuria were sitting on the wide polished planks of the floor beside the stands, their heads together over a partially strung lute.

"It's about time, Domerc—oh, it's you, Allie! Come in!" Liuria said with the flashing smile that lightened her strong, black-browed face and took away all Allie's fears of intruding. "You can chaperone us in case this one gets any ideas."

"Two beautiful ladies," said Fabre without looking up, "will only give me twice as many ideas. We could make beautiful music together."

"Not unless you have another A string," Liuria said.

Fabre moaned. "Always so literal. Have you no . . . no poetry in your soul?"

"Poetry, yes," Liuria said, "but the word you're groping for is 'lechery.'"

"No, I'm groping for my spare strings." Fabre extracted a lutestring from the folds of his rusty black gown and flourished it under Liuria's nose. Allie sat down crosslegged on the cream-and-brown quilt that covered the bed, laughing quietly and enjoying the byplay.

Once the lute was strung, Liuria brought out a wooden flute and blew across it, producing a breathy, wobbly note that made her screw up her face in disgust. "I haven't practiced," she said, fiddling with the head of the flute, "and it shows."

"I need more practice too," Fabre said with a soulful look that somehow made the remark less innocent than it appeared.

"Give me your A."

"And my heart with it." The plucked string of the lute gave out a strong, pure sound that Liuria matched after a moment of making faces into her flute.

"We're going to make music," Liuria said to Allie over her flute. "If Domerc ever gets here . . . Can you play the vielle?"

"Domerc's got it," Fabre pointed out.

"Oh. Right. Want to try the Duhem?"

Allie propped her chin on one hand and sank into the dark, shimmering texture of the music that Fabre and Liuria coaxed from two antique acoustic instruments. When Fabre began singing in a clear tenor quite unlike his speaking voice, shivers ran up and down her spine. Europe was changing her; this stuff sounded like music to her now, even if it wasn't quite as loud and charged with energy as her favorite groups back home.

It could use some jazzing up, though. The lute part had a fast pattering rhythm that should have worked against the voices, but it wasn't strong enough. Without thinking, Allie began to tap out the rhythm with her free hand.

"Keep doing that," Fabre said between verses, in his normal voice. "Tap on a book instead of the quilt, though. I can't hear you."

Encouraged, Allie brought both hands to work on the leather cover of de Heuqueville, slapping out a fast six-four rhythm and pretending she was Skreena Freena's lead drummer. Her right hand still copied the lute part, her left went off into a jazzy syncopated beat that turned the song into a dance.

"Where'd you learn to do that?" Fabre demanded when the song ended.

Allie shrugged. "Listening to Skreena Freena, I guess," she mumbled. And imitating Ted, the lead drummer, for hours on end while Luke's video of the concert played in an endless loop. "I got a *tape* of them upstairs. Want to hear it?" Maybe he was ready to appreciate her kind of music by now.

"A *tape?*" Fabre repeated the word in a puzzled voice and Allie realized that she'd used the English word. Damn! What was it in French? She couldn't think; she never could talk this language when she tried to think it out logically.

But Domerc walked in before Allie could find words to explain what she meant, or to ask Fabre how to say "tape recording" and "Walkman" in his dialect.

"It's about time," Liuria said when Domerc appeared in the doorway.

"Where's the vielle?" Fabre demanded at the same moment.

Domerc's eyes slid away from them. "I haven't got it."

"Well, go and fetch it. We can't do this properly without a third voice."

"We can't do it properly at all," Liuria said, "as long as you insist on drawing out the last two measures like that."

Fabre looked hurt. "It's supposed to be slurred. And Duhem told me himself the tempo slows there."

"It's a *dance!*" Liuria howled. "You want the dancers to remain suspended in mid-air while you do your sensitive rubato?"

Allie didn't hear Fabre's reply. While he and Liuria bickered over the music, she looked at Domerc. His mouth was pinched at the corners and there was something unbearably bleak looking out of his eyes.

"You didn't mean you haven't got it with you," she said softly, beneath the rapid rise and fall of notes as Liuria showed Fabre how she thought the passage should be played. "You meant you don't *have* it."

"Clever girl." Domerc's long, mobile mouth twitched upward at one corner and he eased himself down on the bed beside her. The taut-stretched rope supports for the mattress creaked under his weight; his long-limbed, muscular body made a downward slope on the mattress. Allie tried not to think about leaning into that slope until she rested against Domerc's shoulder. She'd never had to be that blatant to attract a guy's attention back home, and she certainly wasn't going to start now.

"What happened?" Allie ventured as the musical argument between Liuria and Fabre continued.

He looked up and past her, staring at the green vine on the windowsill. "I left it under the triple sign."

"You what?"

"Hocked it," he translated, "put it down the golden gutter, hung it on the handy wagon. . . . I last saw it at Maitre Justin's pawnshop."

That distracted Liuria from the music making. "Domerc, you didn't! If it's the rent again, you know you could have come to me; I haven't nearly spent this quarter's allowance . . ."

"It's not the rent," Domerc said. "I'd a fine to pay. And in actual fact . . ." His voice was so light and airy that it almost broke Allie's heart; all feeling concealed behind the desperately casual inflection. "In actual fact, it's not hocked. Maitre Justin said he couldn't give me that much on loan, but if I made it an actual sale, well, he knows a certain musically minded ship owner who's long wanted a genuine Cazraeus vielle . . . "

"Tord Siofarssen." Liuria snorted. "He doesn't need a better vielle, he needs a new pair of ears and about six hours a day practicing. Domerc, you can't let him have the Cazraeus, Father will spit salamanders. It's been in the family two hundred years. Better let me buy it back for you."

"Our esteemed father can spit as many salamanders as he likes with my hearty good will," said Domerc wearily. "In case you forget, I'm not in the family any longer, never mind my vielle. I've disgraced myself in such fashion as can neither be countenanced nor forgiven by any civilized man. Remember?"

"I never forgot," Liuria said.

Fabre shifted position slightly, and the taut strings of the lute hummed with the ghost of music. He stilled them with his fingers.

"And in any case," Domerc continued, "even if I would take his money through you, your student allowance would hardly cover the cost of the Cazraeus. Justin gave me three hundred Griffons for it."

A lute string snapped under Fabre's hand. Liuria set down her wooden flute, very carefully, on a stack of sheet music. "The robber! It's worth three times that."

"Not," said Domerc with a strained smile, "to someone in a desperate hurry to raise the ready. As Maitre Justin was well aware."

Liuria expelled a long sighing breath. "You're right," she said, "I don't have that much money. Nobody does. Whatever did you need all that for?"

"To pay a fine."

"There isn't anything a scholar can *do* that you'd be fined three hundred Griffons for," Fabre said. "And I should know," he added with a lopsided grin, "I've done most of it."

"It doesn't make sense," Liuria said. "Who'd expect a student to be able to pay a fine like that! Even you wouldn't have been able to if you hadn't walked out of our house with the Cazraeus vielle under your arm. Imposing that kind of fine is as much as expelling someone from the University."

"I believe that was the idea," Domerc agreed. "To get rid of me without the troublesome public procedure of assembling an expulsion committee. You see, he doesn't want to tell his colleagues exactly why he finds my presence in Coindra unbearable. Does he? It might look like a feud. And that might cast some doubt on his story about last spring's events, mightn't it?"

Liuria bit her lip. "Aigar? But you must have given him *some* excuse. And if he was able to impose this much of a fine without a committee hearing on you, it must have been . . ."

"I'll tell you later," Domerc interrupted with a sideways glance at Allie.

Fabre looked up from his lute. "She might be able to—"

"*Later*, all right?" Domerc said over Fabre's last words. "Let's make music. If I can't play, I can still sing."

"I think it's time for me to go to work," Allie said. She grabbed her copy of de Heuqueville and made for the door with her original question unanswered and a whole series of new ones ringing in her ears. Domerc hadn't interrupted Fabre quite soon enough.

What did Fabre think she could help with, and why didn't Domerc want her to know?

The questions mingled with the song in three parts that followed her out of the house, echoed in her mind until the chatter of black-gowned scholars drove them out, and finally went to rest when the Dean himself scowled and asked why she was late and pointed out a mound of fragile glassware that he wanted her to wash.

❀❀❀❀❀

After the Dean left to give a morning lecture, Allie set to work without any great enthusiasm. Basin, cleansing solution, soap. Basket to hold the dirty glassware, not that it looked dirty to *her*, and an open-weave wicker tray to hold the washed pieces while they drained. It was all the same sort of thing, thin-walled glass bubbles in a variety of sizes, from marbles to Christmas ornaments to cantaloupes. What were they for, anyway? She'd never seen anything like them in the Chem lab at Vista View, and Aigar hadn't volunteered any explanation of their purpose.

Allie plunged another double handful of rainbow-bright, fragile glass globes into the basin and sighed very quietly. The water was too hot, and whatever they used for cleaning solution over here stung her hands, and so far her first week's apprenticeship in Magic had been just as boring as high school chemistry lab. She began to wish she hadn't fled Liuria's room so quickly. Maybe she'd been imagining the strange atmosphere and the sidelong looks. Maybe—

Well, anyway, she *had* needed to get to work, and the work *was* making her independent of Dad, which was probably a good thing because he was going to—what was Domerc's expressive phrase? He was going to spit salamanders, Allie thought, when he found out she'd shifted her major from Literature to Magical Arts.

Allie sighed again. She wasn't really the total ignoramus Dad thought her, and she had envisioned the College of Magical Arts as something quite different. A place where people sat around in long black or purple gowns and read *A Midsummer Night's Dream* and had enlightened, intellectual discussions about the symbolism of Ariel's song and whether Shakespeare had Really Believed or had just been pandering to the ignorant superstition of the masses. A place where she could simultaneously drive Dad to a frothing-at-the-mouth fit and learn enough to discredit Mom's half-baked New Age occultism once and for all.

So far, Magic seemed to consist of scrubbing and more scrubbing and a little dusting for variety, with now and then a really exciting task like washing these . . . what had Aigar called them? Voicebubbles. And he hadn't taught her anything special yet, either. Allie sighed again, leaned on the cold-water lever with her elbow and lifted her double handful of glass bubbles out for rinsing.

There was a low muttering sound behind her, a sense of movement, and then an even more alarming movement over her cupped hands. The glass bubbles shivered in the stream of cold water, cracked with a series of high screeching notes, and collapsed into a slithering mass of needle-sharp glass shards. Allie watched helplessly as they poured between her fingers and disappeared beneath the hot soapy bubbles of the washing basin.

"Oh, my poor child," Aigar purred behind her. Allie jumped. When had the Dean come into the lab? Wasn't it far too soon for his lecture to be over?

"What an unfortunate accident," he went on. "You'll need something to stop the blood. Here." He held out a white silk handkerchief. Allie put her soapy hands behind her back.

"No, thank you," she said. "Actually I'm not hurt. And I don't want to touch that. Silk takes water spots, you'd never get them out."

"You weren't cut?"

"No. I wasn't holding them all that tightly, truly I wasn't," Allie insisted. He must think she'd squeezed his precious voicebubbles into little bits. "They just sort of fell apart in my hands." Now he would fire her.

"You weren't injured at all?"

Allie shook her head and blinked back tears. The Dean didn't seem to care anything at all about his laboratory glassware; only about *her*. She was undone by kindness, where she'd been braced to defend against rage.

"How . . . very fortunate." Aigar moved away from her and sat down suddenly on a high stool near the window.

His shoulders slumped under the gray silk gown. Had he really been that worried about her? Warmth grew in Allie, and a conviction that she'd done the right thing by changing her major and begging for a job in the Dean's lab. Never mind Domerc and Fabre and Liuria, with their worried looks and incomprehensible half-warnings. They just didn't understand. Aigar was a good person, really, even if he could be a little intimidating at times.

Why, he hadn't said a word about her carelessness in breaking what was probably a lot of very expensive lab equipment! Overcome by guilt, Allie fished in the hot soapy water, hoping to find at least one unbroken voice-bubble to show the Dean. Her fingers encountered nothing but sharp dangerous slivers; she brushed lightly over them and felt one razor-sharp edge bite the tip of her little finger. A wisp of red coiled through the water.

"I *knew* you were hurt!" The Dean was standing over her again, and this time he wrapped the white silk about her hand with no regard for her protests about ruining perfectly good cloth, and didn't they have any paper towels in the lab?

While he bandaged her, Allie felt the strange unease that often troubled her when the Dean stood too close. Aigar had been staring out a window on the other side of the lab. How had he known about the tiny thread of blood in the soapy water, almost before it happened? Was he, like, psychically linked to her or something? Sheesh. She was starting to think like Mom. Next thing you knew, she'd be babbling about auras and channeling the spirits of dead Cherokees.

She had to get a hold on herself. For some reason, ever since she got to Massat she'd been imagining creepy things about the Université. Of course a lot of things seemed strange to her, the funny clothes and no cars or TV and the strange leather-bound books Domerc loaned her, but things *were* different in Europe. Somehow that was easier to accept now, when she was with the Dean, than at other times.

Allie looked at Aigar and told herself firmly that of *course* things were different here, that was why Dad had made her come here, to learn a different way of life. Everything was all right. Aigar had told her so himself; he had said she belonged here. And he wasn't psychic or anything. There had to be some perfectly rational explanation, only she was too shaken up by the accident to think of it. And it wasn't important anyway. What was important—only for some reason it was too painful to think about—was the care Aigar was lavishing on her cut hand. *No way for a Dean of a College to treat a lab gofer*, a warning voice in the back of her mind chittered, and Allie brushed the warnings away. Some of the other scholars had been at pains to let her know the rumors about Aigar. But that's all they were—rumors. The girl they were talking about wasn't even at the University any more. And she herself sensed nothing remotely sexual in Aigar's attention to her. Those rumors were just jealousy and spite, that was all.

The only possible explanation was that for some reason he really *cared* about her, Allie, everybody's favorite nuisance. When he looked at her, he didn't see some spoiled California brat who'd been shipped off to a nowhere school in Europe to get her out of everybody's hair. What *did* he see? Allie's throat closed tight on that question and she cast about frantically for some neutral topic to take her mind off. Ask him something. She could prolong the moment that way without betraying how weak and wobbly she felt about somebody actually caring about her. And goodness knew, there were enough things she didn't understand about European customs! All week she'd been floundering like the ignorant barbarian Dad had called her, following Liuria and Fabre and Domerc and trying not to betray how utterly lost and confused she was.

"Umm, I was wondering . . ." she started weakly.

"Yes?"

She'd been wondering about all sorts of things during

this first confusing week of lectures and lab demonstrations, but now most of them seemed too risky to ask about. Why hadn't she ever heard of even *one* of the authorities her Introductory Art of Casting lab section leader kept quoting? Because she was ignorant and hadn't learned a thing at Vista View, just like Dad said. Why did the lecturer talk as though he really expected some chanted words and a filament of silk to glow with light when they finally got to the lab exercises? Oh, well, probably he was just being funny in a terribly learned, sophisticated European way and she was just too dumb to catch on to his subtle humor.

But there *were* a few more mundane things that she could ask about.

"I haven't seen a car since I got here," Allie said. "Is, like, the whole town a . . ." The words eluded her, as usually happened when she tried to talk about normal life in California. She just didn't have a good French vocabulary for daily life, she supposed. Not French. Massat-ese. Whatever these people called their dialect. "A *pedestrian zone?*"

"A what?"

"A place set aside for people to walk in," Allie translated. She no longer felt bad about missing a word here and there; the surprising thing was that she'd done as well as she had with the language. It wasn't *exactly* French, she didn't think, because sometimes she would hear the echo of her own voice, and the strong, confident, rhythmically accented noises she was making didn't sound at all like her tentative attempts at conversation in French III. But whatever the dialect, it must be pretty close to standard French, or how come she was able to communicate with anybody?

Aigar was looking at her as though she hadn't communicated at all this time. "Why would you set aside a special place for walking? What else do you expect people to do, fly like Simon Magus? Even our young Masters of Arts are not quite so talented that they can glide the mage-winds without a journey-maze to follow and power to draw on at either end of the link." He put his hand around the scarf and held it down firmly. An ooze of red stained the white silk, and Allie mourned the waste; a paper towel would have done just as well.

She felt uneasy and strangely lightheaded, as though she'd lost a lot of blood instead of the few drops that stained the silk. Cars were clearly out as a subject of conversation. Maybe Europeans were so old-fashioned that nobody ever drove in cities and it wasn't considered worth mentioning. The whole town *did* look like something off one of those travel-agency posters; Allie'd always cynically assumed those photos were carefully framed to avoid TV antennas and telephone wires and cars, but maybe she'd been wrong.

And she was rambling in her thoughts; feeling lightheaded, too. Ridiculous. She hadn't lost enough blood to notice, and she was not one of those silly girls who pretended to faint the first time they had to cut up a frog or something.

"Another thing," she said firmly, to take her mind off the way her head had started to spin. "I must have got all turned around when I arrived here. Because I thought the airport was right across that little hump-backed bridge, only there don't seem to be any roads going out to it from there."

"There is an excellent road," Aigar said. "You know that. Do you not know it?" His voice took on a humming, lilting quality. "You know it, do you not? You know not, do you know?"

Allie felt confused and dizzy. "I . . . what were we talking about?"

"Nothing of importance. It's stopped bleeding now." His hands moved over and under her outstretched arm and the silk scarf unrolled, fluttering scarlet for a moment and then somehow rolling itself up again into a neat package. At least that was what it looked like. Maybe the College of Magical Arts was just a place where people trained to be stage magicians, Allie thought with some disappointment. Next semester she'd be taking doves out of a hat, and by the time she went back home she'd probably have advanced to sawing the lady in half.

"I could wash that for you," she offered, "might be able to get the blood out before it sets."

"*No*," Aigar said again, more sharply than before. The rolled-up scarf disappeared into the folds of his gray silk gown. "That is, I have more important tasks for you this morning, my child."

"You do?" Allie brightened. She'd been hoping that Aigar would eventually entrust her with something more interesting than scrubbing floors and washing glassware. And for him to do it now was especially kind. He must realize how bad she felt about breaking the voice-bubbles, and this was his way of showing her that he still trusted her.

"I need laboratory supplies," Aigar said. "Almoina, cogossia, half a dram of laurat falbenc . . . let's see, what else? Oh, never mind. You can take down the names; I've got work to do. See that shelf?" He pointed to a high shelf along the inner wall, where squat and crooked bottles made an unsteady line on both sides of some kind of lumpish candle-holder. "Check the vials. Make a list of everything that's nearly out and then tell me how much coin you'll need to replace all the supplies."

His long gray robe fluttered across the marble floor; while Allie stared up in dismay at the shelf far above her head, Aigar vanished into the outer room where he kept his books.

She pulled a tall lab stool over to the wall and scrambled up to look at the shelf he'd indicated. Her dismay increased a hundredfold. There were labels on the bottles, all right, but she couldn't begin to decipher the faded, spidery script. She took one down and gazed at it, turning it this way and that in the faint hope that some new angle of light would make sense of the lines and whorls and curlicues of faint lavender ink. That might be an *s*, there, and perhaps that sequence of loops was a couple of *e*'s or *o*'s. "See . . ." she muttered under her breath. "Soo . . . ?" Neither seemed likely; neither had any relationship to the unfamiliar names Aigar had tossed off. Well, maybe she could find a label that looked like . . . what had he said? *Laurat falbenc*, that was one of them. Two words. Should be easy enough to recognize. Allie began methodically taking down bottles, blowing the dust off them, and squinting at the labels. One word. One word. One word. And not a capital *L* to save her soul.

Halfway down the line of bottles, working mechanically, she reached up and touched something that squirmed under her hand. With a gasp she snatched her fingers away and stared at the shelf. What had that been, a cockroach? Nope, it didn't feel like a bug. It felt more like a snake, but not exactly; there'd been the sense of lithe sinuosity, and the dry feeling of a snake's scales, but it had also felt cold and hard and subtly oily.

Like a greasy clay pot.

Or a filthy dirty candle-holder with spiderwebs on its sides, and probably wax dripped all down the far side where she couldn't see. And she'd been imagining that sense of movement, dreaming while she worked, that was all.

The ceramic thing didn't *look* like a bottle of magical herbs or potions. But then, it didn't look much like a candleholder, either, now that she was standing so close to it. It was just a lumpish bit of fired clay, unglazed, like a handful of soil that someone had squeezed in his fist.

With her luck, it would prove to have a cork in the top of it, and it would be the bottle of *Laurat falbenc* that was going to be her Rosetta Stone for deciphering European handwriting. Allie compressed her lips and reached for the clay thing, prepared to grasp it firmly this time.

It writhed in her fingers, and a voice grated in her head. And Allie did something that would disgrace her

forever if the Vista View hockey team ever found out
about it.

She screamed.

It wasn't much of a scream, and she stifled it almost
at once, but the damage was done. Aigar came running
into the room, gray as his robes. "*What are you doing?*"
he demanded when he saw Allie perched on the high
stool. "Leave that alone, you idiot!"

"You t-told me to look at all the bottles on this shelf,"
Allie pointed out. She felt very unsteady. She sat down
on the stool and hooked her heels around the bottom
rung.

"Oh. So I did. Well, what's taking you so long?"

"I can't read the labels," Allie confessed. She decided
not to mention her momentary illusion of something on
the shelf that moved and talked, but she did steal another
glance up at the row of bottles and clay pots. They sat
perfectly still, a few faceted glass bottles winking at her
with reflected light maybe, but not really moving at all.

And definitely not talking.

Aigar looked at his small, forlorn laboratory assistant.
Her white face was almost hidden by the mop of red
curls that flopped around it, and her shoulders were
slumped in defeat. Was it possible that her world had
sunk so far into barbarism as to forget the art of writing? He'd not really taken that hypothesis seriously when
it first occurred to him. But it was certainly consistent
with the other evidence: her ignorance of paper and seals,
the nomad-style tight trews she customarily wore . . .

Clothes, Aigar thought. Why hadn't that occurred to
him earlier? The floor-length student gown she wore
disguised what was under, for the most part, but sooner
or later somebody was bound to notice the barbarian
garments that lay underneath. If nothing else, once she
started getting slashes in her gown, her other clothes
would show through as they had on that first day when
she wore some other scholar's much-used gown. And
she *would* be slashing her gown; chastity was not to be

hoped for in such a pretty little scholar. Particularly one who'd already made the acquaintance of young Fabre.

"Perhaps if you told me the names of the things you want again, slowly?" Allie suggested, and Aigar remembered with a start his original excuse for getting a few hours' peace from the child and her neverending questions. Well, he *did* want supplies. And as long as she was being sent to the merchants' quarter, he might as well see that she came back decently dressed under her gown. Otherwise there *would* be questions asked, in the other direction. And he didn't want his new laboratory assistant attracting too much notice. If people noticed her while she was alive, they'd be that much more likely to ask questions when she disappeared.

"Names? Yes, I can give you the names," he said slowly. No doubt she would commit the list to memory. Folk too barbarous to write often had impressive verbal memories, like the bards of the Misty Isles. "But another thing. While you're at Merchants' Row, why don't you buy yourself some proper clothes so you'll fit in with the other students? One of these days somebody's going to see beneath that gown—"

Allie's face turned as red as her hair, and Aigar chuckled to himself. He'd lay two Dracs to a Hawk that Fabre had already made the attempt.

"I don't know how much things *cost* here," she murmured.

More than his paltry advance on the first week's salary would cover, Aigar realized. With some pain, he extracted a fresh-minted Griffon from his purse and tossed it to her. It fell on her black-covered knees, a small spot of sunny gold that seemed to draw light from the windows and the pale floor.

"That should cover your needs," he said briskly. "No, no, do not thank me. I shall expect you to render an accounting—well, never mind that." An illiterate barbarian would never be able to make sense of the Dracs and Hawks she received in change for her Griffon. "Just show

me your purchases; I'll subtract the value of the supplies and deduct the cost of the clothing from your next
week's pay." Not that a week's pay for a lab assistant
would outfit her in the peacock style of a Coindra scholar,
but she wouldn't know that. Aigar winced inwardly at
the expenses he was incurring. Perhaps it would be best
to take the rest of the child's blood soon, before she had
a chance to entangle him and herself in any more com-
plications.

But not today. She looked so small and defenseless,
and she'd been trying so hard to please him. Not, Aigar
reminded himself, that mercy had any place in the heart
of a master Mage. Well, then. It wouldn't be wise to
remove her so soon after she started working for him;
not with Domerc watching his every action, still searching
for a way to cast the blame on him for that unfortunate affair of last season.

Much, much wiser to keep her here, peacefully working and blending in, attached to him and the laboratory by a binding spell on the blood he'd captured that
morning, until she was just one more face in the crowd
of Coindra scholars and nobody could point to his laboratory as the place where she'd finally disappeared.

And she was still waiting for that list. Aigar sighed
and began recapitulating the ingredients he wanted from
memory, staring at the shelf of bottles to help him recall
everything.

"Almoina," he said, slowly and clearly, "two drams.
Then I'll want half a dram each of cogossia and laurat
falbenc, and a Drac's worth of cabrefolh."

Was he going too fast? He glanced at Allie. She'd
extracted a strange rectangular pad from somewhere
inside her gown, a most peculiar object with a spiral of
metal wire running all along one end, and was scribbling industriously. When he stopped talking, she glanced
up at him with a grin. "Okei!" she said—one of those
strange barbarian exclamations she used occasionally.
Aigar made a mental note to interrogate her some time

about this god Okei. He could never publish the paper, but it would make an interesting addition to his collection of primitive religions.

"I can get it all down as long as you don't go too fast," she went on to reassure him. "Of course the spelling might not be perfect, but I bet the shopkeepers will know what you need. See?"

She proffered the pad to him. It was finer and thinner than any paper Aigar had ever seen, and scored across and across with cabalistic blue lines. Between the lines were scribbles of meaningless symbols.

"Ah . . . interesting," he said neutrally.

"Can't read my writing either, huh?" Allie grinned again. Aigar wished she would stop doing that. It was going to be hard to kill someone who looked so happy over such small things. "Never mind. I got C's in penmanship all the way through school, and that was only because Vista View Day School didn't *give* anything lower than a C to kids whose parents were paying full tuition. But at least I can read my own handwriting. Almoina, 2 drams; cogossia, half a dram; laurat falbenc, the same, cabrefolh, 1 Drac. See?"

"Fascinating," said Aigar. "Some barbaric mnemonic system, I presume. You must teach it to me one day, my child."

CHAPTER FOUR

"Sheesh," Allie muttered as she strode along the flag-stone path that led to the edge of campus, where the shops were. "Barbarian mnemonic system. *Okay*, so my handwriting's not so great, he doesn't have to be that sarcastic about it. European sense of humor, I guess. Great. I don't *like* it here. Funny clothes. Weird food. No real music." As soon as she got her errands done, Allie resolved, she'd go back to her room and get the Walkman. She'd been trying not to play it, conserving the batteries until she figured out where to buy more, but there were some times when nothing but a dose of Pearl Jam or Skreena Freena would dispel her homesickness. She blinked tears out of her eyes, dodged a group of students chanting one of their exotic intertwining songs, and walked into something black and yielding.

"Watch where you're going, idiot—oh, it's you, Allie." Liuria stepped back and nodded. "What's the matter?"

"N-nothing," Allie said. "Really. I've got to buy some herbs for the Dean. Can you tell me where to go?"

"Aigar usually buys from Maître Veuretz," Liuria said, "down by the Cauldron, you know? What does he want?"

"All these." Allie showed her list. Liuria frowned over it and twisted the spiral-bound notepad this way and that.

"I can't make out a word."

"You're holding it upside down," Allie pointed out.

"Oh. This wire thingie goes at the *top*? Oh, I see, and then you flip the pages over. What a clever device. Never mind." Liuria handed it back to her. "I still can't read it. Come along, then, I'll see Veuretz doesn't cheat you."

"I guess anywhere else but Vista View Day School I'd have flunked Penmanship," Allie said with resignation. It sounded as though Liuria had never seen a spiral-bound memo pad before. How odd! But then, probably it was no stranger than her own wondering delight in every feature of Coindra. Golden stone houses crowded so close together they leaned on one another, streets too narrow for cars even if there'd been any, students in medieval-looking long black gowns, lectures full of names and texts she'd never even heard of at Vista View: it was familiar and alien at once, and if they'd pep up their music a little she would be quite willing to finish college here instead of going back to California. Not that she wanted to admit that to Dad, after the fuss she'd put up about coming here in the first place.

When Allie read out the names on her list, Liuria bargained with the shopkeeper and came away with a basket full of strange packets.

"Are you sure that's all?" she asked. "He didn't need to give you a Griffon for this lot; a couple of Hawks would have covered it. Better be sure you return the change. Here it is, seven Hawks and four Dracs." She counted out the money into Allie's hand.

"Oh. Well. Actually, I'm supposed to get some clothes too. He says I should try to look more like the other scholars. Like you." Allie looked up ruefully at Liuria's tall, square-shouldered body, the cap of dark smooth hair and the strong eyebrows that gave her such a decisive look. "I wish!"

"Clothes," said Liuria, brightening. "Oh, this is going to be *fun*. Come on, I'll help you. Not a scarlet like this for you, I think. Would a bright green be too obvious against that hair? Yes," she answered herself, "and you shouldn't wear any soft greens, of course."

"Why not?"

"It might be misunderstood," Liuria said as if that were

an explanation. "But peach, earth tones, or maybe a misty blue would show well under your gown, and better when you take it off. Even lavender, if we can find the right stuff. This way. The cloth merchants are down past the fountain."

Some time later Allie emerged, dazed, from the darkness of the shaded cloth bazaar. Her pockets were lighter by several Dracs and she had the tailor's promise that her new shirts and trews would be ready by day after tomorrow. "Marescal weave," he'd told Liuria, "personally selected by me from this year's market, and not a color will run or fade in washing."

"Hmmph!" Liuria had snorted, "they'd better not, at the price you're charging the fledgling." And she'd set to work to get the price of fabric and tailoring lowered by a full Drac.

It did just occur to Allie that it might be simpler to go to a department store and buy some ready-made clothes in the local style. It wasn't as if she were a hard size to fit. But then, Liuria was so tall, perhaps she had to get things specially made, and it wouldn't be polite to question her.

Besides, it was fun, running the lengths of glowing bright fabrics through her fingers, feeling the softness of silk and the faint scratchy warmth of wool, letting Liuria and the tailor drape great swathes of fabric over her face and shoulders while they debated color and cut. Allie began to think that maybe she'd missed something at home, where she normally limited clothes-shopping expeditions to a quick dash into the mall to pick up some more jeans and T-shirts.

Everything at home was more convenient, she thought, but somehow less fun. Or perhaps the joy came from her Escorrean friends. Liuria and Domerc and Fabre seemed to care passionately about every slightest detail of their lives, from the tuning of a lute to the cut of a tunic to the way a flowered vine grew up the outside of their lodging-house. She thought briefly of Luke, slumped back on the sofa in his apartment, switching TV channels with the remote control while the radio played music to compete with the TV.

And of herself, slumping beside him.

Allie lifted her head fractionally and resolved to learn to live this life as Liuria did. At least while she was here she would take the same joy and interest in the details of life, bring the same energy to it. And to make herself feel more as if she belonged here, she would just quit asking dumb questions that only exposed her American ignorance.

She broke that last promise almost before it was made. They stepped from the darkness of the cloth merchant's shop into a dazzle of sunlight and falling water and discordant voices that broke against one another like the shards of glass bubbles.

"Forty Griffons that awning cost me, and I don't move it on no stinking apprentice's say-so!" a burly man shouted.

A younger, higher voice wove through his like a needle darting through coarse sacking: "I claim Landsenser's right! Your awning blocks light to this garden!"

"Does *not*," the older man growled. "Here, you—"

The slender boy opposing him moved swiftly, knocking out one of the poles that supported the disputed roof and swinging it in a wide arc that kept the man well away from him. "Landsensers!" he cried. "Landsensers to me!"

Everything seemed to be happening at once. The roof of wooden beams and woven slats sagged down and away from the shop it had shaded, gave a groan of timbers wrenched out of shape, and subsided in a clatter of dust and nails around the ears of the shopkeeper and the boy who'd wrecked his awning. Sunlight poured through the newly opened space before the shop, washing the books and scrolls in the front of the shop with pale golden light, bringing out the white face of Domerc where he stood leafing through a work of philosophy. Two women and a man, all dressed in tunics of the same dusty green that the boy wore, arrived not quite at a run and linked hands with him.

"What—" Allie started to say.

Liuria hushed her in a furious undertone. "Wait, can't you? They're Sensing. Oh, poor Domerc," she added.

That seemed a total non sequitur to Allie. Domerc was obviously not hurt; he'd been safely inside the shop when the awning outside came down. He looked startled, and pale in the sudden flood of light, but he was not hurt, Allie thought—and then thought that she must be wrong. His lips were pinched together as if he were enduring great pain, and his eyes had gone blank as though he did not recognize her or Liuria or anything before him. What could be the matter?

"I don't understand," she started to say.

"Then don't," Liuria whispered, "but don't talk, either. Even a scholar-fledgling new from the country should have that much sense!"

Which seemed entirely unfair to Allie, but she could feel Liuria's simmering anger about to explode on the nearest target. And, strangely, nobody else was talking either. The crowd that had gathered around the quarrel was silent, all eyes fixed on the four people in dusty green who stood with eyes shut and hands joined. The tension of the watchers infected Allie; she felt as though she could hardly breathe while waiting for—what? The damage had already been done, the roof had fallen, what more could possibly happen?

When the circle of people in green lifted their heads and unclasped hands, a sigh of tension released breathed through the entire crowd, like a wave moving softly to shore.

"There has been insult to the landvirtue," said the taller of the two women, "but not great harm. The vine that was fading shall grow again, and all shall be well. Come." She nodded at the boy who'd started the trouble; he followed her and the other two, and the shopkeeper began stoically picking up the beams and the shattered laths that covered the walkway before his store.

Allie drew a long shaky breath. "*Well!*" she said, as the people around her relaxed and began talking again. Some of them looked at the wreckage of the shop and scowled at the shopkeeper. "Serves him right," somebody muttered, and there was a murmur of agreement.

"I don't suppose you'd care to tell me what *that* was about? Isn't anybody going to make that kid pay for the damage he did? And what's the big deal about some old vine, anyway? And—Liuria?"

But Liuria was no longer beside her. She had gone into the shop, where she was talking urgently and in a low voice to Domerc. He stared at her as if at a stranger. She put her hands on the edges of his black scholar's gown. They were nearly of a height: Allie looked at the two heads as black as the two wings of a crow, one tilted upward and pleading, one stiff and unmoving.

"You look confused," said a cheerful voice beside her. "Come and have a restorative drink and tell your uncle Fabre all about it."

"Where did you come from?" Allie demanded.

"Domerc and I were trying to read Malcor's *Physica demonstratio* in the shop. That is, he was reading. I was supposed to distract Maitre Benarzi. But as it turned out, the Landsensers did a much better job of distraction. Only trouble is, Domerc won't be able to concentrate now. And Liuria's better for him than I am, when he gets like this. So I thought we could go along to the Blue Pigeon while they get themselves sorted out. See?" And Fabre beamed at her as though he thought he really had explained everything.

"I don't *understand*." Allie felt as though she had been saying nothing else for years. But there was no point in staying to watch Domerc and Liuria staring at each other. And she felt like an intruder. There had been something naked, exposed, in Domerc's tight-lipped expression.

She followed Fabre through the crowd and down the

narrow sloping lane to his favorite inn. At mid-afternoon the place was almost empty. They found a table tucked neatly into one of the curving windows that leaned out over the street. Green glass and green vines filtered the afternoon sunlight into a gentle haze. The dark wood of the table was incised with interwining symbols, too worn with time for Allie to tell whether they were supposed to be pictures or letters. How many generations of scholars had idled away their study time at this table, carving their marks into the wood when nobody was looking?

At the UC Vista View student coffee shop the tables were student-proof plastic, and bright red.

Fabre waved and made signals with both hands above his head, and eventually a girl in a dirty apron brought them a very large pitcher of something fruity-tasting and mildly alcoholic. Allie was thirsty; she emptied her tumbler and held it out for a refill before Fabre had more than tasted his.

"Now," she said, casting all her good resolutions aside at once, "you will explain, please, what all that was about."

Fabre gazed owlishly at her. "All what?"

"Those people in green," Allie said. "Just now. And why that boy could tear up part of a shop and nobody got mad at *him*. And what upset Domerc. And anything else you can think of along the way."

"What upset Domerc——" Fabre began, and then paused and stared into his own tumbler as though he expected to find the right words floating there.

"Is none of my business. I know," Allie said patiently, "but I have to start *somewhere*."

"It's Landsenser business," Fabre said. This time he came to a full stop as though, once again, he thought he'd given a complete explanation.

Allie sighed. "You know," she remarked to the pitcher that stood between them, "I haven't *really* understood anything that's happened since I transferred to the Université de Massat."

"To where?"

"Université de Massat," Allie repeated with strained patience. "*You* know. Here." She waved her hand in a vague circle meant to indicate the inn, the cobbled passageway outside, the partially covered market, and the golden towers of the University itself. The widening arcs of the circle brought her hand into contact with the pitcher. That seemed like a good idea too. She poured herself another tumbler of the fruity punch and was pleased to note that she hardly spilled any on the table.

"Oh." Fabre seemed to be having difficulty thinking. "I could use a refill too." He pushed his tumbler forward and Allie poured again. This time it was harder, though the pitcher was not so full. That didn't seem right; she would have to think it out later. Right now she didn't want to be distracted from the other funny stuff that was going on—had been going on since she arrived, really.

"We call it Coindra," Fabre said, startling her.

"What?"

"You know. *Here*." Fabre waved his hand in a gesture approximating hers.

"Well, never mind all that," Allie said firmly. Perhaps a little too firmly; the slatternly waitress in her smudged apron jumped, startled, and then leaned against the opposite wall and closed her eyes again. "You can call it the Animal House if you want to."

"Why would we do that?"

"Joke. Old movie." Maybe American movies didn't translate well. Come to think of it, she hadn't seen a movie theatre in Coindra. Or a TV. Or a VCR. But that wasn't the point, was it? She was getting distracted again.

"You were going to explain to me," she told Fabre.

"I was?"

"About these people called . . ." Allie couldn't come up with the name he'd used. "*You* know. The characters in the green outfits."

"Landsensers? Oh. Well, I'm not an expert, Coppertop. Don't know any more than you do."

"Just pretend," Allie coaxed, "that I don't know anything at all. It shouldn't be hard," she said ruefully, "I've never felt so ignorant in my life than in the last week. I really don't know much about life outside the States, I guess."

"What States?"

Allie sighed. "Look, Fabre, would you just cut out the wisecracks for a few minutes and tell me about the Landsensers and Domerc? And don't assume I know anything already. Just tell it as if—as if—" She had an inspiration. "As if you were explaining it to a space alien."

"A *what*?"

Fabre was beginning to sound like her, demanding explanations of every other word.

"Somebody from outer space," Allie translated, and then, as he still looked blank, "From another world. Where they don't have Landsensers."

Fabre's face cleared. "Oh, I see. Is this your semester project for Fundamentals of Magical Theory? Old Radegond always has the scholar-fledglings doing something nobody else would think of. Did I ever tell you about the time she made them walk around Coindra for a full week with their lecture notes balanced on their heads? She *said* it was a practical lesson in how people react when unspoken social rules are broken, and it would teach them not to get too wild with the illusions they built in the second semester, but I think she just wanted to get attention for the lecture series. So now she's got you fledglings writing romances of Escorre as if it were the Gard Perilous?" Fabre chuckled. "And you're having trouble getting started, I suppose. All right, I'll help you."

And he started talking even faster than he'd been drinking, while Allie waved her hands and interrupted him as often as she could. "Wait a minute! I don't understand? What's a landmonster?"

Fabre grinned. "You *are* good at this. If I didn't know better I'd almost think you really were a barbarian from a savage world. All right, you understand about the landvirtue?"

"It flows through the land like a river beneath stone," Allie recited from the notes she'd been scribbling, "bringing fertility and health where it runs strong through the earth. It makes our land here beyond the mountains rich and powerful, but it must be served in kind." She was beginning to feel enthusiastic about her notes. All this might be everyday folklore in Coindra, but it would make a great Comparative Religions paper when she got back to Vista View. She might even be able to get it published. That would show Dad! He could hardly go on calling her an ignorant barbarian then. No, she'd be My Daughter Alexandra, you know, her senior paper was published in a real academic journal, great insight into primitive fertility religions . . .

"What kind of sacrifices does this land-virtue stuff want? Nothing too bloody, I hope?" she asked Fabre, secretly hoping the answer wouldn't be anything too yucky and reminiscent of biology lab. She had this thing about blood. But then, these were modern civilized Europeans, and this land-virtue superstition was probably just something they played with. There would be quaint festivals, perhaps, parades, costumes, girls tossing garlands of paper flowers into the river.

Fabre looked as revolted as she could have hoped. "Blood," he said, "would be an insult to the landvirtue. Where *were* you brought up? Oh, sorry; I keep forgetting, you're pretending to be an *alien space*." He looked proud of himself as he brought out the strange words, and Allie couldn't decide whether he was serious or had rearranged them for a joke. She smiled politely and waited for him to explain exactly how the landvirtue was served in the old folk religion of this country.

Two hours later her ears were ringing and her notebook was covered with scrawls that she could hardly decipher. She hoped her difficulty in reading was due to the punch and not to the illegibility of her writing.

Had she been thinking of a paper? There was enough here for a book. Maybe two books.

And Fabre, with what must be more of that sophisticated European sense of humor, had explained it all to her as if it were real and true and going on right now in the modern world. He must, Allie thought, have been waiting eagerly for the moment when she'd gasp and protest that nobody believed in magical fertility currents and monsters growing out of the earth. So she'd carefully kept her face neutral, refrained from commenting, jotted down everything he said as though she were taking it as seriously as he pretended it was.

But what a fantastic cult this Landsensing must have been! Disjointed memories of earth religions and nature cults floated through Allie's head as she looked back over her notes. Instead of a god or gods, it seemed, the people of this region had once worshipped the fertility of the land. Well, that was common enough, although usually they personified it in some fashion. Here, instead of making statues or temples, they worshipped the land by making lovingly tended little gardens and patches of earth all through the city where plants were encouraged to run wild. Fabre would even have had her believe that the flowering vines which choked the windows of their lodging house were there for religious reasons and not because Ma Blood-Puddings was too lazy to weed her garden! And he'd "explained" with a straight face that the vine which was wilting in the shade of the bookseller's new awning had been just such a religious symbol. The boy in green who'd pulled down the awning had been, Fabre said, an apprentice Landsenser who felt the dangerous pressure of the blocked landvirtue—

"Wait a minute," Allie had interrupted at that point. "What do you mean, blocked?"

Fabre looked annoyed. "Do you insist on playing this game out to the point where I have to spell out everything? Oh, all right, though I do feel a fool telling you stuff everyone learns before they're out of leading-strings. The virtue must work on growing things, don't you see? Where stone lies too near the surface for anything to grow, the currents of the virtue part and swirl around it without harm. That's why cities have to be built in the hills, on stone and barren soil. But even here where Coindra was raised there was *some* soil, and the landvirtue wants to flow into that earth and out again as growing things. If it can't do that, it . . . takes other forms."

"What other forms?" Allie demanded.

But here Fabre balked. "Read de Brueil," he said. "*Historia naturae*. Dean Aigar must have a copy somewhere in his study. Rephrase it as you like. It's unlucky to talk of them, didn't your mother teach you any manners?"

"You sound like my father," Allie said sadly.

Fabre patted her hand. "I don't want to be your father. I don't want to be anyone's father for quite a long time, for that matter," he added, "I'm not ready for the responsibility. My ambitions are distinctly lower." He leered at her so comically that Allie had to giggle.

"Does anyone ever take you seriously, Fabre?"

"Never," said Fabre with a mournful look as exaggerated as his leer had been. Even his freckles seemed to droop. "It's the tragedy of my life. Nobody with freckles and hair that stands straight up can be accepted as a romantic hero, so the girls all fall in love with Domerc and cry on my shoulder about it. Although," he added thoughtfully, "crying on one's shoulder can lead to all sorts of interesting things."

"I'm glad you warned me," said Allie.

Fabre sighed. "All right, be that way. Leave me to cherish my lonely passion—"

Allie giggled.

"—and breaking heart—"

"—behind the mask of a clown's smiling face?" Allie suggested.

"Not only is she fundamentally unsympathetic," Fabre mourned, "she steals all my best lines. All right, then,

don't cry on my shoulder. But if you really want to help
Domerc, you could look around Aigar's lab in your spare
time."

"Whatever for?"

"Clues," Fabre said vaguely, waving his hands. "Letters. Evidence. Something to show what a liar he is."

Allie felt her face getting hot. "How can you say things
like that about the Dean?"

"Why, Allie," Fabre said with a reproachful look, "I
thought you liked Domerc."

"I hardly know him," Allie said primly.

"And after all, it was Aigar's lies that got Domerc
thrown out of the Landsensers Guild," Fabre went on
unheeding.

"I don't believe a word of it," Allie said.

"You haven't heard a word of it!" Fabre snapped. "But
you saw how Domerc looked when the Landsensers came
this afternoon?"

Allie nodded, unwillingly remembering that white,
strained look.

"Well, then. Don't you want to help?"

Fabre clearly thought he'd explained everything.

"I might," Allie said cautiously, "if I knew exactly what
was going on." Obviously these people thought the Dean
had done something terrible to Domerc. It was just as
obvious to Allie that he couldn't have behaved badly. She
knew Aigar. He was kind and considerate and not at all
the sort of man Fabre and his friends had made him out
to be. But she wouldn't be able to convince them of that
unless she heard their side of the story, would she?

Fabre looked apprehensively over his shoulder, as if
he expected to see Domerc standing there glaring at him.
"Domerc," he said, "would kill me. He doesn't want it
talked of any more. Wants to put it behind him, he says.
Wants to make a new life. Ha! What Aigar pulled is still
draining the soul out of him. Ah, not literally, you understand. Even Aigar wouldn't use magic that black . . . I
don't think."

"Of course not literally," Allie said, "and either tell me or don't, but I can't do anything to help when I haven't the faintest idea what's wrong."

"It started near Brefania, last spring," Fabre said all in a rush. "Domerc was stationed at the Harendola guildhouse—you know, where the mountains come down into the Harendola valley?"

"Nope," Allie said. "Got a map?"

"Oh, well, never mind. Point is, the valley is held mostly by the Freefarmers of Harendola, except for Astire itself. I suppose I ought to pretend you've never heard of Astire? Right. It's the riverside city; a Greenwall, of course, nothing else would work in such a fertile area."

Allie decided not to ask what a Greenwall was.

"So anyway. Astire is held by Iseu de Brefania, and she mainly supports the Guildhouse. En Savaric ought by rights to contribute to their support, but he says he doesn't need Landsensers because his land is all mountain and rock and even if the peasants cultivate every square *vareng* of soil he still has to run a troop of mercs for cash income. Anyway he doesn't like Landsensers much." Fabre paused and thought this last statement over carefully. "Actually, Savaric—En Savaric, I should say— doesn't like anybody much. Anyway. Mostly the Guild stays off his lands. They've enough to do in the Harendola, anyway, the virtue flows through that valley so strong that it's a fulltime job for a whole House of Landsensers to keep the Freefarmers advised where they need to be planting and which fields can safely be let lie fallow. They just send an apprentice out to ride the border of En Savaric's lands, maybe go a little way up into the hills if necessary. Last spring," Fabre said with emphasis, "Domerc was the apprentice. Third year in the Guild, and he'd have been Robed this year."

"So?" Allie was beginning to wish Fabre would get to the point. This Landsenser business seemed like a cross between a folk religion and a role-playing game, and she was sure it was fascinating to the people who chose to play it, but surely it couldn't have anything to do with Domerc's real problems. People just didn't get that serious about a game. Not normal people, anyway.

"So," Fabre said, "he sensed a flow of landvirtue into the hills, untended, and he rode to follow it and to warn Savaric's peasants. Only on the way up into the hills, he met Dean Aigar and En Savaric themselves. Out hawking, they said. And Aigar—you do know he's a Landsenser as well as Dean of the College—anyway, he took Domerc aside for a private little talk. He said he'd been visiting Savaric as his personal guest and he knew all about the landvirtue and it was going to be taken care of, and would Domerc please not mention anything about it at the Guildhouse because it would just make relations between En Savaric and the Guild even worse than they usually were. So Domerc didn't make a formal report. Which was careless," Fabre said gloomily, "and just the kind of mistake he would make, being from a Seignor family like Savaric's and tending to believe their honor is worth more than ordinary people's, but he didn't deserve what happened to him for it."

"What did happen?"

"Nobody knows for sure."

It had grown dark outside while Fabre talked; the waitress went around the room, lighting torches, and the flickering oblique light slashed across Fabre's round snub-nosed face. Allie could not see the expression in his shadowed eyes. At the far side of the room, two people with heads bent over a music book were softly singing a plaintive love song: something about joy flying away like a falcon untamed. The melody made Allie's chest ache with a sense of loss, and pain, and good things lost forever.

Fabre scarcely seemed to hear the singing; he went on as if they were quite alone in the room. "A few weeks later Domerc was on rounds again. He had asked a senior Landsenser, Biatris d'Eleza, to ride with him. Because he wasn't absolutely sure Aigar had persuaded Savaric to care properly for the landvirtue. It would have meant taking some of his mercenaries off drill and putting them to work in the fields, you see, and Savaric's the kind of idiot who would save a Drac now even if it cost him a Griffon later. So he thought it would be better if Biatris were with him to sense whatever there was. Only he didn't tell her beforehand, you see, because he also thought, being only an apprentice, he might have over-estimated the strength of the landvirtue. So he wanted her to form her own impressions. That was what he said afterwards, anyway. Aigar's version," Fabre said without heat, "was, of course, completely different."

"I wish you'd stop putting the Dean on trial and just tell me what happened," Allie said. Actually she wished Fabre would get through recounting this silly squabble over an imaginary game and tell her the real problem between the Dean and Domerc, but that seemed like an ever fainter hope. Maybe there wasn't a real problem; maybe it was all about this game. People here must take it seriously, if even Dean Aigar played it; he didn't seem like the kind of man to get into games with students.

"Domerc says they Sensed the landvirtue stronger than ever before, and it had all gone wrong. They rode into the hills and found fifty *varengs* of good terraced fields sown with salt, and monsters rising from the earth where the landvirtue should have gone into corn for Savaric's peasants. There were voices like children crying; Biatris warned Domerc it might be a trick, but he rode ahead anyway. Of course he found no children. All the humans had fled or been killed already. He found a mourning-tree and hacked it down, but there were more sprouting behind it; he fled back to where he'd left Biatris and found that she was fading away."

"Going away?" Allie tried to translate, but Fabre ignored her.

"So Domerc put his hands to the ground and tried to take in enough landvirtue to himself to drain the monsters of strength and heal Biatris; but the flow was too

strong. He passed out, and when he came to himself
Biatris was gone, and Aigar was there."

Allie thought this over. The bit about Biatris fading
had to be some idiom she didn't understand. She reduced
the story to what made sense. "Gone? You mean she
was ruled out of the game? Or did she quit?"

"You are cool about this," Fabre said. "Happens all
the time in your Provinces, does it? Or is it just that
you don't care about Domerc?"

"It's just that I've got more sense than to get excited
about a game," Allie told him. If this Biatris had quit
in the middle of the game, she must have more sense
than the rest of this bunch. Allie thought that she'd like
to meet Biatris some day. "So Biatris was out of the game.
And Domerc didn't know Aigar was playing. So what
then?"

"You've a strange way of putting things," Fabre commented. "So—well, nothing, except that the landmonsters
dispersed, and when they got back to the Harendola
Guildhouse Aigar told a rather different story. He claimed
that when he met Domerc in the forest, back when it
all started, he told him to get back to Harendola and
alert the Guild of a major flow of landvirtue into Savaric's
lands. Said he'd been back in Coindra attending to University business, assumed Domerc would have followed
orders and taken care of the matter. Blamed himself,
he did, loud and long, for having left an untried apprentice in a position of such temptation. According to Aigar,"
Fabre said sombrely, "Domerc had deliberately concealed
the landvirtue's flow, salted the land so that it would build
up in that one area, all with the intent of creating a crisis
that would give him his excuse to absorb the virtue into
himself." Fabre looked sharply at Allie. "You do understand that's about the worst thing a Landsenser can do,
under ordinary circumstances, don't you? They're sworn
not to use their Senses and Powers for personal gain.
Otherwise we couldn't trust them, could we?"

"I suppose not," Allie said rather faintly. She was

becoming quite confused among all the rules and conventions of this game. And the intensity with which Fabre told the story made her nervous. There were those kids at Vista View who let role-playing games like Dungeons & Dragons take over their real lives. Was this what had happened to Domerc and his friends? "But if Domerc told one story and Aigar another, how did the gamesmaster decide who won?"

"You do use strange words." Fabre shook his head. "The trouble is, you see, that it was easy to believe an apprentice might be tempted into diverting landvirtue for his own use. Especially as Domerc had done exactly that. He said his reasons were good. Aigar said they weren't. And what could tempt a man like Aigar, Landsenser Emeritus and Dean of the College of Magical Arts, into telling a string of lies to ruin an apprentice's life? He hadn't absorbed any of the excess of landvirtue; the Guild has ways of testing such things. What motive could he have had?"

"You tell me," Allie said.

Fabre shook his head again. "I don't know. All I know is that Aigar set it up, somehow, and he's ruined Domerc's life. He was expelled from the Guild in disgrace, and his family disowned him. Last year he was set for a bright future, Landsenser and Seignor in one; this year he's a starving student, three years older than the rest of his class. Liuria's the only one of the family who's still speaking to him. And I know Domerc. I know he wouldn't lie. He was so damned pure and holy about the duties of Landsensing I could hardly stand him sometimes. His integrity was who he was," Fabre said. "I know I'm not putting it well, but don't you see? Aigar took that away from him—at least in the eyes of the world. Took his life away. And we don't even know why. That's where you come in."

"It is?" Allie felt completely, unpleasantly sober. The only reminder of all the punch she'd consumed was a throbbing headache that started somewhere near her left temple and sank roots down through the back of her neck. "Exactly what," she said slowly and carefully, "do you think I'm going to do for you?"

Fabre blinked. "Help Domerc prove he didn't do it?"

"How?"

"Find out what Aigar's up to. You're in his lab every day, aren't you? There must be some clues. He didn't ruin Domerc's life on a casual whim. He must have some plan that Domerc crossed, and you've a better chance of finding out than any of us. Look at the fine Domerc had to pay for trying to sneak into the lab. He can't raise the ready for another fine like that, none of us can. But you're allowed into the lab. Aigar trusts you."

"And you want me to betray that trust."

"If he's done nothing wrong," Fabre pointed out, "you'll find nothing. Where's the betrayal in that?"

"It's still spying on him. I won't do it. What difference does it make, anyway? It's only a game."

"It's Domerc's whole life!"

"Then," Allie said severely, "it shouldn't be. Tell him to get some new interests!"

Fabre slammed his open hand down on the table. "Salamanders! You may have fire on the top, Copperhead, but you're all ice inside, aren't you? We're good enough to drink and sing with, but not worth troubling yourself when you're in a perfect position to help Domerc."

"A perfect position . . . So that's why you've all been so nice and helpful to me," Allie said slowly. "You're trying to discredit the only man who ever believed I was worth anything. How dare you think I'd do anything to hurt him? Hey, what a great idea. Sure, let's pick up this stupid foreign student, she doesn't know anything, she looks lonely and lost, she'll probably be real glad to go along with whatever we say. She'll even swallow some stupid Dungeons and Dragons type plot and never ask why we really want her to spy on the Dean."

Allie shoved the table back and stood up. The pitcher

rocked violently back and forth and the last remaining drops of punch rolled from side to side. "I may not know much," she said, "but I do have some slight notion of loyalty. And I may be new in town, but I don't need your kind of friendship."

She ran out of the inn while Fabre was still trying to push the table aside, and sprinted down the passageway outside without looking back. At the bottom of the street her right foot skidded on a patch of slimy mud, and she thought she heard someone calling her name; but she turned and ran on through the network of narrow passages and alleys between the tall wooden houses of Coindra. By the time she came to the northern town gates where the mountains overshadowed the city there was no one following her, no one to see her crying into the wide sleeves of her new black scholar's gown.

CHAPTER FIVE

"In sober truth, these Beings called by the ignorant, Landmonsters, be not Monstrous in their Origins. They are but the Spirit of the Land in its full strength arising as vapors from the Ground, and in such Forme bee as Natural as any Creature. Theu doo but become Monstrous in Due Proportion to the Monstrosities perpetrated by Men. . . ."

Allie set the book down for a moment, stretched, and rubbed her eyes. She was curled on the narrow bed in her attic room; she'd pushed it right up against the window so that she could go to sleep and wake up with the sky and the clean air and the green smell of the fields on the far side of the river. It was convenient for reading, too, as long as the daylight lasted. But now the light was fading, and the printed words were growing dim on the page.

She'd borrowed de Breuil's *Historia naturae* from the Dean's shelves. Given that the title was Greek or Latin or something, she'd been surprised and relieved to find that the text was in English. No, not English. Not French either. And the words didn't make any sense on the printed page, but when she read them aloud to herself she could understand them.

That didn't make any sense. Neither did this long serious straight-faced discussion of stuff that had to have come out of some fantasy role-playing game. Except . . .

Allie touched the book and frowned. It was an *old*

84

book: the binding crumbled and rotting at the edges, the paper brown and speckled with age. Maybe a hundred years old, she guessed. They didn't have games like Dungeons and Dragons in the old days, did they? And this guy, this whatsisface de Breuil, made it all sound so . . . so *real*.

Which was, of course, impossible. She just had to keep reading until he got to the catch. Allie picked up the book again, holding it close to her face in the dying light, and murmured to herself as she read.

"They do rise like Steam or Noxious Mists above our most fertile land, called into being by that same Power that does force the green shoot to push through the crusted Soil. Thus did our Fathers meet with many such Beings when they came into the land of Escorre and found it without Human Habitation, and the Land untilled. These did no Harm but did Affright them mightily.

"After the coming of our Forbears unto this Land, it did pass that they found where they had insulted the good land with Wars and Bloodshed, so did worse Monsters arise; and he that did build his Habitation upon good soil found his House beset with Mists and Crying Ghosts, while he that did build upon the Rock held Household in good safety."

Allie scowled at the book. Did this de Breuil character think he was describing an old legend, or preaching a sermon, or what? That last bit sounded more like a Bible story than real life. Well, that explained it, didn't it? He was telling, like, a parable or something. You weren't supposed to believe it really happened.

Which was a good thing. Allie preferred her monsters to stay safely inside the imaginary universes of the role-playing games; and given a choice, she didn't even want to play the games.

The next bit was written like a dialogue, like a student asking a teacher and getting answers. Allie grinned. That was what she needed, all right. Only the student in the book wasn't asking the right questions.

"Then these monsters do take the anger of the landvirtue as well as its life into themselves?

"Even so have we learned by long experience. Thus were the Landsensers formed as a Guild, that those who could sense the flow and manage of the land's virtue might guide us where to build and where to till the soil. If wee do permit the Virtue of the Land to arise in the Natural Form of Vegetation, then shalbe no Mists nor Vaporous Forms to Trouble us by Night."

Well, that was interesting. The question she really wanted to ask was, *How come you people take all this so seriously?* But that wasn't in the book. She'd have settled for some more on the Landsensers, but nooo, the dumb student questioner in the book had to go off asking for descriptions of imaginary monsters. Well, what did you expect of books written by professors, of course they invented students who would ask the questions they wanted to answer. Allie had always suspected Socrates of doing the same thing. Or did she mean Plato? Whoever it was wrote those dialogues. Allie sighed and went back to mining nuggets of information out of de Breuil.

"And what forms do these monsters take?

"At first they do appear as Plants of most unnatural Form; thus may you see weeds that are not green, but a riotous Throng of princely purple, the gold of wealth and the red of blood, all growing as fast as a field of green Corn on a hot summer's day; and so will they grow in despite of Salt or Drouth.

"Can nothing stop this perilous growth?

"If the landvirtue surges elsewhere, the weeds wither and die; if it remains, they grow head-high, a jungle of intertwined stems and sharp knife-edged blades.

"And do they so remain?

"Nay, then follow monstrous and bizarre changes. These weeds do grow heads of grain and spill it on the ground to generate more monsters. They bring forth unnatural fruit that glows with a sickly light under the moon; each fruit on a monster-tree is magic, but none can tell (save by eating one) what its particular virtue is: on the same tree may grow a love potion, a deadly poison, an emetic, a cure for warts, an addicting narcotic. A fruit which, eaten, makes the eater into another such tree, rooted where he stands. A fruit whose seeds take wing and buzz in the eater's mouth, burrowing into his tongue and throat to lay eggs that will in their turn burrow deeper until he is consumed from within. A fruit which removes the power of earth, freeing the eater to soar . . . but not to return. All manner of transformations hide within those varied fruits, some soft and purple like monstrous grapes, others hard as crabapples and, so they say, very sweet."

This guy had a great imagination, Allie thought. This stuff was better than Tolkien, except there wasn't much plot, nothing *happening*.

Rather like her own life at the moment. She hadn't seen much of Domerc and Fabre and Liuria since that evening at the Blue Pigeon. So what? It was her choice, wasn't it? She didn't need them. They hadn't been real friends; they just pretended to make friends with her so they could use her to get at the Dean.

But they were nice to you before you got that job with Aigar, a small voice deep within her pointed out.

Allie told the voice to shut up. Not being friends with the students downstairs still hurt; in fact, it hurt a *lot*. The last thing she needed was to argue with herself about it. Of course she would try to convince herself they really wanted to be true friends. She wanted to believe that so much, she'd be bound to find some argument in favor of it.

No. Anyway, if they did have any use for her except as a spy on the Dean, they could've come around and said Hello, or How's it going, or Let's go to the Blue

Pigeon, or Come play rhythm section while we make music. Couldn't they?

Reading was less painful than thinking.

"And these be only the plants, whose varieties I have not yet begun to catalogue, but never mind; time is limited, let us pass on to the true monsters. These I will not call animals, for they be sprung from the soil like the plants and do begin their life in the same wise, but they are not plants for that they do move freely about the earth, once ripened. And that is their terror.

"Here will I describe the trew Monsters that bestride the earth on legs, that see out of soft jellys for Eyes. So may you see a Man complete save that the top of his head is open and all soft within like a pudding, and the tears drain continually out of his Eyes as he doth walk; or a Woman drest in leaves, with bare branches where her hands should be, doth wail endlessly as one in great grief; or a Child, or Thing about the Bignesse of a Child, whose head hands and feet are all great flowers bursting forth perpetually among the withered ruins of the last ones, ever a flower fading and a new one blooming, and all its flowers it turneth continually toward the Sun whence cometh its Sustenance.

"Surely there can be no danger to men in these pitieful Deformities?

"As with the apples of the dream-trees, so is the danger varied and unpredictable. Yet these may be hewn down by the sword, if they be caught young.

"And if they be not caught in their (as one might say) Infancy?

"Then shal they grow into such beasts as never *Odysseus* dreamt of, when he did adventure among the *Polyphemoi*: with scales as hard as any steel, with limbs like vines to lash at you, to hurl the poison darts which themselves do manufacture out of theyre own Substance, to entangle and slowly strangle you by Contracting with each Expulsion of your own Breath."

"Are they dangerous to the intire Created World, or only until Mankind?"

"They are a part of the Natural Order. If we endanger that Hierarchy of Beeing which doth link the Stone to the Flower, the Flower to the Beest, the Beest to Man, and Man to the Starres, then do the Landmonsters appear to Restore the Hierarchy by destroying Us."

"Then ought we not rather to Soothe them with Sweete Musick and Pleasant Words, as a Man will tame a Horse or a Falcon?"

De Breuil evidently did not think much of the "Make love, not war" approach to conflicts.

"Nay, shalt slay these monsters while they be still soft and vulnerable; have no Mercie upon the Infants, for that the Adults will have none upon you!"

"What shalbe the form taken after the Weeping Man and others which you have described?"

"In due time will these Monsters grow so Great that they Dissolve again into a Vaporous Mist and so sink Back into the Land; but for the great destruction that they may wreak beforetime, let you not wait upon this happening, but take arms against the Creatures from their first appearance."

Allie shivered. She was glad these things were just make believe; this de Breuil guy had a really creepy imagination. Except, what was all this stuff doing in a *textbook*? She flipped to the front and studied the title page.

"Historia Naturae," she read slowly, under her breath, tracing the spidery printing with one finger, "a description of the natural history, geography, and political science of the entire world. With maps of Escorre and the Western Seas. For the use of scholars at university in the town of Coindra, and for such others as may come earnestly seeking knowledge."

Coindra. Escorre. Salmistre. Brefania. This was creepy. There weren't even any names she recognized. Allie glanced over her shoulder. Dark clouds were rolling across the sunset sky, blotting out the last of the light. She'd have to light the lamps . . . She hadn't messed with these old-fashioned oil lamps before; in the evenings they all gathered in Domerc's and Fabre's room to study around the big sturdy table there, or in Liuria's room to sing and gossip and argue.

She wasn't about to go down there now, though. And she didn't have any matches. Oh, well, there was just time to skim a little more of de Breuil. Then she'd walk over to the lab and slip the book back into Aigar's shelves, and maybe on the way back she'd ask somebody where she could buy a box of matches. It was ridiculous, really, the way she'd been depending on Fabre and his friends to help her find everything she needed. It was high time she learned to take care of herself in Europe, Allie thought. Just as soon as she finished reading this book, she'd get started.

She slapped the book down a little too hard, and a loose page floated out and down to the floor. One of the promised maps, it looked like. Allie had skipped those pages, the introduction and all the boring history stuff, in her search for something that would help explain Domerc's problem to her. Now she picked up the map and stared at it, trying to make sense of the outlined shapes. The two islands at the upper left had to be Great Britain and Ireland, though the squiggly printing seemed to call them something else. Allie squinted. The Misty Isles? And over here in Europe, near the Mediterranean, was a neat star labeling the town called Coindra.

There was no town called Massat on the map.

There was no *France*.

There were no country names. Just cities and provinces and rivers.

And to the west, no Americas; only empty space. Well, the map didn't go that far, that was all.

The legend at the top of the page read, "A concise map of the Entire World."

Allie felt cold, and something prickled down her spine. There must be a storm coming. There must be some mistake. She didn't need to worry about maps; she'd never been any good at geography anyway; it was just that it made you feel peculiar, somehow, to be reading a book whose author acted as if your whole *country* didn't exist.

Well, it wasn't her problem. It couldn't be her problem. She just needed to finish reading this section and return the book before the Dean noticed it was missing, seeing that she hadn't exactly asked permission to borrow it.

"Be there monsters of the Air and Watter as well as of the Land?"

"So much may be surmised from the many who have perished while sailing the Western Seas, though none have returned alive to tell their tale."

"Is it not possible that the sea, like unto the land, requireth good Tillage? And that a Regular Traffic of Ships and Sailing Men might be the best means whereby to Tame the Monsters of the Watter?"

"So was it surmised in past ages, but hath none dared to make Tryall of this Hypothesis since the loss of Three Ships at Once under command of the sailing-master Cristoforo Colombo."

Allie set the book down very carefully. She noticed that her hands were damp with sweat. And it was definitely colder in the room than it had been, and the shadows were very deep along the walls.

"Christopher Columbus," she said aloud, "was not lost at sea. He discovered America and gave the Indians measles. Even *I* know that much."

But de Breuil didn't seem to know it.

And there wasn't any map of America in this book.

And everybody, *everybody* seemed to talk and act as if there really were magical monsters that could rise from neglected land. They had a guild devoted to keeping the monsters down, they tore down perfectly good roofs, they wouldn't build towns on anything but rock.

It was all—unreal.

And suddenly, proving it unreal became the most important thing in the world; more important than preserving her pride and staying away from her new false friends; far, far more important than returning this book to the Dean's shelves. Allie slammed the book shut and ran down one flight of stairs. There was a band of golden lamplight under the door of the room that Domerc and Fabre shared. She burst in without knocking, without giving herself time to think and lose courage and anticipate rejection.

Domerc was alone, studying in the circle of lamplight. He looked up in surprise.

"Is something wrong?"

"Not a thing," said Allie, leaning against the door jamb. "Sorry to bother you. It's just—"

She tried to think of a good excuse for the question she wanted to ask. I'm totally ignorant of my own country's history, never mind yours? I'm making a survey to find out how much European students know about American history? I've been assigned a paper on comparative attitudes towards Columbus in Europe and the Old World?

None of the excuses seemed worth it. "Do you know who Christopher Columbus was?" she blurted out.

"Of course," said Domerc. He was looking at her oddly, and no wonder; what a dumb question! Allie felt her body starting to sag with relief; her knees were shaking as though she'd run up four flights of stairs instead of down one. *Silly to get so upset over nothing*, she thought, and then Domerc decided to amplify his answer. "He believed there was land beyond the Western Seas, or that he could get to the eastern edge of the world by sailing west, or some such nonsense; I don't remember exactly, it was a long time ago. The sea monsters ate his ships."

Allie found that she was talking from a small cold place

somewhere deep inside her, a place that ignored the silly girl who wanted to sit down or cry or scream. "If he never came back," she inquired, "how do you know what happened to him?"

"One seaman floated on the wreckage," Domerc said, "three weeks, drinking rain water, until a ship blown off course from the Azores picked him up. Everybody knows that story."

"I don't," Allie said, from the cold quiet stillness inside her. "The way I heard it, he discovered America."

"What?"

"The big continent in the Atlantic Ocean. The Western Sea. *That* way." Allie pointed out Domerc's window, to where the sinking sun was obscured by long dark stripes of clouds.

Domerc looked blank. "Is this some kind of game?"

"You do," Allie said carefully, "know where *America* is?"

He shook his head and started to say something, but Allie couldn't hear him over the roaring in her ears. She backed out of the room, clutching the Dean's volume of *Historia naturae* to her chest, babbling something about having to return this book to Aigar's office right away, before the storm broke.

"He'll know what to do, you see," she informed Domerc, who had risen from his studies and was looking at her anxiously. "It's all right—I'm not sick—I'm just in the wrong place, that's all." She laughed about that, and her laughter came out all wrong: high and shrill. "The wrong *world*. Boy, when Dad said he wanted to get me out of his hair, I never guessed he meant *this* far out. But Aigar will know how to send me back. He has to. If I got here, I must be able to get back somehow. That's logic. Isn't it?" she inquired of Domerc, the student of Philosophy.

"Back where?" Domerc was very white under his sleek black hair; his eyebrows stood out like black charcoal smudges drawn across the pale oval of his face.

"To the real world," Allie explained. "The world where America exists. Where Columbus *discovered* America. And gave the Indians measles." For a wild moment she imagined herself staying in this place that de Breuil called Escorre, mounting another expedition into the Western Seas, discovering the Americas and the golden civilization of Indians undestroyed by Western colonialism, living in harmony with Nature. Then, without voicing the vision, she shook her head. In this world, Domerc said, ships that sailed west were eaten by sea monsters. And *things* came out of the ground at night. "I want to go home, you see," she explained carefully, "only I don't have my ruby slippers. Maybe Aigar can get me some. Don't you think? If I explained everything to him. You see, I really don't belong here. That's why I didn't understand things. You must have thought I was stupid, but it's just that I come from—oh, never mind," she caught herself. Time to stop babbling. "I can't expect you to get it. But Aigar will. *He* believes in me," said Allie.

She turned and ran down the stairs and out into the narrow cloud-dark street where rain was beginning to lash the cobbles, ignoring Domerc's calls after her. If she stopped and thought any longer she was going to start thinking about mists and magic trees and walking jellies, and then she would lose her nerve and not be able to go to campus until morning. And she didn't think she could spend an entire night alone with her new understanding. She would find Aigar, and he would tell her how to get back, and she would do whatever it took, and then everything would be all right again. If only he was working late tonight!

The Dean of the College of Magical Arts was staying late in his laboratory that night, but not for any college-approved work. He'd been bombarded with messages from his impatient partner, and had reluctantly agreed to link by farspeaker that night so that he could inform Savaric as to the progress of the work. But he wasn't fool enough to use the system officially set up and maintained by the University. No telling when some officious member of the University Guild would decide to test the speaker system for maintenance, or some such excuse. No, Aigar had decided, he would use the laboratory voicebubbles to build his own temporary farspeaker. He could certainly hold such a system together with his personal magic for as long as it took to reassure the Seignor. And he would create the system in his own laboratory, with his personal keyspell encasing the room. *And* he would wait until everybody in the administration offices had gone home for the night.

"Took ye long enough," Savaric growled as soon as the contact was made.

Aigar sighed. "Security—"

"Afraid to speak with me by day, are ye? Thought as much." Savaric's scowling face, gray with the bristles of his untrimmed beard, sneered at Aigar from the surface of each shimmering voicebubble in the pyramid of glass spheres.

Aigar clenched his fists under the long sleeves of his gray gown. Savaric always did this to him. Never mind the realities of the situation, the fact that in his public life as Dean of a College he had a certain position to maintain and expectations to meet, that his days were not his own but given over to public service, that he couldn't command the privacy available to a Seignor in his home hold. Savaric never let reality interfere with his assumption that he and his ways were naturally superior to anyone else's way of doing things and that everybody else in the world was either a dolt or a weakling.

The anger and defensiveness washed back from Aigar, interfering with the speakspell. The pyramid of glass spheres trembled, unstable in the powerful wash of emotion, and a mist covered the image of Savaric's face. With an effort Aigar calmed his thoughts and reinforced the chant in the back of his mind, the tones and syllables that held the speakspell together. What did Savaric's petty snubs and jeers mean, after all? He needed the man now. Later he would not need him, and then—well, then Savaric might regret his boorish ways.

If he had time.

Aigar privately vowed to see that Savaric had plenty of time to think over and repent his manners before the end came. The promise steadied his thoughts and his voice. In an even, low tone he recited the steps he had taken since the experiment with Janifer failed. His reasoning was impeccable; even Savaric did not interrupt him now.

Aigar explained that the reason Janifer had merely dispersed the landmonsters they raised, rather than controlling them so that they could add to the strength of Savaric's mercenary army, must be due to his deeply embedded hatred and fear of landmonsters in all their forms. "He was well bound to my service," Aigar insisted, with a glance at the high shelf where Janifer sat in his present form of magically fired clay. "He remains so bound. But he cannot overcome the fear of landmonsters which every child of our land knows from birth. We need to bind a soul from a world that has never known landmonsters."

Savaric cackled at this. "And where d'ye reckon to find such a one? Under a rock? Ye're scairt, Dean Aigar with your fine silk gown, and that's the truth of it. Afeard to stand up and fight like a man, so ye make excuses that ye must have the horn of a mythical beast, or a soul from another world, or some such other thing that ye trust never to have."

"As a matter of fact," Aigar said stiffly, "I have been experimenting for the past month, and have but recently brought such a soul alive and in its human form from the Elder World."

Savaric's repeated image broke into a pyramid of sly grins, and Aigar felt as though he'd just stepped into a trap. Why? All he'd done was to announce his results—a result any mage might be proud of. Could it be that Savaric knew about the white demon-rats and the belching metal monster and the other failures? *Not failures, experimental errors*, Aigar hastily corrected his thoughts.

"If ye've got such a soul bound to yer purpose—" Savaric began.

"Not yet," Aigar interrupted him. "The binding is not yet complete."

"Whyever not? Took ye no time at all to drip Janifer's blood into the clay and fire it with yer spells. I was there, remember?"

Aigar suppressed a shudder. He remembered that day all too clearly. He would never forget the look of surprise in Janifer's eyes, then the dulling of his eyes as the soul left his body and flowed with his blood into the waiting fertile earth. Nor would he soon forget the effort required to bind the four elements together. Human soul to human blood was a natural binding, as was the landvirtue—the earthsoul—to the waiting earth. But to bind the human elements to the earthen ones, and to make both responsive to his wish and command, had required a magical fire intense enough to burn his hands and scorch the stone walls of Savaric's keep. The effort had left him exhausted for days.

"This," he said stiffly, "is rather more complicated. I would not expect you to understand. A soul from Elder World must be prepared beforehand, bound to me by blood. So much I have already done."

"Then what are ye waiting for?" Savaric demanded. "D'ye have any idea how much it's costing me to keep my mercs penned up here, eating like horses and earning nought? Three nice little wars and a siege I've turned down this season, while ye sit on silk cushions and twiddle with the Theory of This and the Hypotreesis of That. And the landvirtue flowing through the Harendola like floodwaters. I tell ye, man, now's the time to move. I've a quarrel going with Iseu de Brefania; I could take over

her valley lands tomorrow and nobody'd think anything
of it but that I'd seized the chance to get me some good
farming lands. It's time to move, ye fool!"

"Fools," said Aigar, "rush in. 'Tis their nature."

"And 'tis the nature of mages to twiddle their thumbs
and let other folk pay the bill when they break their
promises! I think ye're lying. Ye never brought a soul
from Elder World."

"I did." Aigar just stopped himself from retorting, "I
did *so*." Something about Savaric always sent him back
to nursery manners. It would be enormously gratifying
to bash the man with a wooden bucket and rub his face
in the sandbox.

But still more gratifying to use him and his mercenaries until it slowly dawned on Savaric that whoever
controlled the landmonsters controlled the army, and that
he'd handed over his power to the partner he took such
pleasure in affronting.

"I have the child," he said more slowly.

"Where?"

"Well, not here, you idiot! Would I discuss this before
her face?"

Savaric shrugged. "If ye tied her up good first, what's
the difference?"

Aigar almost broke the contact then, so disgusted was
he with the Seignor's casual brutality. He would have
to take Allie's soul. He was resigned to that. But he didn't
mean to make her suffer as Janifer had, with the full
knowledge of what was happening to her. He was going
to do it gently. Perhaps with a sleeping draught or a
slowspell laid over her mind first . . .

"Ye're sure ye can produce the soul?" Savaric nagged
at him.

"Of course I am!"

"Good. Then do it tonight. Farspeak me here when
ye've done, and I'll move my men out to the Harendola.
And after the *unfortunate ravages of war*," Savaric chuckled grimly, "there'll be blood enough on the land, and

fields burnt too, to raise as fine a crop of landmonsters as ever ye could wish to experiment on. Only, Dean, be sure ye get it right this time! I think ye're going soft, afraid to take another soul for yer work."

"Am not."

"Then prove it. Do it now!"

Aigar managed a creaky laugh. "In the middle of the night?"

"Ye said the lass was bound t'ye already. Ye could call her if ye would."

"I won't. Why should I disrupt my plans for your insolent demands?"

"Insolent, is it! I think ye've no soul, no work, nothing to show. And if ye've been wasting my time . . ." Savaric paused menacingly. "Would the Landsensers Guild like to hear the true story of what passed last year in the mountains?"

"You'd never," Aigar gasped. "You'd have to expose yourself too."

"Me?" Savaric grinned. "I'm just a simple Seignor from the back woods, beglamoured and confused by yer magic and lies. I didn't rightly understand yer devilish plot until it was too late, and then, given the bad blood 'twixt me and the Landsensers, I was feared to accuse one of their own, aye, and a high and mighty Warden of the Landguild at that. But if ye don't come up with something better than promises, I'm main feared my conscience will drive me to Tell All. Besides," he pointed out briskly, "the Landsensers have no authority over the Seignors. Worst they can do is decide I'm a right vile and contemptible person. I reckon I'll survive that. I'm not a Senior Servant of the Guild. I don't have high office in Guild and higher office in Coindra to lose."

Aigar pressed his lips together until he could control his voice. "The child from Elder World is called Allie. I brought her here on Fourth Domesci and promptly enrolled her as my laboratory assistant, as a convenient way to keep her under my eye until the magical preparations should be complete. She is bound to me now by blood and silk." He held up the small package of blood-stained white silk that he had worn as an amulet since collecting it. "I have delayed only to collect earth fertile with the landvirtue, suitable for receiving her life's blood and soul force. That earth I have only tonight prepared for the sacrifice." He stepped back and gestured toward the stone bowl on a distant laboratory bench, hoping the wavering vision through the farspeaker would keep Savaric from noticing the cobweb that an enterprising spider had spun from bowl to tabletop.

"Satisfied?" he demanded, stepping forward again to block Savaric's view of the bowl.

"Ah. Mebbe. Ye'll swear the only delay has been for spellcraft and gathering supplies? It's not that ye're afraid to kill the wench?"

Aigar drew himself up and made a grand gesture with one wide-sleeved arm. "You impugn the honor of my office."

Savaric smirked. "Swear."

"The child Allie means nothing to me but the tool of our plan," Aigar said hastily. "By the landsense given to me, her blood shall be mine, her soul shall serve mine."

"Ye mean, serve *us*," Savaric corrected. "Ye'd not be thinking to play me false, mage?"

"Never," Aigar asserted in the firm ringing tones with which he always masked his best lies. "I would not slay her but to further our joint ends," he said, and that, being perfectly true, sounded slightly false. Allie had been a willing and useful servant, and she looked at him with the respect he'd always hoped to see in a student's eyes. It seemed such a waste to use her for Savaric's plans. Couldn't they wait until he had a chance to borrow another Elder World soul?

"I'll be expecting to hear from ye within the hour," Savaric growled. "Else—there's some in your guild would be main interested in the tale I could tell. Remember that, mage." His face blurred, then faded behind a screen of swirling colors. Aigar snarled inarticulately at the voicebubbles. How dare that—that muddy mercenary warrior break the spell before he had been given leave to go?

Something squeaked in the far corner of the laboratory—no, in his library beyond the archway. Rats in the books? Aigar fretted. He needed to summon the child at once. But how could he summon up the necessary concentration while his mind was filled with the image of the white demon-rats from Elder World nibbling away at his precious books? He would have to drive them away. In the morning he could set the child Allie to catching them—no, he couldn't. Aigar cursed Savaric again. Allie had been a most useful laboratory assistant; why couldn't Savaric at least have waited until the end of the semester before demanding her sacrifice?

The rustling sound came again. Aigar whirled, and his wide sleeve caught the pyramid of voicebubbles and sent them flying to the marble floor. A delicate chorus of chinks and tinkles and the whispery remnants of past farspeakings swirled and eddied around the splinters of iridescent glass. But that was only a minor disaster compared to what Aigar now saw.

The source of the noise wasn't a white demon-rat, after all, but the child from Elder World, looking almost as white as those blasted rodents from her home world. Her red hair was slicked down close to her head and water dripped from the hem of her black scholar's gown. With the color drained from her face and her fiery hair hidden, she looked all eyes and sharp pointy nose, like a larger version of the demon-rats.

"*What are you doing here?*" He hadn't summoned her . . . or had he? Was the bond between them so strong that his mere thoughts could bring the child across Coindra in the middle of a spring storm? Aigar touched the amulet of white silk on his breast. It felt softer and more alive than he remembered it; almost like a beating heart.

"I thought you would help me," Allie said. Her voice was a husky whisper without inflection; it made Aigar's skin creep. "That was silly, wasn't it? 'The child Allie is nothing to me but the tool of our plan,'" she quoted, still in that eerily dead voice.

Aigar cursed himself for not resetting the keyspell. The one he used daily, for convenience, was set to recognize Allie and allow her free entrance to the laboratory. It would be a confounded nuisance to have to be present whenever his assistant was working. But this— this was a much greater nuisance. Who could have guessed the infant would be so dedicated to her studies that she'd show up in the lab on a spring evening when she should have been out drinking and singing and doing whatever it was scholars did for amusement?

And, more to the point, how much had she heard?

"Did your parents never warn you that eavesdroppers hear no good of themselves?" Aigar asked with a smile that felt sickly even to him. "If your feelings were hurt, Allie, that's unfortunate, but you must not take statements out of context. I'd hoped to shield you from this unpleasantness, but . . ." He sighed. "Certain narrow-minded people, probably jealous of your rapid advancement in the magical arts, have accused me of taking an unseemly interest in your person. For both our sakes I had to squelch such rumors at once; I'm sorry if my words were too blunt for your taste, but you must see—"

"Come off it," Allie interrupted him. "I heard more than that. You weren't talking about . . ." She paused briefly and frowned. "About *sexual harassment.*"

"What?" Aigar demanded, genuinely confused by the strange syllables.

Allie blinked. "I guess that's another thing you don't have a word for in Escorrean. Like *computer* and *typewriter* and *pedestrian zone.*"

Aigar's fingers fluttered in a warding spell against these

strange jagged syllables, doubtless full of the mysterious power of Elder World. "Think not to cast your outworld magics on me, child," he said sharply, "I have knowledge and deep powers beyond your ken." At least he sincerely hoped that was the case.

Allie sighed. "Who're you kidding? I'm flunking Radegond's lecture series. And that's only Fundamentals of Magical Theory in your course system."

"A minor adjustment in the testing procedure might correct that problem," Aigar suggested. For a moment he harbored the irrational hope that she could be bribed with favors from the Dean's office to forget everything she'd heard, to . . . What was the point? He was about to sacrifice her. He had to. Else Savaric would sacrifice him. It really didn't matter what the child thought of him in her last few moments of life; her soul was half his already, and before midnight she would be cupped in his hands, caught in fired earth to serve him forever.

Strangely, the thought gave him no pleasure.

"I don't want a phony A," Allie said. "*I want to go home*. And I thought . . ." Her eyes were shiny, and one big tear rolled forlornly down to the tip of her pointy little nose. Aigar felt as if he'd been caught torturing a kitten. "I thought you would help me. I thought just maybe, finally, I'd found somebody who gave a damn what became of me. Ha! Big joke, right?" She turned away from him, shoulders slumping. "Never mind. I guess I'll go see if the Landsensers Guild will help me. From what I've been reading, they seem like pretty decent sorts, and they've got a magic of their own."

Aigar felt the white silk amulet throbbing against his chest, sending jolts of pain through him with each pulsation. It must be reflecting Allie's feelings. Poor lost child! He would almost be doing her a favor; she was such a raggle-taggle waif, wandering through the world without sense or purpose, and in such pain that the mere echo of it through the amulet hurt him. At least, once he completed his work, she would have a purpose—what was left of her, anyway.

Besides, he had no choice. She was threatening to expose him to the Landsensers. He could lose his Warden's post, could be toppled from his Deanship by the petty schemers who would be so delighted to have something like this against him. And worse yet, he could be expelled from both guilds, Landsensers and University. For a moment Aigar looked down the icy black slope where a man could fall if he found himself Guildless, saw a future of begging for bread and partch in a Seignor's charity kitchens.

No. Such a fate could not befall *him,* Aigar, Dean and Warden. It would be most inappropriate. Certainly no ragged waif from another world could be allowed to bring him down; it would be against all propriety.

"You're wrong, my child," Aigar said. "You mean more to me than I have dared say." That was true enough, at any rate. "I have but been waiting for a propitious moment to explain all to you; I feared lest the shock might unseat your reason, and waited for the truth to dawn upon you gradually. As I gather it has now done." Allie wouldn't believe that for a minute if her wits were working, but in her present distraught state it might serve for the minute he needed. He moved forward slowly, put one arm around Allie's shoulders and urged her into the laboratory. He could feel her tense shoulders relax under his arm. She *wanted* to believe he really cared about her, Aigar thought with incredulous delight. What a little fool! Really, anybody stupid enough to trust him again, after what she'd overheard, was too dim-witted to live. She'd be much better off as a bondsoul. She could sit on the shelf with Janifer and chatter to her heart's content.

"Just sit here," he urged her to the bench. Where the devil had he put his new glass blade? "You're tired and worried; you can't think clearly now. You need to rest. Close your eyes. Breathe deeply."

She took a ragged, shuddering breath and let it out shakily. Her eyelashes, dark with rain, looked like dark red pencil strokes on her dead-white cheeks. Not a pretty child, Aigar thought, but there was something indefinably appealing about her. He groped in the clutter of laboratory instruments, notes, reference books and steeping solutions, and his hand closed over the sharp edge of the glass blade. A line of blood sprang out on his palm.

"Breathe," he reminded Allie, shifting his grip to the hilt of the blade. If only she hadn't confronted him, forced him into this, he could have done it gently. It was all her fault really.

"Then can I keep working for you?" she asked, eyes closed.

If he said yes, would she guess how he meant her to serve him? It would be so much better if she went to the sacrifice unknowing, unprotesting; he did not want to cause her any unnecessary pain. Besides, there was a possibility that Janifer had become such a craven bondsoul because he'd died in fear. Allie must be kept calm at all costs.

"I fear not, my child," he said.

"I knew it, I *knew* it!" Allie leapt to her feet, knocking aside the glass blade with one flailing sweep of her hand. Aigar's palm was slippery with blood; the knife turned in his hand but at least he did not drop it. "You're just like all the others, just like *him*; if I'm not exactly like you want me to be then you ship me out somewhere else. Nobody wants me! Well, forget the pretty words!" she raged. "I'm not sticking around to hear the story this time. You just want to get rid of me, don't you? So be happy! I'm going. *Now!*"

Incredible! She didn't seem to have noticed the knife; her anger was all inward, all because—what? He didn't love her? Why should he love this little scrap of nothing? And who was the *him* she spoke of with such venom?

Allie jerked her dripping gown back over her shoulders and started for the arched doorway.

Aigar found his voice. "You can't leave!" She shouldn't be able to defy him like this; not with the silken amulet of her own blood beating against his chest.

"Try and stop me!"

He grabbed at the fluttering sleeve of her gown and jerked her backwards to face him, to make her look into his eyes and acknowledge the bond that he had over her in blood and silk. The rainwater that had dripped from her cloak made puddles of slick danger across the polished marble floor; she stepped into one, backwards, and her feet shot out from under her and her head cracked against the carved stone of the arch with a terrible, final sound.

Aigar dropped to his knees beside the small, crumpled figure in her sodden black gown. He pushed the sleeve nearest him up, felt for a pulse. Was that the beating of his own pulse he felt? No, the white silk amulet still fluttered against his chest. And he could feel the warm breath coming from her parted lips.

She lived; and she was stilled, ready for the blood-bonding with earth. He had only to bring her unconscious body to the bowl of earth, or bring the stone bowl to her, to complete the sacrifice.

Aigar stood and groaned under his breath as a muscle in the small of his back cramped. He was too old for all this. The sharp movement he'd made in catching Allie's gown must have made him pull a muscle. He took a step forward and a warning spasm of pain stiffened his whole back for a moment. He couldn't lift such a heavy weight as the stone bowl, not right now. Allie would be lighter, but he'd have to bend to pick her up. And just now he wasn't certain that he'd ever get up again if he bent over.

Besides, he was exhausted from trying to soothe first Savaric, then Allie. Why did everybody pick on him? He needed a restorative potion first. A glass of Brefania Red,

Aigar told himself, and a few minutes of quiet contemplation in the alcove built into the western wall of the laboratory, the one with padded cushions and good thick curtains. He could take his remaining voicebubbles in there and build a small pyramid, just strong enough to farspeak Savaric and tell him the thing was done. Well, as good as done, anyway. No need to confuse these blunt soldierly types with inconsequential details. And once that was over, when he had no more fear of Savaric's approaching the Landsensers Guild, he would be rested and able to complete the sacrifice and soulbinding with full concentration.

CHAPTER SIX

Domerc found it impossible to sit down and continue his studies after Allie ran out of the room. The crazy, impossible things she'd said whirled round in his brain, a mad jumble of fact and fancy. Columbus hadn't died, he'd discovered some lands called . . . Merca? Merike? Whatever. And Allie needed ruby slippers. Why? What for? And she thought *Aigar*, of all people, would help her?

Domerc paced around the study table. A night breeze sighed through the open casement window and all the lamps flickered. He wished Fabre were there. Fabre was probably off chasing a new girl. He'd have to solve this one on his own.

Allie had appeared out of nowhere, exotically dressed, and knowing next to nothing about Coindra and the rules that governed all scholars at the University. Even her name was outlandish.

How far away *had* she come from, anyway?

Her father had sent her away, she said.

What kind of place had he sent her from?

"A Merica," Allie's voice echoed in his mind. "The big continent in the Western Sea."

There were no lands in the Western Sea; nothing but wild water, growing wilder and more full of seavirtue and seamonsters the farther out you sailed. Columbus had proved that to everyone's satisfaction, at the cost of his life and three ships and their crews.

"The real world." He heard Allie again, as clearly as if she were still in the room. "The world where a Merica exists. Where Columbus discovered a Merica."

Was it possible that in Elder World there was such a continent, such a history? In such a world the Western Sea must be without its virtue and its monsters. Perhaps the land also was dead? No virtue flowing through the land, no danger of landmonsters, no Landsensers Guild? It would explain so much about this quick, bright girl who was so ignorant about the simplest things.

It was also hopelessly improbable. No one even knew that Elder World really existed any more; it was a tale for mothers to amuse their children with, a place of legend and wonder from which their forefathers had come hundreds of years ago. It wasn't exactly a location on the net of mage-streams like Astire or Salmistre. Even if it existed, how could one move from there to here without treading the journey-maze? No, much simpler to assume the kid was out of her mind.

But Allie didn't act crazy. Confused, yes. Wrapped up in herself and her social life, like most young scholars. Incredibly ignorant. But not insane.

In any case, mad or sane, she was terribly upset right now. And running to, of all people, Aigar! Domerc snorted. The kid's faith in her precious Dean was about to get a rude shock. He couldn't imagine Aigar putting himself out to help a hysterical undergraduate in the middle of the night.

Unless . . .

Domerc swore under his breath. If any mage lived who did have the power to bring a soul from the Elder World, it would be Aigar. And now the possibility had come into his mind, Domerc could almost imagine how a standard transport spell could be distorted to call objects across the emptiness between the worlds.

"Our forefathers chronicled that they had crossed between the worlds," Domerc said aloud to himself, "by grace and fortune. Could not another soul be brought the same way, by spell and will?"

By Aigar's will? Domerc might hate Aigar, but he had to admit the man was a great scholar-mage. If anybody could figure out how to pervert the spells of the journey-mazes and the currents of the mage-stream, Aigar could. If anybody could muster the strength to use such a spell, it would be the Dean of the College, with his access to all the linked power-spells that kept the University functioning.

Domerc couldn't imagine why Aigar would *want* a soul from Elder World. If he was seeking arcane knowledge, Allie couldn't have been much use to him. Why, she hadn't even known how to trim a quill for a pen before she came to Coindra.

But whatever the man wanted, Domerc felt sure it was nothing good. Else why would he keep Allie's origin to himself? The irrefutable proof of Elder World's existence and the success of his altered journey-maze spell would excite the admiration of all his colleagues. One would expect him to be presenting Allie as Exhibit A in his next scholarly lecture, not hiding her in the back of his lab to scrub benches and wash voicebubbles.

Whatever Aigar wanted with Allie was secret, and probably evil. And she was heading for the Dean's offices right this minute, too upset to know which way was up, and babbling everything she had figured out to anyone she met. Even, Domerc thought with grim amusement, to someone like him whom she didn't particularly like.

There was no way around it; he'd have to go after her and stop her.

It was so late that most lamps were out. To make matters worse, even the moon was half hidden behind flying clouds. Rain spattered the cobbles in fits and starts, precursor of a spring storm just building up its full force. A rising wind whipped Domerc's black gown about his legs and pulled vines free from the walls of houses. He had to hurry, but he could not run in darkness and wind with all the refuse of the alley hiding in shadows to trip him up.

As he strode over piles of refuse and detoured around puddles of standing water, Domerc had ample time to think of all the flaws in his reasoning. If Aigar had not proclaimed his feat of transport, it didn't necessarily mean he had evil plans. A much simpler reason would be that there *was* no feat of transport. Allie wasn't a displaced soul from another world, just a very disturbed kid who couldn't hack University life and had retreated into a fantasy world. And he, Domerc, was about to risk losing his own place at University for the sake of her fantasies. Because if Aigar caught him snooping around the lab at dead of night, there'd be another fine. And he had nothing left to sell.

"Domerc, my lad, you're a fool," he told himself. The rain was coming down full force now, blown into his eyes and under his hood by the wind. Leaves torn loose from the clinging vines whirled about his face, then shot away on the irregular gusts of the rising stormwind. Domerc felt as loose and rootless as one of those stray leaves. What was he doing out here? The thought of all he risked hovered, gaining strength with each step. The University of Coindra was his only Guild. The Landsensers would have nothing to do with him, and his father had formally expunged his name from the family Guild. Get himself expelled from Coindra, and he'd be a Guildless man. No housing, no healers, no food but a bowl of partch in some Seignor's kitchen, and no way out but to join the Seignor's troop of mercenary soldiers.

Was he going to risk that just to get some foolish, headstrong girl out of a trouble that probably existed only in his own mind? The sensible thing would be to go home and wait for Allie to show up again, as she probably would. If she didn't find Aigar in the lab. Or if, as Domerc had almost convinced himself, Aigar had nothing to do with the case.

Of course she'd be back. Where else could she go?

This eminently sensible reasoning had no effect on Domerc's long legs, which carried him across the university campus and through the series of arches and courtyards leading to the Dean's offices. Wind lashed the small fountains and drove the water horizontally over the paving stones, gusted the falling rain into billows of spray that soaked Domerc's unprotected head. He was crazy to be out in this; Allie would have turned around and found shelter when the storm broke. Certainly Aigar wouldn't be in his offices on a night like this; he'd be snug in the Dean's lodgings, enjoying the attentions of a servitor, demanding another flask of Brefania Red to warm his bones against the storm.

But someone was in the laboratory; the glow of an active lightbubble came white through the farthest series of tall pointed windows.

No keyspell blocked the outer offices. Domerc tried to make his way quietly through the dark rooms between him and the laboratory. His sodden shoes squelched on the floor, and he sneezed in the dusty book-room. He could just hear a low monotonous voice, somehow muffled. The voice did not waver when Domerc sneezed. Aigar must be *very* preoccupied.

What business kept him so late in the laboratory on a stormy spring night? Domerc edged through the book-room, hands before him to feel for writing stands or lecterns that might stand in his way. The rainwater soaking his gown coalesced into icy drops that rolled down his back.

The lightbubbble's rays spilled out through the last arch, puddling blue-white on the floor of the book-room like captured lightning. It fell on something that was neither stone nor leather, something that looked like a bunch of old rags dumped at the entrance to the lab. Domerc sighed in relief. Of course. Some servitor was cleaning the laboratory, that was all, and talking to himself while he did it . . .

"That lab was positively *squalid* before I came," Allie's

voice echoed in his mind; Allie before she'd quarreled with them, when she was bubbling over with happiness about her new job. "I think that's why he hired me right away, because he was desperate. That Janifer must have been as big a slob as Aigar, or else it's been months since he worked there. When did he quit, anyway?"

Domerc frowned. Probably it was just his nerves . . . but something didn't look quite right about the pile of rags the servitor had dropped. And he couldn't remember just when Janifer had left the University, or why. Not that it mattered now; why was he fussing over such trivia?

"He won't have anyone in there to clean the place," Allie said in his memory. "I have to do it all. I don't know why; he says someone not trained in magical arts would disarrange things. But you couldn't know less about the magical arts than I do, and I've made plenty of mistakes. He's very understanding though."

Aigar, understanding? Domerc shook his head and edged very slowly around the last free-standing book-case to get a better look at the archway. He must be nuts. He'd be expelled for sure, or more likely slapped with another fine beyond his means, if Aigar caught him snooping around here again. But it wasn't Aigar, wouldn't be, this hour of the night; just some servitor . . .

"He won't have anyone in there to clean the place."

"I have to do it all myself."

"I've made plenty of mistakes."

The remembered statements echoed in his head as though somebody were calling to him. And as he peered around the bookcase, the pile of rags came into sharper focus; a black cloth bunched around a small, limp foot with the shoe dangling half off.

Domerc caught his breath and knelt in the pool of light. Allie!

She lay on the stones just inside the laboratory, eyes closed, red hair tangled as usual. She looked death-pale, but perhaps that was just the effect of the bubble's cold magical light; her foot was warmer than the stone, at least. He bent forward to feel her hands, and his head and hands leaned into something soft, yielding, tensile and tough. The monotonous voice mumbling behind curtains broke off for a moment.

Domerc slipped back into the shadows, cursing his own stupidity. The sight of Allie lying there had made him forget that the laboratory was sure to be keyspelled against intruders. And it wasn't any textbook lock-and-key, either, but something Aigar had custom-designed to alert him to intruders; a spider's web of spells and glamours, quivering at the slightest touch.

And Allie was *inside* the spelled laboratory . . .

Not entirely, she wasn't. And the voice had begun again. Domerc sidled toward the archway, keeping his body flat against the wall, until he could kneel and reach Allie's foot. Would touching her alert the keyspell again? Should he work a minor counterspell against Aigar's web of warning first? No, better not. The use of magic against magic was far more likely to set off alarms than anything else he might do. The only way of knowing was to test it; and if the test failed, he'd have alerted Aigar for nothing. He would just have to draw her out of the laboratory as quickly as he could.

At least this was something worth risking his last Guild affiliation for.

His fingers closed around the bare instep of her foot. Did it twitch slightly in his hand? After a second's thought, Domerc gently replaced the soft leather shoe that was half sliding off the limp foot. She'd need her shoes, if she could be roused. If this didn't bring Aigar down on them with a spell to turn them both to stone. If, if, if . . . oh, why didn't he stop thinking and just *do* it!

One determined pull brought both Allie's feet within reach, and if there was any warning inside the laboratory, Domerc did not hear it. He grasped Allie's ankles and hauled her up onto his back in one clumsy rush, staggering away from the lighted arch, tense with fear of the alarms he might have wakened. Something chittered quietly to itself from a high shelf inside the lab. Aigar droned on behind his velvet curtains. Domerc shifted his grip and draped Allie over one shoulder. She was only a little thing; but he'd gone soft in the months of study at Coindra. Still staggering, he made his way through arches and dark rooms and out into the blackness of the storm. The wind and rain seemed like kind friends, the cloudy sky like the safest of sheltering roofs.

His business with Savaric concluded, Aigar sighed and leaned back in the deep cushioned window niche. The power of the spell died out of the pyramid of voicebubbles, flickering here and there with little bursts of iridescent light and repeated echoes of the conversation just past. Slowly the lights dulled, the echoes grew silent.

There was a flask of stillwein concealed among the cushions; not as civilised as Brefania Red or Enquerre White, but with a fiery strength to it that Aigar sorely needed before he could finish the night's work. Talking to that boor Savaric had not been restful at all; quite the reverse. The man had been standing there in his boots, half-armed, with mercenaries bustling in the far chamber. Any of them might have entered and seen Aigar's image in the matching pyramid of voicebubbles at Savaric's end! The man was blatantly flouting their agreement that no hint of Aigar's involvement in the project should be known until it was successfully completed. He had probably arranged for the bustle of his soldiers as a way of reminding Aigar that he still had the power to ruin him, if this attempt failed.

Under the circumstances, it had seemed only prudent to keep the conversation as brief as possible. And even that had not been easy; Savaric pressed Aigar for details and reassurances on every statement. Aigar had intended merely to report that the project was well on hand and should be completed by morning.

"Scholartalk," Savaric had sneered. "Can ye give me a straight answer for once in yer life, mage? Is it done or no?"

"Consider it done," Aigar replied.

Savaric sniggered. "The child is dead?"

"Yes." As good as dead, anyway. Aigar felt a flash of anger at Savaric, so unfeeling. Couldn't the man sense how it upset him to sacrifice the girl?

Evidently not. "How did you do it?"

"The magic of the blood-sacrifice is not for casual conversation," Aigar said as quellingly as possible. It would be hard enough to take Allie's blood; discussing the process with Savaric was no part of the bargain.

"And ye've fired the earth?"

"I prefer not to discuss the details of the work," Aigar said. "Besides . . ."

Was that a sound outside? Something quivered at his attention, plucking his taut nerves like a lute-string about to snap.

"Wake up, man!" Savaric's voice came tinny through the voicebubbles. His distorted image shivered and formed again, closer, then closer, until he was all monstrous nose framed by receding hair and beard. He must have shoved his face right up against the voicebubbles.

"All is completed," Aigar said. "You may proceed as previously agreed. Now let us break this link. Have I not explained to you that every moment of contact is like an open window through which some skilled mage could observe our converse?" They really should have established a code, he thought irritably. It could have been set up when he was in the Harendola last year for the early tests. He should have arranged the matter then, but he'd been distracted by the need to discredit young Domerc and his wild accusations. In any case, he consoled himself, Savaric was likely too stupid to memorize a code, and it would have been the height of folly to leave a written one in the man's hands. No, there was no alternative to these occasional covert voicelinks, dangerous though they were. But they'd be far less dangerous if Savaric would stop demanding details of the sacrifice and soulbonding and let him get back to work!

Finally the Seignor showed a kind of grudging satisfaction. Hastily Aigar broke the link before Savaric could force him to invent any more particulars of something he had not actually done yet.

Thank goodness that was over! Compared with talking to Savaric, completing the soulbonding of the child from Elder World was a mere bagatelle, a trivial task . . . well, almost trivial. Aigar reminded himself that she had still to be lifted and transported to where her blood could flow into the stone bowl. Was that another warning twinge from his back? Perhaps he had best fortify himself with a little more of the stillwein before attempting the task.

The flask of stillwein was almost empty, and Aigar's back pains had been replaced by a rosy glow of wellbeing, when he parted the curtains and looked out upon his laboratory.

His *empty* laboratory.

Oh, it was not technically empty: the marble work benches and wooden stools were still there. The glassware that Allie had washed and stacked for him glittered along the shelves that lined the wall. But Allie herself was gone. The mirrors and prisms and lightspell holders that dangled from the ceiling swayed gently to and fro, catching and reflecting the cold light of the one activated bubble and sending it to dance in blue-white flashes over an empty floor.

Aigar reeled and caught hold of the curtain to steady himself. There was a ripping sound; the time-worn silk came away from its rod and left him, for a moment, draped in rotting red silk curtains and even more dazed than he had been.

She could not be gone. How could she? He'd only been with Savaric a few moments; surely she hadn't recovered consciousness in that brief time. Well, maybe more than a few moments . . . No. He had not wasted that much time resting in his curtained niche and drinking stillwein while his intended sacrifice crept away. It had definitely not been *that* long. It couldn't have been. Whatever disaster had occurred, it had surely not been due to his own carelessness. It was Savaric's fault for keeping him talking so long.

As the full magnitude of the disaster came to him, Aigar groaned aloud and forgot about placing blame. What matter whose fault it was? He was ruined. His carefully lured soul from Elder World, his key to control of landmonsters and to all the fame and fortune he deserved for this discovery, had escaped. Had lost her trust in him. Would not come so easily to his hand again, even if he could find her in the few hours before dawn. And he had told Savaric that the sacrifice was complete; by morning the Seignor's mercenaries would be marching through the Harendola, burning and killing wherever they went, destroying crops, soaking the fertile land with blood to raise such a crop of landmonsters as had not been seen since the days of the Issart Wars.

He would have to stop Savaric. Aigar staggered back to his pyramid of voicebubbles, rehearsing lies even as he began to chant the tones of the linking spell. He would tell Savaric that he'd tested the bondsoul on a landmonster, a very small one, and she had failed to disperse it? No, Savaric would want to know how he had raised a landmonster in the stony town of Coindra with its strong Landsensers Guild. The impossibility of achieving such a thing had been what drove Aigar to seek aid from a Seignor with remote mountain lands.

Very well, then, he would say that he had dropped the fired earth containing the bondsoul and she had escaped. True, Aigar did not *know* what happened to a bondsoul when its container shattered; but then, neither did anybody else. Perhaps he could try with Janifer? No, he might need Janifer, if he failed to stop Savaric's attack on the Harendola. There was a glimmer of an idea there, some chance at salvation, but Aigar didn't have the energy to pursue it just then; his first attempt at a linking spell had failed. He had to think of nothing but the music, the complex sequence of tones and harmonics and words that would join his voicebubbles with Savaric's.

He gave the charm all his concentration, but still the voicebubbles remained inert and lifeless. He tried a third time, a fourth, with no result. Finally, in desperation, he linked his voicebubbles with the campus system.

He'd avoided using the university communications bubbles because it was too dangerous, too easy for some experimentally-minded junior mage to catch a portion of his conversation by accident. But nothing could be more dangerous than allowing Savaric to march on the Harendola and *then* telling him there was no bondsoul prepared. Aigar reassured himself that few mages would be studying or practicing their communications spells at this hour. None, probably. He commanded the campus system to link him with Savaric's . . .

The dancing lights in his voicebubbles twinkled and dimmed for a moment, then sprang up again in their random patterns. No link had been achieved.

Aigar slumped back against his cushions. Savaric must have dismantled his voicebubble pyramid before he left; a reasonable precaution, and one Aigar would normally have applauded. Now, though, it meant disaster. What could he do? Savaric could hardly have reached the port of Astire yet; perhaps Aigar could warn the Merchanters Guildhouse there, whose voicebubbles would always be ready to receive a communication. No. There was no way to warn them without explaining how he came to know of Savaric's plans; he would be irremediably implicated in the attack, and Savaric would be even more angry with him than if he did nothing.

Such a warning might save the farmers of the Harendola, for the Merchanters could alert the

Landsensers and the Landsensers could call their fellows
from all over Escorre to absorb the upwelling of thwarted
landvirtue, the blood and burning that would create
monsters. But it would ruin Aigar. Shrugging, he dismissed the fate of the Harendola as ultimately unimportant, and returned to considering how he might
salvage his own career.

Perhaps if he brought Janifer to Astire and claimed
he was the newly bound soul? No; the shape of Janifer's
rotund earthform was distinctive, as were the bands of
variously colored earth that had formed in firing. Savaric
might recognize it.

For a moment Aigar was distracted into wondering
whether each soul created its own distinctive form during
the firespell that bound soul to earth. It seemed likely.
It would be an interesting topic for a small paper, once
the usefulness of bondsouls against landmonsters had
been established and the ridiculous prejudice against this
form of research had died away.

But unless he did *something* about Savaric, he wouldn't
last long enough as Dean and Warden to pursue that
or any other research. Aigar groaned again and tried to
think through the fumes of stillwein that warmed his
bones and addled his brain. Not Janifer, then, but another
bondsoul. Any one would do. Savaric would hardly be
able to tell by inspection whether the soul had come
from Elder World or not. Aigar would warn of mysterious dangers inherent in handling the new bondsoul,
dangers that only a skilled mage like him could ward
against; he would keep it wrapped in silk whenever he
was not actually using it.

Perfect! True, the new bondsoul would be no more
effective than Janifer in *controlling* the landmonsters,
since it would be Escorrean and just as afraid of them
as Janifer had been. But it would serve just as well as
Janifer to keep the landmonsters away from him and
Savaric; they would be personally safe, no matter what
happened to the mercenaries and farmers and

merchanters. As for the hope that an Elder World soul would work better, that was only an experimental hypothesis, never tested, and unfortunately now found to be untrue. He would complain that Savaric should have given him time to run the tests as before. The entire debacle would be Savaric's fault . . .

There was just one problem; he didn't *have* a new bondsoul. And how was he to lure one to his laboratory in the middle of a spring stormnight? He must have privacy for the sacrifice and the firebonding; he could not wait until people were stirring around the campus in the morning. Aigar groaned again. Was ever a man so beset by troubles?

"I say!" came a voice from beyond the laboratory's spelled archway. "I can't get in. Is somebody hurt in there?"

Aigar's heart lifted. He must, he decided, be even a mightier mage than he had thought. First Allie, then this new soul had come in answer to his great need, even though he had not consciously invoked the spells of summoning.

"Ahhhh," he groaned loudly. The glass knife was on the workbench where he'd dropped it when Allie tried to escape him. By great good fortune the blade was still whole. Aigar sidled toward the knife, grasped it firmly and called, "I have still enough strength to lift the keyspell. Bless you for coming to my aid!"

And he meant that most sincerely, too. He flattened himself against the laboratory wall and whispered the words that would raise his keyspell. As soon as the young man without stepped across the threshold, Aigar thrust his staff between the boy's feet. He tripped and fell forward; the glass knife met his throat, and he toppled to the floor within inches of the stone bowl that held Aigar's prepared earth. Before Aigar had shoved the bowl into position to catch the flowing blood, the boy's eyes were already glazing over. He stared at Aigar; his lips moved, but Aigar could not hear the words. Then Fabre's snub-nosed, lively face became still, and his wide staring eyes were quite empty of his soul's liveliness.

Before the blood on the floor had dried, Aigar had sprinkled a circle of salt around Fabre's body and the stone bowl that held his blood mixed with living earth of Escorre. He held an arm before his face to shield himself from the magical heat of the firing-spell. The laboratory flamed green and blue and purple; a few overlooked glass vessels cracked from the heat, and a deep ringing chime came from the bowl, as though stone and earth and blood had become a bell of bronze.

When the flames died away, Fabre's body was consumed as though it had never been; and within the stone bowl rested another curious shape of fired earth. Aigar was pleased to note that Fabre's bondsoul did not in the least resemble Janifer's, lending credence to his theory that the soul helped to shape its new form.

At last, everything had worked as it should! Aigar was so delighted with his success that he never thought to wonder what had drawn Fabre to the laboratory on that rainy spring night.

CHAPTER SEVEN

It was dark, and something smelled bad, and her head hurt. And she was lying in a puddle. Allie moaned and tried to roll out of the water. Dripping fabric followed her movements, wrapped around her legs and clung to her arms. She *was* the water . . . No, that didn't make sense . . . but she was falling, falling like rain, so dizzy, and everything hurt. She moaned again and decided to go back to sleep.

"Don't sleep," said an anxious voice too close to her ear. The sound sent splinters of light and discordant noises bouncing off the inside of her skull. "Ooooh," Allie moaned. "Lemme sleep. Too much . . ." Hazy memories of an evening at the Blue Pigeon with Fabre floated to the surface of her mind; the last good day she could remember, the last day when she'd thought she had friends in Escorre. "Too much . . . He never tol' me what we were drinking. Said it wouldn' make me drunk. Can' trust Fabre."

"Hush," said what she now recognized as Domerc's voice. "You're rambling. Try to sit up. I'll help you. It's not good to go back to sleep after . . ."

"Sleep it off, bes' thing for hangover," insisted Allie. She couldn't understand anything, and when she tried to think her mind slid off the things that confused her like droplets of water off a windshield. Everything was blurry. Domerc didn't really like her, none of them did, they just wanted to use her; why was he nursing her

123

through a hangover? And why wouldn't he let her go back to sleep? She wished he would just go away and leave her alone.

And she emphatically did *not* want to sit up. In fact, such a move would be disastrous. She opened her mouth to warn Domerc that he'd better take his arm away from her shoulders and let her lie down, and the disaster came up from her stomach without giving her time to speak.

Now he'll really despise me, she thought miserably . . . he never really liked me anyway, and now I've been sick all over him.

If this had happened in Vista View, Allie thought fuzzily, Luke would have sneered at her for being a stupid little sophomore who couldn't hold her drink. Domerc said nothing, just laid her back down gently and hummed a few notes very quietly into the darkness. A spark of light appeared, grew into a softly glowing shape of cold blue-white radiance somewhere far above her head.

"How'd you do that?" Allie mumbled. "Funny lamp, looks like a bottle."

"It is a bottle." Domerc sounded rueful and amused and, surprisingly, not at all angry. "No lightbubbles here, so I put the spell on one of—my friend's—empty bottles. It won't last, though. Let's get this cleaned up while we can see. Can you lift up just a little, so I can get your gown off? Good. One thing about this place, we've plenty of water."

The cold glowing light showed Allie shadowy shapes, a jumble of furniture and boxes, bowls and buckets placed randomly around them on the floor. Domerc wrung out her gown in one bucket, took a second one to use while he mopped up the floor beside her. There was a steady smacking drip-drop-drip of water on planks while he worked; when he replaced the bucket, it changed to the softer sound of water dripping into more water.

"Not random," Allie said. "Catching the water." She felt better now that her roiling stomach was empty and she wasn't wrapped in a sodden gown, but it was still an effort to make complete sentences.

"Good," Domerc said, "you're starting to make sense. Can you remember what happened?"

"The Blue Pigeon . . . ?" she began tentatively. That evening with Fabre seemed so distant, like something glimpsed through wavy green bottle-glass, or stones lying at the bottom of a river. No. It couldn't have been that; she remembered lonely days afterwards, devoting herself to her studies and her work in the lab . . . "The lab." Something too painful to think of ached deep in her chest; something she didn't want to remember. *It didn't happen I didn't hear it . . .*

"That's right," Domerc said. "You turned up in our rooms. I was studying and Fabre was out. You asked me a bunch of questions about the Western Seas. Then you got all upset and ran out, saying you were going to Aigar's lab. I was worried, so I followed you. When I got there, you were unconscious on the floor of the lab and Aigar was entertaining some other visitor—I didn't wait around to see who it was—behind the curtains. It seemed like a good idea to have you out of there."

It came back to her now, like a dirty flood of trash and filthy water and sewer sweepings. Aigar's betrayal. The words she'd overheard, his clumsy attempts to explain them away or bribe her into silence, and then . . . what? The end of the ugly scene swirled around in her head and refused to come clear.

But what she did remember hurt unbearably. "You were right," she said, ashamed to look at Domerc. "You tried to warn me about Aigar. All of you did. And I didn't want to believe you."

"Loyalty is no crime," Domerc said gently.

"Totally idiotic, unreasoning loyalty is. Or ought to be," Allie said. "I heard—" But Aigar's words were still too painful to repeat. Her mind skittered onto another, related topic. "Oh, and there wasn't anybody else there. He was talking to a pile of glass bubbles. At least when

I came in—" She wouldn't, couldn't think of that now. "Bubbles full of faces," she murmured drowsily.

"A voicebubble link," Domerc said. "Ah! So he was talking to someone far away. And he had to go into the lab in the middle of a storm night to do it. Very interesting."

"Aigar often works late," Allie protested before she remembered that she was no longer defending the Dean.

"On what, I wonder?"

"He doesn't tell me much," Allie said automatically.

"Allie. You just said being deliberately stupid is a crime. I don't know what Aigar had in mind for you, but anybody who could leave you unconscious on the floor while he chats up his friends is not *your* friend; can you try to remember that, and tell me whatever you do know about what he's up to?"

"I wish I knew," Allie said honestly. "But he really didn't tell me anything about his work. Oh, he got mad at me once when I was looking at his bottles and jars and things, but he didn't say why. I guess he was afraid I'd break something. Can't really blame him for that; I'm clumsy and I do break things. It was awfully nice of him to keep me on as his lab assistant . . ." *No, it wasn't.* She flinched at the memory of his voice in the lab, the even tones explaining just why he'd offered her the position.

"What's that about?" Domerc pounced.

"What?"

"You winced."

"It's just . . . something he said about me," Allie protested. "It doesn't matter, I'm stupid, I should have known better, I should have known he didn't really want me because I'm a good worker." When she shut her eyes she felt as though she were sliding into a long dark funnel, a whirling cloud of darkness and empty space where she shrank and shrank until she knew just how unimportant and worthless she really was.

"What exactly did he say?" Domerc prodded.

"None of your business! And I don't want to think of it."

Domerc grinned. "And I didn't much want to get mixed up in it, but I am now. I laid a few trail-breaker spells across our path, but nothing that'll slow down a mage of Aigar's quality for long. It takes at least three voices in counterpoint to chant a cantrip strong enough to hold up against counterspells . . . well, never mind the technical points. Main thing is, it very much is my business. And if you don't mind, I'd like to know exactly what this nasty business is."

"I don't know," Allie protested. "He just said . . ." Domerc was right. Whatever Aigar had planned for her didn't sound good at all. And Domerc, who was already in enough trouble, had risked himself to get her out of there. She squeezed her eyes tight shut for a moment, fighting back an urge to cry, then managed a quick summary of what she'd overheard in Aigar's lab.

"The other guy was talking about moving his men out, and something about burning fields, and a place called Harendola." Fabre had used that name once, but Allie couldn't remember what he had said about it.

"Burning? In the Harendola?" Domerc clenched his fists. "Sorry, go on. What then?"

"I don't remember exactly . . . something about the Landsensers. It sounded like they'd both been up to something, and this other guy was going to tell the Landsensers on Aigar and make it like it was all his fault. I couldn't quite understand what he was saying. He talked funny, and besides I wasn't really paying attention then; I was just waiting for Aigar to finish so I could talk to him."

"Talked funny," Domerc repeated, scowling. "Like this? 'I reckon ye don't knaw much aboot our ways here, laddie.' " He drawled the words out with a sharp twang on the nasals.

"Yes!" Allie exclaimed. "You sound just like him, only not so mean and old."

Domerc's fist pounded his knee. "Savaric. I knew it, I knew it, those two had to be in it together!"

"In what?"

"Never mind. If I'm right, I'll tell you later. I'm just guessing now. What else?"

"Then Aigar started talking about me." Allie bit her lip for a moment and swallowed hard before she was able to go on. "He said . . . he said he had brought me here. To your world. And he hired me so he'd be sure of finding me when he was ready. Then there was something about blood and collecting earth and a sacrifice. Yeccch. I mean, it sounded like a . . . a *horror film.*"

"A what?"

"Never mind," Allie said, unconsciously echoing Domerc, "I'll explain later. Anyway, that's about it . . . he said some more about how he didn't care about me, only about using me. But he didn't say what for. 'To further our joint ends,' but he didn't say what those were. And then he said . . ." She wrapped her arms around her knees. "It's cold here."

"Sorry about the amenities," Domerc told her. "It wasn't easy to find a nice empty hidey-hole that nobody would connect with either of us. What did Aigar say then?"

Allie couldn't stop shivering. "That . . . that he didn't really want to kill me. But he said it like he'd already made up his mind to do it, you know? Only, I couldn't believe he meant it. And then he stopped talking and when he saw that I'd heard him he started lying and saying he hadn't meant a word of it, and promising to see that I got a good grade in Radegond's lectures, and it was all utterly and totally phony and I hate him!" She broke into tears on the last word and had to pinch her own arm, quite hard, to stop the sobs that wanted to come up through her throat.

"There, now," Domerc said, patting her on the shoulder, "That rat isn't worth weeping over. I'd give you my handkerchief, except it's as sodden as both our gowns.

And it would probably be a good idea not to drench what dry clothes we've still got in salt water. So if you could possibly stop . . ."

Allie snorted, giggled, gasped for breath and found that she had stopped crying. She looked curiously at Domerc.

"I don't understand you at all," she said. "You look positively happy. We're wet and hiding in somebody's attic and a master mage is fixing to kill me, and probably you too for helping me get away, and you look as if you'd just won the . . . the *lottery*."

"I do not understand you either," Domerc told her. "What is a latterie? No, never mind. I suppose it is some strange beast of Elder World. We shall just stumble on in mutual incomprehension. At least now we've got something to stumble to."

"We have?"

"Of course we have! From what you've told me, it's perfectly clear that Aigar was hand in glove with Savaric over that eruption of landmonsters in the Harendola last spring. What he had to gain from it I haven't yet figured out, but you're my witness that he was involved. And the talk of blood and earth and sacrifice. I shouldn't be surprised to hear that he's been playing about with blood magic. You know, I wondered what happened to Janifer; he disappeared so suddenly and he didn't seem to've told anybody he was dropping out of school." Domerc looked bright with renewed purpose in the cool light of the bubble. "There is some great evil afoot, Allie, and we've been given the means to stop it."

"We have?"

"At the least," Domerc said, "we know where to go. The Landsensers Guild here . . . no, that won't do. Aigar's a Warden of the Guild, and I'm known to have a grudge against him."

"But it's not just your word this time," Allie pointed out. "I heard him."

"He'd find some way to explain away what you heard,

twist the words." Domerc scowled, got to his feet and began pacing along the worn boards of their hideaway. "New young scholar, misunderstandings, hysterical girl. Probably claim you went to him and offered . . . well, favors . . . in return for help with Radegond's lecture series."

"My goodness," Allie said, "this world sounds more and more like home. We've even got senators and judges who act like that."

"Besides, I do not think it would be wise to let Aigar find you," Domerc concluded. "You may be very important to his plans."

"How?"

"Damned if I can figure it out," Domerc admitted, "but he must be doing something that required him to bring a soul from Elder World. And you're the one he got. The only one. At least, I haven't heard of an epidemic of mildly insane scholar-fledglings coming up for their first year of lectures. Stands to reason he'd want to get you back. No, we've got to find help, but not in Coindra; Aigar has a finger in everything that happens here. Ah! I have it." He stopped pacing and slammed one fist into his open palm.

"Would you like to tell me about it?" Allie suggested after waiting a few moments.

"I haven't quite got all the details worked out," Domerc admitted. "But it's a simple problem in logic. First, we need a place to stay and a voicelink system that's not controlled by the university. Second, we need to keep you out of Aigar's reach. *Ergo*, we leave Coindra without anybody noticing."

"How?"

Domerc frowned. "That's one of the details I haven't worked out yet," he said slowly. "All the mage-transport in Coindra is handled by the University, which means Aigar will be able to keep watch on the journey-mazes from his lab system. That means we'll have to go by land—"

Allie groaned, remembering the rutted track that Aigar had described as a main road out of Coindra.

"—or along the river," Domerc continued without a pause, "although Aigar may be able to watch the docks along the Verenha too—and even if he's not monitoring them personally, he may have thought to tell the university proctors not to let us take passage on a barge. I'd have done that as soon as I noticed we'd disappeared, and Aigar is quite intelligent. He's bound to think of such an obvious precaution. He won't want you getting out of Coindra."

"Oh, well," Allie said, "let's cross that bridge when we come to it. So we get out of Coindra. Sneak out. Where do we go?"

"That's just it," Domerc said, brightening, "we know Savaric and Aigar are planning some mischief in the Harendola, so the obvious thing is to head down that way and warn the people. And it just so happens that I've a good friend with lands along the Verenha near Astire. Iseu de Brefania. Her lands march with the Freefarmers of the Harendola to the south, and with En Savaric's mountains to the north. That's why I was at the Guildhouse there last year—well, never mind that now. Iseu still believes in me, I know she does; we've been friends since I put her up on her first pony. She offered me a place in Brefania when—after that trouble last year—but a man can't be living on charity. Besides, I wanted to be here in Coindra, to keep an eye on Aigar, and a good thing too. Iseu will help us," Domerc concluded, his face lightening, "she's a wonderful person, Iseu, and not scared of anything. You'll love her."

"I can hardly wait," Allie said. Domerc completely missed the waspish note in her voice. He went on telling her about Iseu's stables and Iseu's hunters and Iseu's tall aristocratic grace and Iseu's kindness to her people, and Allie hugged her knees and tried not to feel prejudiced against somebody who was probably, according to Domerc, going to risk her life to help them stop whatever

Aigar had in mind. The longer he talked, the smaller
and more insignificant she felt. She didn't ride, she was
a little red-headed shrimp of a girl instead of a tall gracious lady with some kind of aristocratic title . . . she'd
never achieved much at home, and here in Escorre her
main claim to fame was having been the deluded victim of an evil mage. And now she was going to get to
tell some total stranger, some *tall* and *gracious* and *noble*
stranger, all about how dumb she'd been.

Maybe Domerc was right, maybe with the help of this
Iseu de Brefania they'd be able to stop Aigar doing whatever he was planning. That would be nice for Domerc.
With Aigar discredited, he'd probably be restored to his
place in the Landsensers Guild and his family would take
him back and everybody would fall over themselves
apologizing for having thought ill of him in the first place.
And he wouldn't bother finishing his degree at Coindra,
and she'd probably never see him again. I'm really a hor-
rible self-centered person, Allie thought; I ought to be
rejoicing for Domerc instead of being selfish about losing
one of my friends. And I wouldn't see much of him and
Fabre and Liuria anyway; they don't care about me any
more than Aigar does. Only difference is, they weren't
planning to sacrifice me. That's nice, but it's not exactly a
basis for a long-lasting friendship.

It did, though, remind her of something she'd been
forgetting to do.

"I think you saved my life," she interrupted Domerc's
ongoing panegyric on Iseu de Brefania.

"Hmm? Oh. Yes, I think so. Now, when we find
Iseu—"

"You took a big risk."

Domerc looked uncomfortable. "Oh, it wasn't much.
I mean, granted Aigar isn't a good person to cross, but
it wasn't as if he liked me before. He's already destroyed
my career, caused my family to disown me, and done
his best to force me out of Coindra. What more could
he do?"

"Turn you into a frog?"

"I doubt it," Domerc said, perfectly serious. "The compaction of mass would require an extremely powerful spell. Even Aigar wouldn't have the energy to maintain such a spell for more than a few minutes. Of course he might draw on the University's power net. That would be interesting. I bet all the lightbubbles would dim at once. And even then . . . no, he wouldn't be able to keep it up. After a few minutes his energy would be depleted and I'd resume normal shape. And I'd be very annoyed."

"You mean spells wear off?"

"What did you think," Domerc demanded, "haven't you ever heard of the laws of conservation of energy and mass?"

Allie blinked. How had physics come into this conversation?

"I suppose not," Domerc allowed, "I keep forgetting you're only in Fundamentals of Magical Theory. You can't really understand the conservation laws until you've had calculus. Just take my word for it, okay?"

"Gladly," Allie said. It didn't seem the right time to mention that she'd already taken calculus. Twice. After the second attempt she'd vowed that no power on earth would make her try it again. In fact, the Calculus For Humanities Majors instructor had begged her not to try it again.

"All the same," she said, doggedly returning to her original point, "it was dangerous, and you didn't have to get mixed up in my troubles, and I owe you one. A lot of people wouldn't have bothered. Especially for somebody they didn't much like."

"I do like you," Domerc said. "Not that it matters. I mean, I'd want to rescue anybody from Aigar. I think. Well, maybe not En Savaric. The fact that you can't stand me has nothing to do with it."

"That I *what*?"

"Oh, I know what you think of us," he told her. "Fabre

told me what you said after his talk with you. And speaking of deliberate stupidity, my girl, did it never occur to you that Fabre and I met you *before* you got that job with Aigar? And we didn't steer you into the job, either. When you took it, we tried to warn you about him. Remember?"

Allie winced. "I guess so," she admitted.

"Some day," Domerc said, "we must investigate why you think so little of yourself. Do you think you don't deserve real friends? Or did you look at me and Fabre and m'sister and immediately say to yourself, 'Ah, the kind of creeping sewer rats who'd only be nice to a new scholar if they wanted to make use of her in some nasty and unethical way?' "

"I'm sorry. It was a terrible thing to think. I apologize. I was wrong. I didn't understand. Can you possibly forgive me?"

"I think the blame is rather more equitably distributed than that," Domerc said. "It's true that we like you for yourself, Allie. But after all, Fabre did ask you to spy on Aigar. He should have known better. I could have told him you wouldn't do that. I might have asked you myself if I thought it would work," he confessed. "But anybody except Fabre, whose mind is mostly on lower things—like your legs—could see that you're a very loyal person and much too honest to make a good spy."

"Well, thanks very much!" Allie said indignantly. "So you think I wouldn't have been any good at it?" But the backhanded praise warmed her heart, taking away just a little of the terrible ache left by Aigar's betrayal.

"I think," said Domerc, not looking at her, "we'd better get some rest while we can. As soon as it's light we'll have to get out of here. I really can't impose on Hevr— my friend—to let us stay in his attic indefinitely. It's not fair to drag him into our troubles."

That last statement made Allie feel extremely uncomfortable. It was too close to what she'd just done, albeit unintentionally, to Domerc. He'd sold his vielle to stay in Coindra. Now he was fleeing the University, just as Aigar wanted. Because of her. No matter what fantasies he spun of discovering Aigar's plots in the Harendola and reinstating himself with Guild and family, you couldn't get past the facts: Aigar was snug and comfortable in the Dean's house, and they were hiding in a leaky attic.

Allie opened her mouth to tell Domerc, already half asleep on his rolled-up gown, just how terrible their situation was and just how guilty she felt that she had involved him in her troubles. Then she stopped and shook her head. If Domerc could find something cheerful in the situation, who was she to argue him out of it? For all she knew, his good humor might be the thinnest of deceptions. Maybe underneath he was as sick and scared and miserable as she was. Although, she conceded ruefully, it wasn't likely that his head hurt as much as hers.

And if he could ignore the difficulties and set to rebuilding his life again, after Aigar had knocked it out from under him for the second time, couldn't she just shut up and let him do that?

Allie tried to roll up her own gown into a pillow, but found that Domerc's hasty rinsing in a bucket hadn't been enough to leave it sweet-smelling. Not nearly enough. She found a rotting footstool and used it to cushion her head. Not that she'd ever get to sleep, but she could at least lie still and let Domerc rest. As he fell asleep, the cool glowing light from the enspelled bottle slowly faded. So it took conscious energy to maintain the spell? It would be interesting to learn the laws that governed magic in this world, not that she looked like having the chance now . . . Don't think about that. Don't think about getting home, either, because Aigar brought you here and he's not going to help you get back. Don't think about anything . . .

As she drifted off into a drowsy half-sleep, Allie smelled her sodden gown and wished that they could stop off at the wash-house before leaving Coindra. A hot bath and some clean clothes, that was what she wanted. Should be a basic civil right. Everybody needed clean clothes . . . The ghost of an idea, a memory from her American Studies class, flitted across her mind.

"Domerc?"

"Ummm?"

"This place we're going to. The Harendola. It's on a river?"

"Verenha. Port's Astire. But we can't get on a freight barge. Aigar might have somebody watching the docks."

"I might," Allie said cautiously, "have a way around that. Tell me all about the freight barges."

A rattling snore was her only answer.

"In the morning," she amended.

CHAPTER EIGHT

Aigar didn't bother to clean up his laboratory; the new keyspell he left over it would keep the curious away until he was back from the Harendola. He felt satisfied that he had matters well in hand. He would meet Savaric at Astire, use his new bondsoul to keep landmonsters away from them—well, from him, anyway. If Savaric strayed outside the range of protection and got himself killed by landmonsters, no one would blame him for the unfortunate accident.

While Aigar made his final preparations for departure, he devoted some time to thinking about how to arrange just such an accident. It was a pity that he couldn't take the time to track down Allie, but he dared not risk failing to meet Savaric in the morning. He would just have to clear up this little problem in the Harendola and get back to the University as soon as possible. It should be simple enough to find the child when he returned; no matter how much she wished to run away from him, she would find it painful and enervating to go very far from the bond-amulet of blood and silk. He would simply leave the little bundle of silk safely hidden in his laboratory, keeping Allie as bound to Coindra as though he had her on a leash. He certainly did not wish to draw Allie down to the Harendola with him. In her present form she was no safer from landmonsters than anyone else; indeed, she might be in more danger than most, not knowing what to fear. And it would set his research back *months* if she went and got herself destroyed by landmonsters before he had a chance to bind the rest of her soul to his will and work his spells of control through her.

Just the sort of inconsiderate thing the girl would do, too. No, the silk was better where it was. And Allie was better wherever *she* was; probably hiding in some student lodging around the campus. The bit of her soul that was trapped in the silk would keep her from even wanting to go away; at least that was one thing he didn't have to worry about. Really, Aigar told himself, the whole delay was for the best. When he returned he would have neutralized Savaric's threats—that is, he rephrased his thought, there was a great likelihood of Savaric's suffering some kind of fatal accident in the next few days.

And by that time, Allie might have been lulled into a feeling of safety. The bond Aigar had established with blood and silk should make her want to trust him, even to disbelieve her own memories of last night. She was so ignorant of magic that she would never guess that her feelings had been augmented by his charms and the blood-magic. With her amazing ability to ignore the obvious, she should have talked herself into trusting Aigar again in no time.

She might even be waiting to resume her duties in the lab by the time he had cleared up this other little problem!

With this optimistic daydream cheering him, Aigar left the laboratory and spent the remainder of the night in his rooms, packing a few necessities for the trip and trying to nap. When the University awoke at first light, he returned to his own outer office and informed the assistant dean that he would be away for a few days.

"I have Sensed great virtue moving in the land to the south of Coindra," he said, "and have been all this night consulting with my colleagues of the Guild. I fear their strength may not be enough to contain such an unprecedented eruption of the landvirtue; as Warden of the

Landsensers Guild, it is my duty to add my own poor efforts to theirs. I shall travel from the main University journey-maze to Astire; please see that charges are put down to the College of Magical Arts. No doubt the Landsensers will reimburse us later, but there is no time for such petty questions now." No one should say, later, that he had traveled in secret to the Harendola. True, it might be a bit difficult to explain just which of the Harendola Landsensers had alerted him to the problem; but Aigar could see a way around that. It would be strange indeed if Savaric's invasion, and the subsequent flow of landmonsters, did not result in the death or insanity of some of the local Landsensers. He had only to avoid naming the one who was supposed to have warned him until he knew which ones did not survive the next few days.

And while he was at it, he might as well drop a few hints to get people thinking in the right direction . . . for him. "I fear also . . ." He let his voice trail away artistically.

"What?" the assistant Dean asked.

Savaric shook his head. "No, never mind. It would be wrong to hint at such a thing, when nothing is definitely known yet; still, the force of landvirtue seems to emanate mainly from the valleys bordering on En Savaric's mountain holdings, and we all know what that may mean."

"We do?" said the assistant Dean.

Aigar sighed sharply. Did he have to do *everything*, first drop his hints and then interpret them? Did the woman have no intuition?

"En Savaric is a choleric and hasty man," he explained, "and I am reliably informed that his mercenaries have been without employment since last harvest. If—mind you I say only *if*, for it would be most wrong to leap to assumptions where nothing has been proven—but if he has committed some act of war against his neighbors in the Harendola, there may have been some insult to the landvirtue to inflame this sudden upswelling of power. Indeed, I fear me such an explanation is only too likely."

"Oh!" gasped the assistant Dean. "How terrible! Be sure that I shall look after the affairs of the College in your absence, Dean Aigar, and I do hope you can thwart that evil man!"

Aigar did not reprove her for leaping to conclusions.

The University's transport system was already fully scheduled for that morning. Half a dozen junior lecturers were departing to give a demonstration of the black sciences in southern Issart, a spoiled brat of a Seignor family was leaving classes in mid-semester with his retinue of tutors and advisers, and a party of second-year Magical Arts students was starting a field trip to the Forest of Genebre. Besides all these, there was the usual commercial traffic. Boxes of books and baskets of ready-mixed magic potions awaited transport to the Salmistre of the sea; Frestalar silk and Brefania wine were scheduled to arrive for the town merchanters.

In his capacity as Dean of the College of Magical Arts, even Aigar might have had to wait for an opening in the transport schedule. As a Warden of the Landsensers Guild, upon Guild business, he had to wait only while the junior mage in charge of transport coordination hastily rerouted the science lecturers and told Frestalar to hold the bales of silk.

"What's the trouble?" the boy asked.

"I fear it may be grave," Aigar replied, "else I would not intrude upon your schedule thus. Ah—have there been any other unscheduled transport requests this morning?"

"No, why?" the boy said, and Aigar felt an unsuspected tension along his spine relaxing. *Of course* Allie hadn't tried to escape him by treading a journey-maze away from Coindra. The bond of soul and silk and blood would hold her to Coindra; she wouldn't even think of trying to leave.

"Just wondering why it was taking so long to clear the journey-maze," he said to explain his question. "You do understand that Guild business brooks no delays?"

The boy flushed. "Oh, *yes*, Dean—I mean, Warden— I mean, Dean and Warden Aigar! It is only that I wished to receive voicelink confirmation of the change from Astire. It wouldn't do to have you transported into a cask of Brefania wine, would it now?" He tittered nervously.

"The thought is not without its appeal," said Aigar with an indulgent smile. It meant so much to these junior mages to see that their revered Dean was capable of sharing a moment of light humor. "However, given the pressing nature of my business, perhaps we should delay the experiment until a more propitious time."

The boy turned back to his voicebubbles and whistled the calling chant for Astire once again. Slowly the winking sparks of light within the bubbles steadied and coalesced into the repeated image of a young man in a mail shirt.

"Here, who're *you*?" demanded the boy. "What happened to Daunis?"

Aigar thrust himself between the young mage and the voicebubbles. "Ah, you must be the emergency guard for Astire," he said before the man on the other end of the link could identify himself as one of En Savaric's men. "The situation must be bad indeed. Your people will be glad to know that I intend to transport into Astire immediately to take charge personally. Pray see that no one else rides these mage-streams until the emergency is over."

He hummed a sequence of high, quavering notes that crossed the junior mage's whistled chant in mid-air. The discords thus created quivered about their ears and the image in the voicebubbles dissolved into whirling flecks of light.

"I see no need to waste more time," Aigar said. "Astire has been notified. Now, if you please, I do not wish to dissipate my own magical energies in a simple transport task."

He stepped onto the smooth stones of the journey-maze and began walking along the spiral path marked out by a mosaic of dark stone chips. Behind him, the junior mage shrugged and began the chant that would invoke the linked powers of the University network to join this spiral with the one in Astire. The golden stone buildings and tangled green vines of Coindra grew faint around Aigar; a mist seemed to cover them. The piping notes of the junior mage's invocation also were faint and far away, a birdsong in the mist. The patterned labyrinth seemed to grow into high walls that enclosed him. The sensation of the earth tilting beneath him grew stronger. Aigar reminded himself for the thousandth time that the sense was illusory; nonetheless, his stomach lurched and he tasted bile on his tongue.

The illusory walls of the maze shrank into a pattern of painted wood beneath his feet; he stood on a polished wooden floor inside a wooden hall with high upcurving beams painted in bright blues and reds and picked out in gold. The air he breathed was heavy and moist with the smell of stored grain and wine. Three men, two in mail shirts, stood leaning on their pikes, watching the transport pad of Astire intently as Aigar materialized.

"'Bout time ye got here," said the short one with the prickly, unshaven chin. "What kept ye, then? Feared to face the land?"

"I, too, rejoice in our meeting, En Savaric," Aigar replied with his most courtly bow. "You have moved quickly indeed, to have captured the port of Astire already."

The tall man behind Savaric cleared his throat and spat a gob of brownish phlegm onto the polished wood of the transport hall. "*Captured?* Aye, that's one name for it!"

"Captured," echoed the third man, a nondescript fellow with stooped shoulders and a stained brown Accounter's Guild robe. "The fox running for his life said, 'What fine lands of mine these are!' "

"Any more of yer bloody parables, Lendoman, and I'll hang ye on hooks outside the city walls to feed the landmonsters!" Savaric growled. He faced Aigar squarely, or tried to; his eyes shifted and sought out the far corners of the hall. "It's workin' faster than we expected," he said. "Had to make double-time into Astire after we fired the valley. Didn't kill but a few peasants. Raised plenty of landmonsters, though."

There was a dour laugh from the tall man. "En Savaric tells me that you desire to meet landmonsters. That desire can be satisfied beyond your wildest dreams. And then we shall see the truth of these fantastic claims that you have done what no other mage dreamed of doing. I can hardly wait."

"Enough of your griping, Marin," Savaric silenced the tall mercenary. "The mage here'll take care of all that. And when he's through, who knows?" He leered up at Marin. "You just might find yourself out of work!"

"Oh, aye," sneered Marin, "think you to retire on your new-won lands, En Savaric? Let me tell you, even if this great scholar of yours does cleanse the land of monsters, you'll still be needing us to protect you from the mercenaries Iseu de Brefania will be hiring to get her lands back."

Lendoman twitched fussily at his brown robe, pulling it forward over his shoulders, and cleared his throat. "There is wisdom in Marin's words. 'Who rides the whirlwind may not dismount at will.' My lord Savaric will have need of both mercenaries and magecraft to defend what he has won here."

"I'll have *two* hooks prepared," Savaric growled, "one for each of ye. Lendoman, I've got a *real* mage now, I don't have to put up with your carping. And Marin, wait till ye see what I'm about to have in the way of an army!" He bared his yellowing teeth at Aigar. "Ye brought it?"

Aigar's hand went to the amulet he wore on a thin cord round his neck, between his tunic and over-gown. Under the fabric of the gown he could feel the shape of the amulet, hard and yet somehow vibrant with all the energy and delight and soul that had been drained from Fabre's living body.

"Good, good," Savaric chuckled, rubbing his hands together. "Let's get on with it, then."

"Wait!" Aigar said in his deepest, strongest voice. He infused the word with the harmonics of a compulsion chant. He'd been a fool to stand here in silence and confusion while these little men bickered over little things, but he would not compound his folly by springing to obey Savaric's command like one of these hirelings.

"I must know more of the situation," Aigar went on when the rolling harmonics underlying his command had died away. "Evidently all has not gone as you planned, En Savaric?"

Marin the mercenary snorted. "I should say not! First this fool here—" he swept one arm out, almost hitting Lendoman in the face, "pardon me, this *wisest of mages* took it upon himself to burn out a swathe of the Harendola with magefire before my men had marched through the foothills."

"Magefire!" Aigar repeated. "Used in war? That was banned after the Issart Wars. How could you sink so low?" He was truly shocked.

"Aye," said Marin, "and our noble lord here let him do it without so much as having a Landsenser test the currents of landvirtue first!"

"I *told* ye," Savaric snapped, "we couldna' risk alertin' the Guild! Forbye and besides—"

"I know, I know," Marin interrupted him. "You said we'd no need to worry about landmonsters, that your tame scholar would be here to settle them by some new magic that was beyond the wits of simple soldiers to understand." He gave a short laugh. "Would you care to know what the shades of my men that I lost on the hills of Brefania think of that plan, *En* Savaric?"

"A minor miscalculation," Savaric said defensively. "Fortunes of war. Anyway, now that Aigar's here—"

"Do I gather that landmonsters have already arisen?" Aigar interrupted.

"Arisen!" Once again it was Marin who answered before Savaric could speak. "They've got us penned into Astire. What's left of my men, and what's left of the farmers of the Harendola, *and* all the folk as live in Astire anyway. No way out but over the water. And our noble lordship here had his Lendoman take out the barges with magefire."

"Your men seemed to be losing stomach for the fight," Savaric said calmly. "I'd no intention of seeing my army flee downstream. I've cast the die now; I'll see the game to an end. And ye and yer mercenaries will see it through with me."

"My men are placing odds whether we'll run out of food before the landmonsters will find a way through Astire city walls," Marin said.

"It is well known," Lendoman piped up, "that the monsters which do arise from the virtue of the land do not act against that nature. The living virtue in Astire's growing walls will withstand the emanations of the landmonsters until in time they return to the earth from whence they sprung."

Marin spat. "Theory! As I recall, *mage*, 'twas also well known that landmonsters would not arise but for some nights after an insult to the land. You must have insulted the earth *good* to get a response before the first night was out. And now I'm supposed to trust you and your scroll-learning that these pretty monsters 'ull just turn into vapor before they ooze into the city."

"Better than that," said Savaric, grinning and rubbing his hands together. "Better than that—eh! Lendoman, time ye saw what a real mage can do. The Dean's going to turn the landmonsters into good little mercenaries. Ye should have signed a three-war contract with me when I offered, Marin. I may not be inclined to give ye such good terms after Aigar's worked his magecraft on the monsters."

"Can't be done," Marin said flatly.

Lendoman's mouth had fallen open; he shut it with a click and took a step away from Aigar. "I never read but one manner of working such craft," he said slowly, "and that was— What is it you hold beneath your gown?"

Aigar smiled. "If you are referring to the old cantrip of capturing a living soul between earth and blood, Lendoman, you should be warned that it does not work."

Lendoman looked relieved.

"An Escorrean soul is burdened with too much fear of the landmonsters to control them effectively."

"Aye, we proved that by experiment," Savaric growled. "Souls born in Escorre carry too much fear of the monsters to be good controls. Aigar here had to bring a soul from the Elder World for this day's work. He's got the girl's soul in his hand now. Come on, man. Let's prove the cantrip."

He jerked his head and led the way out of the transport chamber. Marin fell back a pace, so that Aigar had to walk behind Savaric and under the watchful eyes of the mercenary captain. He felt more like a technician and less like the mastermind of the enterprise than he had anticipated.

On the other hand, if Savaric were fool enough to lead the way out of the city, it would be very easy for a regrettable accident to overtake him while Aigar was "discovering" that his Elder World soul worked no better than Janifer for the control of landmonsters.

Lendoman hung behind for a moment, then darted up to Aigar's side and asked in a whisper whether the amulet really contained an Elder World soul bonded to earth.

"You heard En Savaric," Aigar said sternly.

"Strange," Lendoman mused aloud, "I would have thought to sense the essential alienness of such a soul. What you bear feels alive, yet not foreign."

"If we can believe the old chronicles, the men of Elder World are our cousins," Aigar pointed out. Savaric's house mage might be only a marginal Guild member, doubling roles with the Accountants' Guild, but he showed every sign of being a serious nuisance. Perhaps the "accident" could include him with his lord?

"Men," Lendoman repeated. "But this, Savaric said, was a girl-child? And before taking her, you . . . experimented . . . with living souls of Escorre?"

"It is not well to speak overmuch of such matters under an open sky," Aigar said. The less he said, the less chance that he'd be trapped into contradictions . . . although of course Savaric and Lendoman should both have been disposed of before he returned to Coindra to find Allie. Still, there was no point in giving his enemies information they didn't need.

Lendoman's face took on an unattractive pasty shade. "And you looked down on *me* just for using magefire in war," he murmured. "What does the rest of the College think of this project, Dean Aigar?"

Definitely Lendoman would have to go.

The route from the transport hall to the landward gate of Astire took them past a crowded market and through the richer part of the city, where merchants built houses after they'd grown too important to live near the docks and oversee shipping in person. Here each fine house stood within a protective circle of gardens with small stands of trees, banks of flowering shrubs and arches of trained vines to absorb any shift in the underlying virtue of the land. After Coindra's close-grouped houses of stone on golden stone, Aigar found the open spaces of Astire curiously unsettling. The landvirtue seemed to breathe heavy here in the open air, and the silence was almost menacing.

"I am surprised to find the city so empty," he remarked to Savaric. "From your man's tale, I had expected to see the refugees from Brefania encamped in all these pleasant parks. But though the market was busy enough, this quarter of the city is as quiet as ever. What have you done with all the people from outside?"

An unfortunate phrasing; he realized that as soon as Savaric's brow darkened.

"I know what ye're thinking," Savaric growled, "but I didna' kill that many of them. Why-for would I be slaying what's to be my own peasants?"

"Why, indeed," Aigar said courteously. "But by the same token, I should have thought you would be anxious to protect them. With the plague of landmonsters in the open country, surely you would have wanted to take your peasants into the city for their own safety?"

"Couldna' find that many o' them," Savaric said curtly. "They scattered like conies. And there wasna' overmuch time; my men were as fain as any to get themselves behind the walls of Astire. Useless lumps," he added with a jerk of his head towards Marin, "ye'll make me some better soldiers, eh?" And he elbowed Aigar in the ribs and burst into a brief paroxysm of silent laughter. His breath smelled like sour wine.

"I am all eagerness to test this new soul upon some worthy matter," said Aigar. It wouldn't work, of course. Fabre, being of Escorre like Janifer, would be too afraid of landmonsters to send them any more coherent commands than *Keep away from me!* But it would never do to tell Savaric now that the experiment was bound to fail. He would have to wait and "discover" it at the appropriate moment.

The green walls of Astire were at their thickest where the landward gate was set. Aigar glanced up apprehensively at the high panels of growing trees interlaced with growing vines. The broad stretches of living wall stood in overlapping panels here, covering as much space as might have been taken by two plowed fields. The broad arch of the main gate, the straight way through the walls, was completely choked with thorny vines whose white flowers gave off a strong, sickly-sweet perfume. A slender young woman in the soft green tunic and brown cloak of a Landsensers Guild Apprentice accompanied them to the walkway.

Even this series of narrow arched openings was much obscured by a recent growth of the thorny vines. They had to push the vines out of the way, step by painful step, as they proceeded through the walls. The walkway arches were set at oblique angles that led them on a meandering path from wall to wall, never offering a clear line of sight to the outer world. Aigar found, to his annoyance, that he was sweating with apprehension as they approached the open land where he would have to test his new bondsoul's control of landmonsters. What if Fabre proved even weaker than Janifer? He should have brought them both.

Saviric swore at a dangling vine that snagged his beard. When he tried to free himself, the thorns tangled in his sleeve as well. He drew his shortsword and slashed viciously at the vine. The Landsenser apprentice gasped, "No, my lord! You must not!" too late to stop him.

The whole group halted behind Savaric. A viscous bead of sap formed at the severed end of the vine. The tendrils that had been cut off writhed on the ground.

"Idiot!" Marin commented. "These thorns were not so thick yesterday. Couldn't you tell they've been growing apace to absorb the virtue in the land?"

The severed length of vine curled into a thorny sphere and wept aloud.

"It's only a little one," Savaric said contemptuously.

"It'll grow."

"It will not."

The ball of thorns rolled towards the city, past Savaric's boots. Aigar twitched the hem of his robe away from the weeping plant-monster. His free hand sought out the amulet containing Fabre's bondsoul. *Send it away*!

The ceramic form twisted and throbbed under his hand with a fluid motion that should have been impossible for earth that had been hardened in the fires of magecraft. Aigar felt queasy at the living touch of it, just as he had when using Janifer. But the thorn-ball ceased its weeping and rolled back away from them all, into the tangled thickness of the hedge. Aigar had a sense of things uncoiling, roots thrusting into the earth. A moment later, a fresh spray of sweet white flowers burst forth from the hedge at their feet.

Aigar tore his fascinated gaze from the flowers to find that all the rest of the party, even Marin, were gaping at him with admiration.

"You sent it back to root again," Marin said slowly. "I had not credited such a victory were possible." Even more slowly, he bowed his head to Aigar. "Master of mages, I begin to believe you will save my lord after all."

"How did you *do* that?" breathed the apprentice woman.

"The mysteries of the higher craft are not for 'prentices," Aigar said loftily. For once his years of teaching experience stood him in good stead; he was an old hand at sounding knowledgeable while dodging surprise questions from smart-breeched scholars. But . . . what *had* just happened? He had never guessed Fabre's bondsoul would be so powerful. "I have come to render such aid as I might to a land in grievous need, not to spread among the ignorant such knowledge as might do more ill if used without discrimination."

Lendoman half opened his mouth. "I shall, of course, share my art with such mages as prove themselves capable of discretion and worthy of instruction," Aigar went on with a quelling glance at the half-mage, "as soon as the present emergency is passed." And as soon as he himself figured out what was going on.

They moved on, Savaric chuckling in open glee. "When we catch a big one," he murmured, rubbing his hands together, "when we catch a big one . . . !"

Aigar privately resolved that the first landmonsters he encountered should feed on Savaric's soul. All he had to do was persuade the Seignor to stand a safe distance away. His plan was falling beautifully into place. Savaric must go. Marin, who was beginning to show an appropriate degree of respect, could replace him for the time being. As for Lendoman, he could be controlled with half-promises until the time came to dispose of him also.

The meandering series of openings, half choked with vines and flowers, ended like a song cut off in mid-note. Savaric put up his hand wearily to thrust aside one more veil of greenery and stopped dead in the center of the archway. "Come here, mage," he commanded.

Aigar kept his left hand about the bondsoul as he moved to Savaric's side. Behind him Lendoman was whispering protective cantrips in a voice like dry rustling paper. Marin shifted from one heavy foot to the other; Aigar could hear the tiny chinks made by his mail shirt as he moved. The apprentice Landsenser made no sound at all.

He looked over Savaric's shoulder and tried to make sense of the ruined, moving landscape before him.

Aigar knew well enough what he should have been seeing. The rich valley of the Harendola sloped gently upwards from the river bank where Astire lay to the limestone ledges of Brefania. He should have been looking up into that gentle, mist-shrouded valley, with its softly rolling hills, its patches of green and gold and brown marked off by flowering hedges. At the horizon there should have been groups of trees outlined against the sky, and the white limestone of Brefania should have glowed with its own light against the softer brilliance of the sky. To his right would rise the steeper, harsher hills of Savaric's land, like a jagged line of brown and purple bordering the gracious slopes of the Harendola.

Instead, a dark frieze that seemed to be compounded of mist and smoke and ashes surged over the open land, closing off his view of earth and sky and water. Glowing red embers smouldered within the darkness, moving with the tangle of half-seen shapes and almost-glimpsed lines that shifted perpetually within the smoke.

Aigar tried to swallow. His mouth was very dry. "I . . . had not seen monsters of this type before."

Savaric's chuckle sounded as arid as sand grating over bare rock. "Aye, they're none so easy to fight as those we met in my lands. Not wi' sword, any road. Good thing ye're here to tame 'em for me."

Aigar shook his head. "I cannot guarantee that my charms will bind such formless things as these. My research was predicated on the assumption that we should be dealing with the common types of monsters as categorized by de Breuil." It grew easier to talk as he slipped insensibly into lecture mode. "Of these, to wit, the plants of unnatural form and color, the trees of variable and deadly fruit, and the moving shapes after the forms of men and animals, do the works which I have studied treat in such detail as renders me confident of ultimate control. But I cannot promise that my work can be extended to control such formless things as these, En Savaric, nor can I conceive that you truly desire such as this to swell the ranks of your army."

Savaric gave a grim chuckle. "Afeard, are ye, mage? That comes o' too long at the book. All yer spells smell of the lamp. Why, there's naught here but the face of War made manifest; naught to affright a fighting man. And what better mercenaries could I ask for? The spirit of War itself at my command!" He cracked his knuckles and grinned at Aigar.

"The . . . spirit of War," Aigar murmured. "Very well, then. Come with me."

"After ye, Master Mage," Savaric said. He sketched a rough bow and stepped aside to let Aigar through the last archway.

Aigar clutched convulsively at Fabre's bondsoul. *Away, make them go away.*

The moving frieze of coals and ashes parted before him, and through the opening he glimpsed only black smouldering hills where the fair green fields of the Harendola had been. And as he stared, the smoky landmonsters coalesced again and oozed closer towards the gate.

Back, back! Aigar commanded. He felt the quivering motion of Fabre's bondsoul repeating the command, from his soul through Fabre's blend of soul and earth to the earthen spirits of the landmonsters. The shapes of smoke sank closer to the earth, like dogs cringing before their master, and Aigar felt his confidence growing. Fabre was at least as strong as Janifer, perhaps stronger.

"Make 'em form up in column," Savaric's gravelly voice prompted him.

Aigar was sure that even Fabre's bondsoul would not be able to control the monsters so well. But he dared not reveal his foreknowledge to Savaric. Perhaps he could turn Savaric's belief in his powers to advantage.

"If you would step forward to lead the column, En Savaric," he promised, "they shall march after you." If he could just get Savaric separated from the rest of them, perhaps he could maneuver him outside the circle of Fabre's protection.

Savaric grunted and did not move. "Column first. Then we'll see to the next order. They've some way to go before they *shape* for soldiers." He expelled a grating laugh after the last word. "Want to train 'em, Marin?"

"Not I," said the mercenary leader.

"Column," Aigar said aloud. He did not bother to reinforce the word with a mental command directed at Fabre; nonetheless, the bondsoul leapt and quivered under his hand, and the amorphous twisting contours of smoke and fire gradually oozed into a lumpish mass roughly aligned with the outermost wall of Astire. Aigar drew in his breath and tried to conceal his shock.

"Now have 'em stand separate, one by one," Savaric ordered. "I want to see what size each one has."

"Separate," Aigar echoed. Fabre's bondsoul moved feebly against his chest; the mass of oily smoke quivered but remained whole.

"Can't do it, eh?" Savaric sounded almost benign. "Very

well, then, wheel the column and have it move to the
left. Then—"

Under Savaric's instructions, Aigar found that he could
indeed maneuver the mass of smoke and ashes as a single
entity. He could not get it to show its separate selves,
nor did he succeed in surreptitious commands to return
itself to the fires from whence it sprung.

It was time, he judged, for the tempered apology he
had been mentally framing ever since Allie escaped his
laboratory.

"It seems that even this Elder World soul's ability to
control the landmonsters is not complete," he said.
"Nevertheless, results of this preliminary study are most
encouraging. Clearly further research should be funded."
He could dispose of landmonsters safely; that alone
should be enough to justify his work in the eyes of the
College and the Mages Guild. As for Savaric's pipe-
dream of turning the monsters into his own private army,
Aigar had never cared for that idea. He would promise it as long as necessary to keep Savaric happy. If the
Seignor chose to endow a Chair of Landmonster Studies
at Coindra, and if anybody who might know about their
association could be silenced, Aigar saw no reason why
he could not return to his work at Coindra and keep
secretly promising Savaric his monstrous soldiers. Let's
see; they would have to be rid of Lendoman and Marin,
and possibly of the apprentice who'd passed them
through the gates. Only three people. The rest of the
world could be told the same story Aigar had given his
Assistant Dean in Coindra; Savaric's impetuous war had
raised a terrible class of landmonsters. Aigar had nobly
dashed to the rescue, putting aside all thoughts of personal safety in this desperate effort to save the
Harendola.

It was a *good* story. Aigar was already mentally bask-
ing in the acclaim it would bring him. Certainly a minor
matter like his dabblings in blood-magic would be overlooked when people saw the results!

It remained only to dispose of these monsters and to persuade Savaric to go along with him.

"Now," he said briskly, "although this bondsoul is not strong enough to return these monsters to the land as it did with the lesser plant-monster—"

"And how d'ye know that?" Savaric interrupted him. "I didn't tell ye to destroy them, did I? Have ye been playing me false, mage?"

"What else can we do?" Aigar demanded. "They're not suitable for your purposes; would you leave them here at the walls of Astire?"

Savaric stroked his beard and showed yellowish teeth. "Ye can herd them the direction ye want. That's enough for some purposes."

"Yes," Aigar said, "and since these are compounds of fire and air, drawing strength from earth, it stands to reason they can be destroyed by water. I shall command them into the Verenha."

"Not yet—not yet," said Savaric. "Waste not, want not. Ye were asking where the rest of the peasants were. Form up these smoke-things and I'll direct ye where they're to go. Before we drive them into the river we'll just use them to flush the peasants out of hiding."

"That's far too dangerous!" Aigar protested. "You've seen that my control is not absolute. More research is needed!"

"More research, more research, and I suppose I'm to find more Dracs and Griffons than I've already put out for yer materials, not to speak of keeping Marin and his soldiers to kick their heels in idleness these months past. D'ye think I've a magic tree that rains Griffons? It's time yer work paid its own way. Get on wi' it, man."

"But losing peasants will do you no good," Aigar repeated.

"Better a few dead peasants than a gang of rebels plotting to put a knife between my shoulderblades one day when I ride out to inspect my lands," Savaric said. "We'll cross the Harendola and Brefania, collectin' landmonsters and peasants as we go. Any as comes peaceable and accepts me as lord can live. Any as doesn't would be for it anyway, so ye needn't trouble yer tender conscience about them, Dean."

Aigar gave up the argument. At least Savaric's plan would give him ample chances for an "accident." And since the Seignor wasn't receptive to the idea of funding more research, Savaric would have to go in the same "accident" that took Lendoman and Marin and the assistant Landsenser. He liked that better, really. It was . . . tidy. All the loose ends taken care of in one regrettable incident. It would be painful for him, of course, seeing his associates devoured soul and body by unspeakable monsters, but they'd left him no alternative. Never mind. He was strong; he could bear the suffering.

Especially if he came out of it as the hero of all Escorre.

"And while we're collecting peasants," Savaric added, "ye can keep a sharp eye out for Iseu de Brefania. She got away when we took the Stonehold of Brefania, and so did a bunch of her top people. That's the sort we can't have loose in the land to foment rebellion, d'ye see?"

"I thought Iseu had been taken by landmonsters," Aigar said.

Savaric leered. "Has been, will be. I don't pay much heed to these here fine points of grammar. Just ye see to it that she's not around to make trouble after this little excursion—get it?" And he elbowed Aigar in the ribs again.

The man really had no sense of decency. Some things just shouldn't be discussed.

CHAPTER NINE

In the morning the spring rain was still drizzling down. The day was gray and miserable, and nobody seemed to be particularly interested in a couple of wet ragamuffins huddled near the docks.

From their semi-shelter under the edge of a warehouse roof, Allie studied the patterns of movement on the docks for a long time. Three wide, flat barges were moored along the edge of the river. Dock workers were loading parcels and bales of goods onto the first two; the third, already loaded, floated low in the river. A pair of unhappy-looking, wet men came out of a small building some distance from the docks, approached the man standing guard over the third barge and showed him some tokens.

"Paying passengers," Domerc murmured. "You have to have a token of passage to get aboard. You have to get the passage-tokens from the Freighters Guild, over there." He jerked his chin towards the small building. "And there's a University proctor over there watching the Guildhouse."

Allie looked at the cobbled street leading up into Coindra. A shabbily dressed man who looked just as wet and miserable as everybody else lounged against a shop wall, munching a bread roll. "That's a proctor? I thought they had to wear gowns, just like scholars?"

"He's in disguise, obviously. Trying to trap us. Stands to reason Aigar would have the riverside watched. I told you it was hopeless. They'll take us when we go over to the Guildhouse to buy our tokens."

"So we don't buy tokens," Allie said with more confidence than she felt.

"Then we don't get aboard."

"Those guys aren't showing tokens." Allie nodded at the sailors now trotting barefoot aboard the third barge.

Domerc studied them through slitted eyes. "Allie, I don't know about your world, but around here nobody would take a couple of spindle-shanked, soft-handed kids for members of the Freighters Guild. Besides, don't you think the people who work on the barge know each other?"

"I think they need clean clothes, like everybody else," Allie said. "Put that bundle on your head and follow me."

She picked up her own bundle, consisting of some rags from the attic wrapped around her black scholar's gown, rested it on her head and ambled towards the wharf. Domerc followed so closely that he stepped on her heels.

"Move it!" he whispered. "The proctor's looking at us."

"He'll have something to look at if we run, won't he?" Allie answered without moving her lips. "Slow down. Act as if you don't much want to be here."

Domerc sputtered. "That should be easy enough."

Allie slouched up the wharf and snarled, "Laundry," at the man who'd checked the passengers' tickets.

"You're late. Should've brought it back at first light."

"With that storm last night?" Allie screeched indignantly. "Here I rouse meself in the middle of the night and get soaked through bringing your men's shirts in, *and* let them drip all over my nice dry attic so they'll be fresh for you in the morning, and that's all the thanks I get?" She was vaguely aware of Domerc making agitated flapping gestures, trying to shush her. "Look, you're upsetting my assistant, poor simple boy that he is, but a good strong back and a help to me as you never—"

"Oh, never mind. Get on with it. Wheelhouse." He

jerked his head to indicate one of the long, low structures on the deck. Allie trudged past, stooping to make the bundle on her head seem larger and heavier than it really was, and Domerc followed her.

"Now it's your turn," she whispered just as he was about to congratulate her. "You know these boats; I've never been on one before. Where can we hide?"

As soon as the barge pulled away from the Coindra docks and began moving down the Verenha, Domerc relaxed. And a good thing, too, Allie thought. The strains of the last twenty-four hours seemed to have caught up with her all at once. She felt terrified at the thought of leaving Coindra; she wanted to cry as the red-tiled roofs slowly vanished behind the hills on either side of the Verenha. She was totally incapable of dealing with the barge master when he discovered that the "laundress" and her "apprentice" were still on board. Fortunately, Domerc was able to take over at that point.

"I do think you were brilliant, Domerc," Allie told him after they had settled matters with the barge master and escaped the stuffy confines of the crew-house. Surrounded by bubbling stew, steaming wet garments and sweaty barge hands, Allie had discovered that she wasn't as interested in being dry as in breathing clean air. Now she and Domerc had the best of both worlds; their passages were paid, their clothes were partially dry from the heat of the crew-house, and they had shelter from the rain under the eaves of the crew-house. Allie breathed the fresh damp air with appreciation, watched the green and misty shore slide by, and told herself that her throbbing headache would surely go away soon.

Beside her, Domerc shifted uncomfortably. "Oh, it was nothing, the merest threadbare invention."

"I don't mean telling the barge master that we were a pair of runaway lovers trying to escape my cruel Guildmaster," Allie said severely. "That was *most* embarrassing. Besides, I don't think he cared why we sneaked on, as long as he got paid the price of our passage tokens. *That* was what I thought was brilliant of you. How many men would have had the forethought to take a purse of Griffons with them on a rescue?"

Domerc moved his shoulders against the wooden planks of the shed wall. "Forethought. Well. Um. Actually, I'd forgotten all about it. The remainder of what I got for selling the vielle," he explained. "Seemed safer to keep it on me at all times. If I'd been *thinking*, I'd have brought my books."

"They wouldn't have done us half as much good," Allie pointed out. "I still say you were brilliant. And deducing that the man watching the boats was a proctor of the University! How could you tell? He just looked like some bum hanging around the docks to me. What exactly gave him away to you?"

"Well. Ummm. It wasn't any one thing exactly," Domerc said, "just a way of standing, and well—oh, demons fly away with it! I *couldn't* tell, Allie. But it stands to reason Aigar wouldn't just let us take the first barge downriver. Doesn't it?"

Allie leaned her head back against the shed wall. That was no good; all the talk and movement inside seemed to echo right through her aching skull. She dropped her head forward instead and massaged the back of her neck. "I suppose so," she said.

"What's the matter?"

"Headache. Nothing much. You have to expect a headache after being knocked out, I suppose!" But she hadn't expected the way the pain flared down through all her bones until she felt like an arthritic old crone.

"How long will it last?"

"How should I know?" Allie snapped. "I've never been concussed before!" Thinking about the pain seemed to make it worse. "Could we talk about something else?"

"You want to talk about brilliance," Domerc said, "how did you think of smuggling us aboard as a laundress and her apprentice?"

"Didn't exactly *think* of it," Allie mumbled. "Read about it in American Studies 114. Nineteenth century history. Old Underground Railway trick."

"What's a railway?"

"Well, it wasn't one, not really. See, before the Civil War, there used to be this system for helping people get to the free states . . ."

"What's a freestate?"

It took Allie some time to explain slavery, the Civil War, and the Underground Railway. When she finished, Domerc's black brows were pulled together in a dark V.

"*Strange* customs your world has," he said. "Most unpleasant. Why would you want to go back to a place like that?"

"We don't have slavery any more," Allie explained. "Not where I live, anyway." The headache wasn't bothering her so much any more. It was still there, but the dull throbbing in her head was not nearly so bad as the churning in her stomach. Could one possibly get seasick on a river?

Think about something else, she told herself firmly. Distraction, that's the ticket.

"You haven't told me exactly what we're going to do when we get to Astire," she reminded Domerc. "Call the cops, I suppose. But I still don't understand why we couldn't do that in Coindra."

"Copse?" Domerc echoed. "What good would it do us to summon treespirits?"

Another stimulating round of explanations followed. Domerc was horrified to find that Allie's world needed a special Guild of mercenaries charged with preventing random violence. She was equally horrified to find out that Escorre had no police, no army, and no central government. Instead there were several overlapping networks of power. Most things, Domerc explained, were handled by Guilds, and most people in the nature of things belonged to several Guilds. "There's a Guild for every trade, of course. Then if you live in a city, the principal Guilds in that city contribute to keep up a sort of coalition Guild charged with overseeing the affairs of the city. Same sort of thing in a farming area, see, most of the farmers around Iseu's lands belong to the Freefarmers of the Harendola. And, of course, children take their parents' Guild."

Allie frowned. "I don't get it. Why couldn't we go to the Coindra City Guild for help?"

"Coindra doesn't have a City Guild," Domerc explained. "The University Guild runs everything. I suppose the merchanters that supply the University *could* insist on creating a City Guild that would represent them and the University in proportion, but why would they? The University Guild is so big it would still effectively run Coindra, only the merchanters would have to pay their share of the costs. As it is, they get free services. It all works out."

"Until you piss off somebody who practically controls the University Guild," Allie muttered. "Okay, so if the University isn't going to help us, which Guild are you planning to turn to?"

Domerc stared at some birds rising from the forest on the far bank of the river. "You've got the basic idea right," he said. "Usually, someone who doesn't want to apply to his usual Guild for aid would just go to one of the others he has a claim on. Most people belong to two or three Guilds at least. If your trade Guild didn't help, you'd go to your city Guild, and if neither of those worked out, you could try your parents' Guild or your home Guild."

"So which are we going to?"

"None," Domerc said. Allie could barely hear him. "I don't have a Guild any more," he said. "Neither do you. I mean, we'd both be in the University Guild, but we'll probably be expelled from the University as soon as Aigar thinks of it. You're from Elder World, so you don't have any other Guild affiliations. Unless there's something you're not telling me?" He looked almost hopeful.

Allie shook her head, then wished she hadn't. Now she felt dizzy on top of everything else. She would really have liked to lie down in a quiet room somewhere. A quiet room that wasn't *moving*. Oh, well, presumably she'd feel better eventually—though so far she just felt worse and worse. Probably not a good idea to think about that.

"Where would I get mixed up with a Guild? I haven't done anything but start school here."

"Just a thought," said Domerc gloomily. "You see, I— I—well, it just happens that I don't have any other Guilds either. You know about what happened with the Landsensers."

Allie nodded.

"And my father disowned me, so I don't think it would be a good idea to go home and claim home-rights in my village Guild. And of course we don't have a family Guild."

"Why not?" Allie demanded.

"My family's Seignors, both sides," Domerc told her. "It's not that unusual; we tend to intermarry. Everybody's so related that it takes *forever* to work out whether a marriage is valid any more. Take Iseu. If you follow one line of relationships she's only my second cousin, but if you look at second marriages as blood ties she's a kind of step-niece."

"Never mind Iseu," Allie said, although she made a mental note to find out more about this intermarriage business some time when she was feeling better. "What's a Seignor family?"

Domerc explained that Escorre had been settled by Seignors who held power by virtue of their private armies, some eight or nine centuries ago.

"Where'd they come from?" Allie interrupted.

Domerc shrugged. "Elder World, supposedly. Seems likely enough; from what you tell me, Elder World is a terribly violent place and full of private armies."

"It's changed a bit," Allie said, wishing she'd paid more attention in history classes. What was going on nine hundred years ago? The Norman Conquest? Vikings? Attila the Hun? The Spanish Armada? Oh, well, pick a century, you could find some violent types . . .

While she mused, Domerc had been going on with his brief history of Escorre. The Seignors had eventually learned that private wars were a very dangerous way to manage power struggles in Escorre; burning fields and slaughtering peasants raised worse enemies than the ones they'd been trying to defeat. The Landsensers Guild was started by people who found they could sense the landvirtue and could advise others on where it was safe to cut down trees or build houses or found cities. Eventually the Landsensers Guild grew strong enough to break the power of the Seignors. In the centuries since then, wars had been small and limited; numerous other guilds had sprung up following the model of the Landsensers; and the Seignors had gradually become almost irrelevant to the life of Escorre.

"Most of our families go in for farming," Domerc said. "Some run troops of mercenaries for a cash income. That's about all Savaric does, for instance. We're just like anybody else, really. And the Seignor families mostly work together, sort of like a Guild of our own. Except that doesn't help when you've been disowned." He stared glumly at the rippling water and the dense green foliage on the river bank.

"Lose your job, lose your health insurance," Allie murmured.

"What's that?"

"Some other time, okay?" Allie really did not feel up to explaining health insurance to Domerc. She felt hot and cold all over, alternately. And dizzy. And nauseated. She must be coming down with the flu. It seemed a bit much, especially on top of concussion and everything. Allie had a brief vision of her little attic room in Coindra, with its sloping ceiling and its window looking out over the steep red-tiled roofs of the city. She wanted to be back there so much it hurt. She moaned softly.

"What's the matter?"

"Nothing." Allie swallowed hard and tried to think about something else. She couldn't go back to Coindra, and if she was coming down with the flu she couldn't do much about that either. When they got to Astire she would tell Domerc how very ill she felt and ask him if he couldn't find her a place to sleep for a few hours.

"How much longer until we get to Astire?" she asked.

"Not long. It's pretty close to Coindra. We should be seeing the outlying farms any minute now."

"Is that the city, then?" Allie asked, pointing downstream where a dark haze hung over the horizon. She wondered vaguely what industries Escorre had to cause pollution. Obviously it wasn't from cars.

Domerc stared, then jumped to his feet and dashed into the crewhouse. A moment later three men followed him outside, all staring and talking so fast that Allie couldn't catch more than a few scattered words. They pointed and jabbered and Domerc nodded, looking very serious.

"What's the matter?" Allie asked when he rejoined her.

"I might be wrong," Domerc said. "I *hope* I'm wrong. We'll see."

"See *what*?" But within a few minutes the answer became obvious to Allie.

As the boat moved downstream, the dark wall of trees along the river bank was interrupted by smouldering black patches of open ground. Allie stared at wispy plumes of smoke that hung low on the ground instead of dispersing in the air. The smoke seemed thick and translucent at the same time, and the edges of the clouds were *almost* clearly defined. When her eyes tried to make out the shapes, though, she couldn't seem to make herself stare at any one bit of smoke for very long.

"Seems like it would be too wet for forest fires," she said.

"It is." Domerc's mouth was set in a thin line, and

he looked anywhere but at the burnt patches. "It's almost impossible to burn the forest. These were small farms."

Allie caught sight of a blackened heap of timbers in the middle of one of the burnt patches. The smell of roasting meat and burned fat mingled with the general scent of ashes and desolation. Her stomach heaved and she clamped her mouth firmly shut.

"Savaric must be mad!" Domerc exclaimed. "This is going to raise landmonsters enough to destroy the Harendola and all his army."

As they went on downstream towards Astire, they left the forest behind. Now there were only bare fields and blackened heaps of timber. The smoke clouds were thicker here, almost solid-looking, and through them the remains of fire burned as red spots obscured by the shifting gray smoke.

"It can't be Savaric," Allie said after a while, more to distract herself from the oily bubbles of smoke hovering around the burnt farms than because she cared who had done this. "He was talking to Aigar last night, making plans. The way I heard it, he hadn't actually done anything yet. He couldn't have burned all this in a single night."

"Magefire," Domerc said.

Allie wrapped her arms around her knees and wished she were back in Coindra, with no worse problem than the upcoming lab section of Introductory Casting. Magefire. She didn't know what that was, and she didn't want to know. Why had she assumed that a world without freeways was a world without any unpleasant technology?

If you looked too long at the smoke clouds, the glowing coals seemed to move and wink like eyes . . .

"Doesn't work on the forest, of course," Domerc added as if just thinking to mention something any Escorrean child would know. "The wild virtue is too strong in there. Mortal magecraft operates on mortal works." He said it like a maxim repeated too often to be heard.

The bargemaster approached them with bows and apologies. Allie wondered just how much Domerc had overpaid him for their passage. It would be impossible, he explained, for them to put in at Astire under these circumstances. The risk of contagion by landmonsters was too great. Allie gathered that as long as they stayed in midstream, they were safe. This sounded like a very good idea to her.

"Wait till we get to Astire," Domerc argued. "The city might still be all right."

"I'll take you on to the next port at no extra charge," the bargemaster offered.

"Take us past Astire," Domerc countered, "and you can damn well refund the cost of our passage tokens. I paid you to take us to Astire, not to the Western Seas!"

The bargemaster laughed uneasily. "Now, now, young sir. Who said anything about going as far as that? Just past the war area, that's all, and a sensible precaution as any reasonable man would thank me for taking."

Allie would have thanked him, if she hadn't been feeling too sick and miserable to talk. She stared at the planks she sat on, and at the tips of her own shoes, and tried not to listen to the argument or think about the shadowy things she had glimpsed on the burnt shore.

A shout from Domerc startled her into raising her head. "There!" he cried triumphantly. "Astire stands!"

Downstream, the blackened devastation extended right up to a wall of green that came as a sweet shock to Allie's eyes. "What *is* that?" she demanded. "More forest?" But the edge of the greenness seemed too solid, too well defined, for another forest.

"*Astire,*" Domerc said impatiently. "Haven't you ever seen a livewall before? What do you *do* when you need a city in a place where the landvirtue runs strong? Are all your Elder World cities built of dead stone?"

"Ummm. Reinforced concrete, I think. Bricks. Steel. Why are we talking about construction materials?" Allie said absently, her eyes fixed on the green wall ahead.

As the barge glided closer, what had seemed like a solid mass of green stuff resolved into great overlapping curved walls whose colors shifted continually from the spring-green of new leaves to the darker greens of pines and firs and darker still, to the green shadow of tree trunks in a rain forest. The walls swooped and dipped and soared like the construction of an insane child or the masterwork of a topiarist, overlapping and joining and parting in mid-air to form pointed windows and arched doors into the sky. The highest points flung up sprays of green leaves, like towers or fountains or trees; and it all seemed to be moving as Allie watched. "What *is* that?" she repeated in a lost, dreaming voice.

"Astire stands," Domerc repeated. He bowed his head and his fingers flickered before him in a pattern that seemed to linger on the air, a dazzle of green light gone before Allie could be quite sure she had seen anything at all.

"No magefire here, land be praised!" said the bargemaster, a shade too heartily. "And had I known you were of *that* Guild, young sir, be sure I'd have had no objection to landing you here in any case. But you'll understand we plain men have to take care of ourselves, not being rich enough to travel with a Landsenser on board as a regular thing, and very sensible of the honor you done us."

Allie wondered why the man was babbling so; but between her aching head and her wondering gaze, she had little energy to spare for worrying about it. The river curved and swept them downstream across a broad arc of silver water; Astire's crescent-shaped walls reached out to enfold them; a wayward breeze danced over the water. The mist hanging low over the river lifted to reveal a stir of moving figures on the wharfs. Metal glinted in the sudden light, and a triangular black-and-red banner flew out straight in the breeze.

"Savaric's pennon!" someone cried behind her. The man at the helm swore and did something violent and physical that tilted the barge against the river current. They were fighting the river now; it twisted and shook them and water sprayed onto the deck, and the force of the current still carried them choppily down towards the crowd of armed men on the wharves of Astire.

When Fabre didn't show up for the morning rehearsal, Liuria muttered unladylike things about young tomcats who spent all night chasing girls and couldn't be troubled to get up in the morning. Well, just too bad for him if he was nursing an aching head or dallying with a girl; he'd promised to accompany her in the Springsong Fete and she wasn't about to do a public performance with an accompanist who still didn't have his tempos right. She ran lightly up the stairs and pounded on the door to the big room Fabre and Domerc shared, then waited for the inevitable groans and complaints from within. Once she was sure Fabre was up, she thought, she'd go on up to the attic and collect Allie. The kid had an amazing talent for polyrhythms; with her improvising the triple beats required, even Fabre should be able to get the rhythms correct.

But there was no sound from within the room. Liuria banged on the door again and shouted a few insulting comments about Fabre's habits.

Still nothing. She frowned. He never failed to insult her back, if only to demonstrate that he could still think of nastier and wittier lines than she could. And Domerc should have been telling her to keep the noise down and let him study. Well, possibly Domerc had gone out instead of reading this morning. But Fabre?

"Fabre, I don't *believe* this," she called, "here I am finally begging for admittance to your chamber, and you're not even going to answer?" Liuria hit the door again to emphasize her words. This time the ancient latch slipped. The door groaned and swung lazily inward on creaking hinges.

The room was empty and unnaturally tidy. Both beds

were neatly covered with flat patched quilts, with the
extra blankets rolled up to serve as pillows.

"It is *not possible*," Liuria muttered, "that they *both*
got up early, dressed, *made their beds* and went out!"
She flung herself down at the big oak table that filled
the center of the room, propped her chin on her hands
and glowered at the two beds. Domerc might have gone
out early, but he would never have straightened his bed
first. Liuria loved her brother dearly but she was under
no illusions as to the quality of his housekeeping. She
was willing to bet that no one had slept in that bed since
she herself had straightened it the day before. Domerc
had offered to read over her theology paper on the souls
of stones, and she'd picked up some of the mess in the
room and made both beds, ostensibly in payment for
his comments, really because she couldn't concentrate
in a pigsty. She even remembered that she had stretched
the faded quilt flat so that its pattern of interlinked dia-
monds was lined with the natural forces flowing through
the room from north to south—just as it lay now, perfectly aligned.

Fabre's bed was equally neat. Now, Fabre might have
been out all night making music at the Blue Pigeon and
making eyes at pretty girls. He might even have spent
the night with one of the girls, if he got lucky. But
Domerc wouldn't have gone with him. Domerc would
have looked down his nose and made remarks about how
he needed to study and Fabre could stand to do some
reading himself.

All right, said Liuria to herself. So Fabre never came
home last night, he's collecting another slash in his gown.
And Domerc got up early and went for a walk by the
river . . . but no. He never made the bed that neatly.
Try another hypothesis. For once, Fabre talked Domerc
into going out with him. Domerc got drunk. Some girl
took him home, goodness knows there are plenty of girls
who'd like the chance. And I should be glad that he's
finally forgetting his doom and gloom and enjoying

himself like a normal person, instead of sitting here inventing trouble. What am I going to do, anyway? Tell the proctors that my big brother never came home last night? They'd have a good laugh about that. Especially coming from me. They'd look at all the slashes in my gown and tell me I should be able to figure out what he's been up to. Except I don't think so. Not Domerc. Not old gloomy Domerc. He's been worse than ever since Allie quit speaking to us.

A wild hypothesis came to Liuria. She jumped up and dashed up the stairs to Allie's attic room. So what if she embarrassed Domerc and Allie? Served 'em right for oversleeping and worrying her, and besides . . .

And besides, this room was as empty as the others. And considerably neater; Allie kept her books and papers stacked on a shelf above her bed, the bed covered with a quilt even more ragged than the ones Domerc and Fabre had gotten from the landlady, and her curious foreign-looking satchel stuffed under the bed. It was too big to fit all the way under the sagging mattress; a corner of it poked out and reminded Liuria just how bizarre Allie had looked before she got a robe to cover her queer foreign clothes. Even her satchel was outlandish, with its frame of metal rods and smooth unnatural-feeling fabric. There was something very strange about that girl; one of these days, when she got over her huff and was speaking to them again, Liuria meant to find out more about it.

But that mystery could wait. Just now Liuria very much wanted to know where Domerc and Fabre and Allie had disappeared to. If her brother and his friend had made it up with Allie and gone out for a party, why hadn't they told her? It wasn't like them to leave her out. And . . . something *felt* wrong. Liuria closed her eyes and stood for a moment, absorbing the sense of Allie's room. It was the same as the feelings she had picked up downstairs in Domerc's room: fear and surprise and anger.

Something had frightened Allie. She'd gone to

Domerc, still frightened. And then . . . what? Liuria scowled at the open window with its view of the city's peaked red-tiled roofs. They could be anywhere in Coindra. She had nothing to take to the proctors, nothing but a faint lingering sense of strong feelings and her own knowledge of her friends' habits.

There were no clues in Allie's bare, neat little room. Liuria plodded back down the stairs to Domerc's room and cast herself into a chair again. This time the sleeve of her gown knocked over a stack of papers and sent them sliding to the floor.

Domerc would kill her if she got his thesis dirty or crumpled. Liuria knelt on the floor and gathered up the papers, gently smoothing and stacking them; a few pages were out of order, but Domerc would have to fix that, she wasn't about to read over a first-year scholar's work in agonizing detail to figure out the exact sequence of his arguments. Blast, there was another paper that had somehow skittered under the wardrobe. Scratch paper? No, the corner she saw bore Domerc's unmistakable tall slanting letters in brown ink. Setting the recaptured bits of the thesis on the table, Liuria lay down on her stomach and stretched an arm under the wardrobe to recapture the one missing sheet. She breathed in dust and felt something soft and disgusting skittering away from her fingers. Dust bunnies, she told herself firmly, not mice, and—aha! Got it! With a soft exclamation of triumph Liuria drew forth what was, after all, only a spoiled half-sheet on which Domerc had scribbled some kind of a note.

"Fabre," she read, "Allie's upset about, well never mind, you wouldn't believe me anyway, but the thing is she's gone off to the Dean's laboratory in the middle of the night and of course she won't find him there but if she does I'm afraid, oh, it's too complicated, but why don't you check out the College of Magical Arts whenever you get back? We might want your help."

"Blasted first-year scholars," Liuria grumbled. Domerc

might be two years older than her and brilliant, but while she'd been learning how to write papers he'd been busy with the Landsensers Guild. He still wrote like a fledgling. In the time he'd spent scribbling that rambling note to Fabre, he could have put down a coherent explanation of the problem.

Instead. . . . Liuria frowned, trying to reconstruct the sequence. Something or someone had frightened Allie badly. She'd gone to Domerc and then had rushed off into what looked like a nasty wet spring storm, headed for Aigar's laboratory. Domerc had let her go, then got worried and decided to go after her, leaving an inarticulate message for Fabre. Fabre had come home some time later, read Domerc's note, dropped it where a draft could blow it under the wardrobe, and followed the other two.

To Aigar's laboratory.

Luria felt cold prickles up and down her spine. Bad things happened to people who associated with the Dean. Look at that business in the Harendola last year. And then the fine he'd imposed on Domerc this year . . .

"But he hasn't actually *hurt* anybody," Liuria murmured, trying to reassure herself. "Oh, sure, he's destroyed Domerc's career, impoverished him, made him sell his vielle, tried to get him expelled, but he's not violent."

She couldn't picture Aigar doing anybody physical harm. He was too dignified. Too old. Too *clumsy*. Why, if he tried, Domerc would knock him flat! Even Allie could probably trip him up! No, the idea was ludicrous.

All the same, Liuria thought, she could do worse things with this morning than follow her friends to the Dean's rooms in the College of Magical Arts. Not that she was the least bit worried about them. But it wouldn't hurt to just check things out.

Cautiously.

Very cautiously.

There were magics for augmenting one's sense of the

emotions other people sent out. Those spells were popular in the University for obvious reasons, but Liuria had never thought much of the kind of people who resorted to them. If you couldn't tell when somebody was interested in you without spellcasting, she said, you probably had no business chasing that somebody anyway. Now for the first time she found another use for that line of spells.

She was unpracticed in the sensing songs, but it didn't matter; the feelings that had sent Allie out in the storm had been so strong that they lingered all along the narrow street, like spring mist. And besides, she knew now where everybody had gone . . .

Following Allie's fear and anger, Domerc's worry, and Fabre's guarded concern along the street, Liuria left her own trail of doubt and confusion. She felt as if she were visibly shedding the beginnings and ends of her sentences. Any Master of Magical Arts—like Dean Aigar, for instance—would have seen her walking along in a cloud of half-completed arguments. "Oh, surely not—" and "—but what if—" and "—no sense worrying till I get there."

That last, Liuria told herself, was very good advice; and she proceeded to follow it so well that she walked straight into the second courtyard before the College of Magical Arts, and very nearly fell into the fountain, before she realized that she'd reached her destination.

The clouds of emotion were stronger than ever here; Liuria felt as though her friends were standing around her, arguing. And all their forces aligned to draw her inside.

"Here, now, young lady, you can't go back there!" called a sharp-nosed woman in the outer office.

Liuria smiled over her shoulder. "I'm just meeting my roommate for, umm, for a late breakfast," she called. "She said she'd be working this morning."

"Not for Dean Aigar, she isn't." The woman bustled around the writing-desks and into the hallway, as full of importance as a pigeon in a corncrib. Liuria sighed. It was Evgena Fassolaris, the Assistant Dean. She did all Aigar's administrative work and liked nothing so much as keeping students away from the Dean for fear they might disturb his important researches. In general Liuria approved, distantly, of this policy. Aigar was a dangerous man and students were safer if they kept well away from him. But Allie hadn't done that . . . and she had a very strong feeling that Allie wasn't safe at all, now.

And if Allie could get past Evgena, so could she. Liuria made her smile a little sweeter and repeated her story about being there to meet the Dean's laboratory assistant, who'd promised to breakfast with her.

"A likely story!" sniffed the Fassolaris woman. "I suppose you and that precious brother of yours invented it to give you another chance at snooping round Dean Aigar's rooms."

"Did *not*," Liuria protested, even while wishing she had thought of that very thing a little earlier. It would have been a good idea. "I tell you, she's my roommate. We share lodgings at Ma Blood-Pudding's house. In the Rue Jauzion," she added, seeing a trace of doubt cross Evgena's face, "just behind Peire the baker's." All the corroborative detail seemed to be working; maybe she'd throw in a little more truth while she was at it. "But it's true we hadn't planned to meet this morning. The fact is, Allie didn't come home last night. You know how these young scholars are," Liuria plunged on with reckless disregard of her own reputation, "always partying and, well, flirting. They don't understand the importance of studying and keeping regular hours the way those of us who've been at the University longer do. Anyway, I just wanted to make sure she was all right and had shown up for work this morning. I don't think she can afford to lose this job," she added with perfect truth. All semester Allie had lived carefully on her wages from Aigar; it was another thing that made Liuria suspect she'd come to Coindra without her family's sanction.

Evgena Fassolaris' forbidding countenance softened slightly. "You needn't worry about your roommate today," she said. "Dean Aigar's not here and his laboratory is shut up, so he'll never miss her. And she's not been by, either, if it's that snippet of a redhead you mean. Probably sleeping it off still."

Not unless she was sleeping in Aigar's lab, Liuria thought.

"I'd better speak to the Dean," she said.

"You can leave your messages with me. I'm acting Dean until further notice." The Fassolaris' breast puffed up like a corn-stuffed pigeon's, and Liuria began to understand why she was bustling around herself instead of leaving the clerks of the office to do the work. Couldn't miss a chance of telling somebody, could she?

"But you haven't seen Allie," Liuria pointed out, "you just said so. So if you'll just tell me where to find Dean Aigar—"

"Away. Important business. Secret," Acting Dean Fassolaris snapped, and then she relented slightly. "You wouldn't be able to speak to him anyway, so I suppose it'll do no harm to tell you. The poor man was up all night Sensing and linking with the Landsensers Guild in the Harendola. It seems there's been a great current of landvirtue through the Harendola."

"Well, they should be able to absorb it if anybody can," murmured Liuria, envisioning the rolling green hills and golden fields of that fertile valley.

"That I wouldn't know about," said Evgena, "not being a Landsenser myself. But what I do know is that the Harendola Guildhouse spoke with Dean Aigar by voicebubble last night and entreated his aid in dealing with the landvirtue. He said they're in fear of landmonsters, and En Sàvaric from the mountains has been making matters worse by starting a war during spring growing time. By morning the Dean was exhausted, but he's never been one to spare himself. 'Evgena,' he said to me, 'you're the only one I can

trust with the affairs of the College. I have to leave
for the Harendola immediately, Evgena,' he said, 'to
thwart the evil works of En Savaric and help the Guild
there absorb this surge of the landvirtue, and I want
to entrust the College to you. No one else could do
the job.' "

Liuria wanted to ask why anybody else *should* do the
job, seeing that Evgena Fassolaris was the assistant Dean
and the logical person to take over when Aigar was called
away, but she realized that she was letting herself get
distracted by trivia.

"And that redheaded snip wasn't with him, either,"
the Acting Dean added with a sniff. "She may be good
enough to wash bottles for the Dean, but he'd not entrust
her with his secrets, not a mere child like that."

"Of course not," Liuria said sweetly, "she might go
telling everything to the first scholar she met. Although
if there's an emergency in the Harendola, it can hardly
be secret," she added hastily, before Evgena Fassolaris
had more than begun to look puzzled.

Liuria felt reluctant to work her sensing spells under
the eyes of the Assistant Dean. She lingered a few
moments, pretending to read the notices chalked on the
boards just outside the clerks' office, until some other
business sent Evgena bustling back among the writing
stands to upbraid a clerk and show him how the forms
he was filling out should be handled. Then she strolled
casually back out to the open courtyard. The cheerful
splashing of water in the fountain covered her low humming, and she drew her hands back under her slashed
cloak to keep anybody from noticing the subtle weaving movements of her fingers. It was a good thing, Liuria
thought, that generations of students bent on romance
had refined the sensing spells to this sequence of barely
noticeable movements. She would just inconspicuously
stroll round the fountain and pick up the sense of where
and in what direction her friends had carried off their
seething emotions. "Sunside, snowside, moonside,

seaside," Liuria murmured in time to the tones of the sensing spell while she walked around the fountain.

She frowned. There was nothing. The courtyard was unnaturally clean of all traces of emotion. Coming in, she must have been so intent on reaching the Dean's office that she hadn't noticed the sudden blankness in the air. Perhaps that was what had thrown her off so that she almost walked into the fountain.

"They didn't vanish into thin air just outside Aigar's lab," she told herself. "You're missing things. Oh, I wish Fabre were here; I bet *he* knows the spells backwards and forwards." But she knew that was unfair. Fabre didn't need to cheat to get girls; his freckle-faced grin and unassuming line of chatter reeled them in all unsuspecting while they thought they were pursuing some pale proud beauty like Domerc.

She must have missed the trail, that was all. Probably whatever they'd done here had calmed everybody down so that they didn't leave such a cloud of steamy feelings behind them. She circled the fountain again, more slowly, and then again.

Maybe Aigar had turned them all into fountain fish. There'd been rumors that he was working on some magical breakthrough; perhaps he'd found a way around the conservation of mass problem. Liuria scowled at the overfed carp slowly circling the murky waters at the pool's edge and decided that none of them looked in the least human. At least, they didn't look like her friends; the fat-faced one with the twitching whiskers reminded her of Evgena Vassolaris, but *she* was alive and well.

And the morning's contingent of scholars with problems was beginning to show up, disrupting the auras of the courtyard with all their own petty worries and joys. Now Liuria could sense nothing but the sort of free-floating anxiety that visits to a Dean usually generated; a vague feeling of tests and courses flunked, required work forgotten, conflicts with authority.

"What are you *doing*," one of the incoming scholars

demanded, "strolling around and around the fountain like that? You're making me dizzy."

"Getting exercise," Liuria informed him. "Only it's not enough."

"I should think not," the boy said. "You should go for a long walk in the country."

"I intend to," said Liuria, heading out of the linked courtyards and towards the University's main journey-maze.

There she found that all transport to the Harendola had just been cancelled. The scholar-mage in charge wouldn't tell her why, but the way he changed color when she mentioned landmonsters and Savaric convinced Liuria that Evgena Vassolaris had been telling at least part of the truth. Whether there really was a plague of landmonsters she still doubted; she couldn't see Aigar nobly volunteering for dangerous work. But she was quite sure that he had given this story to Evgena, the Transport Mage, and anybody else he dealt with in Coindra. And he'd convinced them enough to close down that branch of the transport net for a time.

She still could see no alternative to following Aigar to the Harendola, though. He was the only one she *could* follow. And he might be the only one who could tell her what had happened in his laboratory the previous night.

Moodily considering her slim chances of getting any information at all out of the Dean, Liuria returned to her lodging, packed a few personal things and the rest of her quarter's allowance, set a minor keyspell on her room and Domerc's and Allie's, and started off for the riverside to hire passage on a freight barge.

CHAPTER TEN

"This looks like a good spot," Domerc whispered to Allie.

She stared at the shore lined with slender reeds and at the grassy hills rising behind the water. As far as she could tell, it was the same monotonous view they'd been looking at ever since the bargemaster headed into midstream at Astire instead of landing his passengers and cargo at the wharf.

"Good for what?" she muttered.

"For us. Tall grass, plenty of cover. Come on. And don't splash!" Domerc glanced at the bows of the barge, where one bored crewman was keeping watch for obstacles downstream; then he wriggled out of his trews and tunic, rolled them into a neat bundle, and slipped overboard with hardly a ripple to mark his passage.

Allie went over the side of the barge without thinking about anything except the need to keep up with Domerc. Later, though, she was going to ask what the hell he had done that for. The water was *cold*; she thought about melting snow and mountain streams, and then about hypothermia. A sleek black shape ahead of her must be Domerc's head, and the oddly shaped lump beside it would be his clothes. She hoped he had remembered to roll up his purse inside the clothes; it was all the money they had. She hoped there weren't any snakes in the river.

The current was too strong for her here; Domerc was

swimming smoothly and strongly, hardly breaking the water, but when she tried to emulate him she was carried downstream and back towards the center of the river. She was too tired. It wasn't worth it. Why not just let the water carry her on to the sea and rest, rest in the sea, the waves rocking . . .

Something coiled around her legs and Allie forgot all about not splashing. She also discovered that she did, after all, have the strength to make it past that strong side-current and into the calm puddles lapping at the shore.

"What took you so long?" whispered a clump of reeds.

Allie decided that she really was going to kill Domerc. Some day. After he got her out of this.

"You could have *warned* me," she whispered back. She grabbed the clump of reeds and hauled herself onto the muddy verge of the river. Nice mud. Nice quiet mud, not going anywhere. She would just lie here for a while and think about Life, and whether she wanted to drown Domerc slowly or just strangle him right now, and various other comforting fantasies.

"Better come up on dry land," Domerc advised her, slithering out of the reeds. "The grass is tall enough here for cover, and you don't want to stay by the river. Tongue-adders like to nest in the reeds. Why didn't you take your clothes off? You're all wet."

He disappeared back into the reeds and made rustling noises like a man getting dressed under unfavorable conditions. Allie stalked up the grassy hill in a dignified silence marred only slightly by the fact that she squelched when she walked and left a trail of muddy drips behind her.

"I didn't have *time* to undress," she said when Domerc caught up with her. "Next time give me some warning, okay? Why are we here, anyway?"

"We had to get off the boat," Domerc said in exasperation. "The barge master is so scared he probably won't stop till he reaches Salmistre of the sea."

"So?" Sounded like a great idea to Allie.

"So we can't abandon our friends like that. And I didn't want him noticing exactly where we left the barge, just in case he's stopped and questioned downstream. We're going to circle back around to Brefania and find out what's going on," Domerc told her. "Iseu may need our help."

"Oh. And exactly what help are two half-drowned, hungry fugitives going to be?"

Domerc drew himself up. "I am a scholar-mage and a fully trained Landsenser," he said.

"Thought you'd been thrown out of the Guild." Allie hated herself, but she couldn't seem to stop being nasty to Domerc. At least quarreling took her mind off her physical miseries.

"They can deny me the right to use my talents," Domerc proclaimed in ringing tones, "but they cannot take away the powers themselves. My sense comes from the Land and not from the hands of men." He stooped, touched the earth at their feet, and rose again while passing one hand over his breast in a quick ritualized gesture.

"Very nice," Allie said approvingly. "Does your Landsense have anything to say about a place to sleep tonight? A warm, dry place," she added with an involuntary shiver.

Domerc frowned. "There are some farms in the foothills, on the edge of the wildlands. It is possible Savaric has not burned those. I saw no evidence that his magefire had gone south of Astire, did you?"

Allie looked over the sea of rippling tall grass that billowed down from their hilltop. Waves of pale gold and moving shadows danced in the wake of every light breeze. There was no sign of anything else at all: farms, houses, or war. She said as much.

"Oh, we're too far south now to see anything," Domerc said. "We'll have to head north through the wildlands. At least there's no danger of landmonsters here."

Allie didn't ask why; she was too tired to care. And the thought of a long walk through nowhere to nothing depressed her unutterably. Why bother? Why bother with anything, come to that? She almost wished she could stay angry with Domerc; anger had been like a little spark of life within her. Now there was nothing but gray clouds and gray depression and the gray sea of grass around them.

Golden, she corrected herself. Why had she thought it was gray? She must be very tired indeed; when she didn't concentrate on what she was looking at, the world seemed to go all pale and wavery, bleached of life and light and color.

Must be the fever, she decided. At least she wasn't cold any longer.

"I wish we could make a fire and get you dry," Domerc said, looking closely at her. "But we'll have to get to a farm first. The wildlands won't burn."

"How come?" Not that she really cared. Understanding Escorre's ecology was too hard.

"The landvirtue," Domerc said. "Same as the forest to the north. It'd be like trying to burn green wood, don't you see?"

"No," Allie said truthfully.

"I'll explain as we go along." He stared at her again. "If you— Are you all right, Allie? You look funny."

"Anybody would look funny after being dunked in a river without warning," Allie said. "I'll be okay. It's a nice warm day; I'll get dry walking." No point in mentioning her vague aches and pains, or the sensation that the world was wavering about her like a heat mirage. She wanted some aspirin, and a hot bath, and a nice soft bed; but none of those things were available, so why worry Domerc about it?

He studied her face for a moment longer and evidently came to the same conclusion. "Well, we have to walk to get to the settled lands, so I suppose we may as well get started."

Heading north made Allie feel a little better. Not much, but at least she no longer had that sense of getting more and more miserable with every minute that passed, as she had felt while floating down the river. "Exercise is good for you," she murmured in time to her steps. "Strength through joy. Arbeit macht frei. No pain no gain. Go for the burn." Vague memories of exercise videos and a lecture on the Holocaust swirled together, dreamlike, until she all but forgot where she was.

"Allie? Allie! Come back!"

Somebody snapped his fingers under her nose. Allie blinked and recognized Domerc's lean brown hand.

"Is something the matter?"

"I was worried about you," Domerc said. "You looked like you were sleepwalking. And I don't think you've heard a word I said about the wildlands."

Allie forced a grin. "You never went to sleep in a lecture?"

"I like to think I'm more interesting than MasterMage Vicintinis," Domerc said.

"Ah. Well. You never know, do you?"

"Salamanders! You Elder World types have no respect," Domerc joked. He looked and sounded relieved, convinced that Allie was all right, and she didn't see any point in telling him otherwise. Besides, she did feel a little better. At least they were going in the right direction—

What a very strange thought. Why should a flu virus care whether you were facing north or south, towards— Allie closed her eyes and tried to remember the map she'd seen in de Breuil. Coindra of the mountains, Salmistre of the sea; what difference did it make? Oh, well, maybe Escorrean viruses were as screwy as everything else in this world; maybe they *cared* whether you were properly aligned with the magnetic poles.

Domerc warned Allie that they'd have to be quiet and move cautiously from now on, as they were getting close to the settlements in the foothills.

"I did notice we seemed to be climbing," Allie said. "Shh!"

She'd been quiet enough before, Allie thought; *Domerc* was the one who insisted on her talking. And now he wanted her to shut up. *Men.* Very well. She would climb quietly and gasp for breath quietly and go back to her speculations about the magnetic Poles. Magnetic Czechs? Be quiet, we're coming to a Czech Point. Check point. Bad checks. Daddy's check floating in little pieces over the red roofs of Coindra. *I want to go back to Coindra.*

"Well, we can't," muttered Domerc, and Allie realized she'd spoken that last thought aloud. "Now hush. Wait here."

She sank down into the shelter of the tall plumed grasses, too tired to care why she was waiting or where Domerc was going so stealthily. Her legs hurt almost as much as her head. It was good to rest, but in a minute they'd have to go on. Why? Because we haven't got there yet. Got where? She couldn't remember; only a feeling that they needed to be moving north. North star to freedom. Follow the drinking gourd . . .

Something rustled among the grass; a dark shape loomed over her. Allie gave an involuntary yelp.

"*Hush,*" Domerc hissed. His face was set in lines that made him look ten years older; she'd seen him look like that once before, when was it? When he had to watch the Landsensers at work in Coindra. *I want to go back to Coindra.*

She knew better than to say that again, though. "What's the matter?" she whispered. "Did they burn the farms?"

"No magefire," Domerc said, "but it's not pretty. I found some food, but we'd better sleep out here."

He had used his gown for an improvised sack; now he spread out the black folds of cloth and displayed a small pile of onions, carrots and hard round knobbly things that looked like malformed potatoes with a skin disease.

"Potatoes?" Domerc repeated as if she'd used another

of her strange foreign words. "These are turnips. And
the purplish ones are rutabagas. They'd be better cooked,
but I don't want to light a fire; might bring Savaric's men
down on us."

Allie's mouth watered at the thought of a hot stew.
"Did you see any soldiers?"

"No. They'd done their work here." Domerc closed
his mouth in the hard line that was becoming familiar.
"But we can't take the chance. Whatever's going on,
Savaric's hand in glove with Aigar. Do you *want* to fall
into Aigar's clutches again?"

It sounded restful; falling, and somebody to catch and
hold you . . . Allie clenched her fists until the nails bit
into her palms. The small, sharp, real pain helped her
to block out the misty dreams and the vague aches that
troubled her thinking. What was needed now was not
dreams, but stew. A nice fire and a nice hot stew. "Can
you find water? And cooking pots?"

"I could," Domerc said, "they didn't bother fouling
the well or smashing the family's goods. But what's the
point? Turnips won't taste any better for being swished
around in cold water; what we want is a fire, and it's
too risky."

"No, it's not," Allie told him. "I remembered another
Underground Railway story. At least . . . would you be
willing to try this?"

Some time later they were back in their hiding place
among the tall grasses, watching a thin plume of smoke
and hot air rising to the sky from the farmyard. Domerc's
nose twitched like a rabbit's as he smelled the aroma
of onions and turnips stewing in water.

"Allie, you're a genius," he whispered.

"I'm only a genius if it works," she whispered back.
"Is it done yet?"

"Doesn't matter. We have to wait until the smoke
stops. And maybe a while after, in case somebody saw
it and came." And that would show Dad, with his snide
certainty that she hadn't learned anything in school.

Ha! Nineteenth Century American History was proving a positive treasure trove. She'd picked up this trick from the same unit on the Underground Railway that held the story about slaves sneaking on boats with laundry. Runaway slaves in the forest would build a small fire and hide until it burnt down to the coals. Then if nobody had come to investigate the smoke, they would go back, cook their food quickly, wrap it in leaves and move on.

Granted, she'd had to make a few alterations to the system. Allie didn't think coals would stay hot long enough to cook a stew, so they'd left the cookpot on the fire. Anybody who did come would know there were people nearby . . . but then, the fire alone would have been proof of that, wouldn't it? Allie assured herself again that it was a *good* plan.

And perhaps by the time the smoke had died down, she would have forgotten what she'd seen in the house on her way to get the cooking pot, and she'd have her appetite back. One thing was sure, she wasn't hungry enough to go after that stew if there was even the slightest sign that somebody had come to investigate the fire. She didn't even want to think about meeting people who could do things like that to a family. The children too; couldn't they have spared the children?

Allie squeezed her eyelids tight shut to close out the memory of the two children, lying pale and still forever in a pool of their own blood. The older one had been a girl; her arm was flung protectively over the small boy's face, as if to keep him from seeing what was about to happen to them. Both their heads lolled back from the wide bloody gashes across the small white throats. And the blood was everywhere . . .

"Wait a little longer," she whispered to Domerc after the last thin thread of smoke had died away. "I'm not hungry anyway."

"Me neither," Domerc said, "but we have to eat." He looked hard at her. "Especially you. Are you feeling sick

or something? Because it's another half-day's walk to the
Stonehold of Brefania."

"I'm fine," Allie lied. "Just, I didn't like what we saw
at the farm." That was true enough. As for the flu, there
was no point in mentioning it to Domerc as long as she
could walk. And she *could*. To prove it, she stood up
and took three unsteady steps forward through the tall
grass before dropping to her knees again.

"Are you *sure* you're all right?"

"Perfectly. But it's safer to crawl, don't you think? If
there *is* anybody watching the fire . . ."

Domerc nodded. "Let me lead, though."

That wasn't sensible. If Domerc got killed, Allie would
be helpless in this strange world. And she didn't even
have the strength to run away. She should be the one in
front. But she was too tired to argue . . . and anyway, the
farmyard was still empty. Allie caught up with Domerc
just as he snatched his burnt fingers from the iron pot.

"Use your gown for a potholder," she suggested. There
were probably cloths inside the farmhouse, not to mention spoons and bowls, but she didn't feel up to going
in there again. It wouldn't be so bad if the little girl's
eyes weren't open . . .

Something whirred between them and sank into the
ground with a menacing, solid *thunk*.

"Ye'd best start running now," called a rough, shaky
voice from across the farmyard. "Next bolt 'ull be aimed
to kill."

Allie looked up, open-mouthed, at the black hole of
the open door in the barn loft. Was something moving
back there, glittering, readying for a second shot?

Domerc gave her a hard shove towards the farmhouse.
When she was on her feet and moving, he took off in
the other direction, ducking and weaving behind the
empty stock pens as if to get as much cover as he could
from the fencing posts. Allie reached the corner of the
house and peered from that shelter. She saw a glittering blur strike one of the wooden posts. Domerc was

still moving . . . now he had the side of the barn between him and the soldiers in the loft . . . but what if they had a window or something on that side? Allie scrabbled in the dirt, got a handful of pebbles and threw them towards the loft. Another bolt buzzed through the air and fell, harmlessly spent, into the open well. She knelt and gathered more pebbles, not enough, she needed something heavy enough to throw all that way. There must be *something* nearby, anything to distract the soldiers from Domerc.

A brilliant blue-white light blazed from the darkness of the loft, and there was a cry of agony. Allie pressed her clenched fist against her open mouth. A truly brave person would run out there and rescue Domerc, not cower behind the farmhouse throwing useless pebbles.

She had never thought herself a truly brave person, but it was not cheering to have the belief confirmed.

And Domerc needed no rescuing. She heard him calling to her, impossibly, from the loft. "Hey, Allie! You can come out now, it's all right."

A ruse? Oh, what the hell. If Domerc was a prisoner, she might as well be one too. They might feed her. They might also kill her, but at least then she wouldn't feel sick any longer. Either way it wouldn't be a total loss.

Allie tottered across the farmyard on trembling legs, feeling a hundred and ten years old. By the time she reached the barn, Domerc was making a labored progress down the ladder, with somebody much broader than he was draped partly across his shoulders. The dark, bulky figure swore copiously and inventively at every step, interspersing the curses with commands to Domerc to mind his bad leg and go gently there.

"Who—what— *What's going on?*" Allie demanded.

Domerc reached the bottom of the ladder and deposited his new acquaintance, none too gently, in a pile of straw. "Allie," he said, mopping his brow, "meet Gaire d'Savaric. Well, formerly d'Savaric. I gather he's renounced his allegiance."

"You got it," growled Gaire. "Give me some of that stew. I an't eaten since yesterday."

"Neither have we," said Domerc. "We'll share, but you'd best come out into the open with us. I don't fancy enclosed places just now." He looked almost as drained as the dead children in the farmhouse.

"What did you *do*?" Allie demanded while they hunted around for a board tall enough for Gaire to use as a crutch and helped him shuffle across to the fire. "What about the others? What *happened*? You shouldn't have gone up there. Were you trying to get yourself killed, or what?"

Domerc helped Gaire to a sitting position by the fire, one leg stuck straight out in front of him. He stood and gave her a long, steady look. "Keep that up," he said, "you'll be able to give my Aunt Almoina a fifteen-minute handicap in the Nagging Females contest. Any child could have figured out that there was only one man up in the loft, shooting one bolt at a time. His aim wasn't any too good—"

"That's what you think," Gaire growled. "Could've taken you both out with my first two shots if I'd wanted to. Happens I don't fancy killing children. Just wanted to scare you away. Then I was going to come down and eat. Been waiting forever to see who'd come back for that stew."

"Didn't you see us when we built the fire?"

"Asleep." Gaire reached a dirty hand into the stew pot and scooped out half a turnip. He crammed the soft food into his mouth and slurped the gravy off his fingers.

"Oh. Well, you're eating now," Allie said. "Wouldn't it have been more sensible to introduce yourself in a friendly manner?"

"You might've killed me before I et," Gaire pointed out. "Wouldn't blame you, neither. Not if you thought I had anything to do with that in there." He jerked his head towards the farmhouse.

"Well, didn't you?" Domerc asked. "If you were one of Savaric's men?"

"Told you I don't fancy killing kids, didn't I?" Gaire grunted and inhaled another handful of stew. Between slurping mouthfuls, he told them his version of what had happened at the farmhouse. According to Gaire, the war had been planned as two simultaneous strikes at the lands of Brefania. The main body of soldiers had been instructed to kill and burn their way from the mountains to the river Verenha, destroy Iseu's keep and secure the port of Astire. Savaric had explicitly told them not to worry about landmonsters, that he had a master-mage coming who'd deal with that. In fact, he'd said, the more they insulted the land, the better. And Savaric's half-mage Lendoman had raised magefire along the line of march, as if Savaric *wanted* the landvirtue to arise as monsters.

All that magefire insulting the landvirtue made Gaire desperately uneasy; after the taking of the Stonehold, he volunteered for a detached group of mercenaries sent out to destroy opposition in these borderland farms. Once in the foothills, the group had split up into parties of three or four soldiers each, fanning out to attack all the farmsteadings at once. Gaire's group had gone a weary way through the hills before coming upon this place.

"I thought we was to run the folk off, 'sall," Gaire said. "Maybe kill the men if they wouldn't go peaceable. That's war. Got no objection to that. But when they started in on the wife and kiddies, I wasn't having no part of it. Told 'em to stop. Then old Ferrat, he was supposed to be in charge of us, he says as the land needs blood and he reckons mine'll do as well as anybody's. Pins me to the ground with a pike through me leg and says, "You can lie there and bleed with the rest of 'em for all o'me." Gaire added a few reflective comments on just what he meant to do to Ferrat when he caught up with him. He was rather vague about how he'd worked the pike out of his leg and dressed the wound, saying that he'd been about out of his head with pain and fever, not to mention hearing the kiddies screaming inside the house before—

"You can skip that part," Allie said quickly. "What did you do after you got free?"

"Holed up in the loft," Gaire said, "figuring to move on in a day or so when me leg got better. Going to head south, some place the war ain't spread to yet. Maybe get a boat down the Verenha. You kids can come with me if you want."

"Thank you," Domerc said, "our business lies . . . elsewhere."

Allie demanded to know how he'd overpowered Gaire.

"Cheated," Gaire growled.

"Climbed a rope up the back of the loft," Domerc said succinctly. "Called magelight to surprise him."

"Damn near blinded me," Gaire said.

"Saw he was wounded, attacked the weakest point—"

"Kicked me right on the bandages." Gaire's face twisted with the memory.

Domerc sighed. "You have my apologies. As Landsenser and Healer I am sworn to do no harm."

"Healer?" Allie and Gaire asked at the same moment.

"Is that another Guild?" Allie went on. "I thought you didn't have any—"

"All Landsensers can draw virtue from the land at need to heal the sick and wounded," Domerc said. "That's one of the reasons there are such extremely stringent rules governing our use of the power. In the days of the Issart Wars there were Landsensers who drew out the virtue of the land only to prolong their own selfish lives. The land and people starved while they lived twice and thrice the span of a man's proper life."

"You don't need to jaw about stuff everybody knows," Gaire grumbled.

"*She* doesn't," Domerc said.

Gaire stared at Allie. "Coulda sworn there wasn't no place farther back of nowhere than me old village, and even there they've heard of the Issart Wars, even if they do think it's yesterday's news."

"The Issart Wars," Domerc explained to Allie, "were over three hundred years ago."

"So where's she from, then? Another world?" Gaire laughed loudly for a moment, then broke off with a gasp of pain.

"You wouldn't believe me if I told you," Domerc muttered.

"Can you heal my leg?"

"Probably," Domerc said. "But can I afford to? We're friends of Iseu de Brefania. You just tried to kill us. Whole and healthy, you might try again with better success."

"Leave me here like this and you're killing me," Gaire protested. "They'll be growin' by tomorrow morning, moving within the week. If not sooner. You goin' to leave a wounded man here to wonder which'll take him first, starvation or the wound-fever or the landmonsters? One as got his wound tryin' to stop the awful things as Ferrat and them others was doing?"

Domerc frowned but said nothing.

"Look," Gaire said, pointing at some vines that wreathed about the posts supporting the low overhanging roof of the farmhouse. "Look, it's starting already!"

Domerc scowled at the vines. "No, it's not. Those are perfectly normal still."

"Look at the new leaves. They got purple edges," Gaire insisted. There was a wild note of panic in his voice. "Don't leave me here. Kill me first! Or—look, I'll swear to you. Be your man. Got no use for Savaric now anyway," he added, and that at least sounded truthful to Allie.

Domerc laughed. "Me, a poor scholar, running mercs?"

"You're out of a Seignor family, aren't ye?"

"How did you know that?"

Gaire shrugged. "Oh, ye've got a bit of the same manner as Savaric, whiles. That way of lookin' down yer long nose at the rest of the world, that go-to-the-landmonsters-for-all-I-care way of speakin'."

"I'm no kin to Savaric," Domerc said quickly.

"Never said ye were. But all you Seignor families act the same. Poor, proud, and private."

Allie sputtered. Gaire had described Domerc to the life.

"Oh?" Domerc asked coldly. "And did Iseu strike you that way, before you killed her?"

"We never caught up with Iseu," Gaire said, "or anybody else in the keep. 'Twere empty when we got there. That was when Savaric told Lendoman to raise the magefire."

Domerc turned to Allie, his face bright with hope. "Iseu's free, and her people with her! Then there's a chance!"

A chance for what? Allie wondered. "How can we find them?"

"Oh, I know where they'll have gone," Domerc said confidently, "they'll be in the—" He bit off the sentence and looked back at Gaire.

"I'll be your sworn man if you'll heal me," Gaire said. "An' I can help you get to the lady Iseu, wherever-abouts you think she'll be. You two young'uns won't never make it on your own. You don't know the first thing about sneaking through a war quiet-like. I'd a' spitted you both if I'd a mind to."

Domerc turned to Allie again. "He's got a point. I was a fool not to search the outbuildings before starting that fire. But after the house I wasn't in a mood to look any farther."

"Squeamish," Gaire said.

"How can I trust your oath?" Domerc demanded again. "It all comes back to that."

Gaire looked pale. "I'll be your man by blood and silk," he said. "But ye've to swear to release my soul at the end o' the war. And I'll trust *your* word on it. Can't say fairer than that, can I now?"

"Where did you hear of the soul-bond? That's black ancient magic."

Gaire glanced at the vine-wreathed porch, then back at the barn. "Been a lot of talk about it. En Savaric, he takes a rare interest in such things."

Domerc wiped his brow. "En Savaric's own soul is in mortal danger. And so will mine be, if I take such an oath from you."

"Thought ye wanted to help yer friend," Gaire said cunningly.

Domerc sighed. "Oh, all right." He knelt beside Gaire. "Give me a bit of the bandage. That's got your blood on it already, no need to shed more. I'll twine it with this." He took out his belt-knife and slashed a short end from his blue silk sash. "Allie, go across the yard; I don't want you mixed up in this."

"Good idea," Gaire said approvingly, "no witnesses, no pack-drill, eh?"

"And while you're there," Domerc added, "can you draw some more water from the well and heat it?"

As Allie rinsed out their stew pot, filled it with clean water and set it on the coals, she caught passing glimpses of Domerc kneeling beside Gaire. Their hands were clasped together; a fragment of sky-blue silk fluttered loose between them. She could not hear the words that passed between the two, nor did she want to. She felt sick, and the palm of her hand throbbed. For some reason she kept remembering the day she'd cut it on voicebubbles in Aigar's laboratory. The Dean himself had stopped the blood with white silk. Blood and silk, blood and silk . . . She fell into an uneasy trance, staring mindlessly at the embers of the cooking fire until it seemed to her that they moved like glowing eyes.

"Allie, is the water warm yet?"

Allie blinked and started from the half-dream. As she lugged the pot across the yard, Gaire protested. "Can't ye heal me through the bandages?"

"Don't be a fool," Domerc said. His voice was deeper,

more resonant than she remembered, and when she looked at him he seemed to be glowing with new life. "I need to see what I'm working with. Do you want me to knit bone and mend flesh cleanly, or shall I meld your filthy trews and that rag of a bandage into your own flesh?"

Gaire's lips paled. "All right. But remember, I'm sworn to you now, body and soul."

"I am hardly likely to forget it," said Domerc. "At least 'twill make the healing easier."

The blood had crusted and dried on Gaire's bandages. Soaking them free was a slow and painful process. Allie kept her eyes shut most of the time, and tried to think about something else.

The last rag came free with a hiss of pain from Gaire.

"Ah. Interesting pattern for a pike wound," Domerc commented.

Allie glanced down for a moment. A line of four blue-black holes punctuated Gaire's hairy thigh. They oozed slightly . . . Her stomach heaved and she swallowed hard, trying to keep the stew down.

"You lied to us," Domerc went on. "You didn't take that wound from another soldier. You were wounded by the farmer here, weren't you? A peaceful man with nothing but his pitchfork, trying to defend his family from you filth. I saw what you did to him for it." And his eyes flickered towards a low shed. Allie guessed that he'd dragged the farmer's body under cover before allowing her to come into the farmyard.

"Not me," Gaire said.

"You would have killed him, though, if you hadn't been out of action. Just as your mates did."

"Not the kids. I swear, En Domerc, I wouldn't have had no hand in what they did inside the house. Tried to talk them out of it. That's why they left me here. You got to believe me!"

Allie put on hand on Domerc's arm. "I think he's telling the truth," she said.

"And how would you know?"

"Well . . . He didn't shoot to kill us; and I think he could have. And he looked really sick when he was talking about the children." Allie swallowed hard. She felt sick, too. There were some pictures she might never be able to put out of her mind.

Domerc sighed. "It makes little difference. He's sworn to me now. I *must* heal him; and I must use him."

He knelt beside Gaire and put both hands over the ugly, oozing wound. His eyes closed and the life seemed to drain out of his face, leaving him pale and still as a wax sculpture. Allie felt as if the three of them were standing at the exact center of a sphere of silence. Outside that sphere, the wind rustled in the grass, a bird sang, clouds marched in formation across the sky. Within it, time slowed, stopped. There was an invisible wall, hard and clear as glass, between them and the world.

A soft sighing sound came from all around them, as if the land itself were breathing. Allie's sense of the glass wall changed to a feeling of something softening, melting, evaporating. Once again she felt connected with the world around them. It was a *good* feeling, the best she'd had since she started feeling ill. Impulsively, she slipped off her shoes and stood barefoot on the earth of the farmyard. That was better yet, but still not quite right. She glanced over her shoulder at the wild grassland from which they had come.

Gaire grinned and sat up. "Pikes and pitch! You done it, me little lordling—I mean, En Domerc."

"If that's the measure of respect you gave En Savaric," Domerc said sternly, "I'm surprised he didn't turn you out of his company long before."

"Ah, but I wasn't his bondsman," Gaire said. "Makes a difference, that. You know now you can trust me. I can't go against you. Don't need so much touch-yer-cap and aye-sir-no-sir 'tween a lord an' his bondsoul, does it now?"

Domerc winced. "I wish you wouldn't remind me of that."

Allie scarcely heard them; she was too intent on exploring her own feelings. The sun-warmed bare earth was like a distant promise of health and strength. She could almost remember what it had been like to feel normal, not to hurt all the time, not to feel overwhelmed by every little thing. Somehow she felt that she couldn't get what she wanted from this hard-packed dry earth, though. She needed to be among growing things . . . wild things. Slowly she backed up, out of the farmyard with its smells of blood and fire and death, until she could breathe in the heady air around the wild grasses that grew right up to the verge of the farmyard. Strange, she hadn't noticed their scent before. Now it was sharp and sweet and intoxicating all at once, like the flower-scented wine at the Blue Pigeon, like drinking flowers, breathing color . . .

She breathed deeply and felt something clearing in her head. The ache that ran through all her bones was still there, but it didn't seem to matter any longer; she had strength enough to ignore it. Her bare feet crushed stalks of prickly wild grass; the green-tinged tips of the new growth waved over her head. She could feel the earth between the stalks of grass, cool and solid and infinitely comforting. All the colors around her seemed brighter than before, the shapes sharper and clearer. She breathed deeply again. This time there was an undertone of spice in the air, and something deeper, something wild and musky and frightening . . .

She ran out of the grass just as Domerc called for her.

"Here I am!" She was almost out of breath, but it was from the deep breathing, she told herself, not from running a few steps. "I was just, just resting."

"Seems to've done you a power of good," Gaire said, looking her up and down with a gleam in his eye that Allie hadn't noticed before Domerc healed him.

"I think the food helped," Allie said.

"Something must've. I was going to ask me young lordling here why he hadn't healed you instead of letting you drag along looking half dead, but now it don't look like there's much need."

Startled, Allie glanced at Domerc. It hadn't occurred to her until that moment that if he could heal an ugly infected pitchfork wound, he might have been able to cure her flu as well. "I didn't tell him I was feeling sick," she said in a small voice, feeling very stupid.

"And he never noticed," Gaire snorted. "That's t'Seignors for you, too wrapped up in themselves and their honor to know or care aught about us commoners. Tell you what, boy, 'twas your lucky day when I swore meself to you. A bit of a common soul is just what ye need to make y'self human like the rest of us."

"It wasn't like that!" Allie cried. "He didn't know—we had so much else to think about—oh, you just don't understand! Besides, I didn't *know* he could do that, so why would I tell him? I don't know anything about your world, and you people don't know what to explain to me."

Gaire looked at Domerc. "Our world? And what world does she think *she's* in, eh?" His chuckle invited Domerc to share a moment's amusement at girls and their silly words.

"I did tell you," Domerc said after a moment, "that you wouldn't believe me." He stooped and began collecting the vegetables that hadn't gone into the stew, rolling them up into a neat pack inside his scholar's gown. "If you think you can walk now, Gaire, we'd best be moving on. It's some distance to the nearest opening."

"Opening?" Allie asked, startled. For a moment she had a lovely vision of some sort of magical gateway to another part of Escorre, something that would just whisk them to their destination with no more effort.

"To the caves of Brefania," Domerc said. "That has to be where Iseu and her people are hiding.

Landmonsters won't come through the solid rock, and the entrances are few and defensible. They're not easy for outsiders to find, but Iseu showed me once." A reminiscent smile crossed his face.

"I'll just bet she did," muttered Allie. She put her shoes back on, took the sack of turnips Domerc offered her and stalked after him and Gaire. Why *hadn't* he noticed she was sick and offered to heal her, if he could do magic like that? And how had he done it, anyway? She was dying to know, but she wasn't about to raise the question for fear that she'd sound hurt and left out and whiny and jealous.

And she still had a headache.

CHAPTER ELEVEN

Aigar suffered deeply as he and Savaric retraced the path taken by Savaric's mercenary army in their devastating march to Astire. The green valley of the Harendola was slashed with broad swathes of burnt, blackened ground. The cinders crunched under his feet as he walked, and evil coils of oily, foul-smelling smoke writhed about his ankles. Some of the coils joined with the column of cloudy and glowing shapes that preceded them. It was one long scene of unrelieved misery; not the sort of thing a man of his position should ever be subjected to. One knew that these things happened in war, of course; they were regrettable but necessary. But one preferred not to experience them at first hand.

The mercenaries Marin had selected to escort them were, if the grumbles behind him were anything to go by, even more unhappy than Aigar himself. But he dared not turn his head to glance at Marin and the soldiers. He kept one hand always on the hard, pulsing, dead-and-alive shape of Fabre's bondsoul, and through Fabre he kept the force of his will on that column of cloudy landmonsters. The Spirit of War, Savaric had called them, and it seemed to Aigar that Savaric had spoken more truly than he knew. He felt as he had on that day when the metal-monster belching clouds of smoke appeared in his laboratory: oppressed by forces greater than he had ever intended to call up.

Marin was fully occupied with seeing that his sullen

troops did not lag or scatter. Lendoman trudged along in his own brooding silence, exuding disapproval of Aigar and all his works. Only Savaric occasionally spoke, usually to announce that he had spotted signs of survivors.

"There's some now!" he would cry, and Aigar would command the cloud-monsters to hold steady while Marin's mercenaries dived into the smouldering remains of a farm to drag out filthy, ash-smeared peasants and crying children.

"It's not safe for you to stay here," Marin would lecture the sullen captives. "You're to go to Astire until the land is pacified. Don't you know better than to stay where landmonsters are rising?"

If any objected, Marin politely invited them to step into the mass of oily smoke and glowing embers, to try for themselves their chances of surviving once Aigar released his hold on the landmonsters. No one ever accepted the offer.

When they'd collected a group of nearly fifty men, women and children, Aigar suggested that some of Marin's men escort the survivors back to Astire. It should be safe enough; the rising monsters they had encountered had already been absorbed into the smoky mass. And the children's sniveling distracted him from his work.

"You wouldn't want me to lose control, would you?" he demanded.

Marin, Lendoman and Savaric all agreed hurriedly that they wouldn't want anything to distract Aigar. There was a momentary tumult as all twenty-five of the soldiers tried to volunteer at once for the task of escorting the peasants back to the city, but Marin sorted that out with a few bellowed orders. Five happy mercenaries took charge of the cowed peasants, and the other twenty fell into line of march again with barely audible grumbles.

"We'll make a sweep south," Savaric announced then. "I'll wager that most of these idiots tried to hide in the hills." He pointed towards the uncultivated rocky hills rising from the valley, where magefire had not yet devastated the land. Only a few plumes of smoke showed where isolated farmsteads had been burnt by the raiding parties Marin had sent out two days previously.

Aigar sighed and tried not to think about how much his feet hurt. At least they wouldn't be walking over the charred remnants of magefired fields. Good plain dirt and rocks would be a pleasure by comparison.

But good plain dirt, Aigar rapidly discovered, bred conventional landmonsters of the sort he'd boasted to Savaric that he could control. More weeping thornbushes crept among the rocks of the foothills, and he could not master Fabre enough to send these back to their origins while at the same time he kept control of the cloud-monsters roiling along behind them. They marched half an hour in wary silence, sidestepping small monsters and listening to the tantalizing sound of a stream gurgling somewhere among rocks. Finally they rounded an outcropping of boulders and saw fresh water falling into a clear pool with a sandy bottom.

"Fill flasks," Marin commanded. Before more than a handful of men had reached the pool, Aigar shouted a warning. "Look at the water, you fools! *Look* at it!"

The sandy bottom of the pool had sprouted a crop of long twisting weeds in greasy, oily colors: dirty purple and muddy orange and a sickly sweet pink predominated. Most of the kneeling mercenaries scrambled back from the edge of the stream. One remained with his wrists in water, begging for help. A long, bright pink tendril snaked around his arms, growing with incredible speed towards his bare throat.

"*Do* something, curse ye!" Savaric shouted at Aigar. The mass of smoke-monsters that had followed under Aigar's command quivered and surged towards them. Aigar put both hands around Fabre's bondsoul and concentrated on keeping the smoky things away. What was the loss of one soldier compared to having them all engulfed by the cloud-monsters?

The pink tendril wreathed lovingly around the man's throat. His screams grew thinner.

Marin leapt forward, swinging his short sword out and down in a glittering arc too fast for the eye to follow. The severed end of the pink vine fell back into the water and Marin leapt back again. His free hand grasped the soldier's jerkin and he dragged the man bodily back from the water's edge.

"Lendoman!" He jerked his head towards the wounded man and occupied himself with cleaning his sword. The accountant-mage, his hands protected by a fold of his cloak, gingerly unwrapped the vine from the man's throat and arms. Droplets of blood welled forth along the white line where the plant-monster had touched the skin. The freed vine writhed on the ground like a blind snake, raising first one end and then the other like hungry heads questing for food. Aigar stared at it and felt his stomach quiver in revulsion. The feeling transmitted itself through Fabre to the landvirtue inherent in the vine; it wriggled away rapidly and disappeared down a minute crevice in the boulders at the head of the waterfall.

The cloudy mass of War oozed hungrily towards the pool. The tangled weeds growing there broke free from the sand and slithered to the bank. The mercenaries all tried to stand behind one another, but the vines were no longer after them; as one, they made for the crevice between boulders where the first pink serpent-vine had disappeared.

Savaric burst into a laugh as the last of the unnatural growths disappeared. "Damn good, master-mage! Even the other landmonsters fear my new soldiers!" He gave the roiling, cloudy mass a yellow-toothed grin. "What can't we conquer now, I wonder?"

"What *I* wonder," said Lendoman prissily, "is where those serpent-vines went, and what they'll grow into next."

Savaric regarded the boulders with interest. "Must be

one of the ways into the caves. Too bad it's too small for us to follow 'em."

Marin and the mercenaries with him looked as if they could support this disappointing news with equanimity.

"Can you chase some more little land-monsters down there?" Savaric demanded of Aigar. "I'll bet you that's where Iseu and her folk are hiding out. A few good monsters ought to kill them or flush them out, makes no odds to me."

"Mightn't it be . . . a good idea . . . to find out where they're likely to come out, first?" Aigar asked. He found it hard to form the words and get them out. A sensation of overpowering heaviness oppressed him. When he took his hand from Fabre's bondsoul, he no longer felt the weight . . . but the mass of oily cloud shuddered and pulsed in a way that made him uneasy. He grasped the amulet again and commanded the smokeshapes to remain still. Even thinking the command felt like pushing his way through water. Worse. Through quicksand. Heavy, clogging his thoughts and movements, and drawing him down, down into the beautiful welcoming earth.

Liuria wasn't such an idiot as to go sailing right up to the public docks of Astire. Not after finding out, first that all the mage-streams between Coindra and Astire had been blocked by Aigar's order, and second, that the bargemasters still in Coindra were willing to sit with their freight on their loaded barges rather than go downriver into whatever disaster had struck the Harendola.

The rowboat she'd borrowed from a friend was never intended for the fast upper reaches of the Verenha, but Liuria told herself firmly that where a great clumsy freight barge could travel, she could certainly take a rowboat. She hadn't reckoned on the force of the current in mid-river, though, or on the broad sweep of water that kept her too far from either shore to make her planned inconspicuous entry into Astire. Besides, the small private dock attached to her Aunt Almoina's summer house wasn't there any more.

Neither was the summer house. Liuria swallowed hard at the sight of blackened ruins and the stench of greasy smoke. She was still trying to control her stomach when the river current swept her up to the public docks of Astire and into the tangle of ropes and nets thoughtfully stretched across the river by one of Marin's brighter subordinates.

No living soul knew the full extent of the caverns underlying the limestone hills of Brefania. Officially, the caverns were the property of the independent lordship of Brefania, which controlled access to the caverns through the keep of Brefania and made a nice yearly profit by charging vintners of the area for the right to store their casks of wine in the deep, cool caverns. Unofficially, every child born in or around the keep had wriggled through the enticing crevices at the back of the wine storage area and explored some distance, with guttering candles, lengths of string to guide them back to the wine cellars, friends to hold their clammy hands and compete in sending echoes around the dark caves. By that miracle which guards small children, fools and drunkards, no child had yet failed to come back from these illicit expeditions. But children don't make maps, at least not realistic ones. "Maps" of the caverns abounded, most of them drawn in rusty ink and berry juice and other compounds intended to resemble blood, all of them showing dragons' treasure hoards and chests of gold and skulls of murdered men, and not one showing the true labyrinth of interconnected passages which linked the larger caverns. The Hall of Bright Rejouissance was a common feature of the maps, though; sometimes called the Stone Candles, sometimes the Gem Palace of the Mountain King, but always firmly (and inaccurately) located in the very center of the labyrinth. Even though few of the children had been brave enough to explore as far as this hall, they had all heard colorful descriptions of its sparkling beauties, and no one would risk the scorn of his companions by leaving it off a map.

When the children grew up and became parents themselves, they petitioned the Seignors of Brefania to board up the entrances to the deep caverns, lest their own children risk their necks in foolish explorations. The known entrances were duly boarded or bricked up, the new generation of children discovered new entrances, and the game continued to everybody's satisfaction.

Iseu of Brefania was one of the few whose interest in the caverns had continued past adolescence. Vaguely encouraged, or at least not discouraged, by her parents, she had over the years furnished the Hall of Bright Rejouissance with cushions and candles, small casks of salt meat and sacks of beans.

"It's dangerous," her mother complained occasionally.

"Not half as dangerous as our neighbor," her father said, frowning towards the mountains where En Savaric kept his troops of mercenaries. True, Savaric had always shown a commendably commercial spirit in running his mercenaries, fighting only for hire and away from his own neighborhood. But there *were* all those soldiers, and Brefanis *was* such a green and pleasant holding compared with Savaric's rocky fastnesses, and he *did* wish that Iseu would quit dabbling with magecraft and go to Coindra where she could study the subject properly and maybe meet some nice strong young man with a bent for military matters. Somebody who specialized in defense issues . . .

But until that happened, it would do no harm for the girl to have a bolt-hole in case . . . well, in case of anything. Iseu's father usually stopped thinking about the whole unpleasant matter about then; it made him nervous, and he much preferred to walk out and inspect his personal vineyards.

It is possible that he never realized just how thoroughly Iseu had furnished the Hall of Bright Rejouissance and the adjoining chambers. Certainly in the winter when the coughing-sickness took him and her mother both, his last advice to Iseu was not, "Buy dried beans," but "You should go to Coindra for a semester and meet some other young people."

"Yes, Papa," Iseu said. Dry-eyed, she closed her father's eyes, folded his cold hands over his breast, and gave all necessary orders for the double funeral. Afterwards, she personally carried a few more sacks of dried peas and coarse-ground corn down to the caverns, and replenished the stock of glow-bubbles. Then she called magelight to a single green-tinged glow-bubble, sat on one of the sacks of peas, and wept for her parents until she was able to return with a calm and untroubled face.

She wanted a friend badly that spring, but her dearest friends in all Escorre had troubles of their own. The scandal of the illicit Landsensing broke over Domerc's head. Iseu didn't believe a word of it, but Domerc left Brefania before she could tell him so; and afterwards, she heard that he had entered Coindra as a fledgling-scholar, two years behind his brilliant young sister Liuria. She felt a passing pang of regret that she could not join them there. But it was too late now; Brefania had only her to guard it. She should have gone while Papa was still alive . . .

That was an upsetting thought. Iseu brushed the tears from her eyes and did what Papa always did when troubled in his mind: She walked out to inspect the vineyards.

That summer and fall passed in peace, and they had an easy warm winter. Nobody died of the coughing-sickness, and Iseu forgot to be worried about En Savaric in her satisfaction at the good harvest and the good prices Brefania wine was fetching. Spring came in, the second spring without her parents, and she did not need to visit the Hall of Bright Rejouissance more than once or twice for her private mourning. On the second visit she noticed that some of the supplies were looking mouldy. Perhaps she should replace them. Then again, perhaps she should clear everything out. She was past the age for childish games.

Then Savaric's men came down, in a night of blood and magefire and screaming, and Rainald the Archer took Iseu by the shoulders and told her not to be a fool and die on the walls of the keep, but to get herself and everybody else she could find down into that place she thought was her secret hideout, and pray while she did it that nobody told Savaric the secret.

Somehow she did it, herding along weeping women and protesting men, anybody she could find: grooms and chambermaids and two of her mother's waiting-women and Druon the cook, who turned out to be possibly the single most useful person she could have brought along. At least he knew lots of things to do with dried beans and strings of onions and the clear water that trickled into a pool on one side of the Hall of Bright Rejouissance.

For the first day Iseu sat on her favorite sack of peas and put her fingers in her ears and tried not to think about what was happening above ground. She could hear the shouts and the clang of weapons in her mind, even if the actual sounds did not penetrate so far below the ground. She could smell blood and fire. Men were dying up there for her. Rainald the Archer would be dead by now. And she could not even go out and walk through the vineyards . . .

Then people started trickling in by twos and threes, children leading their parents, older people who'd remembered the secret entrances of their youth, and Iseu got up off the sack of peas and began organizing her people once again. They needed places to sleep, and most of them wanted washing, and the children were mostly crying, and Druon wanted to know if she'd brought any tartspice powder.

The press of refugees and decisions kept her wonderfully busy for some time; she ate and organized and made plans and fell asleep exhausted and rose to deal with the new people and was thankful not to have time to think of anything else.

In the dark channels beyond the Hall of Bright Rejouissance, narrow passageways far too small for any human child, the vine-monsters dispelled by Aigar crept towards light and life. As they moved they mutated, sprouting multi-jointed legs at strange angles, bulbous visual surfaces facing towards the light, rows of small sharp teeth and piercing suckers. The wild virtue of the insulted land was strong in them, and they were cramped in the tunnels. They moved towards open space and other life, and they changed as they went.

The influx of refugees came to an end. Iseu woke from one of her brief, nightmare-troubled sleeps, prepared to go back to work, and discovered that everything was as organized as it was going to get and there were no new people to be settled in the caverns. Her squire and friend Centor de Briere had thoughtfully cleared the Hall of Bright Rejouissance of everybody but Iseu and her personal staff. Iseu activated a few more glowbubbles, using the most cheerful colors she could think of. Their pink and golden and lavender lights danced over the rocks, making the embedded crystals that lined the walls sparkle like candles at a great ball. Mysterious arches of crystal-studded rock soared like windows opening onto the darkness of the farther caves. Water-smoothed boulders curved into inviting nooks which Iseu had softened with all the cushions and draperies and worn-out tapestries she had been able to abstract from the castle over the years of her childhood play. It was really a very beautiful place. Iseu tried to think about the beauty; but instead she kept thinking about the future. Which was almost as depressing as the immediate past.

"We'll call on the Landsensers Guild to arbitrate the quarrel, of course," Centor said cheerfully.

"What quarrel? There wasn't anything!" Iseu protested.

Centor reminded her of some testy communications from Savaric, claims that Iseu's people were extending their vineyards upwards into his territory.

"Oh, that."

"It was pretext for the war," Centor insisted. "It'll have to be arbitrated. They'll send observers to look at the evidence . . ."

"Evidence!" Iseu gasped. "Didn't you see the magefires burning? *Evidence*? There'll be nothing to see but cinders, and I defy even a Landsenser to tell a Brefania vine cinder from a Savaric weed cinder." For some reason this struck her as extremely funny, and she began laughing and could not stop until her waiting-woman Elli dipped up a gourd of cold spring water and poured most of it into her open mouth. The rest went down her front and sobered her almost as much as a full dip in the icy pool would have done.

"Before the Landsensers arbitrate, we'll have to call on them," Iseu pointed out. "And how will we know when it's safe to leave the caverns . . . if ever?"

"Won't have to call," Druon muttered. "Excuse me, Na Iseu, I want some of the peas."

Iseu got up and leaned against a glittering pillar of crystals while Druon scooped up his peas.

"Look what En Savaric's done to the land," Druon went on as he measured out the peas. "And in planting season, too. There'll be landmonsters raised, no doubt about it. Every Guildhouse in Escorre will be sending someone to investigate. No, my lady, we don't need to go nowhere, I don't reckon. Just sit tight and wait. Dunno what that fool lord was thinking of anyway, starting a war in seedtime, but you can be sure the Landsensers will sort him out in a hurry."

This was a very comforting view of the matter. Iseu settled herself on the sack, now comfortably concave, and tried not to think about how long their food supplies would last, and how long it might take the

Landsensers to arrive and put a stop to Savaric, and whether landmonsters liked caves.

The distant sound of weeping distracted her. Irritably she thought of sending Elli to silence that child, whoever it was; then almost immediately repented her thought. These were *her* people—what was left of them—and what business had she to be sitting on a sack of peas feeling sorry for herself when they needed comfort and leadership? Only, just at the moment, Iseu felt very empty of leadership. She had done all she knew how to do, and now what was there for them but to wait in the caverns and hope for the Guild to arrive?

Well, for one thing, she could comfort the crying child. Iseu listened more attentively, trying to decide which of the adjoining chambers the crying was coming from. The shifting echoes and shadows within the hall confused her; it seemed almost as if the weeping came from the far dark end of the Hall of Bright Rejouissance, where she knew perfectly well there was nothing but a rock wall scored by minute channels far too small to explore; she'd tried often enough.

And it was coming closer.

That was Iseu's last coherent thought before Elli screamed and fell, both hands entangled with something like a length of pink ribbon. The ribbon writhed and hissed and made sobbing sounds, and Iseu saw something that looked like many little legs sprouting from its sides.

Centor's belt knife flashed golden in the glow of the lightbubbles. "Centor, no!" Iseu screamed. She threw her cloak over Elli's hands and the ribbon, grasped whatever writhed and wriggled and did not feel as if it had any bones, and squeezed down with all her might. The wriggling slowed, stopped; the sobbing died away into a silence broken only by Elli's very human gasps of pain.

Slowly and carefully, Iseu unwound the cloak and looked at the bright pink serpent-thing. Where her hands through the cloth had crushed it, the thing oozed clear liquid more like sap than blood; but those *were* legs sprouting from its sides, and the row of small pointed teeth matched the row of bloody dots around Elli's wrists.

"Elli, soak your hands in the mineral springs in the Hall of Vaporous Mists," Iseu directed. There might be something in there to counteract any poison in the bites; besides, she did not know what else to do.

"My lady, you—"

"I happened," Iseu said, not quite looking at Centor, "to be thinking about landmonsters at the time. It's said that some of them, if you cut them in half, both halves grow and you have two to fight instead of one."

She helped Elli to her feet and sent her off towards the Hall of Vaporous Mists with a friendly pat on the shoulder. "Oh, and ask anyone with magecraft, even village wise-women and herb-daddies, to come here," she called after Elli. She turned to face Cantor, her eyes sober. "Well, that answers one question, anyway. Landmonsters can find their way here. And where one comes, we'd best be prepared for more to follow."

The next one had slithered into the Hall before Iseu finished speaking. This one, she noticed as she threw a faded tapestry of a hunting scene over it, was more blue than pink, and it seemed to have teeth at either end.

"Allow *me*," said Centor above her, and his boot ground one wriggling end of the tapestry against solid rock. The other end, with its threadbare picture of a white stag, flopped and shuddered; the stag's head fell down against the floor of the cave. That image stayed with Iseu during the hour that followed, when more vinous things slithered forth than anyone could keep track of or contain, and somehow she and Centor and those who joined them *did* contain them. Afterwards Iseu had no clear memory of just how they'd done it, nor did she wish for one. Impressions and actions swarmed together in her head: the burn of acidulous sap across her bare arm, a pillow writhing as Centor stamped on it with booted feet, an old herb-daddy from the hills calling up magefire he should never have known how to use to annihilate a multi-headed thing that cried like a baby and spat thorns from all its mouths. At one moment there were too many monsters all around them, then the world narrowed to the single hungry thing that was trying to wind about her own legs, then somebody's cane came down on that thing and reduced it to a bruised pulp and whacked her across the shins. And then, as suddenly as it had begun, it was over. The far end of the Hall of Bright Rejouissance was a mass of slime and sap and bruised plant-like things in brilliant unnatural colors; cloaks and rugs lay across the puddled floor, stained and slashed and burnt through by magefire or landmonster sap; Iseu's arm burned from elbow to shoulder, and her shins were sore from the raps of the cane that had saved her from the last *thing*; but nothing moved amid the wreckage except the hall's human defenders. Iseu saw Centor leaning on the wall and nursing a hand that was swollen to twice its size, and the old herb-daddy who'd called magefire, and half a dozen people she vaguely remembered from the vineyards, and Druon with a dripping meat mallet that had best never be used again for pounding anything people wanted to eat. Elli was there, too, crying from the pain of the bites that had turned into red and purple swollen rings around her wrists, but still holding up a rock to smash down on anything that moved under the carpet at her feet.

"Elli, I *told* you to treat those wounds!" Iseu snapped, and then, to her own disgust, burst into tears. She stopped almost at once, swallowed hard, and tried to think what Rainald the Archer would have done. Centor had best take that hand to the hot mineral springs, too; the way it looked now, he might never make music to accompany his voice again. And they had to set a guard here, and—

"Something funny about those things," Centor interrupted her jumbled thoughts.

"Ha, ha," Iseu said.

"No, really. They didn't like it in the tunnels."

Iseu glanced at the narrow holes in the rock and shuddered, imagining being in there with stone at her shoulders, stone at her feet, stone over her head . . . all that weight of earth and stone surrounding her, pressing on her. "Who would?"

"Makes you wonder, though. They're plants really, you know. They need earth and air and sun. Why would they come into a cave?"

"Innate nastiness?" Iseu hazarded.

"Could be," Centor said slowly. "Or . . . Could be they'd been *sent*."

"Don't be ridiculous," Iseu snapped, "nobody can tell landmonsters what to do. Nobody'd want to get that close to them, for that matter."

But Centor's words weighed on her, and so did her own imaginings of the dark heaviness of earth and stone through which the serpent-vines must have traveled to reach them. She felt as though a cloud of evil were sinking slowly through the earth to poison them all . . . Were the glowbubbles darker than they had been? *No*, Iseu told herself. She was tired. And hurt. And probably hungry, though her stomach revolted at the thought of food. And she was letting her imagination run away with her, when what they needed was somebody sensible to see that the wounded got treatment and that a guard was set on these tunnels and that they made a good solid military plan for dealing with any more invasions, instead of screeching and pounding the monsters with boots and sticks.

Iseu drew a deep calming breath and prepared to give orders, when a child came running and skidding into the Hall, stopping herself with a perilous grab at one of the crystal pillars.

"Beg pardon, m'lady," she cried, "but there's strange funny-talking folk outside the light place, you know, up top where me and mum was sleeping."

"The Chamber of Trickling Waters," Iseu said automatically. "What kind of funny-talking folk?" Could

Savaric's soldiers have discovered that entrance? Surely not; someone would have had to show them. It was only a narrow cleft between two rocks, masked by vines and falling water. In Iseu's childhood she'd imagined that she and Domerc and Liuria were the only people who'd ever found that particular way into the caverns. And she knew that Domerc and Liuria were safe in Coindra, with no reason to be caught up in this war.

CHAPTER TWELVE

"This is what we've been looking for?" Allie muttered unbelievingly. It seemed to her that they'd been trudging forever along a series of limestone ledges where only spiky, thorny plants sprouted. Her feet hurt. She hurt all over, for that matter, and the sense of well-being she'd enjoyed in the farm fields was long gone. Now Domerc had stopped with a smile of triumph just where two slabs of limestone rock tilted and folded into one another. A trickle of rusty-looking water seeped out of the ledge, and a tangle of brownish-green vines had taken advantage of the water to grow into the cleft, filling it with a matted mass of leaves and vines and thorns.

"This is it," Domerc said with a grin, "and it wasn't easy to find. Been years since Iseu and Liuria and I used to play here. Liuria was always the one who found it for us; she's got better trail-sense than I have. You probably didn't notice, but we had to backtrack several times looking for this spot."

Allie and Gaire looked at each other. "We noticed," Gaire said at last.

"Oh. Well, anyway, here we are!" With a sweep of his arm Domerc attempted to thrust the matted vines out of the way. They clung tenaciously to the rock; a few dead leaves fell.

"Oh, well. It's been a long time since anybody used this entrance." Domerc thrust both hands into the tangle of vines and pulled vigorously. There were ripping and sighing sounds; the mass of growing stuff moved aside slightly. Allie found that she could not see all the way into the cleft where the ledges met; there was more space behind the vines than she'd thought. The sound of falling water came from somewhere, strangely reverberant, like the echoes of distant bells.

"Come on!"

Gaire and Allie hung back.

"Looks a tight squeeze for a man of my size," Gaire muttered.

"I don't like small spaces," Allie admitted.

"It's bigger once you get through."

Allie stared at the darkness where rocks came together and tried to convince herself it would be all right. Her head was swimming, and strange flashes of colored light interfered with her attempts to see into the cave entrance. There were noises, too. Just what she needed at this point, a full-blown migraine with auras and sound hallucinations . . .

"Hold it right there!" One of the hallucinations blossomed into a globe of brilliant rose-tinged light, almost filling the dark cleft. A sharp stick poked out of the cleft and prodded Domerc in the chest. He stepped back and almost fell off the ledge.

"It's *real*," Allie said with relief.

"Damn right it's real," Domerc said when he'd regained his balance. "I think I know who it is, too. Druon, you old rascal, what do you mean by trying to spike me on a kitchen turnspit? Are you that desperate for food already?"

"Who goes there?" demanded a dark shape in the midst of the glowing light.

"It's me," Domerc said irritably. "Domerc. En Domerc Cantatz ve Falheiras Assombre, if you want to get formal, Druon."

The blackened metal spike withdrew fractionally. "If you be En Domerc, prove it. Ye look too tall to me."

"It's been five *years* since I stayed at the Stonehold,"

Domerc said. "I've *grown*. Look, didn't you see me when I was at the Guildhouse last spring?"

"Did not," said the dark figure. "Heard about it, though. And it's not something young En Domerc would be so eager to chat about. I reckon you be one of Savaric's men trying a Evil Ruse."

"Not half so evil as what you did to the rabbit stew, that time the head cook took your girl to the dance," Domerc said quickly. "Has he stopped sneezing yet?"

The metal spike quivered and withdrew. A sound like rusty laughter emanated from the cave. "I be head cook now," the dark shape said. "Come you in, En Domerc."

"Two of my followers accompany me," Domerc said.

"Followers?" Allie murmured.

"You've *been* following me, right? Don't argue now." With a courtly bow, Domerc motioned to Allie and Gaire to precede him.

Getting through the narrow cleft and the low passage that followed was almost as bad as Allie had imagined it would be. The rose-pink light bobbed ahead of them and showed her the rough rock walls and the ceiling that brushed her head when she tried to stand upright. She felt the weight of all that stone and earth above her head, pressing down like a palpable, evil presence.

Behind her, Gaire kept up a running invective under his breath, cursing equally and inventively all lords, cooks, caves, rocks and slippery water. Allie was grateful to him for giving her something to think about besides the way the passage was narrowing, and what she would do if the rock sides squeezed in and trapped her, and . . . *don't think about that*. Instead she tried to concentrate on Gaire's caustic remarks and to store a few of them up for later use.

And behind both of them, she could hear thumps and muffled sounds of pain as Domerc discovered just how much he had grown since the last time he'd tried to use this particular entrance. Served him right, Allie thought. Shoving her into this as though there was nothing to it. No consideration. No finer feelings.

"*Here* we be," said Druon, ahead of her, with satisfaction. The pink globe Allie had been following disappeared without warning. Soft smothering folds of something fell across her face. She struck out blindly, in a moment of panic, and stumbled through into the light.

It had only been a velvet cloak with a fur border, hung up across the end of the passage to block the light from the outside world. Here there was space, and the glow of many-colored light bubbles filling the space. Allie rubbed her eyes and tried to adjust to this new world. Behind her, first Gaire and then Domerc emerged from the passage. Druon adjusted the cloak fussily, as if to make sure that no chink of light escaped.

There was a handful of people in the cavern, their tired faces illumined by the colored lights. They looked small and dull and grubby next to the sparkling walls that went up so high, into a darkness from which sprays of water fell like rainbow curtains. Allie was still trying to take in the sight when she heard the sound of running footsteps. A young woman with long fair braids burst into the cavern and cast herself on Domerc's shoulder. "I knew it had to be the Falheiras," she cried, "nobody else could ever find that entrance. How did you and . . ."

She paused and looked at Gaire, then Allie, with dawning puzzlement. "Where's Liuria?"

"Not with us," Domerc said. "Safe in Coindra."

"Then how did you find the place?"

"Iseu, I'm not so helpless as all that," Domerc said irritably, "I can do a *few* things without my little sister leading me by the hand. As a matter of fact, I had no difficulty at all in remembering how to reach the entrance."

Allie and Gaire looked at each other again, but said nothing.

"But you will be tired," Iseu said, "and hungry. You shall tell me how you came here later. For now . . ."

She led them through the lighted caverns to a place where the water-smoothed rock curved inward like a giant bed. The niche was softened with mounds of pillows and brightened by gentle glowing light-bubbles. Allie sank into the pillows and listened, half dazed, while Iseu gave orders to Druon concerning spiced soups and hot drinks and other things that sounded too wonderful to be true. In a contented trance of exhaustion, she half-listened while Domerc told Iseu what he thought had been going on and Iseu told Domerc what had happened at the keep of Brefania and Gaire put in a few words now and then.

"Must have been planned a long time—"

"But he isn't afraid that he'll raise landmonsters; that's what I can't understand."

"Wants to raise them," Gaire put in.

"Ridiculous," Domerc said, hardly listening, "nobody *wants* landmonsters. He must have thought it was worth the risk to surprise you in planting-time, when nobody starts wars."

"No risk," Gaire insisted. "Got a tame mage coming from Coindra. Knows how to control landmonsters."

"Nobody can do that," Iseu said, "you don't understand, my good man. If magecraft could control them . . ."

"But this chap isn't just a mage," Gaire said, "He's a Landsenser too. Something about combining the powers."

Domerc and Iseu looked at each other.

"Mage and Landsenser too," Iseu said slowly.

"Aigar," Domerc said. "It has to be."

"I *knew* he was lying last spring," Iseu said, "but I couldn't figure out why. It never occurred to me he *wanted* landmonsters to rise on Savaric's land."

"It never occurred to anyone else either," Domerc said grimly. "If he can really control landmonsters—"

Iseu shivered. "It doesn't bear thinking about." She rose. "I *won't* think about it now. And neither shall you. You need baths and clean clothes. So do I. You remember how to find the Hall of Vaporous Mists, Domerc?"

He smiled. "Still using those grandiose names, Iseu? Yes, I remember. But Gaire and I will wash after Allie."

"You'll do no such thing," Iseu contradicted him. "Allie and I want a nice long soak. In and out with you, while I find something for you to wear, and then you and Centor shall sing part-songs for us while we loll at our ease."

"Yes. I think you could use that," Domerc said, looking narrowly at Iseu's serious face.

Allie decided that she didn't understand anything that was going on and didn't really care. Especially if the sequence of events ended in a hot bath. Domerc and Gaire went off with the young man called Centor; she drifted along behind Iseu while the girl sent people scurrying in search of clothes and soap and Centor's vielle.

Winding passages lit by the ubiquitous glow-bubbles confused Allie; they passed grand halls and pillars of crystal and came at last into an open space where steam rose from a pool at the far end. Domerc's hair was wet, and he seemed to be wearing a tunic that was long enough but far too wide for him, firmly belted over trews that billowed away from his legs. Allie had to look twice before she recognized the pink-faced man beside him, with hair slicked back behind his prominent ears, as an unnaturally clean Gaire.

"Good," Iseu said, "you didn't waste time."

"I can play now," somebody she didn't know said, holding up a hand that looked stiff and swollen to Allie. "See how much better it is after a treatment in the waters?"

"Not enough better," Iseu decreed. "Domerc, you play vielle. Centor needs to rest that hand."

The three men withdrew to a discreet distance and made musician-noises. "Give me an A," Allie heard, and, "Shall we do something out of the Denhatz part-song book?" and from Gaire, unexpectedly, "I don't know your fancy-type songs, but I reckon I could follow along. Used to sing the low parts in the marching group," and he demonstrated with a prolonged low, melodious rumble.

A smiling, pink-cheeked woman with gray braids wrapped around her head took Allie's tunic and trews, standing casually between her and the group of men at the far end of the chamber. Allie slid hastily into the water and caught her breath with surprise. The temperature was just above bearable; the steam smelled of sweet herbs; and there were constant streams of tiny bubbles rising through the pool from the smooth stone bottom, stirring around her like the gentlest of massages.

Allie leaned back to get even more of herself in the hot water. Strange, it felt hot enough to parboil her, but the warmth didn't seem to penetrate deeper than her skin; inside she was still so cold that her bones hurt. Well, give it time. She'd feel warm all over soon enough, sitting in this wonderful natural bath.

Behind her, three voices and the sweet sobbing of a vielle rose in intertwined harmony. Allie could not make out the words at all; it must be one of those confusing things Liuria had mentioned once, the double-songs where one person sang one set of words and melody while the other sang something completely different. Gaire, she noticed, was singing "Hmmm, Mmmm, Hmmmm," in a rich bass that blended nicely with the other sets of words and music. Whatever they were.

Allie decided not to worry about understanding the words, or what geological formation resulted in a natural jacuzzi, or anything else. She would just stay here forever . . . *I want to go back to Coindra*, something cried within her in a sharp twinge of pain.

"What was that?" Iseu said. "You want to go back to Coindra?"

"I, I'm sorry," Allie stammered. "That must sound rude. It's lovely here. I was just thinking I would like to stay right here in the hot water forever, and then . . . I didn't know I'd said anything out loud."

"Coindra must be a fine town," Iseu said wistfully. "At one time I thought to go there, but I'm not really a scholarly sort, and then Papa needed me here." She eyed Allie closely. "But you look quite pale with longing."

"I do?" Allie put one hand to her face. It felt cold to her, but surely that was just by contrast with the steaming heat of the waters around her.

"Give me your hand," Iseu commanded, and then, "That's strange. *Very* strange."

"Just a hand," Allie murmured. "Four fingers. One thumb. Standard model." She felt tired and sleepy and dizzy.

"You shouldn't be so cold, not after being in the waters this long," Iseu announced. "Or so tired."

"Wimpy American. No stamina." Allie suddenly felt like crying. She'd been trying so hard to conceal how she felt, to keep up with Domerc without complaining, and apparently she'd done so poorly that a total stranger could see her exhaustion at a glance. "Don't know why I'm so tired, though," she said, "must be out of shape. Too much studying, not enough hockey."

"What's a hockey? Oh, well, never mind. Have you been feverish? Aching? Your head hurts? When did it start?"

Under Iseu's questioning, Allie admitted that she'd been feeling ill ever since they left Coindra, but that there wasn't anything specific she could point to: she just felt tired and dragged-out and as if there wasn't any reason for living. And the longer they traveled, the worse it got.

"*I want to go back to Coindra,*" she wailed, and then, "I'm sorry. That's not like me. Really. I don't wail and moan and complain about things."

"Who says you do?" inquired Domerc.

Allie glanced up and hastily slid down a few inches more in the pool, until the steaming water was around her neck. Iseu had distracted her so that she hadn't even noticed that the music had stopped.

"She's ill," Iseu said coldly. "I don't think much of you dragging a sick girl all this way, Domerc."

"You don't know the story," Domerc said with a scowl. "Believe me, she wouldn't have been safe in Coindra. I had to keep her away from Aigar. He was going to kill her."

"Why would he do a thing like that?"

Domerc threw up his hands. "How should I know? Maybe he needs human sacrifices to offer to the landmonsters. Now you're blaming me for not letting Allie be one of them. All right, so *go* back to Coindra and be a virgin sacrifice if that's what'll make you happy! Women!"

"She gets worse the farther away from Coindra you travel," Iseu said thoughtfully.

Domerc's black brows drew together, but he said nothing for a moment. "Yes," he said, "I see what you're thinking. And you know what else supports that idea? She was fanatically loyal to Aigar."

"It seemed reasonable at the time," Allie said, but neither of them paid the least attention to her.

"Allie, what kinds of experiments did you help Aigar with?" Iseu demanded.

At the same time Domerc said, "Did you ever give him your blood?"

"Yecch," Allie said, "what do you think went on in that lab, Black Masses or something?" She paused for a moment and clenched her hands under water as a wave of longing swept through her. *The lab, Aigar's beautiful marble-floored lab, I wish I were there right this minute.* Not a popular sentiment to voice just now. And it didn't make *sense*; why should she long to be back there? Perhaps because she'd felt safe and protected and cared for. But it had all been lies. She shouldn't still want it. She *wouldn't.*

After a moment's intense concentration on *not* wanting to go back to the lab, Allie went on. "I never did anything but fetch chemicals and pick up his dirty dishes and wash glassware . . ."

"What about washing glassware?" Domerc demanded when her voice trailed off.

"Nothing really," Allie said. "I was just remembering . . ." It was the day she'd felt sure that Aigar cared about her. What a laugh *that* was! Why should he have cared about her, why should anybody? She should've seen what a fraud it all was from the beginning. "One day when I'd just started on the job I broke a bunch of voicebubbles he'd given me to wash . . . of course I didn't know what they were then . . . but he wasn't angry at all. He even bandaged up my cut hand." She glanced up at Domerc. "I must say, I wish you people would invent Kleenex or something. He spoiled a perfectly good white silk scarf."

"Blood and silk," Domerc said. His voice had a hollow ring.

"Blood and silk," Iseu and Gaire echoed.

"Doesn't she know what that *means?*" asked Centor.

Domerc glanced over his shoulder. "She doesn't know anything, she's from . . . a place where they don't do anything like that. Until recently," he said, his mouth setting in a grim line, "I would have said that *Coindra* was a place where they didn't do anything like that."

"What's the big deal?" Gaire protested. "You took my soulbond yourself, En Domerc!"

"Under emergency conditions," Domerc said, "and you at least consented. In fact, it was your idea. This child didn't even know what was happening."

"Can it be *done* like that?" Iseu asked. "Without the soul's consent?"

Domerc drew a deep breath. "I don't know, I don't *know!* I don't know what you think goes on in Coindra, Iseu, but they don't teach the black bindings in Intermediate and Advanced Cantrips." He glanced down at Allie. "There may have been an element of consent— not to the binding specifically—her trust in Aigar may have been sufficient. It may work like the really good aimerances. Those can build up a powerful love-bond between two people, but the basic liking has to be there beforehand; if you try to work one on people who really don't like one another, it'll dissipate without much effect."

"Really?" Centor asked. "I never knew that. How much would you say one of those aimerance spells would cost?"

"I don't know what any of you are talking about," Allie complained, "and I wish you'd quit looking at me as if I were part of a lab experiment, and—" The other voice, the one that felt like a strange half of herself, took over again. "*I need to go back to Coindra!*"

Iseu found Allie's clenched fist under the water and gently pried the fingers open until they were sitting with clasped hands. "I believe she does need to go back there," she said to the men gathered at the pool's edge. "Don't you?"

Domerc nodded. "And soon. But we should be sure first . . ."

"Allie, try to remember," Iseu said softly, "what happened to the silk that Aigar used to bandage your hand? You wore the bandage home, perhaps, and discarded it in your rooms?"

Tension filled the silence. Allie thought back. Her head ached with the effort. "No," she said finally, "when the bleeding stopped, he scrunched the scarf up and put it in his pocket. I wanted to wash it out in cold water before the stains set, but he was in a hurry to get on to something else."

"I'm sure he was," Domerc said with a groan. "He must have hidden it somewhere."

"It won't be hard to find," Iseu said. "Take her back to Coindra. She'll be drawn to it. The two parts of the soul will long to be reunited."

"I don't *understand*," Allie wailed.

Domerc knelt down at the side of the pool. "Allie, remember the ceremony Gaire and I went through, to be sure I could trust him to serve me faithfully? The soulbinding? It's an old art and not much practiced these days. You wouldn't have learned about it in Radegond's lectures. But we think Aigar did something like that to you, to make sure you would keep coming to the lab and would do whatever he wanted. I don't yet know quite *what* he wanted," Domerc added parenthetically, "but nothing good. Anyway, the point is, you should have found it impossible to leave Coindra."

"I don't think I could have walked away," Allie said, remembering the gray morning when they boarded the barge. "The current carried us away . . . it felt like something being torn out of me . . ."

"And it got worse the farther away from Coindra we came, didn't it?" demanded Domerc. "Why didn't you tell me?"

"I thought it was flu," Allie cried.

"I should have seen it. Even Gaire saw you were feeling ill." There were deep lines etched in Domerc's face; he looked ten years older than the student she'd met on the day she came to Coindra. "I've nearly killed you, dragging you away like that, making you sick . . ."

"Stop that!" Allie said sharply. She felt weak but clearminded for the first time in days. Knowing just what it was that hurt inside her and made her long for Coindra seemed to make it easier to bear. "*You* didn't make me sick, Aigar did. And if you hadn't taken me away, he'd have made me *dead*. Anyway," she said, more optimistically than she felt, "it's no worse than chemotherapy."

"Than what?"

"It's a medical treatment. It makes people feel pretty crummy for a while, but then sometimes it cures whatever was wrong with them and they get better again. I mean, sometimes you have to feel worse to feel better," Allie rattled on, "and if I have to suffer until we get far enough away to break the spell—"

Domerc was shaking his head. "It doesn't work like that, Allie. You *must* reclaim the part of your soul that remains in Aigar's power; otherwise you will die. We have to get you back to Coindra."

A man came half-running into the misty room. "Na

Iseu," he said, "there's more folk at the entrance in the water-room."

"Asking sanctuary?" Iseu demanded.

He shook his head. "No, Na Iseu. It's Savaric and his magician. They've got a hostage. The Seignor's sister, they say." He jerked his head at Domerc. "And they don't want to come into the caves." He pointed at Allie. "It's *her* they want. The little foreign one. Send her out, they say, and the rest of us can stay here as long as we like."

Liuria stood miserably by while Aigar and Savaric bickered. Her arms ached; the two soldiers Savaric had ordered to guard her on the march here had done so by grasping one arm apiece and dragging or lifting her along the trail. Now that she'd completed her betrayal by guiding them to this spot, they really didn't need to keep holding her so tightly. What would she run away for? She didn't deserve to escape; she didn't want to escape. Except maybe to throw herself over this rocky ledge. If the fall was enough to kill her, that would be better than facing everybody after what she'd done.

Liuria peered morosely over the ledge. Not much of a fall from here to the next outcropping of limestone and thorn bushes; maybe twenty feet. She might break a couple of bones, but she wouldn't die; not unless she were really lucky. That would have to wait, then.

She listened without much interest to the wrangling between Aigar and Savaric.

"Ye tellt me yon Elder World soul was ensorceled in yon bit o' clay!" Savaric bellowed, pointing at an amulet Aigar held half-concealed beneath his cloak. His mountain accent was rougher than ever under the stress of some powerful emotion. "Now ye say she's in t'caves with Iseu de Brefania!"

"I . . . slightly anticipated events when we spoke by voice bubble," Aigar said smoothly. "Her soul was already bound to me by blood and silk, the living body lay unconscious awaiting the final transfer, all was prepared. I had no reason to expect any difficulties. And as you see, I overcame the slight problem caused by the girl's disappearance and provided us with another bondsoul fully capable of dispelling the landmonsters. I saw no reason to concern you with this trivial substitution . . ."

"Treeevial, is it!" The word set Savaric off on a prolonged rant. Liuria gathered that Aigar's amulet had been supposed to turn landmonsters into a neatly trained mercenary army to augment Savaric's human forces. Instead it only kept landmonsters away from them and forced them to sink slowly back into the land from which they had sprung.

"Only," Liuria thought drearily. That was a laugh. What wouldn't the Landsensers Guild have done for Aigar's secret? And why hadn't he already sold it to them at exorbitant rates, instead of fooling about with this hill-country, back-lands Seignor and his mercenary troops?

As the argument continued, it slowly became clear to Liuria why Aigar couldn't tell anybody openly what his secret was. He was using a human soul as his intermediary between himself and the landmonsters . . . someone bound to him by blood sacrifice, the soul drawn from the body and captured in that amulet of fired clay he kept fingering.

And it was supposed to be *Allie* in there . . . especially valuable to them because she didn't come from Escorre. Aigar had brought her here from Elder World.

Cold shivers raced through Liuria's aching body as she imagined Allie trapped in stone-hard earth, hung from Aigar's neck to do his bidding forever. Except it wasn't Allie, was it? That was what the wrangling was all about; that was why Aigar had been so excited when she let slip that she'd come to Astire in search of Allie. Because he meant to use her to force Allie to come out and be sacrificed.

Liuria's deep depression lifted very slightly. At least now she had the glimmerings of a purpose. Savaric had sent the captured children from that farm back to Astire;

he couldn't coerce her now by torturing them. Careless of him, that. She would have to find a way to die; then he wouldn't be able to use her to force Allie out. And in her death, she meant to smash that amulet of Aigar's and free whatever poor soul had been trapped there in Allie's place.

Just at the moment there seemed to be no way of accomplishing either of these ends. She would have to be patient and watch for an opportunity.

There were rustlings and stirrings at the vine-covered cleft between the rocks, and Liuria thought she saw the faint glow of a damped lightbubble. "Who's there?" called a familiar voice. "What do you want?"

Liuria forgot for a moment that it might be better if the people inside could not be sure she was Aigar's hostage. "Allie, *don't come out!*" she called urgently. "You must not. He means to—"

A hard hand clamped over her mouth. "You speak when En Savaric tells you to, girl, and say what he wants." The other guard twisted her arm up behind her back and gave it a series of sharp jerks, one to go with each word.

Involuntary tears of pain filled Liuria's eyes. *Good*, she thought. If she looked beaten, maybe they'd not watch her so closely. She hung her head and tried to look limp and compliant.

Inside the narrow tunnel of the entrance, Domerc clasped Allie's hand. "She's right," he murmured. "You must not go out there. There's some way that your soul would give him more power. For all our sakes, don't do it."

"I can't leave Liuria to him!" Allie protested.

"Even if he promised to free her, he wouldn't keep his promise."

"We could set up an exchange," Gaire put in. "Common enough in war. See, you pick a neutral point—"

Domerc rounded on him with a snarl. "You keep out of this!"

"It's your sister we're trying to save," Gaire said with an injured look.

Domerc looked not ten but twenty years older; the soft glow of the damped light-bubble was as harsh as full sunlight on the deep lines in his face. "I am aware of that," he said without inflection, and turned back to Allie. "He wants your soul. It must be because you come from Elder World. Yes. Of course!" He hit himself on the forehead. "I'm an idiot. We're all idiots. You're from Away, you don't know about landmonsters, you aren't afraid of them."

"You bet I am!" Allie said.

"Not the way we are," Domerc said. "We grow up in fear and loathing of them. They're every child's worst nightmare. And these nightmares don't stop when we grow up; they're real, and something none of us ever wants to face. You can't imagine how hard it was for Iseu to fight the landvines that came into the cave instead of screaming and running away in total panic. But to you they're just something nasty, like spiders. Somehow he wants your soul bonded to him, to help him control the landmonsters. Don't you see, we can't let him do that?"

"We can't let him kill Liuria."

"If necessary," Domerc said in measured tones, "I would kill you myself to keep you from exchanging yourself for Liuria."

"Got a better idea," Gaire muttered behind them.

"I thought I told you to keep out of this!" Domerc barked.

"Can't, En Domerc. Bonded t'you by blood and silk. My life's yours. More's the pity. Now come you here and listen for a minute, will you?"

"Keep talking," Domerc told Allie. "Make them think you might give in. And *don't go out there!*"

"I want to talk to Liuria again," Allie called. "How do I know it's her you've got out there? I'm not sure I recognized her voice."

"Oh, aye? D'ye know it now, then?" a harsh accented voice called back. Allie caught her breath at the cry of pain that followed. She took a step towards the cave entrance.

Suddenly Centor and Druon were beside her, Druon holding the long smoke-blackened spit with which he'd greeted her and Domerc, Centor with his belt knife drawn. Behind them, she half-heard Gaire saying something about, " . . . magecraft, then? Now give us time to take position . . ."

"We got instructions," Druon told her in a rumbling mutter. "Anybody tries to get in, I spit 'em like a roast, see?"

Allie looked at Centor's knife.

"And if you try to go out," Centor said, "I'm to do whatever it takes to stop you. Domerc has explained it all to me."

Allie took a deep, trembling breath and tried to steady her voice. "That could be anybody," she called out. "Let me talk to Liuria, or you tell me what you want."

"If ye're so eager to see her, come on out," the rough voice answered. "She's waitin' for ye."

"No, thank you," Allie called back. "I just want to hear what she has to say. I don't believe Liuria would have betrayed us by showing you this entrance. And if she did, why should I care what happens to her now?"

There was a short pause, filled with scuffling sounds that made Allie cold with imagined horrors; then Liuria spoke again, much closer to the cave entrance than she'd been before. Her voice was shaking and she sounded on the verge of tears.

"I'm *sorry*, Allie. It's all my fault. First I let slip that I was looking for you. Then Savaric—" Her voice broke.

"He tortured you," Allie said quickly. "I understand. I don't blame you."

"N-no. The mercenaries brought me up into the hills. They were searching farms; they'd caught some peasants and their children. Savaric hurt one of them, a little boy, he . . ." Liuria swallowed down the nausea rising in her throat. "He would have gone on until the boy died. It would have taken hours. I couldn't stand it. I thought I'd think of something on the way here. I didn't understand what he was after, really. I didn't know what he wanted. Now I do. You mustn't—"

Her voice stopped abruptly, as though someone had clapped a hand over her mouth. A moment later there was a low sobbing gasp, the sort of sound someone might make while desperately trying *not* to scream.

Allie clenched her hands until the nails bit into her palms.

"Heard enough?" the voice that must be En Savaric's called. "Or d'ye want me to break her other arm before ye come out? Or maybe I'll start on the fingers. She used to play the transverse flute, didn't she? All the Falheiras like music."

Beside Allie, Centor stirred fractionally, interposing his shoulder between her and the tunnel entrance. "Don't even think about it," he whispered. "Keep him talking."

Allie gulped and nodded. "Why should I care what you do to her?" she shouted. Her voice cracked on the last word and she had to swallow hard again before she could go on. "Domerc might be soft enough to come out to you if he were here, but I'm not such a fool. She's not *my* sister. I never liked her anyway."

"You like hearing people die slowly, do you?"

"Kill her," Allie shouted, "and you'll have no hold on Domerc. You better wait and talk to him. *He* might care what happens to her." Tears were running down her face before she finished speaking, and she swallowed salt, but she didn't think her voice had wobbled noticeably.

There were low mumbling sounds outside, as though Savaric and Aigar were conferring. Allie strained her ears, desperately trying to hear what they said. What was the good of keeping this up? What did Domerc hope to accomplish by delay? She slipped back in the tunnel to ask him, but he was no longer there. Neither was Gaire.

Allie slammed her fist into the rough stone wall of the tunnel. "*Idiot*," she whispered through her tears. "What good will you getting killed do us?"

"He won't get killed," Centor murmured in her ear. "He's got a plan. A *good* plan. Now you go back and talk. You're doing fine."

CHAPTER THIRTEEN

Aigar kept one hand clasped around the amulet that held Fabre's bondsoul while Savaric and Allie shouted back and forth at one another. He tried not to listen to Savaric's increasingly vicious threats against Liuria. It was probably true that Allie cared for the other girl, no matter what she said to the contrary. And if she didn't, surely Domerc did. Savaric was just getting started; he'd be able to think of tortures that would have Liuria weeping and begging her brother and friend to save her. He was that kind of brute. Aigar pressed his lips together in prim disapproval and stared around him at the limestone ledges, the clumps of thorny bushes, the clusters of trees growing lower down the slope. Anything to take his mind off the fire Savaric was now building on their ledge and the pike he was heating in it. The fire was close enough to ensure that the people inside the caverns would be able to hear Liuria's shrieks of pain. He wished it hadn't come to this. He was a sensitive man, a scholar. He found it extremely painful to be exposed to this sort of brutality.

The low bushy trees growing on the downslope quivered as though a wind were passing through them. Aigar glanced up at the sky; the few clouds he could see were quite still. He was beginning to hallucinate under the strain of this savagery, that's what it was. Perhaps Savaric would order a couple of soldiers to stand guard while he tottered off out of earshot and rested. After all, it would do no good to make him suffer by watching Liuria tortured. He needed to save his strength for the sacrifice he'd have to make when they got Allie out of the caverns. It was for everybody's good, really.

Aigar grasped Savaric by the elbow and tried to make his wants known. His voice croaked unintelligibly. Well, he was a decent man, a man of sensibility; no shame in being distressed by Savaric's vicious methods.

"Eh? Don't *distract* me," Savaric mouthed back.

The crunch of small stones moving ever so slightly went unheard by both of them. One of the soldiers holding Liuria stirred and looked nervously over his shoulder, then looked back at Savaric.

"Oh, aye," Savaric interrupted when Aigar managed to get his request out, "Go off and do whatever ye want. Don't break yer fool neck climbing the ledges, 's all *I* ask. Expect to need ye soon." He gave Aigar a grin full of yellow teeth and looked down at the fire.

A cry of terror from one of the soldiers was their only warning. Savaric's mouth fell open. Aigar turned slowly, with the dignity befitting a master mage, to see what had overset his companions.

They were everywhere and nowhere: shifting, melting shapes of rainbow-colored leaves and singing fruit and weeping flowers. The leaves advanced, uncurling long barbed edges, and winged serpents slithered out of the flowers.

Aigar grasped Fabre's bondsoul and commanded the things to disperse. The ceramic shape that held Fabre leapt and quivered under his hand, but the monstrous plants and distorted trees continued to advance on them.

The only way that remained clear was back down the shelf of stone, the way they had come. The soldier who'd built a fire for Savaric gave a wail of terror and sprang through the glowing heart of the fire just as something too misty to grasp brushed the back of his neck with a cold breathy sigh. The others followed him, tumbling pell-mell down the rocky slopes, while Savaric stood his

ground and shouted at them to return, cursed them for
fools and cowards, demanded that Aigar work his
magecraft: all to no avail. The bondsoul was quick and
responsive under his fingers, but Aigar felt as if his own
fear and disgust for the monsters was being somehow
swallowed up. Instead of sending the messages of terror to the landmonsters, Fabre seemed to be keeping
them all within himself.

Disperse, ye beings! Aigar commanded. He shrieked
the order aloud; still the plant-monsters came closer and
closer yet. As he stared in fascinated horror, something
that clawed and spat like a half-grown mountain klytha-
cat launched itself at his chest. Liuria! How had she got
loose? Aigar just had time to curse the cowards of soldiers who'd run for themselves and loosed the child; then
a cord bit into the back of his neck. He yelped with pain.
The pressure dragged his neck forward, then the cord
broke and his head snapped backwards, throwing him
off balance. He fell to one knee. The rocks bruised him.
The comforting weight of the bondsoul was gone; Aigar
felt cold and naked and alone.

Liuria lay face down before him, one hand clenched
around the amulet. The broken ends of the silk cord
that had held it dangled across the rocky ledge between
them. A red stain seeped out over the shoulder of her
tunic. There was something sticking up from her back,
still quivering slightly.

Savaric gave a dry chuckle. "The old man can still
throw a knife," he said in self-congratulatory tones. "Stand
fast now, ye damned mage, and do something about the
landmonsters. It's just the two of us now. Fool soldiers
ran off."

The fantastically colored pink and purple forms faded
as he spoke. A shape made of leaves turned into the
walking image of a pale, dark-haired young man just
behind Savaric, raising his arm, something long in his
hand . . .

Savaric's chuckle turned into a sickly gurgle. His eyes

rolled up and blood spurted from him as Domerc thrust the turnspit through the back of his neck.

"That's not a clean kill," said a man-high winged serpent. "Shoulda let me do it; so you should." The serpent's scales shimmered and writhed into the form of a soldier, first oddly greenish and scaled, then living skin and a face that Aigar could almost put a name to, one of Marin's men . . . Gaire, that was who. Why were Marin's soldiers attacking Savaric? Treachery!

"He hurt my sister," Domerc said as if that explained everything. He pulled the smoke-blackened turnspit out of Savaric's neck with a jerk and looked across the ledge at Aigar, weighing the spit thoughtfully in one hand.

Aigar stepped backward off the ledge, crashed through stinging bushes, landed on a sharp rock, and discovered that he could, in fact, get up and keep running without pausing to investigate what felt like a broken rib. Maybe two broken ribs. He would think about it later.

"Never mind him," Domerc snapped as Gaire started to take off after Aigar. "Help me with Liuria! Should I take this thing out, or what? Come on, you're a soldier, what do you do for your wounded comrades?"

"Soldier, not a surgeon," Gaire muttered, "and you're making a bad mistake, letting that one go. I coulda stopped him before he caught up with the soldiers."

"I'm not sure you want to keep him from catching up with Savaric's soldiers," Domerc said. "He probably is not too popular with them right now." Liuria's shallow breaths made the knife waggle back and forth in her shoulder.

"Hurts," she whispered into the rocks. "Take it out."

Domerc gingerly pulled out the knife. There was more blood, too much for such a little wound. It welled up over his hands. He glared at Gaire. "Can't you do something for her?"

Gaire knelt beside Domerc and studied Liuria's wound with a professional eye. "Not too deep. Should have left the knife in. She's thin, but it's not easy to get any force with a thrown knife. Probably didn't hit a lung. The arm's going to hurt like hell, though. Probably broken." He felt along Liuria's left arm with surprisingly delicate fingers. She hissed with pain. "You're a lucky little lady; clean break, and none of the joints separated." He turned from her to Savaric and pulled out his belt knife.

"Don't waste time with him!" Domerc snapped. "He's dead. It's Liuria we've got to help."

There was a ripping sound. Gaire stood up with two lengths of Savaric's bloodstained tunic in his hand. "Didn't want him," he said mildly, "wanted some cloth." He rolled one bit of tunic into a compact packet and knelt beside Liuria again. "Keep pressure on till it stops bleeding." He demonstrated. "Then wash it, hope there wasn't anything too nasty on the dagger. That's all I know. Why don't you heal her?"

"Just like that?" Domerc let out his breath in an exasperated sigh.

"Just like you did me."

"The farm was heavy with landvirtue," Domerc said. "I drew on that. The currents don't run through rock; why do you think we're hiding out here?"

"Hold the bandage on tight. I need both hands to fix the arm." Gaire deftly bound Liuria's broken arm to her side, lifting her as little as possible to pass the strip of cloth under her body. She groaned between clenched teeth. "Me, I don't think if I can avoid it, En Domerc. That's your job, not mine. I liked the illusions, by the way."

"First-year magery," Domerc said absently, watching the slow rise and fall of Liuria's back. "If Aigar hadn't been expecting landmonsters, he'd have dispelled the illusions while Saigar's men minced us up. But he was expecting real landmonsters . . . *and* he was expecting to be able to control them. How, I can't imagine."

"Well, it may be first-year magery to you," Gaire said, "but we looked damned impressive to me. So did some of the other illusions you created. They last pretty good, too."

"What d'you mean?" Domerc had stopped holding the illusion-spell when the soldiers fled; everything should have faded out by now. For him, everything except Liuria's pale face had faded out of consciousness.

"Like that bunch over there." Gaire gestured with his free hand; Domerc's head jerked up, and he felt himself going as pale as his sister.

"Pick up Liuria," he said in a level tone. "Slowly."

"Shouldn't move her yet," Gaire grumbled.

"Have to," Domerc replied without taking his eyes from the seething dark clouds at the far end of the limestone ledge, the ones Gaire had been admiring. "I didn't make those. Savaric's blood must have called them. Pick up her feet. I'll take the shoulders. We'll back into the cave. Slowly. Try not to draw their attention."

They shuffled crabwise towards the green vines overhanging the narrow entrance, hardly breathing. Domerc could feel something warm and wet on his hand. Liuria was bleeding again. He couldn't carry her and keep pressure on the wound.

Vines brushed against the back of his neck, and Druon's voice called a warning challenge. "Cantatz ve Falheiras Assombre," Domerc called back over his shoulder.

"*Know* who y'are." Liuria's voice was a frayed thread of a whisper, on the edge of breaking into silence.

"Hush. It's all right. Be still," Domerc murmured while he moved backwards, one shuffling step at a time.

"Give this . . . Allie." Liuria's clenched fist moved slightly. Domerc couldn't see what she was holding; some kind of clay amulet, trailing the broken ends of a silk cord.

The shadows of the cave covered them; the green vines fell back behind Gaire's head. Outside, Domerc could just glimpse the roiling shapes of cloud-monsters feeding on the pool of blood in which Savaric's body lay.

※※※※※

Allie jammed one fist into her mouth and bit down on her knuckles when she saw Liuria's pale face. There was blood all over Domerc's hands. Her blood? Allie couldn't tell if Liuria was even breathing. Gaire and Domerc carried her awkwardly. One arm was bound tight to her side; the other one was laid across her chest.

But her eyelids flickered, and the clenched hand on her chest opened to reveal a smooth hard amulet, an irregular cylinder of fired clay with a hole at the top for its string. "Allie?" she whispered. "Take . . ."

Allie stepped forward. "What? This?" She looked at Domerc. "What is it?"

Domerc shook his head. "Something of Aigar's. She seems to think it's important. It had better be important," he said, "she nearly got herself killed taking it from him. I haven't time to figure out what it's for yet. You carry it until we can get sorted out."

Allie picked up the amulet by its broken cord, knotted the ends of the cord again and slipped it over her neck. The amulet felt greasy and alive under her hand, soft and hard at the same time, still and moving. Just touching it made her head hurt worse, as if somebody were shouting at her. She quickly slipped it outside her shirt, where it wouldn't touch her skin; that felt better.

"She's no lightweight, this long sister of yours," Gaire complained. "How's about we lay her down some place?"

They were clumsy about setting her down; her injured arm brushed against the cave wall. Liuria gasped and her eyes rolled back up into her head.

"She's fainted," Gaire said helpfully.

Domerc, for once, was not looking at his sister; he was watching the faint light that filtered through the green vines at the cave's opening, and murmuring something under his breath while his fingers wove a pattern that danced and dazzled and was not quite there whenever Allie tried to look at it straight on.

"Good," he said. "We'll have to carry her again."

"You did ask for my opinion about her wounds," Gaire grumbled, "and I'm telling you again she shouldn't be hauled about like a leaking wine-sack. Not if you want her to stop leaking."

"The cloudmonsters," Domerc said. He sounded oddly detached, as though most of his mind were on the pattern that flickered between his outstretched fingers. "They're following us into the cave . . . It must be her blood that draws them. I can weave a net that'll slow them down, but we'll have to get her away from here, to some place where I can draw on the landvirtue to stanch her wounds."

Druon nodded. "The Greenway, m'lady?" He looked at Iseu.

"Savaric had soldiers. . . ."

"We'll have to take that risk," Domerc said. His lips were set in a thin tight line. "Better the soldiers than the cloudmonsters. Let's pick her up and go while she's unconscious. I don't know how long this net will hold." He shook his hands out towards the cave mouth, a gesture like someone flicking water from his fingertips. Allie could almost see a network of dark and shining strands, a spiderweb pattern that shifted to a grid, to a spiral, back to a spiderweb before she lost it in the shadows.

The minutes that followed were among the most unpleasant of her life. For some reason which nobody bothered to explain to her, they didn't retreat through the spacious and well-lit caverns. Instead, Iseu led everyone in single file through a series of narrow branching passages.

Domerc wanted Allie to go at the head of the line, where Iseu and Druon kept holding whispered consultations about the best direction to take. She refused and kept refusing until it was too late, until all the other refugees in the caverns of Brefania were ahead of them. "*Why?*" Domerc demanded, exasperated.

"Even Iseu isn't always sure which way to go, to get to . . . wherever it is you want to go," Allie said.

"So?"

"So if I'm about to be hopelessly lost in the depths of the earth," Allie said, "I'd just as soon not listen to it happening. It's bad enough—" She bit her lip. There was, after all, no point in complaining about what they all had to put up with; though Allie did notice with some envy that the Escorreans didn't seem to mind enclosed dark places quite as much as she did.

And that was the other thing she didn't want to admit to Domerc; that the only thing keeping her from breaking into screaming hysterics was being near him. She didn't know whether it was the feeling of safety his mage-chants gave her, or the pride that wouldn't allow her to break down before him. It didn't matter. They had to go on now; the last of the refugees had gone on through the tunnels, and it was their turn to follow.

The nightmare trip through narrow winding passages seemed to go on forever. There were places where Allie would have sworn she couldn't squeeze through if she hadn't known that portly Druon had preceded her; places where water seeped through and made the stones slimy; places where the overhanging rocks came so low that they had to drop to their knees and drag Liuria through. And it was all dark save for the barest glow of magelight from a bubble that floated before Iseu, and all the time Allie felt the weight of stone above her head pressing on her. Her head hurt and her hands ached with a bone-deep chill. And whenever the amulet Liuria had passed on to her swung against her bare skin, she felt as if her head would explode from the imaginary voices shouting at her, trying to distract her from the path they followed. What did the thing *want*? It seemed to want her to stop and wait for the cloudmonsters to catch up with them. Some of Aigar's evil magic, no doubt.

She was on her hands and knees, crawling over slimy rocks, when the quality of the light that guided her seemed to change subtly. The faint rose-pink of Iseu's lightbubble was fading. Allie caught her breath in panic at the thought of being trapped here in absolute darkness, caught between two limestone walls that wept green moss and black trickles of water. Then it dawned on her that she was *seeing* the walls. More than that, she was seeing *colors*. Iseu's lightbubble wasn't fading after all; it was joining with natural daylight, a pallid light interrupted by moving shadows and jostling figures, but true and natural for all that.

"We're *there*," she whispered to Domerc behind her.

"Hmm? Don't interrupt me." He kept up his droning incantation while they crawled the last few feet and stood up in blessed relief. They were in a smooth-walled chamber that rose in a roughly cylindrical shape many feet above their heads. Daylight poured in from above and slithered through cracks in the far side of the chamber. Already most of the refugees had squeezed through those cracks; Savaric's men must have gone. Allie quickly quashed a mental image of soldiers standing silently on either side of each opening, killing the refugees as they emerged. She could hear children laughing outside, squealing with the delight of fresh air and sun and grass to tumble on. It was all right. It *had* to be all right.

But somehow, it felt all wrong.

"That's funny," Domerc said, frowning at the dank tunnel from which they'd just emerged.

Allie's lurking sense of danger leapt at her throat. "What? What's wrong?"

"It's good, really," Domerc reassured her. "Only, I don't understand it. All the way through the tunnel I couldn't use my hands to keep casting the net behind us, but the cloudmonsters stayed the same distance away. And they still haven't come through the tunnel.

"Good," Allie said, hugging herself. She was so cold now that she ached all through and shivered continuously. The only warmth she could feel came from the evil amulet of Aïgar's, burning through her shirt as if it wanted to fill her head with Aïgar's spells. "Wonderful. You must be a better mage than you realized, if words alone kept them away. How about some more words?

In fact, how about building the net, *now*, before we go outside?"

"I want—I need to understand what's happening," Domerc said in a slightly abstracted tone. "Besides, that won't work. The net doesn't hold them forever, it just slows them down. Eventually they'll ooze through it, and if we're all outside then, they'll follow us and attack us in the open space where I can't cast a big enough net to contain them."

"Oh." That was a nastier picture than Allie's earlier idea about the soldiers. "Well, what do people usually do about cloudmonsters?"

"They dissipate in a few hours. Or days," Domerc said, still in that remote voice as if he were discussing a purely academic problem.

"And until then?"

"Nothing. They absorb whatever life they come across. I understand," Domerc said, "that some people have tried to outrun them. But it's difficult to tell, because nobody's survived being in the same valley with an infestation of cloudmonsters." His hands moved as he spoke, and Allie was relieved to see the almost-invisible shimmer of a mage-net building across the tunnel. Even if all he was doing was buying time, right now that seemed to her like an excellent thing to buy.

"They should have caught up with us and devoured us by now," Domerc said, still in the abstracted tones of a scholar following a trail of obsolete references. "I can't understand it."

Allie shrugged. The slight motion brought the clay amulet against her skin. Jagged lines of noise and pain lanced through her head; she swayed and put one hand to her forehead.

"Here now, don't faint on me," Domerc muttered while his fingers wove the net of light and magic.

The noises inside Allie's head coalesced into a single strident voice. "All right, all *right*, stop shouting," she said.

"I wasn't shouting," Domerc protested.

"Not you. I . . ." It was too hard to explain. Allie put two fingers gingerly to the amulet. It *wanted* her to touch it, and she was too tired to fight Aigar's evil magic. Besides, it didn't feel evil; it felt warm and comforting, the first warmth her bone-chilled hands had known in so long . . . She grasped it firmly, wrapping her fingers around it, and this time the sensation of something living and moving inside the hard glazed earthenware did not revolt her. It was almost like having a little purring cat to hold.

A *little purring kitten*! The voice inside her head was indignant. *Even now, I don't get any respect. It's not fair*. An image of Fabre's freckled, snub-nosed face filled Allie's mind.

"Fabre?" she whispered.

"What?" Domerc demanded.

"Hush up," Allie said impatiently, "I can't hear both of you at once. It must be some of your Escorrean magic. Funny, this doesn't *look* like a farspeaker bubble," she added, glancing at the amulet where it rested in the palm of her hand.

"Why should it?"

"Well," Allie said, "Fabre seems to be talking to me through it . . ."

More flashes of sound and light dazzled her, jolting through her head and bringing an understanding that turned her stomach. She sat down abruptly on the water-smoothed cave floor.

"En Domerc, what's keeping you?" Gaire shouted from outside. "Your sister's still bleeding. I can't stop it. And I think the bastard nicked a lung after all. And this place is *lousy* with Landvirtue; everybody can feel it. You'd better get out here before we have more landmonsters coming from this side."

"Just a minute," Domerc called back. "Allie's sick."

Allie shook her head. "Not sick. Just felt like—like I'd touched a live electric wire. Silly me, you don't have electricity here, do you? 'S all right," she assured Domerc,

"I know I'm babbling, I'll stop in a minute, I always do this when I'm really shaken up." She glanced at the amulet, now hanging harmlessly against her shirt. "I just hope he doesn't feel it necessary to do that again."

"Who? Have you run mad?"

"Fabre," Allie said. She gulped in a deep breath and let it out very slowly, willing her racing pulses to slow down. Wouldn't do to come over all dizzy and faint at this point. "Fabre's soul is in this amulet. He's been bonded with blood and earth. He can speak to us and he can speak to the land-monsters. He's been what kept them away from us."

Domerc slumped to the ground beside her. "Allie, I know you've had a hard time, but . . ."

"If you don't believe me," Allie snapped, "hold the amulet for a minute. Here!" She took the silken cord by two fingers and held it out away from her chest so that the amulet dangled in mid-air between them.

Domerc touched it with the tip of one finger, jumped, and put his finger in his mouth.

"Go *on*," Allie said, "he won't shout if you hold it so he can speak inside your head."

This time Domerc let the amulet rest on his open palm. He drew in a long shaky breath. "Fabre," he whispered. "*Fabre?*"

His face changed a dozen times in the next few seconds. When he let the amulet swing free again, there were tears in his eyes.

"It was all there," he said, "all the pieces, and I didn't put them together in time. And Fabre died for my stupidity."

The amulet swung and quivered against Allie's chest until she placed one hand on it to still it. *Dear girl, please tell my idiot of a roommate that I am* not *dead, merely changed in form. And if you would wear me inside your shirt instead of out, one of my dearest dreams would be fulfilled . . . to lie between your breasts.*

Allie sputtered. "It's Fabre, all right. And he's very much alive, Domerc."

"Alive and trapped," Domerc muttered.

"And able to keep the landmonsters away," Allie pointed out. "Now about Liuria . . ."

When they squeezed through the narrow opening, sun and sky dazzled her. They were standing on springy green turf under an arch of bending trees like willows, but with silvery white bark. Fabre, now tucked safely inside Allie's shirt as he had requested, quivered against her bare skin. She drew in a deep breath of clean, fresh, warm air and felt more alive than she had since they found Gaire at the farm.

Domerc scowled at her. "Don't you go all silly on me like the rest of them." He jerked his chin at Iseu's refugees. The children were turning cartwheels. Some of the adults had joined hands in a round dance, hopping and skipping as if they had forgotten everything in the joy of sun and wind. Druon lay sprawled full length on the grass, his massive belly rising and falling in deep, regular breaths, a blissful smile on his face.

And amid all this unthinking exultation, Gaire knelt beside Liuria, and the pad he held against her shoulder was soaked through with fresh blood.

Allie shook her head to clear it. "They *have* gone mad," she murmured. "What is it?"

"The landvirtue," Domerc said. "It is rising like a river in spate. Most of the folk around Brefania have some touch of Landsenser blood, enough to feel it and be renewed from it. They're drunk on it now."

Allie felt bubbles of happiness floating through her. "Heal Liuria," she said. "You needed landvirtue. Here it is. Fabre will keep the cloud monsters away. Heal her now. If it's strong enough to make everybody drunk, surely it's strong enough for healing."

"Too strong, maybe," Domerc muttered, as he knelt opposite Gaire and placed his own hand over the blood-stained pad. He closed his eyes for a moment in concentration.

Allie blinked. Domerc seemed to be flickering like a

failing picture. No, that wasn't it. He wasn't fading out; he was growing more real, more intensely *there*, in short bursts that made the moments when he was just an ordinary young man seem as if he were fading out. The brightness around him hurt her eyes.

Liuria stirred and mumbled something. Domerc laid his other hand on her strapped-down arm. A moment later she sat up and said, quite clearly, "Get this damn bandage off me!"

Gaire started to unwrap his bindings. But Domerc knelt without moving, and the brilliance that flashed and coruscated around him was almost blinding now. Allie thought in a confused way about electric wires, and overloads, and a lot of things she had never understood either in Physics 101 or in Fundamentals of Magical Theory. Then she did not think at all, but moved forward to lay her hand on Domerc's shoulder.

Strength and energy and light poured through her. She felt one moment of incredulous joy, as her body remembered what it was to be whole and free of cold and aching pains; then the light was almost too strong for her to hold, and all she could think of was the need to contain and absorb it. She could feel in her blood and bones what the Escorreans had tried to explain to her, the surging energy of the land that must grow and make life, that would make monsters if it could not flow freely into the crops and the animals and the people.

Iseu was singing now, and so were the others; or perhaps the singing was all inside her head. Later she was never able to recall the melodies that intertwined there; she could only say that it was the most beautiful song she had ever heard, the different lines of melody arching and intertwining like growing vines, blossoming like flowers, rising to a peak of ecstasy beyond anything she had felt before. The song vibrated through her; she was glass, she would shatter on the next note. No, she was crystal, she was light and ringing sound. . . .

The sound died away slowly, and Allie saw the

Greenway around her again, changed and yet unchanged. The slender trees were vibrant with life; the playing children were charged with all the beauty and possibility and heartbreak and joy of their future lives; the blades of grass beneath her feet were living emerald, translucent and glowing with life.

Domerc rose shakily to his feet. "It was too much for me," he said, "it would have consumed me. How did you *do* that?"

"Do what?" Allie said, noting ruefully that whatever had just happened didn't seem to have made her any more intelligent. More alive, yes—more alive than she had ever dreamed of being.

"She's a Landsenser," Liuria said. She was free of bandages now, rubbing the arm that had been broken with a bemused look as though she still expected to feel pain and splintered bone there.

"She can't be," Domerc said. "She isn't even Escorrean; she's from Elder World."

"So were we all, once, if the histories are true," Liuria reminded him. She gave Allie a cool measuring look. "Perhaps that landsense helped her to cross between the worlds."

Gaire, who had been squatting on his heels while his betters argued about things he didn't have to think about, jumped up and dashed through the archway of trees with a wild shout and hurled himself into a clump of thorny bushes.

"Now what's bitten *him*?" Domerc demanded.

Gaire emerged almost at once, his face streaming blood from the thorns. With him he pulled a bedraggled figure, a tottering old man in a torn and filthy gown. "It's that there wizard of En Savaric's," he announced triumphantly. "Sneaking around and spying on us!"

"I was not!" Aigar straightened and tried to flick some of the mud off his gown with the tips of his fingers. "I was peacefully making my way back to the University. Shocked and dismayed though I was to be caught up in Savaric's evil war, it seems he is dead now and you people are fully competent to restore order without my aid. Therefore, since my duties as Dean of the College of Magical Arts require my presence in Coindra—"

"It won't work, Aigar," Liuria said, almost kindly. "There are too many witnesses to swear to your helping Savaric. Me, for starters. You stood by while his soldiers broke my arm."

"It doesn't look broken now," Aigar said, "and really, my dear girl, what did you expect me to do? I was as much his prisoner as you; surely you could see that."

Domerc groaned. "He can't talk his way out of this one. Can he?" He appealed to Allie.

"I—don't—think—so," said Allie. "Talking isn't really the point, is it?" Aigar could talk rings around her or anybody else. He could probably outthink her, too.

"So what?" she murmured to herself. "So *what?*" She felt giddy with freedom, and maybe with the power of the landvirtue too. In this new clear light she might not be any smarter, but she could *see* clearly. And what she saw was that as long as she didn't need his approval, Aigar couldn't control her. No matter how many clever tales he told.

They had better move fast, though, before he got his wits back and worked some magecraft on them. Allie stepped around Liuria and walked slowly up to Aigar, her hand on Fabre's bondsoul.

"You might as well tell us everything," she said. "Starting with what you and Savaric were up to in these hills last spring."

I haven't the faintest idea what you're talking about," Aigar said shakily. "There's no crime in visiting an old friend, is there? *I* wasn't responsible for Savaric's greed—"

"But you took full advantage of it," Allie interrupted him. "You were going to raise landmonsters and turn them into a mercenary army for him, weren't you? Then the two of you would own all Escorre. But something went wrong. I suspect your first bondsouls couldn't control the landmonsters adequately. They kept them away from you and Savaric, but no more. They killed Biatris Landsenser, and you put the blame on Domerc. Then you brought me from Elder World and tried to bind my soul to use against the landmonsters."

"I *did* bind your soul," Aigar said. He seemed to stand taller as he gave up his lies and evasions. "By blood and silk and the seven Names, your soul is mine and I command you to cease this meddling with affairs beyond your understanding."

His voice was a grating pain through her bones; she felt herself shaking with the desire to fall down and beg forgiveness. The weight of the command was too heavy for her. She sank to her knees, bent forward, rested the palms of her hands on the ground.

Strength flowed into her from the grass and earth; not enough to stand up, but enough to raise her head and look at Aigar. His attention was no longer on her; the terrible syllables of the mage-chant rolled on over her head, and the stones beneath the grass shook and she could feel the echo of that quivering in her bones, in Domerc's, in Iseu's. Somewhere one of the children wailed; the sound ended in a frightened gasp, as though Aigar's magery had sucked the child's breath out. They were all caught in the intricate weave of sound and sense, flies in Aigar's web, and Allie's protests were no more than an impotent buzzing.

Where's a land-monster when you need one? she thought. But the virtue was drained out of this part of the earth now. She had seen to that. All the strength and wild magic of the earth was in her and Domerc, and it was less than nothing against Aigar's years of training. The chant pressed her body down flat against the earth, and she felt as breathless and weak as she had that time Judy Scher hooked her ankle and brought her down in the middle of a hockey game.

Breath knocked out of her.

There was something in that, if she could only *think* through the droning of the chant. Aigar wasn't even looking at her now, he didn't need to, she was so weak, nothing, all her reasonable arguments no more than a fly buzzing against a window. He was standing so close. She couldn't think about defying him; her mind skittered away from any attempt to plan, deafened by the thrumming tones of his voice that told her *obey, obey, obey*.

There was a crooked branch on the ground a few inches from her hand; one of the children had been improvising a game using a rounded stone for a ball.

Like hockey.

Judy Scher.

Breath knocked out of her . . .

Allie didn't think about it. Her fingers flowed like seeping water towards the stick and she *didn't think about it didn't think about it don't think about a blue monkey*, someone said in a story out of her childhood, *and the pot will be filled with gold*. Judy Scher charging down the hockey field with that terrifying grin on her face, and the stick catching her ankle, not fair, not fair, but nobody saw. Allie held the anger of that moment when she'd found herself face-down and breathless while the game swirled around her. She could be there now: she could be hearing the screaming of the coach instead of the deep surging mage-chant; she could take revenge on Judy now, think about Judy, only about Judy . . .

Her fingers closed about the stick and she jerked it sideways and forwards in a convulsive motion. *Somebody* was standing in the path of the stick; *somebody* stumbled and fell on top of Allie, and the bone-shaking sounds stopped, and then there was even more weight on her and she squeaked in protest.

"Sorry," said Gaire, heaving Aigar up. There was a rag stuffed in the Dean's mouth, and Gaire had one hand clamped over the rag to keep it in place. "Didn't mean to squash you, little one. Needed to shut him up, though, and quickest way was to fall on him."

Allie nodded and concentrated on getting her own breath back. Two of her ribs hurt when she breathed in, and she felt light-headed and sick to her stomach; but that was nothing compared with the relief of having Aigar's chant stop before it dissolved her like water.

"Can you folk make magic without your songs?" Gaire demanded of Domerc.

Domerc shook his head, looking dazed. "No—the theory of harmonies—well, never mind that. How did you *do* that?" he demanded of Allie, sounding more indignant than properly grateful. "Even I couldn't move, and you- you're just a first-year—"

"I didn't think about a blue monkey," Allie told him.

CHAPTER FOURTEEN

By the time Iseu had led her people back to the Stonehold, Savaric's mercenary army had melted away into the hills to the north and the scrubby bushes to the south, the long sloping lands leading to the sea.

"They'll be back," she fretted.

"Not they," Centor said. His hand was still red and swollen, but he was already trying to pick out a dance tune on his vielle. "Mercenaries go where the pay is. Savaric gone, and for all they know, landmonsters raging out of control, and you in a fine position to make counterclaim to Savaric's lands? They'll not wait around to see who takes the lands; in a week they'll be serving the Coast Merchants' Guild or the Pirates' Guild, whichever has the fuller coffers this month."

"How did they all find out so fast?"

Centor shrugged. "Lendoman. Or mercenary magic. I don't *know* how they find things out so quickly, but haven't you ever noticed how mercenary troops show up about three minutes after somebody's decided to increase the war budget? Knowing who's got a purse full of Dracs and Griffons is part of their business. And it's obvious," he added thoughtfully, "that there won't be many Griffons to spare around here for a while. Savaric made sure of that."

"That he did," said Iseu. Her lips set in a tight line, she left Centor tuning his vielle and went on to deal with the hundred and one other matters requiring her immediate attention. She had delegated tasks wherever possible: Druon was in charge of finding out just what foodstores they had left and dividing the stocks so that nobody would starve while they reclaimed burnt fields and destroyed steadings. Domerc, eyes red with fatigue, was using one of the voicebubbles to make contact with anybody and everybody who might buy Brefania wine before they found out just how badly Brefania was going to need money for rebuilding. Allie and Liuria were asleep on a pile of cushions, red hair and dark twined like a pair of exhausted kittens. Iseu longed desperately to join them, but there were other tasks first. Someone had to see that Aigar was delivered over to the proctor-mages of the University; somebody had to make it safe for Allie to go back to Coindra and retrieve the partial soulbond Aigar had made from her blood. Iseu squinted at Allie's sleeping face. She was so pale that her skin was almost translucent. How much longer could she last without the soulbond?

At least Aigar himself was no immediate problem. Tatiragno, the old herb-daddy who'd surprised himself and everybody else by calling up mage-fire to destroy a landmonster in the caves, had gone off to investigate Iseu's stillroom as soon as they reached the Stronghold. The sour-smelling brew he'd produced from laurat falbenc and a few unspecified roots was guaranteed, he said, to give anybody a sore throat for a day and a night.

"Good for a scolding wife," he cackled, "or to silence a nasty mage."

Aigar had been persuaded, not without some difficulty, to swallow the brew as soon as Gaire removed the dirty rags from his mouth. Now, hands loosely bound, he whispered angry phrases as Iseu borrowed Domerc from his task of wine-selling long enough to make contact with the great system of voice-bubbles at Coindra. His voice, even in whispers, sent little snakes crawling up and down Iseu's spine. But he could not chant the mage-songs. He could not call upon any power except his own persuasive way with words.

"Give him some more of Tatiragno's tea," Domerc suggested after he'd reached Acting Dean Fassolaris. The woman had simply not *heard* anything he tried to tell her about Aigar's plots with Savaric.

"If she's determined to believe whatever he says," Iseu said glumly, "what difference does it make whether he can chant or not?"

Domerc rubbed his eyes. "Well, for one thing, Evgena won't be coming herself. It makes her sick at her stomach to tread the journey-mazes. She'll discover some crisis in Coindra that demands her personal attention, and send a couple of proctor-mages to get Aigar and 'straighten out those young fools,'" he quoted the Acting Dean wryly. "And the proctor-mages *may* be inclined to listen to reason—as long as we make sure that reason is all they listen to. I do hope they don't send Rollan, though," he added. "He made proctor through sheer seniority. I don't think he has the necessary equipment for listening to reason."

"I just hope they send somebody soon," Iseu said. She had half a dozen people clamoring for her instructions. By the time she'd straightened out the quarrel over use of the still-room and seen to having clean straw laid down in all the outbuildings that were used for sleeping quarters, the proctor-mages delegated by Evgena Fassolaris had reached the Brefania journey-maze and were being escorted to the chamber where Aigar sat.

One of them was Rollan.

Aigar sat up straighter when the proctor-mages entered the room. "About time you got here," he rasped in the husky whisper that was all Daddy Tatiragno's tea had left of his voice. "We need someone to talk some sense into these young fools. They meant well, I'm sure. Stress of the war. Shock, probably. They actually think *I* had something to do with Savaric's folly!"

"Not think," Domerc corrected him, "know. I saw you with Savaric."

Aigar raised his brows. "The boy still bears me a

grudge, I fear, for reporting his dereliction of duty some time since."

Rollan nodded. "Remember the case. Bad show. Expect better of the Seignor families."

"*Salamanders!*" Domerc exploded. "I tell you he had his hands in the dough of every pie Savaric cooked."

"The story," Aigar yawned, "is familiar." Somehow he managed to infuse his whisper with infinite patience and boredom.

"This time," Domerc pointed out, "I'm not the only witness."

Liuria woke up first; Allie groaned and muttered something incomprehensible and fell back among the cushions. She was so fine-drawn by now, Iseu had the momentary fancy that she could see the cushions through Allie's slender body and translucent skin.

"I heard Aigar tell Savaric that he had made a soul-bond with my friend Allie's blood," Liuria said, rubbing the sleep out of her eyes and pushing her mop of black curls aside. "And he told Savaric to break my arm. To make Allie come out of the cave."

Rollan looked curiously at her. "Which arm?"

"The left—oh. Allie healed it."

"This scholar Allie," the other proctor-mage said. "Where is she?"

"That's another thing," Domerc interrupted. "You must take her back to Coindra at once."

Rollan looked down his nose. "First-year scholars do not say *must* to proctors, young man. But I do have every intention of hearing what this girl has to say in the matter."

Allie came out of her dreamy sleep like a swimmer floating up through murky water. It would be so easy to stay under there. But Domerc and Liuria kept talking at her until it was easier to wake up, even if it was only to tell them to go away. And when she understood what they wanted, she had to stay awake, however reluctantly.

She confirmed everything Domerc and Liuria had said; Aigar countered with bland comments about young girls and their imaginations and hinted that Allie resented him because he'd refused the bribes she offered him for a passing mark in Fundamentals of Magical Theory.

"Oh, really," Allie said. Disgust lent her voice the illusion of strength. "Sex for grades, huh? I bet you've done that one before. Fool some poor kid into playing up to you for a grade, and then turn her in to the proctors for attempted bribery, and fail her anyway."

From the expression on Rollan's face, he recognized the story. Allie wondered briefly how many times Aigar had done that, and to whom; but she was too tired to care. The proctors were arguing among themselves now in hushed voices that she couldn't follow. Perhaps she could just take a little nap and wake up again when they were ready . . .

"Wild accusations," the one called Rollan said sourly, and the other proctor nodded.

"No *evidence*."

"Wait a minute." Allie stood and was disgusted to find that the effort left her dizzy. "You want evidence?" She reached inside the neck of her tunic and hauled up the cord that held Fabre's bondsoul.

"What an ugly piece of pottery," said Rollan.

"I think it's rather cute," said the other one, "in a pudgy sort of way."

Rollan snorted. "You would. Don't you see what it's shaped like? Girl must belong to one of those back-country fertility cults."

Lemme at them! Fabre's furious demand vibrated through the palm of Allie's hand.

"I plan to," she told him.

"Plan what?" Rollan demanded.

By way of answer, Allie slipped the cord over her head and held out the pendant to Rollan. "Here. Hold this." Prudently, she kept a firm grasp of the cord. As soon as he took the pendant from her, Rollan gasped and dropped it.

That makes me sick! Fabre complained as soon as Allie caught him. *How would you like to be flung through the air and dangled on the end of a little string?*

"I'm sorry! I didn't know you could feel it!"

I can feel anything I touch.

There was more than a hint of smug satisfaction in the thought. Allie's cheeks flamed. "In that case," she said firmly, "I'm wearing you on the *outside* of my tunic from now on."

"Has the girl run mad?" the other proctor appealed to Rollan.

Rollan, his lips gray with shock, shook his head. "No. It's dark magery, or else a mommet; I can't tell."

Lemme at him, lemme at him! Fabre demanded when Allie touched him. *Coward! If he'd held me a moment longer he'd have been able to tell! I'll fry his fingers, the chicken-brained cackler!*

Allie held out the pendant. "If you'll just hold on to it this time?" she suggested.

Rollan and the other proctor reached out simultaneously. For a moment, while the three of them all held the pendant, Allie could feel all their thoughts mixing and twining around the furious burst of leashed energy that was all that remained of Fabre. "That red-haired scholar who roomed with Domerc . . . *That's me, Rollan, you prick-faced fart* . . . Never did have any manners . . . *Sorry, Allie, but I've got to shock some sense into them* . . . Didn't he turn up missing a few days ago? . . . Not missing. Dead. A nasty killing. *Now listen for once in your sorry life, Rollan. I am Fabre. Aigar trapped my soul in this thing of clay and fire . . .*"

Allie found that she was crying as Fabre went through the story in enough detail to convince the slowest and dullest of proctors. She let go of the pendant and leaned back against the wall. It was too much, having to hear it all, hearing the sadness under Fabre's belligerent tone. She was too tired. She was too far from home—wherever that might be. At least they might let her sleep!

She felt as though she had just nodded off again when someone grabbed her wrist and yanked her to her feet.

"What did you do that for?" she said, or tried to say. She had the feeling that her words were dissolving into the mist that floated between her eyes and Liuria's.

Instead of answering her, Liuria looked at Domerc. "She's getting worse," Liuria said. "Do you think she's strong enough to tread the mazeways back to Coindra?"

"She'll have to. Nothing but getting her bondsoul back will cure her." It was Domerc's voice that answered, firm and know-it-all as ever. Allie groped at her neck and felt Fabre's pendant heavy in her hand. *Go with them, go with them, go with them,* Fabre urged, *or end as I am. You must rejoin your soul.*

"Don't b'lieve in souls," she mumbled. "Channeling, reincarnation, loada b.s."

"Now she's delirious!" Liuria sounded as though she were about to cry. "I don't understand why she got so much worse so fast."

"Lot of factors," Domerc said. "She should have collapsed hours ago; I think she's been drawing strength from the landvirtue all along, without noticing it. So what did we do? Brought her into the Stonehold, with three levels of stone and flagstone between her and the land. Not a good move. Then, when they took Aigar back to Coindra, the bond between them attenuated and she couldn't take it any more."

"They took Aigar back to Coindra?" Allie repeated. "Already?"

"Salamanders! You really did go back to sleep sitting up, didn't you? Yes, the proctors already escorted Aigar back along the mazeways. That's probably why you're feeling so tired. You need to be near him."

"Ick," Allie said. "I do *not*."

"Not impugning your taste," Domerc said. "It's the bonding spell. You're mostly drawn to the bondsoul itself, but also to Aigar, since he's the one who set the spell."

"*Ick*," Allie said again.

"Well, at least that woke you up! Don't worry; we'll get you back together."

Allie followed Domerc and Liuria through the halls of the Stonehold to the room where Brefania maintained a private journey-maze. For convenience, it was a part of one of the great underground storage cellars, rather than a separate room. People were piling straw-packed baskets of wine along the far wall, ready to sell off Brefania's reserve stocks for money to get them through the season of devastation. Domerc ignored them and led the way straight to the corner where the beginning and ending patterns of the journey-maze were marked with red and ochre lines on the stone flags. He and Liuria began to chant two opposing melodies while they guided Allie's steps along the ochre lines. As they sang, the lines extended themselves, creating a looping path over the stones. The intricate counterpoint that created their path rose about them. Interesting magic, Allie thought sleepily. Too hard for a first-year scholar, though. Too many different rhythms mingling, too many melodies twining and branching . . .

The sense of things intertwining and separating coiled like snakes in the back of her throat. Her stomach wrenched in revolt as the world around her turned briefly inside out, then reformed itself in the shape of the Journey-Maze Hall in Coindra.

Through the open door Allie could sense mist and light and the bustle of a university in session. She made for the door without waiting for her companions, took a deep breath of Coindra air, and sat down ungracefully at the edge of a stone walkway. She felt better already; but she needed to touch the ground. There was bare damp earth just beyond the stone, and a riot of squishy green vines coming out of the soil and bursting into improbably bright flowers. Allie wrapped one of the vines around her wrist and laid her palm flat on the earth. She could feel the beating of the landvirtue like a pulse in the earth, strong and steady, not insulted or wild here, a binding strength that flowed through land and vines and hands and blood and bone.

In the damp morning air she could feel something else, the tug of the invisible cord that bound her to the amulet Aigar had created. "Blood and silk," she said, standing. She took two steps along the tug of the cord. It was drawing her straight to Aigar's laboratory, in the heart of the College of Magical Arts. With every step the tug grew stronger, and so did she.

"Aigar won't be there," Domerc reassured her before she thought to worry about it.

"I assumed he would be in jail."

"What's a jail?"

"Place where they lock up bad guys and don't let them out," Allie wondered whether Escorre had anything like a parole board. "Not for a while, anyway."

"Oh." Domerc jerked his head at a graceful building of serpentine marble, to the right of the Magical Arts complex. "We call it the Faculty Center. As Dean, he's entitled to appeal to be heard by the general faculty and to have his case discussed by them as long as they need before reaching a decision. Personally," Domerc said, "I'd rather take the decision as read and go Guildless, but then I know how it feels to be on the wrong side of a Guild hearing; Aigar doesn't. I suppose he'll do anything to put off the decision as long as possible."

"But he will—they won't let him—"

"There are ways," Domerc said, "to strip a mage of his powers. Permanently. There's no way to take away his landsense, but once he's expelled from that Guild too, there'll be no way for him to use it." He shivered in the watery morning light. "Then again," he said, almost inaudibly, "I suppose I might want to put it off too. There is nothing worse than having the sense and being blocked from using it."

The bleak note in his voice reminded Allie that Domerc was still banned from the Landsensers Guild. He knew exactly what he was talking about.

And the triple arches of the main building in the Magical Arts complex rose before them. The fountain splashed and black-robèd scholars hurried through the courtyards, chattering about Laboratory Magic and who could lend them some notes on de Breuil and whether anybody had enough Dracs to pay for a round at the Blue Pigeon. Allie put one hand on Fabre's bondsoul, and the other hand in Liuria's, and stood for a moment just outside the arches, savoring this moment of home-coming. A few scholars glanced curiously at the shabby trio. One muttered, "And not a decent gown among the three of them! Honestly, I don't know what the new scholars are coming to! Better not let a proctor catch you children without your gowns," he warned them.

Allie grinned. "I think this is where I came in." The pull of the amulet was very strong now, a tide sweep-ing her forward. She had only to let it carry her through the dim antechamber where clerks paged endlessly through the black-bound rolls of the College, through the cluttered library and into the laboratory whose door no one had even bothered to shut, since everyone knew the Dean kept it keyspelled whenever he was absent.

Domerc and Liuria stopped at the open doorway as if they'd been caught in a spider's web.

"I *thought* so," Allie said over her shoulder. "He set the keyspell to admit me, when I was working for him; and why bother to reset it, when he thought I was dead? Aigar never did pay attention to details," she said with a grin. "Look at this mess!"

"I am looking," said Domerc, somewhat hollowly. "It could take the rest of the semester to find a little scrap of bloody silk in here. Can't you sense where it is?"

Allie shook her head. "Too close, now." It was like trying to pick out one line of melody when a dozen rock bands were playing on festival stages.

"Maybe the faculty could ask Aigar," Liuria suggested, "during the hearings."

"Maybe," Allie said, scanning the cluttered shelves with a frown, "maybe there's somebody else we could ask."

A faint chittering and squeaking came from one of the high dusty shelves where Aigar kept his bottles and potions. Allie dusted off a stool with the palm of her hand, dragged it over to the wall, climbed up and stood on tiptoes, feeling along the top shelf for something she'd touched just once before. She knew what it was now, that touch of something at once warm and cold, moving and still, alive and dead.

She had been carrying its counterpart around her neck since they fled through the caverns of Brefania.

Now she touched the thing that had startled her so much once before, and grasped it carefully in one hand, and gave it its true name.

"Janifer," Allie said. "You are Janifer, aren't you? And we're going to get you and Fabre out of this, only first I would appreciate it very much if you would tell me where Aigar hid my bondsoul."

She held Janifer in her hands for a long moment, then set him down gently on a low shelf and went to the overflowing wicker basket of trash in the center of the room.

"Aigar," Domerc said from the doorway, "is crazy. What if somebody had emptied that?"

"Nobody ever did clean up in here," Allie said, hanging over the trash basket, "except me. And— Ha! What a slob," she said, pulling out the once-white silk bundle. It was stained with some red sauce from one of Aigar's laboratory meals, and it smelled like stillwein. And as soon as Allie had it in her hands, she felt as if she'd just drunk three cups of espresso at the Cappucino Cat in Vista View.

"You look more awake," Domerc said.

"Awake?" Allie bounced on the tips of her toes. "I'm *wired*. Let's go conquer the world!"

CHAPTER FIFTEEN

Wired or not, though, her body was still exhausted. What Allie really wanted was to sleep for three days and then go home. Unfortunately, neither of these was an option at the moment.

"You have to testify in the hearings," Liuria said.

Allie smothered a yawn. "Can't I do that tomorrow? Domerc said they were going to drag on forever."

"All right," Liuria said, "but let me take Fabre and Janifer. They're what will destroy Aigar. And remember, you can't go home until you've testified. It wouldn't be fair."

"*Home?*" Domerc demanded. "You want to take yourself and your landsense back to Elder World? Don't be an idiot. You have to stay here and join the Guild."

"Who died and made *you* God? I don't have to stay here. I don't *belong* here."

"Well, you don't belong in any world without landsense," Domerc snapped, "and you'd find that out soon enough if I did let you go back. Besides, we don't know exactly how Aigar's 'tween-worlds spell worked."

"I bet Janifer does," Allie said sweetly.

"We'd have to test it first."

Liuria patted her brother on the shoulder and took Allie's hand. "I think what my retarded brother is trying to say, Allie, is that he'll miss you. We all will. Go on, Domerc, admit it. It won't kill you."

"Of *course* I'll miss her," Domerc said, glaring at his

sister, "but that is not the point. Sending somebody with the landsense into a world where they can't use it would be criminal. If Allie has been given this talent, she has to use it. Otherwise it would be like—like—like never getting her bondsoul back together with her body."

"You don't know how that feels," Allie protested.

"And you," said Domerc, "don't know how it feels to have a talent you're not allowed to use."

Domerc, she has to *go* back to Elder World," Liuria said slowly, "but she doesn't have to *stay* there."

"I see no reason to allow her to risk the journey-maze in the first place."

"You're a fool, Domerc. She can't just disappear. She has to go back and tell her family what happened." Liuria frowned for a moment. "Well, perhaps not that exactly. But she has to tell them where she's been and where she's going." Another frown. "Oh, salamanders! Well, anyway, she can't just disappear. She has to tell them *something*. How would you feel if I took off into Elder World and never came back?"

"Better than if it's Allie who never comes back," Domerc said promptly, "I never wanted a bratty little sister anyway."

Allie cleared her throat. "Excuse me for butting in here, but isn't it my future we're discussing? Don't I get some say in it?"

"What do you really want?" Domerc demanded. "To stay here where you have a place, a talent, a Guild, people who like you—"

"Love you," Liuria corrected.

"Oh, all right. Anyway. Do you want all this?" His arm swept a circle that somehow encompassed the stony streets and red-tiled roofs of Coindra, the green living walls of Astire, the caves of Brefania, the river Verenha flowing down towards a sea Allie had never seen. "Or do you want to go back to a world where there's no virtue in the land and no proper work for you to do?"

"I want," Allie said, "to have the *choice*."

She insisted on that through the weeks that followed, while she was called in again and yet again to tell her story to the assembled faculty. Domerc and Janifer and the senior mages all worked daily on the task of releasing Fabre's bondsoul; at night, Domerc conducted his own unauthorized laboratory experiments on what Janifer could tell him of the journey-maze spell.

The night work went better than the day; another proof, Domerc said drily, that committees never accomplished anything worthwhile.

"If it's going so well," Allie demanded, "let's see the results."

Domerc pointed at the demon-white rats they'd trapped in Aigar's lab. "See that cage? It's been to Elder World and back."

"Then you can send me back now?" It had been six weeks. And Allie kept just happening to meet new people, all of whom just happened to wear dusty green robes, and all of whom welcomed her like a long-lost and much-loved cousin. The Landsensers Guild really wanted her. And Allie's resolve was weakening. It would be so easy to stay here, to take up the work and place that belonged to her. If Domerc or somebody else didn't work out the alterations to the journey-maze spell soon, she would be too comfortable and too happy in Escorre to take the risk of going home. And it wasn't right. A person couldn't just disappear and leave other people who loved them, in their own way, forever wondering what had happened. Allie might not have understood that at the beginning of the semester, but she knew it now. Besides, she had some suspicions about Mom. This landsense of hers had to come from somewhere.

"There were two cages of of demon-rats," Domerc said. "The first one I sent did not return. I think it has something to do with the phases of the moon. You want to be stuck in Elder World forever?"

"I might," Allie said slowly, "decide to stay." The thought *hurt*. But how would her parents feel if she disappeared forever? They might hurt just as badly. She couldn't know.

"You're not going," Domerc said flatly, "until we are sure you *can* come back if you want to. You owe us that much."

Allie nodded. She felt torn between debts and desire. Could her parents stand it if she disappeared into Escorre? Could she stand it if she didn't come back? Could she make a place for herself in the world that used to be home, find a use for her landsense there? And what about her friends in Escorre, who had saved her life and shown her how to live it?

There was only one way to settle the questions. And when Domerc finally admitted that the journey-maze spell was completely worked out, Allie told him she was ready to go back. It wasn't true, of course. She would never be ready. But that was no one's business but hers.

"I just hope the moon there matches ours," Domerc said.

"It will. Everything else does . . . sort of." The shapes of the continents, the seas, the color of the sun, the changing of the seasons. "And it takes twenty-eight days from full moon to full moon, just like here."

"*Sort of* completes no cantrips," Domerc said darkly. "Check the moon as soon as you're back in Elder World. You leave here on the waning crescent, return on the waxing crescent. We'll be here three moons running to call you back."

"Don't I have to match the chant?"

Domerc gave her one of his Seignor looks, all long nose and hauteur. "*Think*, Allie. How would the rats have come back if they had to do anything intelligent? I've improved on Aigar's original spell, naturally."

"Naturally," Allie echoed. Domerc missed the trace of sarcasm in her voice.

"All you have to do is be in the same place at the right time."

❧❧❧❧❧

That sounded simple enough when Domerc said it. But when Allie actually walked blinking from sun-dappled grass to the glittering lighted windows in Orly Airport, when the journey-maze chant faded behind her to be replaced by the shuffle of feet and the squeaking of baggage carts, she pinched herself and rubbed her eyes and could not quite believe that Escorre had been anything but a dream—much less that Domerc or anybody else would be able to bring her back.

The world she had once been used to crashed upon her ears and eyes like surf on a rocky beach: so many lights, so much noise, so many machines and people rushing everywhere! In a daze, like a jet-lagged tourist, she followed signs and stood in lines and eventually fished out of her backpack, battered and stained, her return ticket to New York.

While the clerk was checking her documents, she stared at a calendar on the wall and noticed that two months had passed since she left America. All right. She'd certainly been *somewhere* . . .

"You've certainly been *somewhere*," Dad said when she got to New York, "but it wasn't the Universite de Massat. Did you think I wouldn't check up on you? You never even registered there. Your mother would have been worried sick if she'd known."

"You didn't tell her?"

Dad snorted. "What was there to tell? You made enough of a fuss about going; I should have realized you'd have to show your independence in some half-baked manner like running off. Where've you been, anyway, shacked up with some boy? No, don't tell me. I don't want to know."

Allie stood a little straighter. "Actually," she said, "I was studying. I happened to register at the wrong university."

"Oh? And what exactly did you study?"

Fundamentals of Magical Theory, Allie thought. Introductory Art of Casting (Lab Section). *Algebra*. Oh, and there was this real interesting field trip and practical demonstration of Raising Landmonsters . . .

"Oh, just your basic intro survey courses," she said finally. "You were right, Dad; there was a lot I didn't learn at Vista View. In fact, I'm going back where I was studying to learn more."

"Oh, no, you aren't," he contradicted her. "I'm not paying for your pleasure jaunts around Europe. You could have had a semester at Massat; you blew it; that's the end of it."

"You don't have to pay for anything," Allie said. "I've been . . . offered a job back there."

"What kind of a job can you get without a degree? Flipping burgers?"

"Better than that," Allie said. She searched for words to make the translation, but couldn't find any. No matter how she tried to explain the Landsensers Guild, Dad dismissed it as "youth hostel work," "day labor," or "freelance gardening."

It didn't really matter, Allie decided, that she couldn't explain the magic and the landsense and what the Guild was really about. Her father wasn't about to listen long enough to grasp any of that anyway. He *knew* that nobody could get a decent job without a college degree, and he *knew* that Allie had no skills or talents, and it was eighteen years too late to convince him otherwise.

"I'm sorry," Allie said at last. "You can't understand. I can't tell you. I don't suppose it's your fault. But it's not mine either."

"Kids." Dad shook his head. "You think you can screw around, do whatever you like, then when it doesn't work out you can wail *you don't understand me*. You're gonna be just like your mother, a perpetual adolescent looking for Never-Never Land."

"Dad," Allie said, "I might not come back for a long time. I'd like to say good-bye without bickering."

"Nonsense. You'll be crawling back as soon as you run out of money."

And that, Allie supposed, was that. Perhaps she would have better luck with her mother.

At first it seemed that was true. Allie didn't get the instant rush of homecoming she had expected when she finally reached Vista View; instead she found herself noticing the smog and the freeways and the new housing development that had filled the valley below University Heights. All those buildings on what had been good fertile soil made Allie nervous now.

Mom agreed instantly that the new housing development was a terrible thing, and would Allie like to join her in a protest march on Saturday?

"It's too late," Allie said gloomily. Sitting cross-legged on one of the Indian print cushions that Mom used for furniture, she bit into a sesame bran cookie and admired the forest of hanging plants and crystals with which Mom had transformed this one-room apartment. "The houses are already there. Nobody *respects* land here."

"The Indians used to respect Mother Earth," Mom asserted. "All Indian culture was based on worshipping the land and taking only what they needed to survive."

A partial semester at Coindra had taught Allie something about the dangers of sweeping generalizations. "Um . . . maybe," she said diplomatically. "But listen, Mom, what would you think if I told you there was a place where people *really* respect the earth—they *have* to— and I know how to get there? I've *been* there. Dad wouldn't listen to me. . . ."

Mom listened, all right. She let Allie tell her the whole story of her arrival in Escorre, giving little cries of delight and inserting comments like, "You should learn to read auras. I'm sure Aigar's was almost black."

When Allie finished, though, her mother gave a deep sigh and said, "Isn't dream travel wonderful? I'm sure there is an important Life Lesson for you in all this, Allie."

"Mom. It *happened*."

"Of course it did," Mom said instantly, "you know I believe in psychic power. It was probably a message being channeled to you by one of the Older Ones, and your subconscious turned it into a story about being at school in a very strange place. Now we have to meditate and find out what the true underlying message was."

"You could come with me," Allie said. "Didn't you ever wonder why both of us are so good at growing plants?"

Her mother shrugged. "Some people just have a green thumb. It's not important. Do you think you'd be able to practice your astral travel if you wore one of the crystal medicine bags my friend Nekh-ra-Lissa makes? That's not her birth name," she added at the look on Allie's face. "It's her True Name. She discovered it when she regressed through past lives and discovered that she was once . . ."

"Let me guess," Allie said wearily. "An Egyptian priestess."

Mom clapped her hands. "Wonderful! You've inherited my psychic gift!"

"No, Mom, but I think I got something else from you. I'm a Landsenser, and I think you could be too. I'm going back to take that job they offered me," Allie said. She was certain now. If she stayed in this world, would the pressure of the unused landsense make her start babbling about channeling and reincarnation and pyramid power? That must have been what happened to Mom. Allie felt strong and sure. She would save both of them. Mom would come to Escorre with her and find out what she could really do with that sense of hidden power that she'd never been able to use here.

But Mom shook her head and smiled. "I don't understand exactly where you think you're going, Allie, dear, but I couldn't possibly take a trip right now. There are too many important things going on. I've been invited to be a co-leader in my candle meditation class, and there's a lecture on Moldavian crystal power next week, and the Psychic Fair the weekend after that. You really ought to stay here," she said earnestly. "Northern California is where it's all happening."

"Not for me, it isn't," Allie said. "But I can't go back until the next quarter-moon, so I'll go to the meditation class and the Moldavian crystals lecture with you. Have to pass on the psychic fair, though. That's the weekend when the moon is waxing, and . . . Oh, no!" *All you have to do is be in the same place at the right time.* Why hadn't she thought of that?

"What's the matter, dear?"

"I have to be at Orly Airport in two weeks," Allie said. "No. There's no way I can earn the money. They said they'd try for three moons, though. Do you think I could earn enough for a standby ticket to Paris in three months? I could get a job waiting tables at the Tofu Shop. Tips are crummy, though," she said, remembering her last summer stint there. "Maybe I'd better try some upscale place like the Steak Shoppe."

Mom stood up and began rummaging through the bricks-and-board bookcase filled with paperbacks on astral travel and inner children and star visitors. "No daughter of mine," she said calmly, "is going to spend three months in a place full of red meat and death vibrations. Besides, I don't think you could save enough. I have an emergency fund somewhere. . . . Ha! I knew it had to be some place logical." She opened a copy of *Inner Peace, Outer Wealth* and took out a slim white envelope marked, "Dream Notes."

"I figured nobody would bother to open it just to read about my dreams," she explained, tearing the envelope open. "Here you are." She held out ten crisp one-hundred dollar bills.

"Mom! Where did you get that?"

"I've always had a green thumb," her mother said calmly, "as you pointed out. I have ways of supplementing my income that I thought you were too young to know about."

"That's enough to get both of us to Paris!"

Her mother shook her head again. "No, dear. It's very kind of you, I'm sure, but I really don't want to leave Vista View. All my friends and classes are here, and Nekhra-Lissa says I'm on the verge of a really major spiritual breakthrough."

"Mom, I might not be able to come back for a long time."

Her mother swept her into an incense-scented embrace. "Darling, I know, and I'll miss you, but don't be afraid. We'll check on your soul travel every week in meditation class. I don't understand exactly what you're going to do," Mom added, "or where you're going, but the important thing is that it's what *you* want. Remember, each of us has to find her own path through the forest. Mine," she said so firmly that Allie gave up arguing, "is here."

Two weeks later, Allie walked through the mirror-bright confusion of Orly Airport once again. And again. And again.

By three A.M., the few travelers passing through the airport were too tired to care about a red-haired American girl with tears in her eyes who seemed bent on wearing a path down one of the side corridors of Orly with her cold, bare feet. The shops were long closed. But the cleaning people and the night staff were beginning to give her Looks.

Why wasn't it working? Domerc had been so confident. Hah! Arrogant Seignor. She should have made Liuria check his lab notes. He'd gotten it wrong after all . . . or perhaps they weren't chanting her back . . . perhaps they'd forgotten her already. The old sense of being worthless and belonging nowhere swept over Allie again. She avoided the eyes of the janitor who had been about to approach her and slouched away from him, down the hall. *I'm nobody. I'm not here. You don't see me. Nothing is real nothing nothing nothing . . .*

But the cold glass window at the end of the hall was real and solid enough. Allie rubbed her nose and blinked back tears. Never mind why; it wasn't working. She'd said she would take that risk to come back once and say goodbye, but had she really meant it? No, of course not. She'd assumed Domerc would rescue her. She'd even spent the money left after buying her ticket on a stock of tapes and batteries to keep her Walkman going whenever she missed Elder World music: Nirvana, Turquoise Jelly, Sonic Youth, Rotten Jocks . . .

Sonic Youth. Allie's shoulders straightened. She'd been playing their new release on the Walkman that first day. Could it hurt to try again?

She tugged the Walkman out of her backpack, clipped it to the waistband of her jeans, fitted the headphones and started down the hall once again. As she walked, she half closed her eyes and whistled along with the tape, not quite in tune. She couldn't remember the variations she'd improvised that first time; she could only hope that something would repeat and match the journey-maze chant harmonies. If that was important. If anybody was even trying to reach her . . .

The lights seemed to be dimming around her, and she could no longer hear the creaking wheels of the janitor's cart. She was alone in a tunnel that was somehow not quite *there*.

Hope stabbed through Allie's chest; she thought she could hear voices singing outside the tape, twining in one of the complex multi-part melodies of Escorre. She closed her eyes and joined the whisper of not-quite-there voices, and they grew louder around her as she sang.

The sun was warm on her head, and the green weeds were chest-high all around her. Allie opened her eyes to an explosion of light and green and flowers. Liuria burst through the growing grasses to give her an explosive, smothering hug.

"So I don't have to do anything intelligent," Allie said

witheringly to Domerc. "Hah! Next time I trust myself to one of your spells, I'm checking the lab notes first."

"What?"

She pulled off the Walkman and handed it to him. "You might want to learn something about my kind of music. It seems to help with treading the journey-maze." The details could wait until later.

"Fabre came with us," Domerc said. Allie looked around in confusion, then understood as Domerc pulled a clay pendant out of his gown. She felt a lump in her throat.

"You didn't succeed in re-transforming him and Janifer?"

"Not yet," Domerc said. "Actually, Janifer says he prefers to stay in this form. He says you can get much more done when you don't waste time eating and sleeping and chasing girls."

"And Fabre?"

"Says he will be able to endure the term of his imprisonment more patiently if he can be, ah, close to you." Domerc held out the pendant. "Take him. *Please* take him. He hasn't given us a moment's peace since you left."

"He can only transmit his thoughts if you're touching him," Allie pointed out.

"He has been . . . ah . . . extending his range."

The pendant in Domerc's hand seemed to be jittering and trembling with suppressed fury. Cautiously, Allie touched it with one finger, then lifted it up and slipped the cord over her head.

That's better. Somehow Fabre had managed to insert himself under her shirt. He snuggled against her skin and made purring thoughts of contentment.

Domerc and Liuria were watching her anxiously. Allie looked over their shoulders to the golden walls and red-tiled roofs of Coindra, and a lump of pure happiness filled her throat. She blinked away tears of relief. Domerc, predictably, misunderstood.

"Regrets?"

"None," Allie said.

And Fabre, as usual, had the last word. *Next time, take me with you. I want to meet some more Elder World girls.*

Paksenarrion, a simple sheepfarmer's daughter, yearns for a life of adventure and glory, such as the heroes in songs and story. At age seventeen she runs away from home to join a mercenary company, and begins her epic life . . .

ELIZABETH MOON

THE DEED OF PAKSENARRION

"This is the first work of high heroic fantasy I've seen, that has taken the work of Tolkien, assimilated it totally and deeply and absolutely, and produced something altogether new and yet incontestably based on the master. . . . This is the real thing. Worldbuilding in the grand tradition, background thought out to the last detail, by someone who knows absolutely whereof she speaks. . . . Her military knowledge is impressive, her picture of life in a mercenary company most convincing."—**Judith Tarr**

About the author: Elizabeth Moon joined the U.S. Marine Corps in 1968 and completed both Officers Candidate School and Basic School, reaching the rank of 1st Lieutenant during active duty. Her background in military training and discipline imbue The Deed of Paksenarrion with a gritty realism that is all too rare in most current fantasy.

"I thoroughly enjoyed *Deed of Paksenarrion*. A most engrossing highly readable work."
—Anne McCaffrey

"For once the promises are borne out. *Sheepfarmer's Daughter* is an advance in realism. . . . I can only say that I eagerly await whatever Elizabeth Moon chooses to write next."
—Taras Wolansky, *Lan's Lantern*

*   *   *   *   *

Volume One: Sheepfarmer's Daughter—Paks is trained as a mercenary, blooded, and introduced to the life of a soldier . . . and to the followers of Gird, the soldier's god.

Volume Two: Divided Allegiance—Paks leaves the Duke's company to follow the path of Gird alone—and on her lonely quests encounters the other sentient races of her world.

Volume Three: Oath of Gold—Paks the warrior must learn to live with Paks the human. She undertakes a holy quest for a lost elven prince that brings the gods' wrath down on her and tests her very limits.

*   *   *   *   *

These books are available at your local bookstore, or you can fill out the coupon and return it to Baen Books, at the address below.

HARRY TURTLEDOVE:
A MIND FOR ALL SEASONS